CAUGHT UNAWARE

Jill S. Flateland

Copyright © 2024

ISBN 978-1-966012-20-7 (paperback)
ISBN 978-1-966012-31-3 (hardback)
ISBN 978-1-966012-30-6 (digital)

First printing: June 2024

This is an original Publication of Jill S. Flateland.

Website: JillSFlateland.com

Cover illustration by Kendra Petersen

Printed in the United States of America

10 9 8 7 6 5 4 3 2 1
First Edition

Dedication to My Family

I dedicate this book to my husband, Byron B. Flateland. I am grateful for his continued support. He is my greatest inspiration and the love of my life. I feel blessed knowing he loves me and will stand beside me always. For this, I am truly grateful.

Byron has blessed me with his intelligence, humor, and love throughout my life. His honesty is unquestionable, although at times, I don't fully appreciate his feedback, but my superhero will stand beside me always. He is my greatest inspiration and the love of my life.

Fortunately, Byron is also a curious man who loves to travel. We take several weeks every year to experience new adventures. We've been to India, Italy, Spain, Ethiopia, Ghana, and Kenya. More exotic trips included safaris in the Serengeti National Park in Tanzania, the Okavango Delta in Botswana, and bird watching in Kenya.

Over the years, we've visited 86 countries, and we have barely touched the surface of the world. Wherever I go, I meet new people and learn about their culture. It's been thrilling to weave bits of their personalities, insights, and inspiration to create the soul of my characters.

My true blessings are our daughters, Kirsten Sielaff and Crystal Fletcher, and their husbands, Tim Sielaff and Jason Fletcher. Kirsten set aside time to edit my novels, making many corrections and patiently reviewing my rewrites. Her technological skills have bailed me out on many occasions. Thanks to Crystal for her great sense of humor, honest appraisal, and for supplying me with updated criminal, forensic, and pharmaceutical information I can weave into many more novels.

Special Acknowledgements

Special thanks to my dear sister, Cindy Lea Williams, who has diligently taken on the challenging task of editing this series of novels. I'm truly indebted for her unwavering guidance and constant upbeat attitude when I get bogged down with details, and I appreciate how she springs into action at a moment's notice to tackle whatever looms ahead. Cindy is always my sister. However, she has also blossomed into a partner who brainstorms through any situation and a friend for life. My love for her is eternal.

I want to also thank Jeri Lou Maus and Mary Ann Fraser, friends who gave their time and effort to help produce a better, stronger manuscript. I'm amazed at their thorough feedback and rapid turn-around time. Jeri Lou has been on several trips with us, including whale watching in Baja and visiting Vill-Angel Medical Clinic in Endebess, Kenya. Our trip to Africa was a wonderful adventure.

Regrettably, Mary Ann passed away on May 18, 2022, following a car accident. I miss her kind words, genuine insight, and talented music, as she was also our church organist—loving gratitude, always.

I am blessed to have a terrific graphic artist, Kendra Peterson, who creates the most wonderful book covers depicting the story within. I never know what I'll get, but I've never been disappointed.

Last, but far from least, I give thanks to the 93rd Street Irregulars, my writer's group colleagues, who I'm privileged to call my sounding board for creating this rapid-paced, suspense-filled novel. They helped me refine the characters and chapters to bring the story to life. Without them, this book would never come to fruition.

Agent Dr. Joshtine Cordelia-Hastings Cyber Crisis Series
By Jill S. Flateland

In *Caught Unaware*, the fifth book in this series, Cordy has been promoted to a cabinet position to head up the new Cyber Crisis Agency. Now pregnant with twins, she and her husband, Braun, face life-changing events when General H.Q., the fourth most deadly terrorist on Earth, targets a shipment of missiles to arrive in Iran, threatening a nuclear war. H.Q. knows he must weaken the U.S. to succeed. Washington, D.C., becomes a deadly battleground as a massive cyberattack crashes subway trains, diverts funds overseas when selling stocks short on the NYSE, and launches a drone attack on the White House. Cordy and her team must end this now. Their lives depend on it.

If you read *Sweet Revenge*, the first novel in the series, you have already met Dr. Joshtine Cordelia-Hastings. Known to most as Cordy, she is a peculiar breed, enrolling in MIT at sixteen, and earning dual PhDs in computer science, and forensic jurisprudence, and criminology by the age of twenty-three. She is adventurous, quick-witted, and energetic—any man's equal, although absolutely female.

In a world of complex electronic puzzles, Cordy's skills as the leader of the FBI's Research Analyst team are put to the test to analyze, decrypt, and decode information. Cordy's strategic thinking and ability to plan ahead is similar to the chess games she played as a youth, helping her to stay three steps ahead of the enemy.

Join Cordy as she fights bioterrorism in the second novel, *Rapid Response*. Her adventures continue in the third novel, *Crashing The Grid*, where a terrorist organization has taken down New York City's power grid and water treatment plants. *Combating Chaos: All Systems Down* is the fourth book in the series. Cordy discovers terrorist plots involving major international cities, in London, Paris, Berlin, and Rome, plus an attack on the U.S.'s largest oil corporation near Wichita Falls, Texas. Cordy and her team unite with foreign agents racing to prevent further disaster as the clock ticks closer to destruction.

Character Summaries

Major Characters:

Dr. Quint Altari, PhD – Former lead IT intelligence analyst, MIT graduate with PhD in computer science, Cordy's Cybersecurity team leader

Dr. Joshtine Cordelia-Hastings, PhD, DFS, JD (Cordy) –Recently promoted to chair the new Cyber Crisis Agency, former lead Cyber Threat and Research Analyst, FBI Intelligence Analyst, MIT graduate with dual PhDs in computer science and forensic criminology, also passed the bar exam last year with a doctorate in forensic medicine and criminal law

Vice President Thomas James Harris, JD (Tom) – VP under President Spendorf sworn in as acting president during Spendorf's recovery

Agent Braun Hastings – Commander for a Ghost Unit within the Joint Special Operations Command (JSOC), former FBI agent, negotiator, and SWAT commander, Cordy's husband, Usher's brother

Special Agent Usher Hastings – Special agent foreign affairs, FBI agent, former SWAT, Braun's brother, Zina's husband

Agent Zina McLoughlin-Hastings – U.S. FBI agent foreign affairs, former FBI liaison officer from Dublin, Ireland, stationed in London, UK, sent on original assignment to hunt down Cracker in Russia, partnered with Usher to track down General Okueva in Russia, Usher's wife

Mo Hendrum, JD – Secretary of State, former Governor of New York City, former attorney, Sophia's husband

Judge Sophia Hendrum, JD – Newly appointed Supreme Court Justice, former public defender, Mo's wife

Chief Jackson – Private Investigator, former FBI agent, previous boss of Cordy, Braun, and Usher

Special Agent Alyosha Krackovitz, JD, nicknamed Cracker – IT specialist, Russian lawyer, special ops in the Russian Rebel Army, FBI liaison officer for International Operations Division, Rozalina's husband

Agent Dr. Rozalina Krackovitz, MD – Russian medical doctor, computer researcher, and FBI liaison officer for Russian Operations, Cracker's wife

Svetlana Orlov – Seventeen-year-old recent U.S. citizen who emigrated from Russia, attending MIT online, currently Cyber Crisis Agency intern, Perry's best friend

Perry Smirnov – Twenty-year-old recent U.S. citizen, a former hacker who created the stolen Big V Virus used by a terrorist to wipe out the NYC grid two years ago, volunteered to reverse Big V hack, currently Cyber Crisis Agency resident, Svetlana's best friend

U.S. President Isaac (Zac) Spendorf – Recovered from Virus X

Guy Weimer – Secretary of Dept. of Homeland Security (DHS)

Winston Willoughby – President Spendorf's chief of staff, formerly his personal secretary

Carl Wyller – Secretary of Dept. of Defense (DoD), Peggy's husband

Officer Peggy Wyller – D.C. Metropolitan police officer, 4th District, Carl's wife

Farzad Zahair, alias Ingram Freeman – Iranian terrorist who sabotaged military drones, attempted a covert coup against the U.S., kidnapped the Secretary of State, Mo Hendrum, and the Director of FBI's wife, Emma Sloan

<u>Secondary Characters:</u>

Amir – An undercover Iranian Revolutionary Guard who teams up with Zahair, the police force has been hunting him for months

Mierzany K. Ansin – CEO for Ansin Associates & Securities, Inc., a private security firm renowned for its plush private jet services used by many Congress members on the Hill

Agent Kyle Benson – Head of Secret Service Agency

Russ Bracken – SWAT Team Leader of Federal Forces in Colorado, former Navy Seal Special Ops Explosive Breacher, served in Afghanistan, Cordy's past boyfriend

Admiral J. L. Browning (Jud) – Navy Seal Admiral, serving on Joint Testing Ops with DoD

Nick Chambers – Secretary of Transportation

Marshal Albert Chernyshevsky (Uncle Albert) – A Russian hero who retired at the highest military rank as a Marshal, he is now the leader of the Rebel Army, Rozalina's uncle

Chico – SWAT member under Bracken's command, served in Afghanistan

Agent Marvin (Marv) Crane – Secret Service agent, the personal bodyguard assigned to President Spendorf

Desmond – Bomb expert under Bracken's command, former Seal, newest team member

Colonel General Dimitri – Pilot, 2nd in command of Marshal Albert's Rebel Army

Agent Evans – FBI IT analyst, forensic specialist

Sergeant Foley – Bomb expert under Bracken's command, served in Afghanistan

Agent Neil Gray – FBI Deputy Director

Casper Grest – Co-pilot who kidnapped Cordy

Lady Tiffany Hadsy (Shady Lady) – Major investor of IYFHI shares, who created a remote access Trojan setting sell-short stock prices at New York Stock Exchange

General H.Q. – Number 4 on the top 10 terrorists list

Kayman – SWAT member under Bracken's command, served in Afghanistan

Congressman Conrad Justuso – Texas Republican who ran for president against Spendorf last year and lost

José Carlos Justuso – Former leader of the Zeta criminal syndicate, regarded as one of the most violent Mexican drug cartels providing illegal drugs and weapons across the U.S. border, heads covert Iranian operations in the Western Hemisphere, Conrad's brother

Kip Kahooly (Rusty) – U.S. Air Force Special Ops, serving on Joint Testing Ops with DoD, Braun's close friend and college roommate

Azinnea M. Krysin – CEO of Intercity Future Transport, Inc. (IYFTI)

Lieutenant Colonel Leo – Serves in Marshal Albert's Rebel Army, Vlad's military partner, and friend

Agent Mitch Masters – Newest Secret Service agent

Officer Ian McMurchein – MI-6 foreign intelligence spy for the UK

Dr. Nat Ping, MD, PhD in Internal Medicine – Recently promoted to National Security Advisor, retired Secretary of Health and Human Services (HHS), former Central Intelligence agent for counter-terrorism, former Senate Foreign Relations Committee member

Chief Amos Polack – New chief of Metropolitan Police Department in Washington, D.C.

Poncho – SWAT member under Bracken, 2nd in command, served with Bracken in Afghanistan

Ranger M. B. Ruthmyer (Max) – Marine Corp Special Operations SOCOM, serving on Joint Testing Ops with DoD

General Hunter Quincy Shyler – Chairman of the Joint Chiefs of Staff, a four-star general known for his ill temper, yet, well-respected by most, Desert Storm hero responsible for DoD testing of RCV and Maven II drone

Agent Loran Sloan – FBI Director, Braun's and Usher's boss

Pilot Stone – The pilot who kidnapped Cordy, rerouted her private jet from Fort Collins, Colorado, to Washington, D.C.

Agent Vern Trudo – A twelve-year Secret Service veteran, Supervisor for the Department of Homeland Security

Crayton Udesky – Major investor of IYFHI who implemented remote access trojan setting sell-short stock prices at New York Stock Exchange, murdered in White House

Captain Vlad – IT expert, was Usher's Russian contact for Special Operations last year, serves in Marshal Albert's Rebel Army, Leo's military partner and friend, Perry's cousin

Chet Yelson – DoD's Deputy Director, steps up to fill Carl Wyller's place while Carl recovers from a stab wound

Einar Zinmansky – DoD's contractor, whose laptop went missing, heads up Maven II Drone Project

Abbreviations

ATC – Air Traffic Control

ATF – Bureau of Alcohol, Tobacco, Firearms, and Explosives

BATT – Ballistic Armored Tactical Transport

B/P – Blood pressure

CDT – Central Daylight Time

CIA – Central Intelligence Agency

Code Q – Quick response, in this case, the author is using it to indicate a cyberthreat to the U.S.

Code 2 – Urgent (may be officer down)

Code 3 – Emergency, red lights, and siren

Code 10-3 – Stop transmitting

Code 10-4 – Acknowledge order

Code 10-54 – Dead body

Code 10-999 – Officer down, needs help immediately

Code 11 – Identify frequency/transmitting too fast/didn't catch request

Code 11-99 – Officer needs help

Code 30 – Officer needs emergency backup

Code 31 – Crime in progress

Code 211 – Armed robbery in progress

DFS – Doctorate in Forensic Science

DHS – Department of Homeland Security

DoD – Department of Defense

DOJ – Department of Justice

ED – Emergency Department

EDT – Eastern Daylight Time

EMP – Electrical Magnetic Pulse

EMS – Emergency Medical Services

EMT – Emergency Medical Technician

FBI – Federal Bureau of Investigations

FDA – Food and Drug Administration

FEMA – Federal Emergency Management Agency

HUD – Housing and Urban Development

ICU – Intensive Care Unit

ID – Identification

IED – Improvised Explosive Device

IP address – Internet protocol address, a logical address assigned to each device to identify personal data

IRST – Iran Standard Time

IST – Integrated Service Telephones used in the Bunker

IT – Information Technology

IYFTI – Intercity Future Transport, Inc.

JLTV – Joint Light Tactical Vehicle

JD – Juris Doctor, graduate degree in law

JSOC – Joint Special Operations Command

LYA – Love you always

KGB – Komitet Gosudarstvennoy Bezopsnosti, which translates to Committee for State Security

MD/PhD – Doctor of Medicine/Doctor of Philosophy

MDT – Mountain Daylight Time

MSK – Moscow Standard Time

NSA – National Security Agency

NYSE – New York Stock Exchange

RAT – Remote Access Tool or Remote Access Trojan

RCV – Robotic Combat Vehicle

RV – Recreational Vehicle

SOCOM – Marines Special Operations Command

STAT – Medical term from the Latin word statim, meaning immediately

STRATCOM – U.S. Strategic Command is one of eleven unified commands under the Department of Defense

SUV – Sport Utility Vehicle

SWAT – Special Weapons and Tactics

TMI – Too much information

TOR – The Onion Router-a network that provides web privacy and hides IP addresses

UK – United Kingdom

UPS – Uninterruptible Power Supply

U.S. – United States

VPN – Virtual Private Network

Washington, D.C. – Washington, District of Columbia

White House WAVE or WAVES – Log of Workers And Visitor Entry System

WHO – World Health Organization

WMATA – Washington Metro Area Transit Authority

WW – World War

Table of Contents

Cyber Crisis Agency

It was a blustery winter morning in Washington, D.C. Unable to sleep, U.S. President Isaac Spendorf was on his usual prowl in the White House to fill his grandmother's old china teapot to brew his fifth cup of Morning Thunder tea. On his way back to the Oval Office, he stopped mid-stride, listening to a large-screen TV blaring from the conference room: "…Cozy Bear, a pro-Russia hacker group, rerouted a full bomb's worth of highly-enriched U.S. uranium to a nuclear plant in Iran."

"Oh my God!" Zac nearly dropped the teapot and set it down as his heart skipped a beat and then pounded like a jackhammer hitting his ribcage. Icy fear clutched his gut, while acid reflux caused a burning sensation in the back of his throat. He'd grown up hearing horrific war stories. His father, a paratrooper during WWII, had stormed Normandy on D-day and relived the nightmares every night for the rest of his life. *How did this slip by the Department of Defense?* The urgency of the situation bubbled to the surface, and Zac felt the weight of the responsibility fall heavily on his shoulders.

Eager to learn more, he stood outside the door as the news continued, "…a suspicious rock sample, weighing 95 kilograms, was obtained covertly by the University of New Mexico from a Texas laboratory that has been on the national watchlist. It turned out to be weapons-grade uranium."

How could this happen on my watch? He remembered visiting the Hiroshima Peace Museum, seeing the horrific photos from the raid, and watching testimonial videos of survivors of the first atomic bomb, Little Boy, which took only 65 kilograms to level Japan's city, killing 140,000 people. *This cyberattack could be the highest threat in our history.*

"…the rock, shielded to protect against radioactive exposure, was shipped back to Texas, but it never reached its destination. It arrived in Iran two hours ago. Cozy Bear also hacked four other countries, including the UK…"

Spendorf vowed to tackle the crisis head-on. He dashed to his office, barking orders at his Chief of Staff Winston Willoughby, as he passed his desk. "Get Carl Wyller on the line immediately. Send it to VidChat—no security leaks."

The VidChat was already ringing when Spendorf entered his office. Recognizing Carl's image on the screen, he didn't bother with a greeting. "Why wasn't I notified of the missing uranium?"

"I was about to call you," Carl muttered. "I just got off the phone with Dr. Ping—"

Spendorf's temper flared, "So our Director of National Intelligence knew about this, too, and I had to hear about it over the news? I hate being caught unaware!" The tension in the room went up a notch. Refusing to procrastinate, Zac was direct and to the point. Punctuality was a must in his world, pulling out all stops to complete the job. Perhaps he wanted too much of his team, but in his opinion, it was his job to be aware of small details and the large looming ones. "This is the fourth massive cyberattack in the last year. It's time to act. Cybersecurity falls under the Department of Defense. What are you doing about this?"

"Well, sir. We're working with SolarWinds, FireEye, and CrowdStrike to secure our military networks with upgraded operating systems, and DoD is busy replacing outdated equipment." Carl sputtered. "You know my SUV has a better GPS—"

Spendorf snapped, "If you're too bogged down, I'll take action into my own hands," then bit back his anger. His eyes narrowed, jaw clenched, and he gave the familiar glare he was so well-known for.

Carl held up his hands. "Okay, Zac. I've seen that look before, and I'm not stupid enough to get in your way. Why, even you—Um, never mind, I'll get right on this," Carl hesitated before adding, "I'll have a word with the Russian president."

"No. If they are responsible, they'll be held accountable. Swift sanctions speak louder than words. We'll cut off all funding to

Iranian and Russian banks and restrict their oil exports. Targeting personal assets will also impose severe financial burdens. I'm sure the EU will join us in imposing additional sanctions."

Carl cleared his throat. "I can—"

"You just get our military back on track, and I'll take care of the uranium crisis. As far as our cybersecurity, I have a better idea." As usual, Spendorf's innovative thinking blossomed. "I'm creating a new cabinet post. We'll call it the Cyber Crisis Agency. It will be responsible for coordinating all cybersecurity efforts across different government departments, ensuring a unified and effective response to cyber threats. And I know the perfect person to run the department. I'm sure the Senate will agree."

Carl heaved a sigh. "That would be a relief, sir. Who do you have in mind?"

"I need someone to get this off the ground while launching at full speed." He added, "Dr. Joshtine Cordelia-Hastings has worked with me in the past. She's renowned for her IT and security skills, and I hear she just passed her bar exam in forensic law."

"Cordy? She's well respected on the Hill, too." Carl sounded grateful. "You're right. I'm sure she can get Senate approval."

"Cordy will be perfect. She's brilliant, adventurous, quick-witted, and energetic. I'll keep you posted." He disconnected the call. Zac needed this post now. *This position will oversee all cybersecurity operations and strategies and carries enormous responsibility. I must find funding in the budget.* Without hesitation, he called Cordy to ask if she'd accept the nomination for the new cabinet position.

Cordy was a lot like Spendorf—honest to her core, loyal, and would fight for what was right, refusing to admit defeat. "I'm deeply honored, Mr. President."

"Call me Zac. We've been on a first-name basis for years, and just because you're joining my Cabinet doesn't change how we address one another."

"Thanks, that means a lot. Tell me more. What will be my responsibilities?" Cordy tapped away on her keyboard in the background as Zac laid out his expectations.

"You'll report directly to me and work closely with Homeland Security, the Secretary of Defense, and the Director of National Security. You've worked with them in the past. We'll get input from you and the directors to draft a job description for all to review and revise as needed."

Cordy, a close friend, and seasoned security data analyst at the FBI openly expressed her concerns, "It's not just about protecting the government's critical infrastructure as we know it. The pace of our technological advances significantly impacts how we protect our national interests. Both our government and corporations are ill-prepared for a cyber war. The DoD and Homeland Security lack the legal authority to enforce our strategies on private sectors. I'm skeptical that social media giants or private employers like Amazon, Microsoft, or Boeing have the necessary safeguards against cyberattacks."

Zac nodded. "We've made significant progress with the banking and financial industries, the Securities and Exchange Commission, and healthcare."

"True, but they still encounter breakthrough malware," Cordy said. "Spyware today is getting smaller, more complex, and easier to implant even when standard firewalls protect our systems. Did you know that nearly 3 million Google searches are done every minute of every day and 12 websites are hacked during that minute?"

Zac's eyes flew open. "Really? I had no idea."

"We must implement proactive security measures to protect our systems." Cordy rushed on, "We would lose the battle if hit today. How can we unite everyone around a cyber defense system to combat current and future attacks? The nature of that conflict changes on a daily basis. We can find a solution today, but tomorrow, there will be some new threat. Even CrowdStrike, a leading cybersecurity firm, experienced a security breach that grounded planes worldwide, leaving families stranded in airports, either trying to get back home or traveling for business. The flawed update crashed Microsoft Windows, too, causing server outages and displaying the infamous 'blue screen of death' worldwide."

"You're right. Our nation is vulnerable to foreign cyber threats. We need an experienced team, and with your expertise, we can develop effective strategies to combat cybercrimes." Zac's plea was sincere, "I understand it's a lot to ask, and there may be no way to fully compensate you for your efforts, but I truly need you. We're navigating uncharted waters, and time is of the essence."

By the end of the call, Cordy said, "Yes, I accept the nomination. I'm anxious to start and have been jotting down ideas and questions as we speak."

Zac eagerly arranged a face-to-face meeting for the next day, ready to delve deeper into the cyber defense initiative.

Cordy gushed, "I can't wait to tell Braun. He's already in D.C., so I'll catch the earliest flight. Maybe he can meet me at the airport. See you tomorrow."

Zac said. "You and your husband make a good team, and we're lucky to have both of you working with us. It could be weeks before the Senate approves your nomination to head up the Cyber Crisis Agency."

In the meantime, Cordy had a lot to do.

***

Oh my, this is really happening! I need a top-notch team. Deep down, Cordy's goal was to make the U.S. the most secure cyber-superpower in the world. Challenged with concerns about fulfilling this enormous responsibility, Cordy spent a restless night, her stomach in turmoil, and by 4 a.m., she scrapped the whole idea of sleep. She brewed some tea and popped a slice of wheat bread into the toaster. After adding cream to her cup, she grabbed her phone and flipped through her contact list.

Cordy's first call was to Dr. Quint Altari, who had worked with her analysis team after getting his doctorate at her alma mater, MIT. His skills surpassed her expectations and would make him a strong team leader. She grabbed the phone while munching her toast—no time like now to gather talent. Between bites, she interviewed Quint and hired him on the spot.

Sept. 8 — 11:00 a.m. EDT, U.S. Cabinet Meeting, Washington, D.C.

At twenty-eight, Cordy was at the top of the world—married to the love of her life and ecstatic to be pregnant with twins. Her most challenging adjustment was that her husband, JSOC Commander Braun Hastings, was frequently away on special ops missions. She absolutely trusted him, but her greatest fear was for his safety—she never knew where he was stationed or how long he'd be away from home.

She also loved her new promotion, which took effect three weeks after Zac's proposal to the Senate. However, it meant frequent trips between her home base in Fort Collins, Colorado, and Washington, D.C. The job was challenging but didn't seem like work most days. It was fun. She used her ability to plot strategies like a three-dimensional chess game, staying a few steps ahead of most problems.

Her team updated security across various agencies during the last seven months. They analyzed, decrypted, and decoded complex applications, avoiding multiple foreign cyberattacks. Implementing an effective and efficient server-based backup system was critical to the network's security. All members were exceptional in their own rights, held accountable to one another, and carried their workloads with minimal complaints. They worked countless late hours and weekends to build a more robust and diverse network. She had every reason to be proud of their accomplishments.

Zac also seemed pleased with the team's endeavors and asked Cordy to give an update at tomorrow's cabinet meeting.

Cordy woke up early the next day, excited to inform the Cabinet on the team's progress. Preparing for the meeting, she slipped into a navy pantsuit instead of her usual black jeans. One glance in the mirror made her sigh. It was essential to look her best. Makeup was a pain, but being a strawberry-blonde, her eyebrows appeared non-existent, and no one could see her long eyelashes, so she touched them up with an eyebrow pencil and a bit of mascara. After another assessment in the mirror, she pulled her shoulder-length hair into a French braid rather than her usual, casual ponytail. That was enough primping for one day, and she headed out the door.

When President Spendorf called for Cordy's report, she smiled. Despite the butterflies in her stomach, she was eager to share the team's results. "Thanks, Mr. President. With the help of many of you around this table, we managed to recover the uranium from Iran before it got into the deadly hands of General H.Q., who funded the latest attacks on Israel. The cybersecurity team worked tirelessly for the last seven months to cleanse our government systems of all traces of past cyberattacks."

Every eye was glued to her as she continued.

"Our internal network was riddled with challenges. The Pegasus worm had infiltrated our government's infrastructure, particularly our phones and emails. This spyware posed a significant threat, allowing adversaries to eavesdrop on conversations, read texts, and access data searches. It could even download photos and track GPS locations without the user's knowledge. Despite the difficulty in tracing the subtle footprint left by Pegasus, the cybersecurity team successfully plugged these leaks. All programs are now encrypted, and we are confident that we are fully shielded from future hacks, at least those known today."

President Spendorf and his senior team congratulated her on their significant achievement.

Cordy rushed to board a plane for Fort Collins, Colorado. It would be great to be home for the weekend. As she buckled her seatbelt, her cell phone rang. "Hi, Quint. I can't talk for long—the plane's about to take off."

"Glad to hear your Cabinet meeting went well, but I have some bad news." Quint sounded exasperated. "The Department of Justice has been calling for the past twenty minutes to complain that their screens froze after logging in this morning. Ten seconds later, the screens turned dark, and the system won't reboot. I thought it might be a hard drive issue, maybe the motherboard or an overheating CPU, but not all of them at the same time. Any ideas? We need to act fast."

Cordy's heart raced. Her cabinet report still echoed in her ears. *The potential threat is significant, as it could compromise the entire Department of Justice system, leading to data loss and potential disruption of operations. The implications are dire.*

Quint asked, "Do you think someone hacked into the DOJ? Were there any problems mentioned while you were on the hill?"

Cordy thought back to a major debate during the Cabinet meeting. "Yes, the Department of Justice is checking into possible illegal activities by traders who sell short."

"Why only those who sell short?" Quint asked.

"I don't have many details," Cordy wondered aloud, "but small investors are outraged over their losses, and Congress is demanding more government scrutiny. So far, the Securities and Trade Commission has tasked the DOJ with tracking how short sellers determine bets that stocks will fall. This investigation could have potentially angered certain parties, who might want to disrupt the DOJ's operations."

Quint said, "Do you think there's a connection between the DOJ's investigation and today's computer glitch?"

"Good question. We need more research, but my main concern is that we just upgraded everything with new servers and modified security access. What if we missed something? We can't afford to overlook any detail in our investigation."

Quint heaved a sigh. "Hey, Girlfriend, you don't think China hid more of those microchips in their electronic devices, do you?"

Cordy's mouth felt bone-dry. "Quint, you're scaring the hell out of me. They could collect and alter data and jeopardize our justice system. Everything is at risk."

"Criminy, Cordy. What if they recoded those chips as we did at MIT?"

"Exactly." Cordy felt her heart race. That gnawing feeling made her gut clench, and it wasn't the twins. "What if we can't stop it? Once activated, the screens go black, just like you described at the Justice Department. All files can disappear, and they don't even need to connect to the Internet. Low-frequency radio waves could trigger the malware—and easily take down the nearest power grid. Check for any sleeper surveillance components."

"Right. We found that old malware on the motherboards. I'll check into it."

There was a sudden commotion on the plane. The screens lit up with a video of safety rules when "Breaking news flashed across the screens. At first, the plane became silent, then passengers began talking at once and pointing to their TV screens. Cordy read the crawler scrolling below the newscast, "Intercity Future Transport, Inc. just made a bid to take over the Washington, D.C.'s Transit System." The screen flipped to the New York Stock Exchange floor, showing bidders waving their arms and shouting. The camera panned to a jagged line rising sharply, a visual representation of the stock prices soaring. The crawler read, "IYFTI stock has risen from \$62/share to \$280 and continues to rise."

A man sitting beside her pulled out his cell phone, his voice filled with excitement. "Nancy, buy 100 shares of IYFTI. Oh, why not? Make that 1,000 shares…"

A flight attendant tapped Cordy on the shoulder. "Please, turn off your phone." She glanced around. "Everyone, put your phones on airplane mode, now. We are about to take off."

"One second." Cordy rushed to disconnect. "Have the team backup all servers and do the same systems-wide upgrade we just completed on our network. I'll rerun everything through our analysis program when I get there. It should trap any spyware." The flight attendant's disapproving glare was unmistakable. "Sorry, Quint. Gotta go."

Home. At last. It had taken her entire team the rest of Friday and most of today to trap, quarantine, and backup data to new servers, but the Justice Department would be up and running smoothly when they returned to work.

Cordy was exhausted. Of course, fighting off dry heaves didn't help. Once again, she hugged the great white porcelain bowl with both arms. Her cell phone chirped as she was about to turn in for the night. She recognized the unique tone she'd assigned to her husband's texts.

Braun wrote, "Hope the twins let you get plenty of rest. I'm off to Maryland—testing a new weapon at Aberdeen Proving Ground early this a.m. I'll see you next weekend if all goes well. Miss you terribly. I can't wait to see you, and I'm counting the minutes until I can hold you again. LYA."

Cordy smiled at the initials—Love You Always. She wanted to talk to him in person, but he'd be heading for bed at this late hour, and with the two-hour time difference, he'd get up early.

As far as the twins letting her sleep, that was debatable. One moment, she felt ravishingly hungry and then nauseated the next. It's hard to believe she was already seven months pregnant. She'd lost her shapely waistline, had outgrown her jeans, and wore comfy maternity clothes. Resting her arms over her belly, she felt a ripple beneath her fingers. A warm glow rushed through her. *Twins.* She could hardly believe it.

It was dark when she stumbled to the kitchen in her stocking feet, grabbed a box of crackers, and went to her office. She made double-sure everything was locked behind a secure firewall before logging into her darknet account. Quint had sent the DOJ server files through her system's analyzer one last time. No hiccups so far, so she headed for bed.

Sleep at last. It will be nice to have a peaceful Sunday.

Disaster Strikes

Sept. 10 — 11:10 p.m. EDT, Washington, D.C./
9:10 p.m. MDT, Fort Collins, Colorado

Even though the freezing weather was miserable for D.C. fans sitting in the cold metal seats, excitement rippled through the stadium when the Washington Nationals faced the New York Yankees. Competition grew fierce. Tension rose as the two teams tied twice, again going into an extra inning. The Yankees got another run, and it was the Nats' turn at bat. The whole team lined up at the dugout railing dressed in rally caps—their caps turned inside out and put on backward. Six minutes later, there were two outs, and the bases were loaded.

The umpire yanked the mask from the top of his head and pulled it down over his face. "Batter up!"

A crowd shouted as the home team's first baseman approached the plate. His fingers tingled, and his mouth was dry. Wiping the sweat from his palms down his pants, he gave an audible gulp. Offering a silent prayer, he gripped the bat. The first pitch was a fastball reaching 100 mph. Fear nearly paralyzed him, and he misjudged the ball. He didn't even swing. It was a perfect pitch.

"Strike One," the ump called.

"Why didn't you swing?" came from his teammates.

"Just swing!" his manager yelled. "Do something! The bases are loaded. At least get one home."

The second pitch was a screwball. Anxious to hit the ball this time, he stepped up and swung too early.

"Strike Two," echoed in his ears. A low groan rippled through the crowd.

"Are you blind?" the manager yelled. "Watch the ball!"

The Yankees were in the lead. Bases loaded. This hit would determine the game. The nervous batter wiped his hands once more and got into position. The bat felt heavy, and his hands slicked on the wood. All eyes were on him. The stadium was so quiet you could hear a gnat fart. The catcher patted his bare hand into the pocket of his mitt, then flashed a brief signal—two fingers, a curveball.

The pitcher shook his head, and the catcher gave another sign. The pitcher's eyes narrowed. His hands flew over his head as he wound up for the pitch, gripped the ball with his fingernails, and let her fly. He beamed a grin as the air's turbulence wobbled the ball streaking for home plate—sure, it was an unhittable pitch. It was time to win this game, so he opted for a knuckleball.

The crowd leaned forward, their eyes widening in anticipation, as the ball hurtled toward the batter.

The batter crouched over the home plate, his bat poised to swing, as he eyed the ball. Confused by the pantomime between the pitcher and catcher, he had only a nanosecond to calculate the speed. When the ball hit the bat's sweet spot, he slugged it with all his might. The ball soared clear over the right-field wall and into the stands. In a daze, he ran—a grand slam. The fans erupted in joy. There was a continuous roar as he met his team at home plate and was engulfed in massive bear hugs. The scoreboard lit up with bright fireworks, mirroring the jubilation that filled the stadium.

With this win, the Nats were heading for the World Series, playing against the Astros a week from next Friday at Minute Maid Park in Houston, Texas. The park was expected to be at total capacity with 40,960 bystanders. President Spendorf would even be there to deliver the first ceremonial pitch.

After leaving the stadium, the team joined in as the city celebrated. Metro Park pulsed with cheering people dancing in the streets. Horns honked, and fireworks sparkled through the sky. All went well until the rain turned to sleet. Then, there was a mad rush to escape the foul weather.

A quarter of the fans had ridden the Metro lines to reach the stadium due to limited nearby parking. The closest station, the Green Line from Navy Yard, was crowded with passengers. The Capital South Station's Blue, Orange, and Silver Lines transported three times the number of passengers compared to the Green Line. Although it was a twelve-minute walk, it was better than waiting outside in the cold.

The Blue Line was also a rapid transit to and from Reagan Airport. When it finally arrived, more people packed onto the train than disembarked. There were no more places to sit in any of the four cars—standing room only, but the passengers were still in the afterglow of the great win. It felt more like the height of the evening rush hour instead of thirteen minutes after midnight. The elated fans were unified over the joy of victory. For the moment, the adrenaline surge even wiped out political conflicts in a city renowned for diversity, but that attitude didn't last long.

"Next stop, Metro Central Station," the automated voice sounded over the speakers. A stampede of passengers shoved through the opening doors, pushing and shoving to get off the train while others fought to enter. Too soon, the doors closed, leaving dozens of restless people to await another train. Many, unable to exit, would need to get off at McPherson Square, the next station, and turn around.

Locomotive Engineer Gammet Banngs knew the train was dangerously overcrowded and opted to close the doors to prevent more riders. Sleet covered the train's windshield, and the engineer had trouble seeing through the haze even with cranking up the defrost and turning the wipers to high. He knew his boss expected him to keep the train on schedule, but he was already twenty minutes late and stuck working overtime. Trying to make up time, Banngs throttled the engine to full speed when the lights went out throughout downtown D.C. He kept the old girl spinning along the tracks as fast as she could go.

As they rounded a wide corner, the new battery-operated computer system routed the amped-up train through the tunnel. The metal siding of the long curve reflected a strange glow on the signal panel. Banngs' eyes flew open when he realized it was a yellow warning light—a train ahead. "Holy shit! It can't be!"

Grasping the trip arm to stop the train, his jarring hands held firm. The engine kept barreling forward—going too fast for the gear to grab hold. A whoosh of air shot from the compressor. "Shit, the air lines are freezing." Instinct took over. He flipped off the A/C and thermostat, changed the air filter, and forced the de-icing system on.

Banngs wiped the sweat from his brow as the automatic brakes briefly caught. A red light flashed, warning his brakes were overheating. The train shuddered. The brake alarm blasted, and the engine regained its speed. The train cannoned through the darkened tunnel toward disaster. Frantic, he pulled on the manual levers, throwing his body into the desperate maneuver. The brakes growled and screeched, slipped, and grabbed again. The noise echoed underground.

Hank, the conductor, called over his direct intercom, "What's going on?"

"Train ahead!" Banngs yelled over the commuter's radio. "Before station!" He tried again to raise the other train operator's attention. "Move. Incoming train. Take sidetrack!"

"Jeez!" the conductor's panicked voice yelled again but was drowned out as Banngs blasted the horn—two longs, a short, and another long—cautioning everyone to get out of the way. A train was on the tracks and moving fast.

The train ahead still didn't budge. "Move!" Banngs radioed the main switchboard operator. "Runaway train approaching another engine stalled on tracks. Emergency brakes applied but failed." His heart raced. The station's warning light blinked from yellow to red.

Sweat dripped from his forehead and stung his eyes. "We're not going to make it!"

"Switchboard down!" the panicked operator rushed on. "No power. Electricity out. On diesel backup. Can't rouse engineer…"

"It'll be too late," Banngs swore. "No help. It's up to me." His options narrowed by the second. He blew the iron devil's horn in a desperate death shriek—a constant blast for a whole five seconds while his mind grasped at other options. Releasing the horn, he blasted three short toots—ordering the conductor to the rear of the train. The dashboard shook so hard he could barely read the panel, but his experienced hand instinctively grabbed the throttle and shut her down. He knew the consequences of going against the rule book. *Rules be damned.*

The throttle popped with a grating noise as it shifted down one notch. Banngs knew he'd stripped the gears. *The boss will have my hide.* The cars bumped into one another with a loud clatter as the engine slowed, and the cars continued at the prior speed—bang! Thump, thump, thump. The brakes grabbed once again, slowing the cars.

Sounds emanated from the dispatcher's radio as he issued orders. The station ahead had finally sprung into action—a glimmer of hope. *May they respond in time.*

Friction wore through the brake pads, making a high-pitched squeal that grew ever louder. The acrid smell of burning rubber filled the air. Metal-on-metal ground out an imminent warning as sparks flew up in front of the window from the locked wheels rasping against the rails, and he worried they'd set the train on fire. Banngs felt the heat already warping the wheels, causing the cars to wobble and sway. His muscles ached, a throbbing cramp, and the physical strain of the situation was evident in every movement.

As he approached the rear end of the stalled train, the reflected light from the engine grew brighter. He sounded an SOS blast with his horn, the wail undeniable, and again tried to stop the engine by grasping the trip arm. But it was an impossible endeavor. The train was still going too fast, and Banngs' efforts seemed futile in the face of the unstoppable force.

"Move, for God's sake!" The passenger cars rocked, and the clutch shuddered, causing the brakes to slip in and out of gear. The engine wheezed, and the brakes still wouldn't hold, a stark reminder that even the manual brakes would never stop the train in time.

As the train lurched, nearly derailing from the tracks, a wave of fear swept through the passengers. Banngs, glancing up at the security cameras, could see the terror in their eyes. They strained their necks to see an eerie red glow and the stalled train around the curve. The passengers' screams, a symphony of panic, grew louder.

Hank, a bulky, tall, strapping man, had already taken it upon himself to trigger the all-alert warning to the passengers to get into crash position, which was impossible with so many standing. The message echoed through the engine and every car to the rear.

"Help me!" the engineer's desperate plea echoed in the engine. He considered jumping, but it would be futile, and he wouldn't save the train. Images of his wife and their three young children flashed through his mind. Four cars, loaded with people, trailed behind him.

He swiped an arm across his brow, threw the reverse gear down as low as it would go, and pulled her wide open to reverse the engine's torque. He'd been instructed never to do this UNLESS DURING AN ABSOLUTE EMERGENCY! The sound frequency of the brakes climbed to a deafening roar. The engine's sharp kick surged the gear into reverse, but the train was still going forward. The belt drive chirped with a high-pitched sound like steel against steel. The wheels stuck and slid across the rails.

Under maximum stress, Banngs powered through the excruciating muscle spasms, manipulating heavy levers, and activating every bell and whistle. Battling against gravity, as the train navigated the final curve, he managed to pull the swaying horn's cord once more, dislodging the rattling brake valve, which nearly fractured his right shoulder. A ripping pain brought tears to his eyes as he transferred the cord to his left hand. It was his last chance. "Toot, toot, toot," repeating the break cars signal—then the emergency whistle signal, two blast segments repeatedly, long-short, long-short, all the while watching the rear end of the train ahead draw dangerously close.

Banngs had a sinking feeling. *Where was Hank? Why didn't he break the train's link between the cars and set them free?* Banngs couldn't save himself, but maybe the other cars would stop in time for the passengers to live if he could free the cars from the engine.

The conductor shouted over the radio, "Can't release train decoupler…" There came a big cloud of dust, a roar, and the sound of chaos up ahead from the station's radio. Maybe help was on the way, at least for some. The train ahead tooted, and its engine gave a slow whine but didn't move. The rear red light glowed brighter.

Banngs realized he had only a few breaths to draw in this world. Possessed by a kind of devilish frenzy, he used both leathery hands to yank the breaker bar back and forth, trying to loosen the locked grip. He slammed all his weight against the lever. At last, his fist rammed forward. It felt as if God herself came down, grabbed his hand, and jammed that metal stick in place. It gave with a snap. The train cars released, the gears no longer had any impact, and the engine leapt forward, no longer tethered to the rest of the train.

"Bang! Crash! Crunch!" The screams, the groans, the explosive fire, and the deafening clatter merged as the engine plowed into the back end of the stalled train, upending that train's rear car. The impact hurled Banngs from the engine. He felt his body rise in a cyclone—*on my way to heaven* were his last thoughts.

Sept. 11 — 12:15 a.m. EDT, Washington, D.C./
Sept. 10 — 10:15 p.m. MDT, Fort Collins, Colorado

The blood froze in Hank's veins as if his heart had stopped pumping. He had been in the rear of the train, moving heaven and hell, trying to uncouple the engine from the rest of the train. He could not remove the locking pins any more than a child could stop an earthquake. How had Banngs managed? The crash ahead was deafening. Hank knew Banngs was gone. He had died a hero amongst flying metal and glass, leaving Hank helpless, with the tremendous burden of rescuing these passengers.

The remaining cars flirted with the tracks in a whip-like motion, and no longer being pulled forward, they slowed. Bang!" came a tremendous smashing sound, a grinding, and piling up of metal as the first car hit the crumpled engine. It flew into the air, twisted, and landed upside-down. People were thrown against the windows. Some kept going through the glass, hitting the ground. Passengers screamed and moaned, and others lay silent, battered beyond recognition. Over half of them lay under debris—buried and fighting for their lives. Smoke and fire filled the tunnel as people rushed up the tracks from the nearest station—EMS personnel, police, and firefighters in the lead.

The second and third cars fared better. Screams erupted as the ground rumbled, and the tracks shook. The air filled with flying debris and bodies as the car landed upright. Many hung onto anything within reach and scrambled to get their legs beneath them.

A whirlwind blew the last train car backward. It continued to rock back and forth, jostling Hank from one side to the other, and finally, he ended up wedged between two seats that had broken free. Holding his aching head, he gingerly stood. His joints moved—no broken bones, and gratefully, both legs were still intact. A large knot on his temple oozed blood, and he felt dizzy, but others were in much worse shape. People were milling around him—some groaning, others moaning, and many lying at odd angles, bleeding with a few bones protruding.

Hank was responsible for evacuating the passengers from the train and ensuring their safe return to ground level. His cell phone had no power, which was not uncommon inside the tunnel, so he searched through the debris until he found his radio. As he reached through a dark crack beneath an upturned seat to retrieve the device, he accidentally bumped into a dark blue backpack that felt warm to the touch. He thought he heard something coming from the backpack, so he leaned in closer and was able to discern a faint ticking sound.

Carefully opening the flap, he found a timer that read 15 minutes 28 seconds in bright red block numbers. It had wires wrapped around a bundle that generated heat, and Hank was sure it was an explosive mechanism. The seconds ticked down as he gently tucked the bag away from the crowd and radioed, "Dispatch, train crashed, multiple injuries—requesting police, emergency backup, firemen, and a bomb squad." When he mentioned the bomb squad, people panicked, breaking out windows. They nearly trampled each other as they pushed and shoved toward the exits.

"Copy that." The dispatcher sounded stressed. "Requesting emergency backup. Get everyone out of the car and head toward Metro Central Station. The tunnel is nearly blocked on our end and could collapse at any moment."

"The metro is 11 miles from here, and many people are injured. Can you send several cars to offload the passengers?"

"No," Hank noted fear in the dispatcher's voice. "I turned off the Blue Line's electrical and diesel power to prevent electrocution from the third rail. We'd have to power up again to send another train, which would be extremely dangerous."

"There has to be another way," Hank grew frustrated and felt abandoned. "There's a bomb ticking. We only have ten minutes! You have to help me get these people to safety."

"Then get a move on it," came from the radio. "My hands are tied."

Hank clutched the radio tight enough to crush it. "What about buses at the end of the tunnel? That would help."

"We'll consider that," the dispatcher said, "I'll have to check with the boss."

Fireworks

Sept. 11 — 12:17 a.m. EDT, Washington, D.C./
Sept. 10 — 10:17 p.m. MDT, Fort Collins, Colorado

A slight, short man dressed in black jeans and a dark sweatshirt pulled the hood over his head, shadowing his dark brown eyes. He crouched, hidden in the silhouette of the nearby Metro Station. People rushed to get off the subway, swarmed the streets, and paid no attention to the man. He heard fireworks in the distance, but there was no time to celebrate. His cell phone vibrated. He glanced at the caller ID and answered in a whisper, "Where are you?"

"Be there in 20 seconds. Are they planted?"

"Yeah, I barely got off the train before the doors closed," the man said. "It's a zoo down there."

Three SUVs pulled up to the station. Their tires squealed on the pavement, and the doors flew open. Armed men in full gear poured out of each and headed inside. He counted nine shooters, three more than he was expecting. Ready to approach the lead SUV, he swore when the doors slammed shut, engines revved, and they sped away.

"Hey, what's going on?" He spoke louder than he planned and ducked once more for cover. Feeling a surge of betrayal and helplessness, he accused, "You left me behind."

"No. I'm in the alley." A set of headlights flickered. The passenger door of a green sedan opened. The sight filled the man with a sense of salvation and hope. "I'm here. Get in."

The man shoved his cell into his back pocket and sprinted into the dark, his heart pounding in his chest. Slipping on the slushy street, he regained his balance and hopped into the car. Impatience dripped from every pore, "Hurry, I hear sirens approaching!"

***

The driver flipped on the headlights and drove the speed limit, passing a patrol car as it pulled up to Metro Central Station. Ambulances and fire trucks soon followed—their wailing sirens and rack lights flashing at full bore. "Let the fireworks begin," the driver counted off the moments in his head—his devoted team would take it from here. In the rearview mirror, newly lit fires sparked through buildings in his wake. *Right on time.* He met two more SUVs, dropping off additional armed men a block away. Breaking glass and gunshots echoed as he drove out of town.

The initial plan had been a success. The hacker had come through. Everything was going as planned, and he'd done his part. *It cost a few colleagues' lives but the train's new flawed software worked as planned. Now, to move on to phase two—the White House.*

Sept. 11 — 12:18 a.m. EDT, Washington, D.C./
Sept. 10 — 10:18 p.m. MDT, Fort Collins, Colorado

Traffic grew after the Nats won. Going off duty, Officer Peggy Wyller and her long-time partner, JD Parker, drove through Penn Quarter to drop off the police cruiser at the Fourth District Substation. They planned to pick up their cars and meet their spouses for a late-night dinner. Her husband, Carl, was the Secretary of Defense and worked late at the White House. It would be nice to kick back and relax for once. People were still celebrating, and she was glad they had a reservation at their favorite restaurant.

The police radio blared, "This is car 12. Code 10-999 Shots fired! 11-99 Need emergency backup."

Peggy tapped the steering wheel. "Dinner plans may be on hold."

The radio beeped again, and something unintelligible sounded, followed by dispatch alert, "Car 12. Repeat message."

"We got 10-54s. Unknown number dead at Metro Station."

There was more gunfire, and the radio blared. "45 Baker, Officer down. Repeat, Officer down. Code 31. Requesting backup. Armed robbery at 600 block, on 13th Street NW. Unknown suspects…"

Dispatch replied, "Okay, noted gunfire at 0015. Requesting backup. Are there officers down in the Metro or at the robbery?"

"45 Baker, Both areas."

Dispatch replied, "10-4. Units en route. What's your status?"

"10-999." 45 logged off.

Parker turned to Peggy. "He's requesting help from any officer in the vicinity. We're close." She nodded, and he radioed dispatch, "Car 37. Put us in."

The radio sizzled, "All units! Backup needed. Proceed to Metro Central Station. Active shooters, uncontained. Suspected explosive on-site near McPherson Square—bomb squad en route. Proceed with caution."

Peggy could barely hear her phone over the blasting sirens that followed them through the city. The captain sounded breathless. "… sniper alert, Blue Line derailed—train at max capacity—unknown number injured. Repeat Sniper alert. Bomb Squad at scene."

Flipping on the rack lights and the car's siren, Peggy heard more radio emergencies blaring over her call with the captain. An unknown voice sounding edgy, "Car 22. 211 in progress. Looting at 607 13th Street Northwest. M Shop and Gallery Place also hit. What's your ETA?"

"ETA two minutes." Parker had to shout to be heard over the deafening blares, and the shrieks of skidding vehicles.

Captain replied, "Car 37—Target Metro snipers."

"Roger. Over and out." Parker let go of the transmission button.

Peggy crouched low behind the steering wheel and veered around two vacant cruisers already parked at the curb in front of the Metro Station. Officers zigzagged along the street against sniper fire coming from M-Shop. Cranking the wheel to the right, she avoided an oncoming green sedan and parked in the alley away from the gunfire. Feeling that familiar adrenaline burst, she bolted from the patrol car, popped the trunk, and geared up.

Parker's flashlight bounced beams off the grayish walls, searching for a safer, unblocked entrance. Proceeding with caution, they found a locked side door.

Peggy picked the lock, rushed inside the Metro station, and climbed over the toll gate.

Parker's foot caught on the top rung and stumbled, but he made it after dragging his size 13s off the metal barrier. Other officers filed in behind them. EMS and firefighters briefed each other before heading downstairs, not knowing what to expect.

Peggy's heart raced as adrenaline coursed through her body, leaving her breathing heavily in short pants of air. She swiped beads of sweat that broke out across her forehead. More shots came from the third level down. Shouts and sobs echoed through the large lobby.

It seemed like all of humanity rushed from the gaping belly below, scrambling to climb up the non-moving escalators, and trampling each other. Flashlights from multiple cell phones bounced through the crowd, struggling to navigate through the pitch-black station.

Peggy radioed dispatch, "Armed men below. They're shooting at us."

"Help me!" A pale, disheveled man cried as he reached the top of the stairs while carrying a crying girl, probably about four years old, in his arms. The child's wrist hung at an odd angle. Blood dripped from the man's left sleeve as he raced straight for Peggy. "Please, help my daughter."

Peggy yelled, "Medical assistance needed."

A paramedic joined an EMT and darted to the man's side. "We'll take it from here."

"Thanks." Peggy didn't wait for more details. It sounded like the Fourth of July outside, and more shots echoed from downstairs. Overwhelmed with panicked people—screaming, crying, and wounded, she grabbed her radio, "Need SWAT and EMS ASAP. Notify hospitals for incoming!"

The bomb squad had already made it down the steps, so Peggy and her partner followed. Rounding the stairs, past the landing, she heard a ping—chunks of concrete bit into her ankle from the step in front of her. Peggy hopped back up a step, ran into Parker, lost her balance, and tumbled down the rest of the stairs amidst gunfire. When she landed, one of the bomb squad members lay on the ground, unmoving in a pool of blood. She stopped to check. "No pulse."

A few more shots pinged off the cement floor near her. Instinct took over. Peggy ducked behind a massive concrete post.

Parker was already on his radio, "Officer down. Code 3. Armed assailants on track level." His light caught a paramedic dashing forward, but before he reached the downed man, a warning shot drove him back.

"Take cover," Peggy yelled. "Leave him. He has no pulse."

Parker grabbed the paramedic's arm and pulled him sideways to join them behind the barrier.

Peggy flashed her light toward the tracks. They were only fifty yards from a parked train where snipers took advantage of the prime space hidden from the police. Spying a glint of a rifle hoisted out of an opened window, where snipers hid from the police, and blasted rapid fire in an arc. Glass from cars two and three exploded into fragments.

She heard a gun clatter to the ground, as a man's large body lay sprawled over the shattered window. He didn't move. Blood dripped down the side of the car. *Probably dead.*

Peggy heard return fire erupting as she zigzagged her way to the rear of the train.

Sniper fire directed next to the emergency team coming down the steps, and hit one officer, missing another who dodged back around the corner yelling, "Max is hit!"

Six officers darted forward in formation, firing their automatic rifles. Bullets pinged against the metal of the first subway train car. They cut through the thin aluminum coating, and the remaining windows in car one burst into fragments. An EMT snatched Max's vest around the sleeve and collar opening and dragged him back up the few steps to the landing.

Knowing most of the officers, Peggy's gut clenched, but shoved her helplessness aside. When Parker placed his hand on her shoulder, they moved forward, resolute and determined. She wedged the train's rear door open. It was the fourth and last car after the engine, and it seemed empty, but they ducked behind the closest seat to assess the situation.

Peggy scanned her light along the walls and aisle of the car, saw no threats, and inched herself upright. Her muscles felt tight. The scarred tissue over her left ankle ached like it had been torn open again, but there was no time to worry about such little things. A gust of wind greeted her as the door between the two cars opened. Instinct told her to shoot. Her finger nearly pulled the trigger when Parker's flashlight lit up a familiar face, a face she had seen all of her life.

The man was chiseled, hard like a rock, and not just any rock, but solid like a small mountain. His face was seasoned, with deep lines etched by years of living on the edge. Although he was in his mid-sixties, he'd weathered well, like he'd been exposed to the elements for a few eons. He shifted in the shadows, nearly invisible.

Blowing out a deep breath, Peggy squeaked, "Jeez, Dad, I could have killed you! What are you doing here? You're retired." The shock of seeing her father added another layer of tension to the already intense scene.

"Peggy, stay down!" He rushed toward her and dove between two seats as a man dressed in military gear blasted through the door.

This time, Peggy fired nearly at the same time as Parker. The man flew back. She saw flickering lights in the train car ahead, and a shooter yelled, "Cops breached the rear car, and more are at the front."

Dad peeked around the seat and sprinted the last five steps. He ducked and grinned at her, as if thrilled to be in the action, however inappropriate it was for a retired cop to be joining the fight. "I heard the call over the police scanner and knew you'd be in the fray. Your chief is still green as spinach, and you know how much I loathe spinach. I thought I'd lend a hand or two."

"He's going to croak when he hears," Peggy said.

"Oh, yeah, green as a frog." Dad nodded. "I like your analogy, but let's face it, I counted six more snipers on this train, and who knows how many are downtown. He can use the help."

A series of shouts and rapid gunfire drowned his words. Bullets tore through the windows, spraying them with splintered glass. Peggy ducked and covered her eyes but felt the sting as shards etched her face.

Officers stormed the train. She felt the carriages sway with the weight of heavy footsteps headed up the aisle from the front. "Car one, clear," someone called out.

Dad turned off his flashlight and whispered, "I'm going back through that door to trap the shooters between the officers at the front end and us. Cover me." He tapped Peggy's knee. "On three— one, two…"

By the time she reached three, her father had disappeared. Peggy had no idea where her dad had gone and didn't dare shoot for fear of hitting him. Meanwhile, Parker was inching forward, and she could hear rustling near the door between the cars. Fear clutched her soul when a blast of air hit her face. Someone had come through the exit, and she feared the worst.

Chancing a look, she turned on her torch. Two men had pinned her dad to the wall. A gun barrel poked against his chest. "Another step, old man dies."

She recognized the taller sniper—a face she had seen in the police station's most wanted list: Amir, an Iranian Revolutionary Guard. The force had been hunting him for months. He could disappear like a phantom and was as dangerous as a grizzly bear. She doubted Amir was the ringleader, but he was running the show down here, no questions asked.

Peggy's plan of attack changed in the blink of an eye. "Don't shoot!" She dropped her gun.

Peggy's dad took advantage of the distraction, giving him a moment to react.

***

It had been years since anyone caught Amir off guard, and the sudden blow stunned him. He lost control of his gun, which was knocked to the floor and accidentally fired upon landing. The bullet ricocheted off the metal door and struck his partner, killing him instantly. Amir, taken aback by the fact that a man at least twenty years his senior had caught him off guard, was furious. He rolled across the floor and coiled like a cobra.

"Dad, look out," the woman shouted, but it was too late. Amir struck out with a sharp kick to the officer's mid-section.

The old man landed hard, but like a street-wise panther, he pounced with agility, grabbed Amir's ankle, and twisted it, bringing him down nearly on top of himself. Soon, they were grappling on the floor, tearing each other's clothing, scratching, clawing, and belting one another with their fists.

Amir threw his left arm over his face and punched with his right.

The old man took the blow to the jaw and came up fast, striking Amir in the back of the head. Before Amir could defend himself, the officer bounced upright and hooked his arms viciously around Amir's ribs, lifted him, and slammed him against the metal frame of the opened door.

Amir back-heeled the man, turned, and threw his weight toward the officer, trying to drive his knee into the old man's belly.

Instead, a fist exploded into Amir's gut. He grunted in pain as his knees buckled.

The officer swiped blood from his swelling lip, grasped a knife from his boot, and slashed at Amir. The blade bounced off the Kevlar vest and caught Amir in the arm.

More shooting. "Car two, clear," sounded from somewhere in front of him.

The woman shouted, "Get down, Dad."

The old man dropped to the floor as shots came from the front of the car.

The woman fired and hit another man dressed in camo, racing toward her father. The exit between cars two and three whooshed open as armed officers dashed forward.

Amir could hardly breathe as he dove from the train through the exit at the other end of the car. He was the last of his men standing. The battle with the old officer had been more grueling than he expected, but Amir couldn't stick around any longer. It was time to meet Zahair and attack the White House. He heard the woman shout, "Cars three and four, clear."

Back on the streets outside of Metro Central, the newly appointed Chief Polack fought the traffic, getting angrier by the second. Stalled a good two blocks from the train station, he seethed as vehicles darted around him. To be honest, it wasn't the stalled traffic that triggered his ire. It was the cumulative effect of all the wrong choices he had made in the past few hours. He'd been warned of a potential terrorist attack but didn't take heed. He radioed his captain. "It's gridlock. Must be two dozen squad cars parked along the streets. Flashing lights are blinding—too many. I can't see anything but shadows in the distance. Gunfire is coming from above and below ground, and I can't determine our teams from the assassins. I'm calling the mayor to send in the National Guard—"

"How long before they get there?" the captain asked.

"Don't know." Polack made his way closer when someone grabbed his arm. "Take cover! To your right!" Polack crouched behind a trash can. Sirens sounded. The whoop, whoop, whooping sound of helicopter blades cut in.

Armed men bolted from a black Humvee—five of them with semi-automatics.

Polack's sweaty fingers hit the wrong number twice as he speed-dialed. "This is Chief Polack, Mayor—dozens of shooters downtown." Muffled shots rang out like distant fireworks. "Need National Guard and SWAT teams. Our police force is under attack and overwhelmed. They're using tear gas."

An officer yelled, "Get down, Polack!"

A bullet hit the chief's chest. Polack dropped the phone as he flew backward, and air rushed from his lungs, but the Kevlar vest had saved his life. He moaned as he turned to his side. *I hope the mayor got this message. Better call up the chain of command.* He scrambled to get his phone, still sheltering behind a trash can, dialing with trembling fingers, "Dispatch, get me Secretary of Defense Carl…"

Send In National Guard

***Sept. 11 – 12:26 a.m. EDT, White House Oval Office, Washington, D.C./
Sept. 10 – 10:26 p.m. MDT, Fort Collins, Colorado***

President Isaac Spendorf felt the intense strain of his presidency—his nerves were frayed, and it was only the first year of his second term in office. How had he gone from being a Medal of Honor Marine to having silver streaks in his dark black hair? He was eighteen when he'd set his course against terrorism in the Middle East, then at home. Now, he had no time for sleep.

The recent surge in selling short prices and cascading risk of consumer losses had put a heavy burden on his shoulders, and the upcoming speech to Congress was crucial in addressing these issues. Sitting at his desk in the Oval Office, Zac ran through his speech for a second time. He'd deliver it to Congress on Monday morning.

His chief of staff's voice crackled over the intercom, shattering the silence in the Oval Office. "Carl Wyller's here to see you. Says it's urgent, and the mayor is on line 1." Winston's unyielding calm during a crisis sounded unnerved.

Zac set aside his speech, his mind racing, anticipating reasons for the mayor's unexpected call. "Thanks, Winston. Send in Carl. He may know what's so important on the mayor's mind that he called me." Concerned, he had to remain calm.

One glance at Carl's face told Zac volumes. Visibly shaken, unlike his long-time friend and trusted advisor, who rarely showed fear. *This can't be good.* Zac briskly gestured for him to come in.

Carl hurried across the plush navy carpet and paused, standing on the national bald eagle to catch his breath.

Zac noted the symbol representing the United States' strength, courage, and freedom. He was responsible for the nation's security. "Don't hold back. I want all the details."

Carl brushed sleet from his dark brown hair. "The mayor called," his voice trembled with fear, "and now I have the chief of police on the phone demanding we send in the National Guard and FBI SWAT teams. Polack says his officers are under attack, and all hell is breaking loose downtown. Zac, Peggy's out there!"

"Okay, I understand. We'll do everything we can." Zac backtracked, "So, did you send in the National Guard?"

"Aah, not yet." Carl's frown reflected deep concern. "They're on standby, but I wanted your approval and came as fast as possible. Remember what happened the last time we sent them to Texas? The press had a heyday over it. And the lives lost, the damage done…"

Zac's glare conveyed his determination to handle the situation. He wasn't worried about the press, and if downtown was in as much chaos as Carl described, there was no need for chit-chat. "Let's see what the mayor has to say." Zac grabbed the phone from his desk and punched line 1. "This is President Spendorf."

Carl towered over Zac's ornately carved, file-cluttered walnut desk, hands trembling and still clutching his cell phone. A deep crease ran across his brow, his eyes wide with concern. "What's he saying?"

"Yes, Mayor, so I've heard. Secretary Wyller's here with me. One moment, I'll put you on speaker." Zac clicked the button. "Go ahead." Zac's direct approach was a testament to his hands-on leadership style.

"This is Mayor—" A radio squawked in the background, drowning out the mayor's voice.

Barely able to decipher what the mayor shouted over the radio, Zac caught, "…a 911 call…Metro Station…riders trapped… shooters…bodies… downtown's ablaze." The mayor's voice rose over the chatter, "I'm requesting you send in the National Guard—"

Muffled shots rang out like distant fireworks on Independence Day. Zac said, "The mayor must have the police scanner on in the background."

Carl's breath hitched, "Oh God, keep Peggy safe," he murmured beneath his breath.

Screams and coughing erupted over the phone. Sirens wailed, and loud popping sounds blasted. Zac wiped his brow and heaved a sigh. "Yes, Mayor, we'll send in the Guard and anyone else you need. Keep us informed." He motioned for Carl to make the arrangements and disconnected the mayor.

Carl released his breath. "Thanks." He shouted to Chief Polack over his cell phone, "National Guard is approved. I'll send in SWAT?"

"Go, Go, Go! All units, another officer down!" squawked over Polack's phone. "He has a pulse. Where's EMS?"

"I told you to stay down, Polack," someone screamed. A clatter of footsteps and gunfire erupted. Polack's phone call went silent.

Carl disconnected and hit a preprogrammed number. Two rings later, he spoke with the chief of the National Guard, "It's a go."

"We're on our way." The chief barked orders as he disconnected.

Carl hung up, walked to the door, and gave orders to a few aides as he speed-dialed the director of the Special Ops Division. "Are your SWAT teams ready to roll?"

"Polack already called, so we've been in the wings," the Director said. "Geared up and ready to roll. Metro station—two minutes out."

"Great. Keep me posted." Carl hung up.

Who Is This?

Sept. 11 — 12:30 a.m. EDT, Congressman Justuso's Apartment, Washington, D.C.

Congressman Conrad Justuso couldn't believe he had lost the election to President Spendorf back in November of last year. The Texas Republican had been confident of winning and knew he would make a far better president. After counting the early mail-in votes, he woke up on Election Day leading in nearly all of the state polls, some by as much as 20%, but suffered a crushing defeat by the early hours of the following day. It had been numerous hours of speeches, campaigning, fundraising, and sleepless nights—all for naught, leaving him completely shattered.

Conrad couldn't even remember his concession speech, but he would get back on his feet. He was still young, forty-five, a known charmer, and smart. Plotting for another run, he knew he'd win next time. At least he wouldn't run against Spendorf again. It was the president's second term in office. His mind was already strategizing, finding ways to outmaneuver his opponents in the next election.

Conrad spent the entire day preparing documents with Zogster's lawyer for an upcoming Supreme Court hearing. The lawyer cautioned, "If you're not careful, you could face Congress with charges that could lead to impeachment."

Conrad stiffened and directed his anger toward the lawyer: "What you're about to hear is way above your pay grade, so listen closely. You will be asked for an analysis and advice. You'll hear questions that may not make sense, so don't be afraid to say you don't understand. Words can become a noose. Don't hang yourself, and definitely, don't hang me. As far as the court is concerned, you're Zogster's lawyer—not mine. Keep my name out of this!"

The Zogster case, a high-profile legal battle, was crucial as it was allegedly linked to illegal trafficking into the United States by

Mexican drug cartels, primarily the Zetas, which is a significant concern for every American citizen.

The Zetas, known as one of the most violent cartels, are involved in brutal torture and murder, money laundering, and the illegal trafficking of drugs, weapons, and humans across the U.S. border.

Initially, Conrad's political platform focused on family values, economic growth for the middle class, and a strong stand on ICE's ability to secure the borders. Then, his whole world turned upside down when he discovered his older brother, José Carlos Justuso, had gone rogue and was discovered leading a Zeta criminal syndicate.

Caught in a crisis, Conrad and his father staged his brother's death. Their father had promised to keep José safe and removed him as far away from Mexico as possible. Still, it was questionable how secure José could be while involved in covert Iranian operations in the Western Hemisphere.

After José's death, Conrad inherited 55% of Zogster's shares, a shell company for money laundering. It became a perfect ploy for raising funds, and Conrad used it to his advantage. He had to conceal his direct involvement in his bid for the top office. Conrad's political career would be over if news of how the Congressman raised campaign funds leaked. He ensured his legal counsel kept his name out of the spotlight.

This was challenging since he had gone public, questioning ICE's handling of suspected raids.

A tragic incident had occurred at the Texas border over nine months ago, resulting in the loss of forty-three lives. It was a convenient incident, and according to ICE's records, one of the victims was Conrad's brother, José Carlos Justuso. Conrad took the opportunity to launch a campaign to raise more funds for ICE while also chastising them for mishandling their border raids.

In retrospect, Conrad regretted his actions, as they led to a prolonged and high-profile criminal offense. Three trials related to the raids had been held, with the first resulting in a hung jury. Another prosecution led to a referral to the Texas Supreme Court, which expedited a case petition before the U.S. Supreme Court on the docket for last Friday.

Fortunately, the DOJ had a software glitch, postponing the hearing by two days. This unexpected delay allowed the Congressman to cover up some unforeseen details that had recently emerged, which didn't bode well for his family.

By 9 p.m., with his legal business wrapped up, Conrad was exhausted and flipped on the local baseball game, hoping to wind down for the day. It had been a spectacular win for the Nats, but what happened next, watching D.C. erupt into chaos under Spendorf's watch, was too good to be true. He could use this to his advantage. Maybe even get Spendorf impeached.

Gloating at the idea, the Congressman walked across the plush carpet of his newly remodeled apartment to the corner bar and refilled his glass with bourbon. The crackling fire invited him to relax in his recliner as he downed his drink.

He had just drifted off when his cell phone rang, jolting him awake. "Who is calling at this hour?" Staring at the ID, he didn't recognize the caller. It was probably a wrong number, so he didn't bother to answer. Five minutes later, the phone rang again—the same number. He finally answered the third call. "Who is this?"

"You don't know me, but I know all about you," a mechanical voice said. "And unless you meet me in the next half hour, I'm taking your little secret public."

"What secret?" Deep down, he worried the caller might know the truth, but how did anyone else find out? Reeling with fear, he felt his legs wobble as he hopped from his chair. Conrad's fingers felt numb as he fumbled to click the record button on his cell phone. "Can you repeat that? I don't think I heard you correctly."

"You can't lie to me," the disguised voice said. "I know your family secret and where you got your money."

Conrad hyperventilated so hard he nearly passed out, missing part of the call. "What are you talking about?"

"Check with your brother…that is if you can find him."

"I no longer have a brother." Conrad was wide awake now. "I haven't a clue what money you are talking about." His lungs found it hard to breathe. *Where is my brother? I haven't heard from José in nearly a year.*

The voice snapped Conrad back to the present. "Meet me in half an hour at the West Executive Avenue parking lot near the White House if you want your family to remain alive. I'll give you further directions from there."

"Where? That's a large lot." Conrad's mind raced.

"Your usual parking spot, third row toward the end of the lot," the voice said. "You drive a blue pearl Subaru Outback. I'll find you. Just be there." The call disconnected.

Conrad glanced down at the pistol in his hand. *When did I retrieve the gun from the top desk drawer?* He threw on his black leather jacket, shoved the loaded firearm into his pocket, and raced for the elevator. He plugged in his earbuds and replayed the phone's recording on the way down. He had to notify Ansin immediately.

Of course, the CEO wouldn't be caught dead with the Congressman. He never made personal appearances. Conrad tapped *13, a contact number he'd been instructed to call only if there was an absolute emergency. The call went to an encoded service that scrambled the message to prevent prying ears from understanding. "This is CJ42. I need your help." He replayed the recording for Ansin and hung up.

Rushing to his car, he ducked inside the parking garage and stood in a dark corner, watching for any shadows lurking outside. Waiting for what seemed like an eternity, he felt his world crashing in around him, pressing against his chest so tightly he could barely breathe. His throat felt on fire.

He nearly dropped the phone when it finally vibrated in his clammy hand. The sudden sound was a relief, a break in the tension that had been building. Glancing up at the sky, he whispered, "Thank you." Ansin had seen fit to answer him.

A text message popped up, "This message will disappear in thirty seconds, so get the details on the first read. Do not meet this schmuck, and you never made this call, no matter what happens. Understood? I'll deny everything." The words sent a chill down his spine. Seconds later, the text disappeared, leaving him in a state of fear and uncertainty.

"Shit!" Conrad was about to pocket his phone when it vibrated again with another text. "Drive your car two blocks from the entrance to the designated lot, park, and get out. Do not remove the keys from the ignition and walk away. Leave everything to my boys, and make sure you're seen with someone credible over the next two hours." This time, it didn't surprise Conrad when the text evaporated.

His mind quickly went back to his days on the campaign trail. "I need someone I can trust, someone who can provide a reliable alibi," he mumbled, his voice filled with desperation. Confronted with a threat to his life, he felt on the verge of panic. Entering a fight-or-flight mode, his fingers felt numb and trembled as he called Secret Service Agent Jerry Gardria.

Lights Out

***Sept. 11 — 12:35-1:40 a.m. EDT, White House, Washington, D.C./
Sept. 10 — 10:35-11:40 p.m. MDT, Fort Collins, Colorado***

To avoid distractions, Secret Service Agent Vern Trudo removed his earpiece, working quietly in his sound-proof office on a special Department of Homeland Security assignment—tracking a contractor's recent activity. Red flags kept popping up the more he researched Ansin Associates & Securities' background. Mierzany K. Ansin was a Russian immigrant who became a U.S. citizen eight years ago. Now, he was the CEO of a firm renowned for its private security services, which offered plush private jet transportation used by many Congress members on the Hill.

His history was a bit sketchy, but so far, Trudo noted that Ansin had started on a shoestring budget—his first office consisted of a metal coffee table in his garage, a phone, and a laptop. Nevertheless, he managed to get a third loan on his house and borrowed enough money to purchase his first jet. Ansin also had ambition—plenty of ambition. Within two months, he had hooked up with an oilman from Texas, who invested enough money to buy a whole fleet of planes. Ansin began flying merchandise across the Mexican border. He had a well-honed security team that ensured his cargo made it safely to its destination. But something about his rise didn't quite add up and piqued Trudo's curiosity and set his investigative instincts on high alert.

Ansin's initial financial records smelled fishy. As Trudo poured over them, he felt the hair prickle on the back of his neck. *I don't know yet what it means,* but after his 12 years of service, he'd learned to trust the instinct that told him he was getting close to something meaningful. He dug deeper, his determination to uncover the truth unwavering. *It will be here. I know it.*

Ansin had been approved as a government contractor for the past two years. Corporate taxes were paid, although at a lower rate than anticipated. Government invoices seemed within legal limits for services rendered. Then, something shady lurked in the shadows.

Wait! A lump rose in Trudo's throat. *What happened this past year? Everything's missing. No one could stay that anonymous. He has no personal records.*

His Social Security number showed Ansin as deceased. He filed no tax records nor one from a living trust. There were no lawsuits, driver's licenses, or pilot licenses in Ansin's name, yet no formal death certificate was on file. It became an accountant's nightmare, with no way of tracking personal data, and Trudo was no accountant.

Tingling with anticipation that he might find something important just around the corner, he was interrupted by his ringing telephone. The caller ID read Kyle Benson, Head of the Secret Service Agency. Reluctantly, he answered, "Hello. This is Agent Trudo. How may I help you?" His frustration at the interruption made the tension in the room grow thick.

His boss didn't bother to identify himself, but the image on Trudo's phone was Kyle's. "Oh good, you're awake. I need a huge favor. Four Secret Servicemen on the graveyard shift are out sick. The agent in charge of White House security is running a fever, and I'm sending him home. I need someone with experience to take over the rest of his shift. I know it's Sunday, your usual day off, but can you bail me out?"

Trudo thumbed through his notes with a wistful look. *Not now. I'm so close.*

Kyle paused, his expression grave. "I've just received vital news from the president. A power outage has plunged downtown into chaos, putting the White House on high alert. I need an experienced agent to take charge. You're already in the West Wing, so I'm not asking, I'm telling you—report immediately."

"High alert?" Trudo's sense of duty was steadfast, and he promised to return to his research on Ansin as soon as possible. "Okay, fill me in. I'll make the first rounds and report in to update you."

"Thanks," Kyle paused again. "Hold on, President Spendorf is calling. Notify me when you get to the office." The call disconnected.

Trudo was used to working overtime—averaging fifty extra hours a month. He was expected to be on duty virtually around the clock when accompanying the president on trips. It was so uncommon to work only eight hours that he felt as if he hadn't done his job on a rare day it happened. But, of course, being on salary, he never got paid for the extra hours.

Trudo didn't mind. The benefits were good, and his private life was non-existent—he had moved in with his widowed Irish mother six months ago. He had no wife, no children, and no regrets. His work defined him. He lived, ate, and breathed his job, except on Sundays. As a devout Catholic, Sunday was reserved for mass and working at the soup kitchen.

White House security is kept behind the scenes and will not be fully revealed to the public, nor should it be, but the job was easy enough for Trudo. He'd monitored multiple images from security cameras inside and outside the building to detect any potential threats on thousands of shifts over the years. Gathering his Ansin research, he filed it into his lower right drawer and powered off his computer.

With duty calling, Trudo prepared himself. He plugged in his earpiece and adjusted the tiny microphone resting in his right sleeve, ensuring it was in the perfect position for communication. This system, though part of a complex IT world, was second nature.

He'd barely left his office when Kyle spoke through the earpiece, "We have a critical situation unfolding. Riots have erupted in the streets near Metro Central Station and McPherson Square, where two subway trains collided, resulting in numerous casualties. Active shooters are targeting people underground, and a suspicious backpack—with a possible bomb—has been discovered in one of the trains. President Spendorf has called in the National Guard." Kyle's voice underscored the severity of the situation.

Trudo's pulse quickened, knowing he could face immediate danger.

Kyle swallowed loud enough to be heard. "SWAT teams have been dispatched. Secure your area and check the employee entrance. I will keep you updated."

"Roger." Trudo became hypervigilant. Protecting the first family, vice president, and their surroundings was a monumental responsibility, especially on a night when chaos erupted throughout the city. On November 11, 2011, Trudo recalled when shots rang out from the south lawn and hit the Truman balcony. The president's daughter and mother-in-law were inside. He was determined to prevent a repeat of such an event on his watch, knowing that his role was crucial in ensuring their safety.

It was fifty-five minutes past midnight, and sirens sounded in the distance. Given the proximity to McPherson Square, Trudo's first priority was to check the security of the multiple sites of President's Park. He spoke into his wrist microphone, "Checking in on the Eisenhower Executive Office Building. Please give an updated status report."

The guard came back with, "All clear." Trudo also contacted the guards at the Treasury Building and grounds, the Visitor Center, Lafayette Square, and The Ellipse, and each reported, "All clear." Relieved that systems were running smoothly, he moved directly to the White House. The reassurance of the "all clear" reports brought a sense of relief, affirming the effectiveness of the security measures in place.

Being diligent, he made a quick trip outside to verify the grounds were also secured. The first line of defense was quite visible—an iron barricade around the property. Some guards greeted him, "Evening, sir."

Trudo ran the latest software monitoring reports of different protection perimeters inside the fences—every inch covered by infrared sensors and alarms to detect intruders if rioters attempted to breach the grounds. "All clear."

A gust of wind blew sleet against Trudo's face and stung his cheeks. Pulling up his collar, he turned to scan the area, noted the bullet-proof windows of the Oval Office, and captured glimpses of agents' silhouettes atop the roof—counter-snipers at the ready. "What's your status?"

One rooftop agent waved and gave him an all-clear sign, meaning the Avenger Missile System was also functioning. Trudo trudged inside to check one more contact.

Washington, D.C., is a no-fly zone with surface-to-air missiles throughout the city and high-tech lasers designed to detect possible threats. He wished he could see the full one-mile radius from the park's perimeter, but he had to content himself with calling on each watch commander. This time, he used a phone instead of his wrist microphone. Being on a high alert status, securing the fly zone was a top priority before calling his boss with updates.

Keenly aware of his surroundings, he remained watchful. Even though the areas outside the White House were on track, he had ongoing concerns to consider. Many employees, including the president's personal staff, such as the chefs, butlers, maids, guards, and Secret Service officers, came and went at all hours of the day. Numerous personnel worked in the West Wing—the vice president, senior advisors, chief of staff, press secretary, and support teams, to name a few. High alert meant meeting additional security guidelines, and entering with a badge and logging in using an assigned code wouldn't be enough. All employees must be scanned and, if in doubt, even fingerprinted.

Trudo felt confident that all was secure and headed back to the office. He noticed it was 1:22 a.m., and the usual bustle within the White House had died down. Phones rang in the background as agents helped themselves to coffee, tea, and refreshments.

Agent Mitch Masters met him with a nod and gave Trudo a fresh cup of java. "I rarely see you on the graveyard shift."

"Thanks." Trudo took the cup offered. "I love working these hours. I get more done in one night shift than a whole week of day duty." He checked in with Kyle as ordered.

Masters, the rookie of the bunch, ran a hand over his shadowed chin. "I want to keep this job and move up to days, so teach me everything." The rotating screenshots reflecting from his blue-tinted computer lens glasses made his wide eyes appear even bluer than usual.

"Okay, stay alert and ask questions." Trudo sipped his coffee and set the cup on his desk.

Masters moved toward the monitors. "I see President Spendorf is still in the Oval Office. Doesn't he usually turn in by this hour?"

Trudo knew Zac Spendorf often suffered from insomnia and rarely slept for more than three or four hours at night. He glanced up at the screen and saw the president sipping tea as he chatted on the phone. Zac loved Celestial Seasonings teas of any variety, but his favorite was a cup of steaming Morning Thunder, which he brewed next to his desk in an old china teapot that had belonged to his grandmother. "He's probably already up for the day. He's addressing Congress regarding a new immigration bill before the vote on Monday."

The overhead lights flickered. "This storm is creating havoc—better backup everything." Trudo opened his desk drawer and fished out a thumb drive.

"Snow in September?" Masters exclaimed under his breath, "I never saw that in Florida."

Trudo inserted the drive into a USB port and downloaded the Ansin files, which he had neglected to take the time to back up earlier. "It's not the snow. It's the sleet and wind we have to worry about." He pocketed the thumb drive a few minutes later.

A loud pop sounded, and the lights went out. "What happened?" one of the agents asked.

Others mumbled their dismay in the background. "Did someone hack into the power grid?" "Relax, you always expect the worst. We do lose electricity from time to time, you know."

Trudo flipped on a flashlight he'd pulled from his vest pocket and spoke into his wrist mic, "Marv, what's your status?"

Masters asked, "Who are you talking to?"

"Checking on the president." Trudo waited for an answer. "I'm sure Marv's with him. He's guarded the president for years and knows what to do during an emergency, but better to be safe than sorry."

"Hey, the computers just went down," a voice echoed in the room. "My cell phone isn't going through either."

"It's probably on overload." Trudo knew he had to reign in the team's fears, but it wasn't easy during a crisis.

Marv spoke calmly, "President Spendorf is safe and working late as usual. Don't worry. I know we're on alert status. I have his back."

Trudo thanked Marv and entered the following information into a manual log, "0130—White House lights out, 0132—President Spendorf safe in Oval Office."

Masters checked the uninterruptible power supply sitting on a shelf under his desk—the light continued to blink. "UPS is working. I see it flashing. The emergency generator should kick in shortly."

"If the UPS was working, these computers shouldn't have gone down," Trudo felt a flutter in the pit of his stomach. *What's going on? Kyle mentioned we're on high alert. I need boots on the ground to gather intelligence.* He spoke over his mic, "All agents spread out and keep eyes on your zone. Cameras and landlines are down. No cellular activity. Report anything that appears unusual." The Secret Service agents' vigilance was unwavering, even in the face of uncertainty.

There was a pause. Kyle panted out of breath, "I'm heading that way to check on it now."

Masters was on his hands and knees checking out his workstation. "I hear an electric magnetic pulse can target a network. Do you think it's possible?"

"That would be a real feat in this protected zone. Check the breaker box." Trudo tapped his chin in thought. "Maybe they were knocked out by a power spike."

"Where?" Masters backed away from the desk, stood up, and dusted off the knees of his slacks.

A short, stocky agent whose eyebrows formed one continuous gray arch over his eyes said, "I'm on it."

"Thanks, Jerry." Trudo was glad to see a familiar face among the team. Jerry Gardria was experienced and reliable. "Take Masters with you and introduce him to the power room."

"Come on, son." Jerry motioned to Masters. "Today's your lucky day."

After jotting a note into a logbook, Trudo flipped through a manual he'd pulled from the shelf detailing procedures during threatened security. The Secret Service staff ran mock breach drills every three months. Trudo was sure that if this had happened during the day, everything would still have run like clockwork, but tonight, he knew they were understaffed and had an unprepared team. It could challenge his skills. Mentally ticking off each item, he felt confident he had followed everything according to the letter. His gut remained unsettled. He would rely on a motto his grandpa had passed down, "When in doubt—fake it. Never show fear to the public or your team."

Trudo checked his watch and realized it was nearly time for the next shift to arrive. He closed the protocol book on his desk, opened the office door, and turned. "I'll be back in fifteen minutes." He used his torch to light the hallway and darted from the room to check the staff entrance as requested. It was the only entry point to the White House at this hour. With downtown chaos and no electrical power or phone service, he would ensure the White House stayed secure.

As the Supreme Court's newest member, Justice Sophia Hendrum had inherited the traditional Canteen Committee appointed to oversee the Court's Cafeteria. Her tenure was unremarkable to date—nothing as great as Justice Elena Kagan's acquisition of a frozen yogurt machine or Brett Kavanaugh's pizza additions to the menu. It was way past closing time, after midnight, and Sophia didn't want to walk the twenty minutes in the pouring rain to the nearest open eatery, Union Station's Food Court. On the other hand, she had a key to the cafeteria and could nuke a meal if needed, and her husband, Mo, had made plans to meet her. "Where is he anyway?" she wondered aloud.

He had called it a romantic midnight rendezvous, but she wasn't surprised when her husband, now the Secretary of State, had to work into the wee morning hours. Their life wasn't much different from when he was the Governor of New York, but then he usually worked from home after hours. Now, he met his team at the office to make many international calls to accommodate important contacts overseas.

Sophia nearly collided with a short, heavy-set male dashing her way. A black umbrella covered most of the man's face.

"Sorry I didn't see you," he squeaked. "Will this tunnel take me to the White House? I'm running late."

"No, you'll have to go back in the rain. It's fifteen minutes west of here." Sophia pointed to the exit. "You can take the tunnel from the Department of Treasury Annex."

"Right. Thanks." The man turned and caught his umbrella on her coat pocket.

She shuddered when she saw the ivory handle was an odd-shaped snakehead—she hated snakes. The rude man nearly tore her coat as he dashed away without apologizing.

He must be a new employee. Sophia remembered her first few days on the Hill—it could be confusing. She was still miffed by the man when she reached the cafeteria, but thoughts of seeing her husband uplifted her mood.

Mo finally called three minutes later. "Sorry, honey. I had an early morning call to Iran. The royal family members don't like being bothered in the middle of their night, so now it's daytime there. They're furious with the additional sanctions we added yesterday. They say I'll soon regret these actions. See you in ten minutes. Are you already at the cafeteria?"

"Yes, I'm thinking crème brûlée. It's the new item I'm planning to add to the menu. I want to see how you like it. Sorry, no wine, but I brewed some coffee."

"Anything as long as I can spend some time with you," Mo said. "As usual, I have another early morning conference call—this time with a Russian oligarch. I'll barely get home, shower, shave, and change clothes before I have to turn around and come back."

Sophia laughed. "Same old Mo."

"Wow, I just exited the tunnel, and downtown is ablaze! Several buildings are on fire." Mo gave an audible shiver, "Brr, it's freezing out here."

She could hear the rain splattering on the sidewalk. "I'll give you a warm hug when you get here. Rap on the door twice, so I know it's you. Love you."

"You, too," he disconnected.

Five minutes later, Sophia heard two loud raps on the Supreme Court Cafeteria door. She opened it, and even though Mo was drenched, his dark hair dripping rain onto the floor, she reached inside his raincoat and hugged him. "I'm glad you finally made it."

"I hate to eat and run." Mo filled her in on his day, and Sophia did the same with hers, chatting between bites of the most delicious, creamy custard covered in caramelized sugar that cracked beneath his fork. "Too bad I'm full, or I'd order a second helping. The blueberries make an excellent addition. I'd rate this ten stars!" Mo licked his fork and probably would have licked the plate, too, but Sophia gave him that "evil-eye look" that always made him feel like a mischievous child caught in the act. He gently set his silverware on his napkin and smacked his lips.

"You'd rate this a ten. Not bad, especially since we only rate five stars tops." Sophia laughed. "I know you need to leave, so I'll clean up and meet you at home."

Mo drained his cup, wrapped up the last piece of dessert for later, and slipped it into his coat pocket. "Where are you parked? I'll help with the dishes and walk you to your car. I don't know what I'd do if anyone kidnapped you again like they did last year. I thought I'd die of worry."

"D.C. is not New York City." Sophia cleared the table and dumped the remaining coffee. "Besides, I parked underground today. I'll be safe. Your car is in the West Executive Avenue parking lot, right?"

Mo nodded.

"That's in the opposite direction." Sophia plugged the sink drain, turned on the hot water, and poured in the dish soap.

"Okay, but be sure to call for an escort." He leaned over and kissed her on the cheek. "Don't stay too late. See you at home." He left the building.

Sophia cleaned the dishes, put them away, and locked up. She slipped the cafeteria key into her pocket as the lights went out throughout President's Park. For some reason, she had a bad feeling in her gut. It was odd that she should worry about Mo's safety, especially in the secure environment of the Supreme Court. She shrugged against a cold blast of sleet and met an agent at the security scanner. "Do you mind walking me to my sedan? I forgot my flashlight."

The agent smiled. "This way, Justice Hendrum."

Sept. 11 —1:45 a.m. EDT, Washington, D.C.

Agent Vern Trudo heard urgent voices reverberate in the dark hallway inside the White House as he hurried toward the employee entrance. At first, Trudo thought he caught a glimpse of someone darting in the shadows, but upon shining his light in that direction, he found no one. The critical nature of the situation made him consider doubling back to investigate, but the clamor from the scanning area demanded his immediate attention.

"I already told you, 'This is my ID badge. My name is Einar Zinmansky.' I am the man in the photo, and I entered my code, so let me through."

Trudo hastened his steps. The light of his torch bounced off the hard walls as he approached the security station.

"I can't! We have no electricity." A strapping young agent held his ground, arms crossed over his chest, feet apart, unwilling to budge. "Your code hasn't been accepted."

"That's not my problem." Zinmansky, a short, pudgy, dark-haired man dressed in a soaked beige trench coat, stepped forward, and shook out his black umbrella, holding it by the crooked ivory snakehead handle. Water flew into the agent's face, but Zinmansky paid no attention and pulled a pen from his pocket. "Now, I have work to do. I want to sign in."

The agent grabbed the radio. "Let me call my supervisor."

"I'll save you the trouble." Zinmansky signed his name on a sticky pad beside the scanner and jotted the date and time. "Initial this. It will have to do."

Trudo came closer. "What's going on here?"

Zinmansky wiped a chunk of mud from the knee of his slacks. His shoes were soaked and muddy. He stepped closer to Trudo as the agent lamented, "This man has a clearance pass, but he can't enter his passcode with the power outage, and I can't log him in, nor can I scan him or document his entry on our security camera. The early morning workers will be checking in soon to make matters worse. What am I supposed to do? He signed this sticky note."

"Maybe you can help me." Zinmansky showed Trudo his ID, a blue badge with two gold asterisks in the bottom left corner. "See, I have top clearance."

Trudo turned to the young agent. "We have protocols to follow when the power goes out. Where's the paper log?"

"I can't find it," the agent said, "but I'll keep looking."

"Please, I'm late for an important meeting." Zinmansky clenched and unclenched his fists. "I'll come back and sign in later if you want." Then, spying Carl in the hallway, he yelled, "Wait, Secretary Wyller, can you vouch for me? I'm Einar Zinmansky."

"What?" Carl paused mid-stride. "Zinmansky? Oh, yes, he's one of our contractors. Have you seen Kyle? I need to talk to him ASAP."

"I spoke to him a while ago." Trudo pointed toward the door. "I think he went outside to check the grounds."

"Thanks," Carl waved and dashed in that direction.

Trudo turned back to the agent. "I'll track down the proper paperwork. Add the sticky note to the logbook, and when the power returns, enter it into the database. For now, take his photo with your cell phone, and use the wand to assure security," Trudo added, hoping the batteries were charged enough to allow the device to function until the generators kicked in.

"Thanks, I hadn't thought of that. I can take it from here." The young agent moved in front of Zinmansky. "Remove your coat."

The man dropped the coat and umbrella on a chair nearby. His light gray suit jacket was damp at the cuffs.

The agent's cell phone flashed as he took Zinmansky's photo. "Now, hold out your arms."

Zinmansky did as he was told while the agent waved the scanner over his body. The wand did not beep. "All clear." The agent sounded relieved.

"It's about time." Zinmansky folded his umbrella, placed the crook over his arm, picked up his raincoat, and turned to Trudo. "Thanks for all your help. I hope the rest of our team is spared this hassle." His footsteps faded as he headed down the dark hallway.

After verifying that the staff entrance was secure, Trudo asked an aide to take a paper logbook to the checkpoint. Once that was done, Trudo contacted Agent Kyle to determine why the backup generator had failed and ensured the external defense systems were still working. A few minutes later, he saw Masters returning to the main office and asked, "Were the breakers tripped?"

"No." Masters wiped away a trickle of sweat dripping down his cheek. "We had to take the stairs. To be sure, we reset all breakers, but there is still no power. Jerry got called away. Congressman Conrad Justuso forgot the keys to his office in the Capitol building, so Jerry went to meet him and sent me back here. Do you need me to run any other errands?"

"You can write down your trip to the power room in the log." Trudo opened the office door and placed his torch on the desk. "I ran into Kyle in the hallway. Thankfully, the perimeter's infrared lasers are working, but they're running on battery backup. That gives us 24 hours."

Carl Wyller entered the office, water droplets dripping off the stubble on his chin as he finger-combed his rain-soaked hair. His wide brown eyes scanned the room. "I checked outside, but Kyle's not there, and he's not responding."

"I just ran into Kyle about 100 yards from here." Trudo jotted another note into the log. "He was checking on Avenger."

"The House, Pentagon, and State headquarters are all without electricity, and the backup generators have failed." Carl rubbed his hands together as if to warm himself. "Potomac Electric says there's a downed transmission line in Southern Maryland. Agitators are rioting in the streets, spraying downtown buildings with graffiti, and setting stores on fire. At least twenty businesses were broken into and looted."

"What about the subway system? Did SWAT find any bombs?" Trudo asked.

"They defused one bomb, but they're still searching for more," Carl paused with his hand on the doorknob. "The police are still clearing passengers from the tunnels. Our 911 emergency services are overloaded, and surveillance is down. Set up temporary generators according to policy and be prepared to deal with rioters."

"This can't be happening," Masters said. "We're in Washington, D.C."

Carl stood in the doorway. "Electric feeders are down, and who knows for how long. Fortunately, the Capitol building has backup power. So, do what you must and get these monitors up and running. Override the automatic switches and boot up the generators manually. Keep me informed."

"Then what?" Masters asked.

"Reboot the whole system if needed, but get these operational ASAP." Carl let the door slam behind him.

Sept. 11 – 2:08 a.m. EDT, Washington, D.C./
12:08 a.m. MDT, Fort Collins, Colorado

Carl had just reached the Oval Office when the lights suddenly came back on. The power in the White House had been out for thirty-eight minutes, much longer than the most recent blackout. The sudden burst of light, the hum of the generators, and the return of air conditioning eased the tension in the room.

Agent Kyle Benson met Carl in the hallway. "That was close. If the electricity remained out for two more minutes, I was ready to sequester the president just to be safe after the downtown riots, planted bombs, and hundreds dead only half a mile from here. Did the generators finally kick in, or did the electricity return?" His concern was etched across his face.

"I don't know about the generators, but we're on full power," Carl said. "My cell phone just vibrated to life, too."

President Spendorf called from his office, "I refuse to hide just because of a power outage. I'm not afraid of the dark. Are all systems working?"

"It looks that way," Carl wiped his brow, "but downtown is still fighting chaos. Fortunately, we got lucky, it's back to business as usual."

Caught Unaware

However, business, as usual, was far from the truth. At 12:40 a.m. MDT, three shrill beeps shattered the silence of Dr. Cordelia-Hastings' home in Fort Collins, Colorado.

Adrenaline surged through Cordy's veins as she leapt out of bed. Her heart pounded as the urgent message, "Code Q! Homeland and national security systems breached. Report immediately," reverberated in the stillness. *Code Q—a grave threat? Or a direct assault on the U.S. government? Not even the 9/11 attack had prompted such a high alert. Who had set off this alarm? Russia, China, Syria, or perhaps North Korea?* She shook her head, realizing that any country could launch cyberattacks—even those without nuclear weapons.

Static electricity flowed through every nerve cell as Cordy grabbed her encrypted Satphone. Cybersecurity was huge, overbearing, and her responsibility. She punched the numbered buttons with trembling fingers to summon her team. "Code Q. Report immediately! Pack enough to stay for a few days."

The situation was rapidly unfolding and cloaked in uncertainty. All federal security agencies were required to respond immediately, without any delay, and to be on high alert to find answers as quickly as possible. Cordy nearly stumbled on her way to the bathroom. She splashed water on her face, washed, brushed her teeth, and quickly dressed. Grabbing her pre-packed overnight bag, she stuffed her computer and a few last-minute items into it and hurriedly left her home.

Cordy climbed into her silver Toyota RAV4. She notified her office security that a Code Q Alert was in effect, instructing them to prepare for her team with full security measures, ID badges, and body scans, with no exceptions. Despite the queasiness she was struggling to suppress, she had a persistent feeling in her gut, and this time, it wasn't morning sickness. She was restless and completely in the dark, a sensation that only heightened her anxiety. Patience wasn't her forte, and uncertainty was her greatest nightmare. But she was determined, and she needed to be in control.

So, what triggered the alert? Stop guessing! She flipped on the radio to hear the latest news. "...thousands of Washington, D.C., residents are without power..." *Okay, I suspected as much, but what else?* She hit the scan button on her radio. The first station frequency played for eight seconds before moving on. "... D.C.'s deadly train crash killed 62 so far. Many more still buried under rubble..." "...police hunting snipers. Six officers dead, ten in critical condition..." "... rioters looting downtown...arsonist setting buildings on fire..." "... minivan spun out of control causing horrific traffic jam..." "...multi-car pile up after semi-truck collided with Metro bus on 14th Street Bridge." "Damaged bridge closed for repairs..." *Nothing about the White House. Maybe Homeland is keeping this under wraps.* The thought took her breath away. She flipped off the radio.

Power outage. What else is in danger? Her mind flooded with what-if scenarios. *What if they hacked the power grids, water supplies, or the Pentagon's weapon systems? Did they attack the financial industry? Failure to access credit cards will create a run on banks. What about medical corporations? What if the hacker shuts down E-medical records, denying healthcare to millions of people or, worse, disables life-saving electronic equipment? According to the latest news, there's already rioting in the streets.* The danger of these scenarios only triggered more adrenaline, but she couldn't stop her mind from racing. Driving at 90 mph, she was thankful for the deserted streets at this hour.

Ten minutes after the alert, updates made her datawatch nearly vibrate off her wrist. "White House strobe lights down." *So, the power outage reached President's Park and the White House. It would be completely dark at this hour. What happened to the backup system? Surely, we tested for that.* Her mind flashed to the last test of the system. *Yes, I know we did.* The crisis of the situation was credible, and she was determined to get to the bottom of it.

Impatient to get to work, she swiped her ID card at the secured parking lot entrance, drove over the security grid that electronically checked the underside of her vehicle for explosives, narcotics, or other hazards, and nodded to the guard, who was barely old enough to vote. *These gun-toting soldiers seem younger every day.*

The guard signaled for her to open the SUV's rear door as he walked around the vehicle. It took a few precious moments to check her car before he hit the automatic close button. The hatch door whined and shut with a click. He moved to her side window, smiled, and tapped the roof of her car, indicating she was free to go. Cordy parked and darted into an attached anonymous two-story brick building.

Clipping her ID to her jacket, Cordy's mind spun into action before she reached the office's front door. *The strobe lights are down.* She remembered reworking the strobe light code over a month ago, and it had worked perfectly. For the past several months, her team, with their expertise and experience, had been tasked with rebuilding government security and updating the digital infrastructure. They had prioritized, analyzed, and walled off all government systems, adding security upgrades to identify, track, and protect files from cyber espionage.

What went wrong? How had someone hacked into a major defense program protecting the White House? Did it have anything to do with the screens going black in the Justice Department two days ago? Did we miss something? Cordy knew failure wasn't an option. Her team would stop whatever threat the attacker planted.

A security officer stepped forward and greeted her at the front door. "It's nice to have company at this hour."

"It's good to see you, too." Cordy set two bags and her laptop on the conveyor belt. "Has anyone from my team arrived yet?"

The officer entered the time and checked off her name on the thick pad in his hand. "You're the first. As usual, I'll log them in as each member enters. Code Q. We can never be too safe. Think you'll find anything?"

This officer is too chatty. Cordy stepped through the scanner. "We'll track down whomever or whatever triggered the alert." She paused at the end of the conveyor belt as he checked her bags.

"Why all the crackers, Ma'am? Are you planning on staying the week?" The officer's right eyebrow lifted as he grinned.

"Morning sickness." Cordy placed a hand on her belly, rolled her eyes, and grabbed her stuff. He seemed confused. *No time to educate this man.* "Hope you have a nice day."

"You, too." He nodded and went back to work.

Cordy's office was spartan of decor, in deliberate contrast to her immediate boss's accommodations—the president of the U.S., who lived in the White House. Honestly, the space was a bit cramped, but it wasn't about the rooms. It was about who worked there and the decisions they made. The office was deliberately placed across the country from Washington, D.C., to safeguard national assets and separate vital functions in case of an emergency. However, she frequently flew to the nation's capital since her recent promotion.

She glanced at her watch. Sixteen minutes had flown by since the initial alert. *It'll be a while before I get another break.* Cordy made a quick pit stop while considering what lay ahead. Her thoughts felt like they moved in slow motion, but in reality, they ticked through her mind like scene clips from a movie, generating a constant stress that never seemed to ease.

Would motion-detecting strobe lights going dark cause such chaos? That didn't make any sense—they turned off and on all the time. I wonder what else triggered the cyber alert. Flashes of nuclear threats from Iran, Russia, and Syria flooded her mind, but those attacks were DoD's responsibility—hers was cyber warfare, a threat that could potentially disrupt the entire nation.

She had dedicated years of her life to fighting all threats in the FBI. If the U.S. blew up a missile base in Syria, all that would be left was rubble, and the danger would be neutralized. It would take time to rebuild. But with her new job of protecting against cyberwarfare, she could take down servers filled with malware, phishing links on apps and emails, or recruiting videos, and the hacks would reappear on a different server within a few hours.

Cordy quickly washed her hands, darted from the restroom, and took the elevator to the second floor. Her mind kept spinning with possibilities.

Sept. 11 –2:58 a.m. EDT, Washington, D.C./
12:58 a.m. MDT, Fort Collins, Colorado

The strobe lights were off, but Cordy's instincts told her that something else triggered the alarm. The White House and its surrounding park were at risk, which meant that the president of the United States was in danger. As the leader of her small but dedicated team, Cordy felt the weight of responsibility on her shoulders. Her team was a crucial part of the nation's diverse security system, and they had successfully contained any crisis before most people knew about it. However, today's utterly unpredictable situation caught Cordy off guard. As a team, their daily challenge was to avoid or contain all cyber threats at any cost.

The elevator stopped on the second floor. Outside Cordy's office was a third, more sophisticated security system. She stared into a retinal scanner and used the fingerpad to unlock the reinforced steel door, opening into the fire-retardant chamber—her office. No one entered without passing through the scanner and gaining approval first. Cameras throughout the building also recorded all movement 24/7.

A heat wave greeted Cordy when she opened the office door. Multiple computers working in the background made the windowless room swelter. She caught a drip of sweat sliding down her cheek with her left sleeve, checked the AC, and found it was already on full blast. A temperature gauge on her desk read 68°F, which was usually in her comfort zone, but since her pregnancy, her personal thermostat ran hot.

The refrigeration's low hum mingled with the buzzing fluorescent lights overhead and interfered with Cordy's focus on the multiple emergencies set before her. A wall of screens directly in front of the desk allowed her to monitor government operations comprehensively. Cordy's fingers flew across the keyboard, searching through the plethora of data streaming over her network. She felt relief when she noted the Code Q alarm had nothing to do with the Justice Department.

A red alert flashed the problem. The highly sophisticated infrared laser system protecting the White House's perimeter and nearby federal buildings had also gone down eighteen minutes ago. Her mind snapped to attention, forming mental images and codes as she struggled to assess the national security risks and set to work. President's Park was wide open for attack without federal grounds protection, and chaos ran rampant in downtown Washington, D.C.,—less than a mile from the White House. *I must act fast.*

Ten Days Earlier

Sept. 1 – 5:48 p.m. IRST, Qatar Airlines flight from
Mashhad, Iran, to Washington, D.C.

Qatar Airbus, Flight QR707, was stuck on a wet tarmac outside of Mashhad, Iran. The A-320 was at maximum capacity, and a flustered hostess repeated for the umpteenth time to the passengers packed in the aisles, "Please take your seats. All overhead bins are full. You must check any luggage that you're unable to stow under the seat in front of you."

The jet bounced as disgruntled passengers inched their way forward, some shoving, others swearing. One middle-aged man was incredibly obnoxious. "This is ridiculous. I want to speak with the person in charge."

Seated passengers glared at the man, but the plump, gray-haired lout refused to shut up as he elbowed his way in the opposite direction of traffic flow.

A petite purser, dressed primly in the airline's maroon uniform, met the irate passenger head-on. Her cheeks flushed, nearly the same color as her tight-fitted jacket. "Sir, I'll help you check your luggage." She reached for his travel case.

"I won't check my bag," he retorted as he pulled away, accidentally banging the luggage wheels into the shoulder of a passenger seated in 2B. The jerk didn't apologize.

The purser leaned toward the seated passenger. "I'm sorry, sir." Playing tug-of-war with the man's suitcase, she demanded, "Give me the bag. There's no more room in the overhead bins." By now, her knee-length pencil skirt had hiked up to mid-thigh. She managed to wrestle the bag away from the man and yanked at the hem of her uniform. She handed the bag to an attendant at the front of the plane. "Check this, please."

***

The passenger in 2B, Farzad Zahair, tried to calm the fury growing inside. *That idiot could blow my cover if I'm not careful.* He patted his suit pocket, making sure nothing had been stolen during the recent commotion. It could have been a set-up to distract one's attention, and it's what Zahair would have done if he planned to swipe one's personal belongings. Relief flooded through him as he felt his passport. Of course, terrorists don't fly to the U.S. under their real names—his passport read Ingram Freeman. The blue-tinted contact lenses irritated his brown eyes, and he felt a headache coming on. The idiot's booming voice didn't help.

There was still a commotion in the aisle nearby. The purser rose on her toes to glare at the foul-mouthed man towering over her and tried to appease him as he waved his hands toward the door where she'd sent his bag.

The man continued to swear—growing more irate. "There's been one hell of a mistake." The loudmouth shoved his boarding pass into her hand and leaned closer to read the purser's nametag. "I only fly first class, Arianna. I refuse to take a trip to the U.S. flying in a f____g chicken coop. Find me a better seat."

Agitated by the jerk's behavior, Zahair suspected the man demanded special perks because he felt entitled. He was throwing a fit worse than a two-year-old just because he hadn't gotten an upgrade. *You should have paid for first class if you wanted to fly up front.* He felt his calm demeanor slipping into something far more primitive.

Arianna's dark brown ponytail swished from side to side as she shook her head, but she didn't back down. "Sir, you must take your assigned seat. The plane is full." She checked the boarding stub and returned it to him. "Go back to 30E now." She repositioned the maroon cap that had slid from her head.

The irate passenger pushed his way to the front of the plane, but she blocked his path. "No, you can not go in there. The cockpit is off-limits."

"You have no idea who you are dealing with. I'm Dirk Young, CEO of—"

"I don't care who you are!" Arianna's dark brown eyes sparked a gold glint of anger as the man shoved her aside. "Sir! Take your seat now, or I will call security. They will remove you from this plane, and you will never fly with us again."

"I'll move back to that shabby seat, but you will bring me a ton of free champagne after all this hassle!" Dirk the Jerk said.

Zahair's head throbbed. He wanted to jump up and crush the guy's skull, but that wouldn't bode well for him. He had to play the part of a successful businessman, not a thug.

Finally, Arianna convinced the grumpy man to sit in his assigned seat and offered him a complimentary glass of champagne as a token of peace.

Zahair rubbed his forehead. *I doubt this will be the last we hear from that bastard, but thank you for now.* He went back to reading his book, doing his best to zone out a screaming child. A teenager reclined beside him, playing Flapping Birds on his cell phone. Every time a bird leapt into the air, the phone beeped. Zahair grabbed his lime-green earbuds and tossed them at the teen. "Use these if you want to live through the flight."

The teen snapped his chewing gum. "Thanks, bro. These are cool buds." He plugged them into his phone and continued chomping his gum like a cow chewing cud.

At last, the flight crew closed and sealed the door. It's time to settle back for a boring flight. *Twelve hours until I can optimize my plans. Hopefully, that kid spits out his gum soon.*

The flight crew crept along the aisles, their faces drawn as if they had been up all week. They were probably on their second leg in three days and saw no end in sight.

Two hours later, Zahair had finished a mediocre meal and nodded off when Dirk the Jerk started up again. He was back in first class, asking to trade seats with anyone.

Dirk made the mistake of poking Zahair's shoulder, the one he'd bruised earlier in the flight, waving money in his face. "I'll give you $100 if you change seats with me."

"You, again. Go away!" Zahair's patience was wearing thin.

A ding sounded overhead, and Zahair saw the seatbelt sign light up. "We are encountering turbulence. Please return to your seats and buckle your seatbelts," came over the intercom.

The plane lurched, causing Dirk to stumble in the aisle. Arianna came to his aid. "Are you okay, Mr. Young?"

"No, I'm not," Dirk said. "I don't belong back there. I expect one of these passengers who got an upgrade to trade seats with me." He turned to the first-class passengers and announced, "I'll pay extra to change seats. Name your price. I can afford it." He waved five $100 bills in front of the teenager sitting next to Zahair. "You there, young man, surely you can use a few extra bucks."

A man across the aisle stood up. "Leave my son alone."

Dirk turned. "You going to make me?" His beefy hand shoved the father's shoulder, knocking his head into the overhead bin.

Arianna grabbed Dirk's arm. "Sir, this is intolerable. Go back to your seat now. I'm tired of dealing with your antics. You've caused nothing but chaos since you boarded the plane. I'm reporting you—"

"Leave me alone," Dirk bulldozed his way past the purser and plowed into a host who had come to her aid.

"Go back to your seat now," he said. "I'm not going to ask you again."

Dirk swore at the man and was getting more agitated.

People craned their necks to see what was happening. One young mother covered her child's ears.

Zahair sensed his own pulse with each heartbeat throb behind his irritated eyes—a side effect of his recent concussion. He took a deep breath and tried to relax, but the man wouldn't shut up. He clenched and unclenched his fists. Stress always made his headaches worse.

Arianna wasn't arguing with Dirk, but she shook her head. Zahair knew you should never shake your head when confronting someone whose ire is up. She made the mistake of closing her eyes, saying, "Uh-uh. I can't."

It was all it took to piss off Dirk. His face turned redder than a radish as he bellowed obscenities and slapped her across the face.

She brought her hands up to protect herself. "You're crazy."

Had she really said that? Zahair had seen this in hostage situations more than once. When an unstable person reaches this point, no amount of talking will change his mind. His options were narrowing every second.

Other passengers shouted for Dirk to leave them alone and to sit down.

Dirk was now so out of control that he was performing as if on center stage, punching anyone sitting along the aisle. "Shut up. Do you hear me? Shut up!" Enraged, the man's bulging eyes cut back to Arianna. "Get me the pilot, now!"

"I can't," she crossed her arms in front of her face as he again swung a fist at her.

"Where's your security?" Zahair asked. *Why am I getting involved?*

Dirk swiped a punch at Zahair. It was more than Zahair could tolerate. His breath hitched. Sweat poured down his armpits. A rapid tattoo beat like a drum in his chest.

The host yanked Dirk away, but the man spun around and struck the male flight attendant in the gut. Dirk headed for the cockpit.

Responsible for the flight's crew, Arianna bravely dashed down the hall behind him. "You can't go in there."

Dirk yelled back, "Watch me."

The co-pilot opened the door with such force it smacked into Dirk. "Move. Are you trying to crash the plane?" The co-pilot shoved Dirk away from the cockpit.

Dirk turned and rammed a fist into the co-pilot's face, sending him into the drink cart at the front of the plane. Water and blood sprayed across the cart. The co-pilot backed down the aisle, holding his nose.

Dirk headed for another blow.

Zahair shut his eyes, forcing his fingers into claws. *Stay where you are. Let it play out without you getting involved. Don't draw any attention.* He tried to obey his inner voice. *Don't do it,* but his mind snapped. "Enough!"

As the two men reached Zahair's seat, his book slid to the floor with a thud. In an instant, he stood between the co-pilot and Dirk.

The jerk launched for Zahair, who ducked in time to grab the idiot around the waist and body-slammed him.

People screamed, "Yes, get the bastard." "Get him." "Subdue the jerk." "Tie him up."

Zahair heard the air rush from Dirk's lungs as he hit the floor. *Shit, what am I doing? Too late now. Just finish the job.* Zahair's breathing sped up. He felt light-headed, the first sign of hyperventilation. Thump, thump, thump—his heart throbbed against his ribcage. Without thinking, his fingers slid around Dirk's neck.

Dirk grabbed Zahair's hair, tugging, trying to breathe. The teen that sat next to Zahair grabbed his shoulder. "You're killing the guy. Let him breathe."

Zahair eased up and tugged Dirk upright. "Breathe, buddy, but don't you dare take another swing at anyone. You hear me?"

Dirk gasped in a deep breath and choked. "Yes," he finally wheezed. Then he brought his arm forward and swung his elbow into Zahair's gut.

Zahair grabbed the back of Dirk's head in his beefy palm, yanked a chunk of hair as he pulled back his head, and smoothly wrapped his other arm around Dirk's neck. With an experienced move, Zahair pulled the man close to his knees and lifted him off the ground, whispering, "Do that again, and it'll be the last breath you take. I'll snap your neck like a pretzel, and you'll be a drooling quadriplegic, breathing out of a tube poking through your neck like a straw. Do you capeesh?"

Dirk nodded as best he could as Zahair set him back on his tiptoes.

The whisper was so low that only Dirk could hear it. "Good. Now, I want you to apologize to the flight crew. Ask for forgiveness like a good little boy." Zahair's hand tightened around Dirk's carotid when he tried to shake his head. "Do it."

Dirk nodded.

"I'm not done yet. The police will arrest you when we land, and you will not resist." The whisper was barely audible as Zahair smiled at Arianna, now standing before them.

"Thank you, sir. I'll take it from here." Her eyes showed fear and gratitude.

"Sorry, Miss." Dirk's hot breath eked over Zahair's arm.

"I'll hand him over as soon as we come to an agreement," Zahair said.

The stewardess nodded.

Zahair whispered again in Dirk's ear as he squeezed until he felt the jerk's Adam's apple bob while Dirk tried to catch a breath. He became limp as the blood supply to his brain dwindled. "You'll return to your seat after formally apologizing to the plane's co-pilot, flight crew, and everyone on board. Do I make myself perfectly clear?"

Zahair feared he'd gone too far when Dirk didn't move and thumped him across the back as he guided the jerk toward the purser. "He's all yours. I believe Mr. Young, as you called him, would like to take the microphone and apologize to all these nice people."

Dirk gasped in a breath. His eyes darted between Zahair and Arianna and then to the host, who stepped closer with zip ties in his hands. "Yes, that's exactly what I'd like to do." Dirk stepped behind the purser. "Please, Miss, and I'll quietly take my seat…the one I'm assigned to." He glanced toward Zahair and nodded.

Zahair sat back down to a loud round of applause. "The crew deserves all the credit." He lowered his eyes, smiled, and scooped his book from the floor.

The teenager beamed a toothy grin. "That was so cool."

Passengers whispered, pointed, and stared at Zahair, probably wondering how he subdued Dirk while hardly breaking into a sweat— if they only knew. He hoped to disappear into the background as an everyday "Joe." Usually, he passed like a shadow in the dark, dressed in plain clothes that hid his ripped abs, sculpted muscles, and lean body. He was a gentleman who opened the door for ladies, allowed older men to cut in line before him, and walked with his head down. Rarely would he look someone in the eye. He kicked himself for letting this jerk get to him.

After Dirk apologized, the host escorted the jerk back to his original seat with his wrists zip-tied in front of him. Dirk didn't grumble once.

Now sporting a bandage under his oozing nostrils, the co-pilot knelt next to Zahair. "The pilot and I extend our deepest gratitude. We have a reporter who will meet you at the gate. They want a first-hand interview—"

"No!" Zahair said. "No interviews. I mean, your crew has dealt with this in such a splendid manner. They deserve all of the credit." His mind raced. He had to think fast. Any exposure to the press could mean his death. "If anyone deserves an interview, it should be you. Look at you. You're a hero." He could see the co-pilot wasn't buying it. "I will ask a favor, however. I am running on a tight schedule. I only ask that you allow me to be the first off the plane. Then, the medics should come on board to treat those who have been injured. You can arrange that for me, right?"

"Of course," the co-pilot said, "but the pilot has already radioed ahead. You're the hero."

"I'm no hero."

"It's already in the works," the co-pilot said, appearing baffled.

"I understand, so make sure they interview the proper people." Zahair lowered his voice. "This is only for your ears. I am on a mission, and I can't be late."

"I knew you were in the military," the co-pilot said, louder than Zahair expected. "Purple heart?"

Zahair was a terrific storyteller who could make up tall tales on the fly. He made the lie as close to the truth as possible. It was easier to remember. He had earned a two-pointed sword of Ali in Iran, so he said, "Two, while I was fighting for my country, my family back home was murdered, but we don't talk about it." He spoke loud enough for those around him to hear. "It brings back a lot of…" He swallowed. "My little girl…my wife…you know…sad memories." He leaned over and whispered into the co-pilot's ear. "I'm working undercover. I can't be spotted, and no mention of my name can be released to the press. Do you understand?"

The co-pilot nodded. "You are a true hero. I'll make the arrangements."

"Thanks for your understanding." Zahair heartily shook the co-pilot's hand. He could have easily crushed the man's fingers in his firm grasp.

"The flight crew will be sure you are the first off the plane before bringing in the paramedics." The co-pilot stood, gave a salute, and went about his business. "Arianna, I need a word with you."

The co-pilot returned a few minutes later. "Mr. Freeman, please move to the front of the plane and bring your luggage. You can ride in the jump seat and be the first to deplane."

Zahair knew he needed to leave the airport without going through Customs and disappear undetected as soon as possible. He sent an Instatext to his contact, Einar Zinmansky, who had only twenty seconds to read the message before it was deleted—erasing and overwriting to prevent detection. "Plane landed. I need to bypass Customs." He used an encrypted code and entered the gate number. "Co-pilot says press will be on standby. Bring disguise. I'll pose as a reporter to make my getaway."

Second Alert

Another surge of adrenaline blazed through Cordy's veins when a second alarm blasted. It had been only thirty-five minutes since the initial Code Q alert. So far, Cordy had struggled unsuccessfully to get the ground lasers back online. *What's happening now?* Springing into action, her mind acutely alert, she pulled up her analysis program. The latest drone program had been hacked. "Not the Pentagon, too!" *Do that drone program and the loss of the laser system have anything to do with one another?*

Cordy hit the communication button marked Quint. "Where are you?"

"I stopped by the forensic lab," which is what Quint called his office, "to pick up my burner cell, and I'm heading your way. Did you catch the Nats game last night? They won and are heading for the championship."

"Baseball?" Cordy said in disgust. "There's no time for sports! Oh, wait. I just remembered what happened in Florida before the Super Bowl. No, forget it. My mind's on overload."

Quint paused. "Do you mean the hack causing a water treatment plant to add 100 times the lye content above the normal amount? What made you think of that?"

"You did with that Nat's comment." Cordy surprised even herself. She rarely watched sports. It wasn't the game that caught her eye but the hack. "Fortunately, an astute engineer caught the discrepancy before any contaminated water reached the public, but it could have been a nightmare." *Nightmare. Right.* Her brain had detoured again. *Or had it? Is something planned during the World Series? That's a little over a week away.* "Where are they holding the games?"

"The Nats will play the Houston Astros, first in Texas, and then back to D.C.," Quint said.

Houston? Another detour. Her mind bounced from one idea to another. Something she did when stressed. *Focus, Cordy! Get the strobe lights and laser systems online.* "Back to the Pentagon. Return to the lab and check the Department of Defense files. I'm worried someone's hacked into the Maven II project. The WAMI capabilities are said to be a thousand times more powerful than those of any drone in our arsenal."

"Whammy?" Quint asked.

"Wide-area motion imagery—eyes in the skies." Cordy's breath hitched. *Is that the weapon Braun's testing this morning? I know he wouldn't tell me even if I could ask him, and he's already on full alert by now. No personal calls are allowed for two hours before any test.* "Make sure the Maven II project is secure. It has built-in artificial intelligence to track and attack threats, far superior to any person or a whole army of trained soldiers. This can't fall into enemy hands."

"Oh, WAMI. Got it! Not happening on our watch." His voice was hoarse with emotion.

Cordy tried to open the back door to the laser program, still wondering why her thoughts kept drifting to hacks during sports events. What were her instincts trying to get her to see? Struggling to sort out the jumble of ideas that flooded her mind, something kept drifting just out of reach. She grabbed a sticky note and jotted down the World Series in Houston as a reminder for later. It might be nothing, but it eased her mind. Gripping her keyboard, she inhaled deeply. "We're swamped with data here. I need another set of eyes. Find out who's hacked into the drones and stop them while I get the laser and strobe light systems back online. I've called in Perry and Svetlana, too. Get any help you need."

"I'm on it," Quint said, "but not Perry. I'm not having some Russian geek hacker—"

"Just do whatever it takes and reverse this." Cordy disconnected on his mid-grumble. *Now is not the time to get involved in their spat. We have to work together.* She knew there had been a rivalry brewing. Both professional jealousy and trust issues wedged between her teammates, although Quint's snarky attitude toward Perry did not include Svetlana, the second Russian to join their team. She studied hard to become a U.S. citizen and earned her GED before Cordy hired her last month as an intern. Svetlana had great expertise, could accomplish complex actions, tasks, and processes relating to computational and physical techniques, and had a diverse insight into other venues—beyond average skills for her age. She had proven her worth to Cordy.

Some Cabinet members also questioned adding Russians to the cybersecurity team, but even President Spendorf agreed they were a benefit. Perry, a first-year resident, faced a challenging path to obtaining a security clearance. He had written the primary virus code that shut down New York's power grid, but he hadn't planted it. His misfortune was that a notorious hacker stole the code, enhanced it, and embedded it into the grid. This had earned Perry some distrust.

However, amidst the chaos, Perry came to the team's rescue, proving his unwavering loyalty to the U.S. He not only reversed the hacked code but also worked tirelessly to reform the corruption of significant business and financial systems, contributing to the country's defense against cyber warfare. This brilliant teen had a unique journey, attending high school while also taking online college courses. He graduated from the University at sixteen, worked briefly for the Russian government, and was wooed away to Red Panda in South Africa until two years ago. Spyware was his specialty. Perry's insight into Russian hacking allowed him to quickly recognize familiar malware patterns. In Cordy's opinion, he was definitely an asset to the team. *If only Quint could see it, too.*

Sept. 11 – 3:26 a.m. EDT, Washington, D.C./
1:26 a.m. MDT, Fort Collins, Colorado

Another message from Guy at Homeland Security startled Cordy out of her reflections. "FYI. Rebooting strobe light system—should restart soon."

Hasn't he already done that? It would have been my first response. It's been forty-six minutes since the initial Code Q alert, and it takes at least five minutes, yet that still might not work. A key piece of the puzzle snapped into her mind. *Why didn't I think of that before? Check for any modifications to the channel code that knocked out the system. If that little demon is in here, I'll find it.*

When her phone chirped, Cordy had barely bridged an interface to her analytical program to connect directly to the strobe light and laser systems. *Homeland Security again.*

This time, Secretary Guy Weimer began talking without an introduction. "… won't reboot, and—" A loud vibration came over the line. "Hold on a moment, it's from Secret Service Agent Kyle Benson." There was a pause.

Cordy heard snippets of the conversation. "Agent Trudo reported…" "…breached no-fly zone…" "We're short-staffed, and this falls to Homeland Security."

Guy asked, "Is the camera already installed?" "Thanks. We'll take care of it."

"Guy? Are you free to speak?" Cordy asked.

"Yes. I just got word that a sharp-eyed guard patrolling the perimeter of the White House reported unusual activity in progress on top of a building a block away. It looks like a huge crate. This is unbelievable but true. A chopper hovered over the rooftop, made a delivery drop, and then zoomed away! Entering a no-fly zone is not allowed, yet it happened. A quick check of the city's records shows no permissions applied for, and that building has a direct line of sight to the White House. My gut tells me that an enemy has taken advantage of this blackout or maybe even caused it, but that isn't a heating system going in at 3:20 a.m. It's too much of a coincidence, and I don't believe in such things."

"Neither do I," Cordy said.

"We've sent in a team to investigate. Secret Service is on high alert, and I'm asking for continued surveillance. I know you're halfway across the country, but we are bogged down and need your help."

"What do you need from me?" Cordy asked.

"I'm sending you the GPS coordinates and a VidCam link the team just set up. Monitor it for any cell or computer activity from the area—signals, emails, text messages, or conversations. Everyone's on overload here with the lasers down. Get me information as quickly as you can!"

Cordy swallowed hard when another wave of nausea pulsed through her. She munched on a cracker as she typed the GPS info into her latest WatchDog and CyberCheck programs to detect any signal traffic. "Anything else?" she asked, but Guy had disconnected the call. As a precaution, she also entered the GPS coordinates into Avenger. Unless Homeland Security or DoD launched a missile, it wouldn't attack—but the coordinates were available if any threats developed.

While her programs searched in the background for any activity at the GPS site, Cordy discovered the modified channel code, a crucial piece of data that had been tampered with. She replaced it with the original data to resume the strobe lights and laser systems, and hit enter.

A blasting third alert shook her to her core. The loud beeps added a headache to the nausea she was already fighting. The lasers and strobe lights were now working, but the Avenger Missile System, a crucial defense system protecting the White House airspace, had crashed. It happened right after she entered the revised code. *Did I cause the alert?* Cordy reviewed her entry one more time. *No, it wasn't me.* Fear went up another notch when the National Terrorism Advisory System status jumped from Alert to Activated.

Cordy rushed to enter Avenger's internal program to review any updates to the code, but the Department of Defense had taken over the controls. They were the only department that could override the system. *Thank God it wasn't something I did to raise the alert, but who shut down Avenger?*

Cordy fought to log in. She was determined to get Avenger operating again and wouldn't let a few denied access attempts stop her. "Now what!" She exclaimed, refusing to be deterred. She was forced to use a workaround and entered a code she never thought she'd need to use. Initially, she refused to code in a backdoor on their latest upgrade, but Quint and her team insisted. It worked.

Three minutes ago, Carl Wyller – Secretary of Defense, was the last person to log into the system, or so she thought. But something wasn't right, as she'd suspected. The name entered was "Karl Wyller"—Carl with a K. The mystery deepened.

It took less than fifty seconds to quarantine all entries made over the last 12 hours—except her own. The shrill beeping ceased when the Avenger System resumed operations, but four attempts to regain control from external sources had been initiated in that timeframe. She traced the IP addresses of the intruders—all remained anonymous. She could only trace the intruders' locations. Two originated from Ryazan, Russia, and one from a Museum in Tehran, Iran. A fourth came from the West Bank of Israel. Whoever orchestrated this multi-pronged attack was highly skilled.

"Wouldn't the WatchDog program alert us?" Perry shoved his glasses, which had slid down his nose, back in place.

"It should have, but we haven't been pinged." *Trap door? Who said that, and what does he mean? What vault? Our vault where we keep all government backup servers? No, it couldn't be.* Cordy hopped from her chair to get a clearer picture on the screen, but it was only a grainy, green shadow. Even using Upscaler to enlarge the image, filling the whole screen didn't help—*night vision lens.*

She hit the direct line to Homeland Security, her fingers trembling. But Guy didn't pick up, even after four rings, so she tried Carl Wyller, and he answered on the first ring.

"I'm on VidCam," Cordy rushed on, "Do you still have eyes on that building across the street?"

"What building?" Carl sounded stressed—his voice high-pitched and sharp-toned. "What are you talking about? One moment, I have

Washington PD on the line, and I may lose the call if I put them on hold."

"Listen. This is urgent!" Cordy rushed on before he could say no. "Guy called, gave me GPS coordinates of a building across from the White House, and asked me to monitor activity on the VidCam. Something's happening. I can't see exactly what, but a male voice said, 'Trap door triggered! Hit vault first. Five minutes.' Any idea what that means?"

"Why didn't you call Guy?" Carl said something else, followed by a rustling sound in the background. "…I'm busy…" "Yes, Chief Polack, hold on a moment. I'm on two calls."

Cordy wanted facts. "Guy didn't answer, and while I have you on the phone, did you shut down the Avenger System?"

"What? Avenger? No. I've been tied up all day with…wait, Guy's heading this way." There was a shuffling sound. "Guy, Cordy's on the phone. She says something's going down somewhere—take the call. I'm in up to my eyeballs in alligators already. I'm transferring her to you."

More static. "Guy, here."

Cordy repeated her concerns about the GPS site. "That was two minutes ago. What do you see on your end?"

"Nothing from here, but I'll check into it." Guy's calm voice was reassuring.

Someone in the background shouted, "Guy, over here. Hurry!"

"Sorry, Cordy. Gotta go." Guy disconnected.

Cordy nearly dropped the phone when her VidCam image flickered. A male with a thick Middle Eastern accent said, "Seek target—fifteen minutes and counting." Cordy, a seasoned intelligence analyst, got closer to her screen, hoping to see a more precise picture, when a shadowy figure came into view. The male appeared to be a soldier dressed in camo gear. A helmet hid his face, but he held up his cell phone. She zoomed in and read the message but wasn't sure what it meant, "IS confirmed." Someone in the background screamed, "General, we've been sighted. Launch! Launch!"

Another voice, unaccented and commanding, filled the room. "Track seeker and jam signal. Lock onto target. Time to strike!" The screen went black, leaving Cordy in a state of panic. Her breath came in short, sharp gasps, and her heart pounded in her chest like a drum.

Breaking News

Sept. 11 — 3:36 a.m. EDT, Washington, D.C./
1:36 a.m. MDT, Fort Collins, Colorado

Fifty-six minutes after the initial Code Q! Cordy's mind spun out of control as every little thought grabbed her attention. *Focus!* A man in military gear was on a rooftop across the street from the White House and had just given the order, "Track seeker and jam signal." *Everything went dark. Did someone discover our GPS?* "Time to strike!" *Strike where?* "Lock onto target." *Where? The White House? Our vault?* That cell phone message read, "IS confirmed." *What is confirmed? Why IS in caps?*

A seismic wave of fear crashed through Cordy as she scrambled to reboot the WatchDog program. The signal remained blocked. She was sitting atop a ticking time bomb, unable to stop an explosion. *What if they track everything back to our GPS?* In a split second, the world she knew could end. Five minutes had passed since the general's fifteen-minute warning, and time was flying by too fast. Out of habit, she set her timer to go off in nine minutes, wondering what was about to happen.

Frustrated, Cordy had tried everything in her power, and she could think of nothing more to do on her end. She hated being left in the dark but had to leave this threat up to Homeland Security and the DoD. As usual, Guy had sounded calm, able to face any crisis. Carl, however, seemed in over his head. Her only ray of hope was that the Cyber Crisis Agency had backup copies of all government data or most of it. As a precaution, she had placed the rooftop militant's GPS coordinates into Avenger for all the good that would do if security services didn't act in time.

The door burst open as Svetlana, the team's newest member, dashed into the office. Her blonde hair, usually in a neat French braid, was still damp, wind-blown, and in a riot of curls. She swiped back a stray lock with one hand and held out a cell phone with the other. "Cordy, Perry's on the phone." A blush blossomed over her cheeks when she said his name, making her appear younger than seventeen. "He says to turn on CNN! They just reported someone hacked the Pentagon."

"I know. Quint's working on it, but how did CNN get that info so quickly? Hang on." Cordy opened a link to the major news stations—CNN, BBC World News, MSNBC, and Fox News came up on the screen. She muted all but CNN, heaved a sigh, and took the phone. "Hi, Perry." The shock of the news was evident in her voice, mirroring the disbelief in the room.

"I got your message, threw on my clothes, and headed to the office." He sounded out of breath.

Cordy kept one eye on the screen as she spoke, "Give me the latest news."

Perry's voice cracked in excitement. "Your forensic program pinged, and someone attacked our latest drone technology. It's sending a steady stream to our WatchDog data analysis system, and one is scheduled for live testing in the next few minutes. I'm afraid it's too late to call it off. According to our sources, jets have already taken off for the war games. Germany and the UK also reported being hacked. Be there in a sec." He disconnected.

Cordy's heart skipped a beat, not for the first time today. *Braun's testing a new weapon system this morning. Please, let it be anything but this hacked drone.* She punched the intercom. "Quint, give me an update."

No one responded.

"Quint. Answer me!" Cordy shouted as her fingers flew across her keyboard, searching for Quint's latest entries. Five minutes ago, he had typed several lines of code and ended with Kuint. A gasp escaped her lips. Her pulse skittered into overdrive—*name's misspelled with a K like Carl's. What does that mean?*

A slender, fair-skinned man opened Cordy's office door. She was amazed at how professional Perry always looked, even at this hour—

dressed in Dockers with sharp creases pressed down each leg. His navy blue suit jacket hung loosely over a light blue shirt.

"What's going on?" Perry gulped. His unbuttoned shirt collar revealed a jagged scar running from his left ear to his Adam's apple that bobbed as he swallowed. Today, he wore Coke-bottle lens glasses that kept sliding down his narrow nose instead of his usual contacts. *He didn't even take the time to put them in.*

"Look at this." Cordy waved Perry forward. "Something's wrong." Her voice rose in pitch as she paced—every nerve fiber on alert. "I don't like what I see."

"What's wrong?" Those intense blue eyes peered around the room. "Did you talk to Quint?"

"Ten minutes ago, but now he doesn't answer." Cordy clenched her fists, returned to her station, and sat staring at her laptop. "Five minutes ago, Quint logged off as Kuint." She pointed to the code. "It's spelled with a K, just like Karl before shutting down the Avenger system."

"Avenger went down?" Perry's concern etched furrows across his brow.

"Yes, the strobe lights, laser system, and Avenger all shut down before someone on top of a building near the White House gave orders to launch."

"Launch what?" Perry asked.

"I don't know. What next?" Cordy's mind raced, frantic with fleeting thoughts. She muttered, "I'm worried they may have access to our vault data. Malware, defense system vulnerability, access…but how? Everything is encrypted to keep it secure."

Perry piped up, "Maybe like what happened to SolarWinds? Cyberpunks linked into upgrades to track and take control of secure devices."

"I hope not." *It's like a locksmith picking our security codes. It is as easy as opening a trapdoor—Trapdoor. Oh no, that's what the guy with the accent said. Once entered, it would allow access to our data. They could confiscate intellectual property and seize millions of federal, corporate, and personal accounts. The hacker could shut down healthcare, financial, and banking systems, where they could funnel funds into overseas accounts.* Rubbing her throbbing temples, she said, "This could be devilishly hard to track. It would give hackers the keys to everything and be next to impossible to retrieve."

Perry gasped, "Even the defense system and the drones?"

"Yes, I'm afraid so." Fear climbed another notch. "When Avenger shut down, I ran our analysis program, caught the hack, and reversed it. I'll do the same for the drone program, but we're running out of time." Cordy gnawed on her lip as she logged into the Pentagon files. Her main worry was the Maven II drones. *What if Braun ended up testing a hacked drone? A cyberattack could be deadly.* She had to keep her husband safe.

The CyberCheck program popped up on two screens. One displayed the current file, and the other had their latest backup code. "We can't stop whatever is lurking on that rooftop, but we aren't totally stymied. This can run in the background. It will warn us if there are any changes to the code."

Perry shoved his cell phone into his back pocket and walked over to Cordy's desk to review the code as it ran across the screen, line by line, while comparing the two data files.

Cordy noted that Perry was peering over her shoulder, but she was still deep in thought and repeated, "Trapdoor triggered. Hit vault in five minutes. Our vault? Is that what that soldier meant? Did someone unlock our encryption?"

"Why didn't the WatchDog program alert us?" Perry shoved his glasses back in place.

"It should have." Cordy gulped at a horrific thought. *Whoever has access to our vault codes could sell them to other countries, making everything we've created to prevent hackers from stealing vital information useless…if anyone can safeguard it, Quint will. He'll seal up whatever loophole the hacker discovered, but it's a lot to do on his own, and I need him here. No, the vault must be in jeopardy. Why else would he leave*

The vault kept track of all their security and intellectual property. The tools used to research, analyze, and block potential access to software and hardware had been the key to their security efforts. That was why it resided away from its home base. The thought made her hands tremble. If stolen, nothing was safe. Her fingers fumbled as she texted Quint, "Did someone hack into our darknet accounts?"

Cordy was sure they had caught the attack early on. Still thinking aloud, "The attacker will segregate its initial phase from any follow-up action. So, we need to stay one step ahead." However, time was not on their side. Her team worked well together. Quint was excellent at the initial discovery phase, which reviewed past hacker events. Cordy excelled at the follow-up stage, looking into the future to determine how the attack would progress, and together, they would create a method to trap and secure the system, but it took precious hours they didn't have. Her analysis program gave an alarm and started quarantining line items.

Perry tapped a highlighted string of code on her screen. "This is like a game to hackers. Look at these timestamps. They check the data every five minutes to make sure only one instance of their malware is running at a time."

"That's deliberate," Cordy said. "They are in it for the long haul. The hackers probably plan to prevent detection by only intermittently attacking high-security environments, but we will outsmart them."

Although Braun's safety was her highest priority, she had other pressing issues requiring the team's attention. She grabbed her phone and typed in critical concerns, forming a to-do list:

1. Protect the U.S. cybersecurity network
2. Keep strobe, laser, and Avenger systems online
3. Reverse hack into Pentagon—find bot and block it!
   - ✓ Maven II Drone Program code

    - UK drones hacked—call Cyber and Government Security
  Directorate
    - German drones also hacked—need Chancellor
  Huffenmeister's permission to ✓ with their IT dept
4. Safeguard vault! Monitor Quint and be ready for backup
5. Track and trap, reclassify, and abort
6. Who's responsible?
    - Inside job? A mole?
    - Karl Wyller or DoD? Carl denies shutting down Avenger.
  Then who?
7. How did anyone get access to sign off as Kuint?
    - China?
    - Russia?
    - Iran?
    - North Korea?

Fortunately, the team had encrypted all federal government data, but a few agents still refused to use secured systems for their personal emails and cell phones, which could be breached. That was one of the problems with a Secretary of State's server years ago, but surely today, no one tolerated linking unsecured lines to the network. Or was there a device out there that slipped through the cracks?

Perry continued to stare at the code on her screen while he rubbed his hand over his chin, which had only recently begun to sprout a few wiry blond hairs, leaving it looking remarkably like some exotic peach. "Cordy?"

She flinched when Perry tapped her shoulder.

"It has a familiar Russian fingerprint—several different network management system pathways exist. They're talking to every device on the network."

"I know. We blocked direct access to the Internet, but I'm sure the attacker is aware and already retooling their malware." Cordy turned to Perry. "Do you feel comfortable contacting your cousin, Vlad?"

"That's a good idea," Perry said.

Cordy's fingers nervously tapped her thigh as she thought. "Or better yet, has Vlad kept in contact with Cracker? They came to our aid last year."

"I haven't spoken with Vlad for a few months, but we can reach Cracker and his wife directly if needed."

Cordy speed-dialed her key government contacts, but there were no answers at any of them. Unable to reach National Security, Homeland Security, DoD, or even the president directly, Cordy sent a quick encrypted text message to all of the above. "FYI: The Pentagon hack looks like it might be coming from Russia. Time is crucial, so I'm contacting an FBI Russian special agent."

Perry headed for the door and paused. "We didn't hear from anyone in the UK, but did you get the message from Germany? Unfortunately, I don't have access."

"Oh, right. I nearly forgot." Cordy hadn't opened the file yet and was grateful Perry had reminded her. "While I do that, check Quint's office and see if he left any messages."

Perry nodded and departed.

Cordy opened the text sent from Germany, "Hacker attacked our drone rootfiles and replaced them with malware." She opened the darknet account and searched for the Maven II drone's rootfiles. It took three attempts to open the program, where she found a more sinister problem than expected. *The hackers used revised rootkits to send messages to erase code as soon as it activates. I thought we had blocked our data. Even after repairing the hacked files with the latest backup code, the malware repopulates the code every five minutes and automatically removes any repairs. We have to re-encrypt our vault backup code to remove the rootfile malware. I bet that's what Quint's doing. I hope.*

Agent Vern Trudo, an experienced security officer with a sharp eye for detail, had barely completed his rounds when he received a message from President Spendorf's trusted bodyguard, Marv. Marv's voice crackled through Trudo's earpiece, "I just found two bugs planted in Winston's office. Checking Oval now."

"Roger, keep me posted." Trudo punched an access code into a special security device he wore on his wrist. It was a sleek, black device, a marvel of modern technology, linked to SatSurveillance, a secured system that runs via satellite and works independently from the network. The access code, a complex sequence of numbers and letters, changed every thirty minutes. Only Kyle, Trudo, as a shift supervisor, and key security personnel could log into the system that allowed eyes on the Oval Office.

Trudo's wrist screen activated a security camera used only for emergencies. As the lights in the hallway started blinking, Trudo rushed to the main headquarters to get a clearer view of the camera footage on a larger screen.

Masters glanced up when Trudo flung open the office door. "What's going on?"

"Heads up, everyone. Oval Office may have been breached," Trudo's voice crackled with tenacity, sending a shiver down his spine. He pulled up a computer grid of the building. Red lights blinked, indicating computer network problems. The grid's flashing lights started at the East Wing. New lights rapidly marched across the screen, moving westward, each blink adding to the mounting tension.

Masters hopped from his chair, his face a mirror of the growing concern. "The network is going down. What do we do?"

"Cut the links." Trudo typed frantically on his keyboard, trying to stay one step ahead of whatever was powering down the White House electronic devices. The computer grid running on

SatSurveillance continued functioning as the remaining computers shut down inside the main office.

"Can't override nor reboot the system," Masters said, his voice tinged with a sense of helplessness. "I have no access to the network."

Trudo called Marv. "Check on the president. Turn off all electronics, including computers. Get him out of the Oval Office if breached."

Trudo saw the president was on a phone when Marv entered his office.

Marv shone a flashlight around the room. He spoke into his wrist mic. "Just got here. Powers out in Oval." Marv moved toward Zac's desk. "Please, sir, save whatever's on your computer and turn it off. Then get out of your chair and wait in the hallway." Marv rushed to the windows, scanned outside, and closed the drapes.

Zac turned toward Marv. "What? I'm on the phone with Kyle."

"Let me talk to him and turn off the computer now!" Marv stepped behind Zac's chair, blocking him from the window for protection, pushed his chair to one side, and took the phone. "Hi, Kyle. It's all clear here. The president is secure and in my care." Marv disconnected the call.

Zac turned to protest, but after one look at Marv's determined face, Zac reached across his desk, saved, closed down the Word file, and then hit the power down button before scooting back his chair. He stood and glanced at the screen. "I tried to turn off my computer, but it doesn't respond, even after unplugging the power cord."

"Are you sure? Maybe it's on battery power." Marv tried to shut off the laptop.

Carl darted into the office. "Zac? Oh, good. Marv's with you—just checking."

Zac threw an arm over his face. "Don't shine that light in my eyes. I'm okay."

"Sorry. Gotta go." Carl popped back out of the office without another word.

Marv hit the computer's power button two more times with no results. The computer image flashed a few times, but the power remained on even after disconnecting the power cord.

Trudo heard a pause over the mic, followed by, "The president is okay, but the office has no power." Marv lifted the mainline phone and listened. "Phone's down, too. Even with the power off, his computer's flickering, there's a high-pitched buzz, and I can't shut it down. What's going on?"

"I think it's a power surge," Trudo said.

"Or worse." Marv beamed his flashlight over the president's desk. "Is someone trying to hack into our network?"

Trudo watched the grid continue to light up with more flashing red lights. Every computer throughout the House blinked red on the grid and had shut down except in the Oval Office.

"Another blackout!" Master's voice trembled. "Twice in one shift—I don't like it."

"I reprogrammed the backup generators after the last outage, and they should go on any minute now." In fact, Trudo had rebooted the entire network system.

"All electronics in the Oval Office, except Zac's computer, are off. Cell phones, too," Marv said.

"We don't have a moment to spare." Trudo rubbed his chin, his mind racing with the potential threats.

Zac picked up the desk phone. "Nothing yet. White House phone is still dead."

"What is this?" Marv pulled Zac further away from his desk. "There's a flashing green light on the president's webcam."

"That doesn't look good," Trudo brought his wrist to his mouth, "Kyle, the red lights on my grid marched all the way to the Oval Office, where they stopped. Marv's reporting a flashing green light on the president's computer—oops, the green light just went out. It might be a security breach. This isn't some kid sniffing around. It's—"

As predicted, the lights flicked on. Trudo breathed a visible sigh of relief, the tension in the room dissipating.

Even though the green light on the president's computer had stopped flashing, Marv ripped a sticky note from a pad on the desk and slapped it across the camera lens to prevent any spying into the office. He knew that in the world of cyber espionage, even a seemingly innocuous camera could be turned into a powerful tool for surveillance. He disconnected Zac's computer from the network, pulled the laptop from the desk, and stashed it in his top desk drawer.

"What are you doing?" Trudo asked. "Why did you put the computer into Zac's desk?"

"What if someone can access this room using his laptop? It won't turn off no matter what I do."

A loud beep sounded for three seconds, and the grid cleared all blinking lights. "What just happened?" Masters asked.

"The systems network is rebooting," Marv said. "Phone's working again."

The computer screens blazed to life in the main office, starkly contrasting the recent blackout. Trudo, with a mix of relief and caution, ordered an immediate shutdown. "We're in the dark here. Close down everything. We might be dealing with a network virus."

Marv grabbed the cell phone and motioned to the door.

"What?" Zac's voice was firm. "Am I expected to abandon my post?" He looked around the fully lit room, the printer humming in the background. "No. I'm staying until I get the green light from the cybersecurity team." He activated his VidChat, the emergency line to Cordy. "I'm not moving."

"Are we all clear?" Marv asked Trudo over the mic.

Trudo checked in with Kyle. "We're still on high alert, but there are no known threats now."

"Guess we're staying then," Marv reported. "Follow up on every lead and keep us updated."

"Will do. Kyle, can I send analysts to check out every computer before anyone touches them?" Trudo asked.

"Yes, stay on SatSurveillance, shut down power to all network computers, and get the cybersecurity team leader out here ASAP," Kyle said. "Everyone, keep this event quiet."

"Remember, this is strictly confidential," Zac reminded everyone. "We're to treat this as just another day at the office. No leaks to the press."

"Roger." Trudo entered the disturbance into a SatSurveillance log using a secret code known only to key personnel.

Cordy's timer blared, a stark reminder of the ticking clock. Fourteen minutes had vanished since the soldier's ominous announcement from the rooftop near the White House. Cordy's nerves were taut, her senses heightened to the extreme. She had to consciously release her death grip on the chair's handles. In the background, the obnoxious sound from CNN made Cordy flinch, adding to the pressure of the situation.

A newswoman announced, "We interrupt this program with more breaking news." The TV went momentarily to white static, then returned, "…is missing and feared dead."

"Missing? Feared dead? Who?" Cordy's breath caught in her throat, her heart pounding as she waited for more details. The suspense was thick in the air.

As the TV screen came back into focus, reporter Lisa Pagetti stood before the camera in stunned silence. Her mouth gaped as she tried to say her lines in a vast departure from her display of professional confidence and attire. Besides a dab of red lipstick, she wore no make-up, and her bleached-blonde hair lay limp against her head. The cameraman cleared his throat and whispered, "Lisa!" It snapped her from her trance. In a strained voice, as if she was lost with no script, she stammered, "This just in—"

Cordy hit the TV's remote record button and leaned forward, wanting to catch every word. The direct VidChat line from the U.S. president rang, causing her to jolt upright. The hair on her arms rose to attention, and a shiver convulsed through her as adrenaline flooded her system. Trying to calm her racing heart, she had to focus. Pull yourself together, and stay calm. She whisked the phone from her desk with a clammy hand. "Cordy here. What's happening? Are you safe?"

President Spendorf blurted, "I got your message. Yes, I'm fine, but we need you here at the White House."

Cordy felt relief flow through her, knowing Zac was safe, but she rushed on, "I tracked a voice. A man warned, 'Lock onto target. Time to strike!' My screen went black, and now CNN has just reported that someone is missing. Who—"

Zac spoke over her, "Systems are going down before our eyes. Lights are blinking, intermittent alarms squawking, and I'm afraid Carl is about to have a stroke."

"Which systems?" Cordy poised her fingers over the keyboard, ready to type. "We can work from here."

"No, we need you here in D.C. Marv found two bugs in the foyer by Winston's desk, and who knows if there are any others?" Then, as an afterthought, Zac said, "Wait a moment. How did you know someone was missing?"

"It was on CNN," Cordy added to her list. "There was a security breach near the Oval Office. I'm not sure if they know who."

"Already in the news? Do you see what I mean?" Zac sighed heavily. "I can't keep anything a secret. I swear my office is bugged, too. I had hoped this would remain confidential. Are you sure you removed every instance of the Pegasus virus from the building? Did someone find a workaround?"

"There is no evidence of Pegasus. Who is missing?" Cordy held her breath, awaiting a response.

"Secretary of State Mo Hendrum—at 2 a.m., a parking attendant found Mo's car with the door left open and the windshield shattered."

"Any other clues?" Cordy asked.

"Mo's office cell phone was on the ground next to a pool of a sticky substance and blood outside the driver's door. He must have dialed 911 before being attacked. When he didn't answer, the operator tracked the call to White House security."

"Did anyone see Mo leave the lot?" Cordy asked.

"No, everything happened while the power went out. Mo just disappeared—you remember him, don't you?"

Cordy remembered when New York City's power grid went down. His wife had also been kidnapped at that time. "Yes, I worked with him when he was the Governor of New York. But who was the real target? His wife, Justice Sophia, or the Secretary of State? They are both high-profile."

"True," Zac said. "The Supreme Court is ruling on the Zogster case later today." Zac rushed on. "The Department of State is dealing with controversial issues, too. Iran promised revenge when sanctions targeted their top allies, but I didn't expect anything to happen on home soil."

Cordy made another note on her list—Mo Hendrum is missing. "Any other leads?"

"The guard said a blue Subaru next to Mo's car was also damaged. Sophia is beside herself with worry. She knows the first 24 hours are crucial, so she called in Chief Jackson."

"Good. The chief will stay on it like glue." Cordy swallowed a lump in her throat, recalling her previous boss. She saw how Jackson had been dragged through the depths of despair when his wife was held hostage four years ago, ending in her death, although she probably would have died from her cancer within the year. "If anyone knows the fear of losing a loved one, he does, and he'll do everything in his power to save Secretary Hendrum?" Cordy respected and trusted the chief. *But who would kidnap Mo and why?* "So, you think the blackout was planned?"

"Yes, definitely, and we need to plug internal leaks. I need you here. Catch the next flight to D.C."

"I just remembered something. That soldier I saw on the security camera screen had a text message on his cell phone. I zoomed in, and it read, 'IS confirmed.' That is a capital I and capital S. Do you think that's a reference to Mo's kidnapping? Or," her heart skipped a beat, "what if 'IS confirmed' stands for your initials? Isaac Spend—" An alarm blasted in the background.

A male shouted over the alarm, "President, let's go!"

"What's happening?" Cordy asked.

"Marv, what are you doing? I'm talking to Cordy." Zac's demeanor grew more agitated.

"We're not staying this time," Marv said.

Loud voices came over the newscast on Cordy's screen. "What's that? It can't be!" Reporter Lisa Pagetti yelled, "Oh my. It's heading our way!"

Cordy's heart jackhammered against her rib cage, and a roar resounded in her ears. "What's heading your way?"

The Secretary of Defense opened the Oval Office door. "Oh, good, Carl, what's going on?" Zac said.

"Mr. President," Carl yelled, "Hurry. Move out of the office, pronto!" He said something else, but Cordy didn't catch it.

"Cordy, just get here ASAP! Now what, Carl? Marv? I'm busy—"

"No choice, Zac." Marv sounded like he meant it. "If you don't leave at once, I'm carrying you over my shoulder."

A spark of fear entered Zac's voice. "Gotta go. We're under fire."

Booted footsteps and a loud commotion ensued in the background. Marv snapped off orders in a clipped voice. "Everyone out. This way. Move it, people."

"Zac?" Cordy asked, her voice filled with concern. CNN's news report caught her eye. A fuzzy photo zoomed from afar onto a large white structure. Cordy gasped, "It's the White House."

Spendorf's strained voice came over the phone, "They're hustling me to a secure place. Send a message to your husband, Pronto. I need both of you here. Hang on, Carl."

"Eagle is leaving his nest," she heard Marv say. "Make way for—drop that phone." Then, there was nothing over VidChat but static.

Glancing at the TV, Cordy saw the newscaster's camera pan upward toward two diving aircraft heading directly for the building. Lisa shouted, "Drones!"

Muzzle flashes burst from the rooftop of the White House as the view cleared. A missile flew like an eagle straight for its target, weaving and bobbing in unison with the attacker to strike its prey. A mid-air explosion disintegrated the largest drone and rocked the remaining aircraft. Fluid spurted from the engine and caught fire, shooting bursts of flames in all directions as the object plummeted. The screen's photo flickered to a blurred image as Lisa and the cameraman ran, ending with a picture of the ground growing closer. Cordy heard a clunk. The TV's screen became a random flicker of dots and a high-pitched hiss.

"Zac! Are you there?" Cordy asked over the phone. "What just happened?" Her voice rose when he didn't respond. "President Spendorf, can you hear me?" Still, no answer. She'd been disconnected, and CNN was no longer broadcasting.

Madly searching for an answer, she switched to MSNBC with the same result. Cordy scanned through all the channels—nothing but static. She jotted, "Drone attack—? our Mavens or another," on her list. She returned a call to President Spendorf using the Bunker's communication network. It went directly to voicemail, which disconnected. *I know Braun isn't supposed to have any personal calls when on a special mission, but this is an emergency.*

With Braun's input, Cordy had designed him a unique gold wedding ring that she called a smart ring. Similar to a smartphone, it acted as a backup system during emergencies. The ring contained a tiny hidden chip that gave a GPS reading and alerted Braun when she sent him an urgent text or phone call. A clear stone turned to red for a text and blue for a phone call. It was a two-way communication system, allowing Braun to trigger an emergency notification to her by turning the stone from front to his palm side. However, Braun rarely used his smart ring as an alert unless he was on special ops missions. Today, he hadn't triggered an alert, which was unusual given the circumstances.

Cordy checked his smart ring's GPS and saw that Braun was between the Pentagon and Aberdeen Proving Grounds, probably flying to Maryland by helicopter for the trial weapon's test, a crucial part of a top-secret project they were working on. She sent an urgent text, expecting a response within two minutes, "Call me immediately. President Spendorf is in trouble and wants to talk to us ASAP."

Next, she tried Guy Weimer, head of Homeland Security. That call also went to voice mail. Feeling overwhelmed, she left a message. "Pentagon's security system has been breached. What's happening at the White House? Was that a drone launched from the building across the street? Zac called and said, 'We're under fire.' I was disconnected when he was escorted to the Bunker, and I can't get through to him. Call me back when you get this message."

Front-Line

Sept. 11 – 3:58 a.m. EDT, Aberdeen Proving Ground, Maryland

At thirty-four years old, JSOC Commander Braun Hastings was at the pinnacle of his career. As an FBI tactical aviation pilot with more than 3,500 hours in Delta 1 Special Forces, Braun had earned his reputation for having an analytical mind and self-determination. Tonight would be no different. He knew he was trusted and was aware of the responsibility of that trust. He set the radio frequency to 246.8000 for Aberdeen Proving Ground and received permission to land. His alert, gray eyes drank in his surroundings. The helicopter briefly hovered while making the final approach before safely landing.

As a special operations team leader, he collaborated with the Department of Defense to test the Army's newest unmanned system—a battery-powered robotic combat vehicle. Equipped with artificial intelligence, the robot was designed to detect the enemy's location, monitor their activities, and gather data on humans, the environment, and military operations. Its most valuable feature was its ability to identify and disarm booby traps, explosives, and other dangerous devices. Additionally, it could deploy a computerized drone equipped with cameras and ammunition if required. The robot automatically sent the images to satellites and uploaded them to the Department of Defense.

Braun's team would run the third and final test of the RCV in as many weeks, each progressively more complex. These tests were crucial in determining the RCV's effectiveness in various conditions, such as cold weather in Fort Drum, New York, and semi-arid terrain like Fort Hood, Texas. This last test at Aberdeen Proving Ground, Maryland, was to assess how well the RCV functioned over land, air, or open water. If successful, the military would deploy RCV/drone units to more than 20 locations where the U.S. faced armored warfare.

Three more men completed Braun's team. His favorite was Kip Kahooly, Braun's college roommate, now a U.S. Air Force special ops officer. His flaming red hair, ruddy complexion, and freckled face had earned him the nickname Rusty. They had been through many missions together, and Braun knew he could always count on Rusty. Night vision goggles hid the man's ocean-blue eyes. He was a man of few words, but he was unusually verbose tonight.

"Here. It's a foggy night and bitter cold. The sleet is getting worse." Rusty handed him a navy blue scarf. "Brit sent this for you and says, 'Cordy will appreciate you staying warm and healthy.'" He snorted a laugh. "Those two women."

"Thanks." Braun gladly wrapped the soft cashmere wool scarf around his neck to ward off the raw wind that threatened to chafe away his skin. He had been the best man at Rusty's wedding last year. "Did your wife come along to Maryland?"

"No." Rusty beamed with pride. "We're pregnant with a son. How's that for a surprise? Due date is around Thanksgiving. Can't wait for Christmas. Britney's parents are coming."

Navy Seal Admiral J. L. Browning stepped up behind Rusty and patted him on the back. "Congratulations!"

"Thanks, Jud." Rusty turned toward the silver-haired man, who only came up to Rusty's shoulders and shook his hand.

Jud's smile radiated up to the crinkles around his hazel eyes. "Wait until you become a grandpa. That's the best life has to offer. You can spoil the kids rotten and send them home." He chuckled and then became all business. "Braun, Max wants to see you in the office."

Braun tensed. "Anything wrong?"

Admiral Jud shrugged. "He's not sure."

"We'd better see what's on his mind." Braun adjusted his night vision goggles and scanned the area. "Have the waters been cleared?"

Jud nodded. "I cleared the Chesapeake Bay from 0300, and no entry is allowed until 0600. There are no unaccounted-for ships, and coast defense is on standby if there's a mishap. You checked the air. Did you find any threats?"

"North and East cleared for now," Braun said.

"South and West, also," Rusty added. "Testing is scheduled in a few minutes."

"What about Bush and Gunpowder Rivers?" Braun asked. "You remember our last test. The general warned us of two potential threats and then sprung a third on us—unannounced."

"As it should be," Jud said. "They try to make it as real-to-life as possible, and the rivers were Max's assignment."

"Let's go." Braun grabbed his pack, motioned the men forward, and sprinted to the designated headquarters. The team was in high spirits, ready to face the challenges of the upcoming test. He spied Ranger Maxwell B. Ruthmyer, the fourth man of his team but far from the last. Max was a member of the Marine Corps Special Operations Command, SOCOM. The "been there, done that" Marine strode forward with confidence.

"This will be the toughest test yet." Max's smooth, bass voice echoed through the BATT chosen as their headquarters. The men always brought in their own communications devices and tactical gear.

Max's smile tugged at a white scar running from his left temple down to his chin, earned when he'd led a major offensive on a Taliban-held town in Afghanistan, killing more than 380 insurgents. Wounded more than once during the battle, Max continued to fight to save many of his men. His uniform covered numerous other scars, but he was steady as a brain surgeon, and Braun had handpicked him for the team. Max was determined, persistent, insightful, and loyal.

Braun held up a brown envelope, "General Hunter Shyler's orders." He tore open the flap, drew out a sheet of paper, read it, and glanced around the room. "Did we get anything over the network? Anything about terrain or weather for the attack?"

"Nope." Max shook his head.

"Radio? Satphone?" Braun asked.

"No. Why?" Max asked as he took Braun's paper. This sheet only says, "Good Luck, men. Report back to me at 0530."

"Right," Braun said. "It's up to us to identify and deal with any threats."

"Done." Max nodded. "I noted a red flag hoisted over Howell Point Tower."

"So, we'll be firing over the water." Braun patted Max on the back. "Good catch. Gear up, and be ready for enemies on land, air, and open water."

Rusty caught Braun's nod and grabbed his gear. "I'll inspect the RCV and load the drone's bomb sniffer. Meet you on the field."

"Move it under a few trees to make sure the radar doesn't mistake the branches blowing in the wind for targets like it did the last time," Braun said. "I'm told they fixed that flaw, and we need to test it."

"I know just the spot." Rusty dashed outside.

Braun motioned for Jud and Max to join Rusty. The men headed into the night in full gear, ready for the war games. Braun took the rear, watching his men's backs.

Rusty adjusted the camera, activated the bomb sniffer, and launched the drone toward the water, where it would complete a full five-mile radius circle. The team's goggles had a built-in screen to display any images captured.

Fifteen minutes later, a black Oshkosh joint light tactical vehicle drove through the woods. The JLTV sat higher than a Humvee and was 70% faster even while running with its lights off. The missile launch turret turned in their direction.

"We've been spotted." Braun motioned to his team. "The driver is using night vision goggles. Stay low, and be ready for—"

Rusty bolted to the left as the test RCV automatically maneuvered, nearly running over him. A low whistle erupted as the robot fired, and a thundering explosion burst mid-air as the double-detonating Javelin missiles collided. The robot launched one, and the JLTV fired the other. They lit up the area brighter than a full moon as hot metal shards erupted into the night.

"Good, all went well as planned." Braun grinned at his team. "Nice job."

The team members beamed back broad smiles. "We'll be heading home soon," Rusty said.

The drone weaved and bobbed, making its way back to home base, when without warning, a second, more deadly explosion, came directly from the drone, sending metal shards in all directions as it self-destructed.

Braun was so close that his body felt the powerful force of the explosion rock through him, sweeping his legs out from under him. Pain throbbed behind his eyes. His ears keened like a siren. He couldn't hear anything distinctive as he stood, moved his fingers, and flexed his knees. Every joint hurt, but they all worked. He didn't know how that was possible.

Dust, grit, the smell of burning flesh, and something else indescribable, yet he'd never forget that odor. It's not quite like scorched almonds or plastic, but intense. "What just happened?" Braun shouted. "If we didn't set off the drone, then who the hell is in control?"

In the distance, the RCV's machine gun turret swung 180°. An injured Rusty shouted something one second, flew through the air the next, and plowed directly into Braun. Rusty's uniform was in flames—the right side of his face in bloody shreds. His helmet was missing. Metal shards protruded from his vest and legs.

Braun shut down the RCV as his mind snapped to autopilot. He flipped Rusty over and threw himself onto his buddy, trying to suffocate the blaze. He didn't even feel his chest on fire. The embers smoldered until the nylon lining of their wool jackets melted onto their shirts and skin. Their clothes tore apart as Braun peeled himself away to help his friend up. The cashmere scarf was nothing but shreds.

Rusty shuddered while lying on the steaming ground—dead weight, unable to stand. Teary eyes locked onto Braun's. "Tell Brit..." a gasp for air, "so sorry." He coughed.

Braun grabbed his friend's shoulders. "Rusty, stay with me! For Britney's sake. For your son. Look at me!" Rusty exhaled for the last time. His eyes glazed over.

Braun checked for a pulse. "No, Rusty!" Braun reached for his Satphone to call in the medics. Then it dawned on him. He wasn't in Afghanistan anymore. There were no medics. He dialed 911, wedged the phone to his ear with his raised shoulder, and rammed his fist into Rusty's chest. Unable to hear anything but a loud ringing, he shouted into the phone, "Man down!" He repeated three times, "Need ambulance. Aberdeen Proving Ground—hurry!"

He peeled back Rusty's shredded Kevlar vest and continued CPR, but his hands were caked in blood after three rounds of compressions. Rusty's rib bones were exposed. Braun knew his attempts were useless. He squeezed his eyes shut. Tears leaked down his cheeks as he held his breath. "Please, no." Even with his eyes closed, he could still see Rusty lying on the burned-out ground. Forcing himself to open his eyes again, they filled with horror. "How did this happen?"

Braun's hand flew to his mouth as if to cover the scream welling from deep inside him. Inhaling the stench once more, he steeled himself and pried a metal bullet from Rusty's vest and a few shards from his neck and torso, pocketing them as evidence to prove the drone had been weaponized. He'd send them to Cordy for analysis. His heart tried to escape the scene as wobbly legs threatened to collapse. A knot twisted his gut. He held his arms across his chest and scanned the area through the smoke and haze. *Where are the others?* "Where's my team?" he wondered aloud. It wasn't like Jud and Max to disappear when a buddy was in need.

"Over here," said an unknown man dressed in camo with a fire extinguisher in his hands. Another man leaned over Jud, and Braun guessed it was their "enemy." They had witnessed the downed men and came to their aid.

Braun dashed toward Jud and tripped over Max, lying unconscious—blood dripping from his left temple. A blackened tree branch lay at his side. Braun slipped his fingers over Max's carotid artery. "There's a pulse—rapid and weak but steady."

The man in camouflage nodded. "Yup, we checked." At least, that's what Braun thought he said. The camouflage guy pointed to where the JLTV had been. "…enemy saw team down, game over." He made a plus sign with his fingers and waved his hand at Jud and Max.

Braun guessed he said, "Ambulance is on its way."

Admiral Jud's blackened face distorted in pain. Pools of firefighting foam covered his chest, arms, and legs. There wasn't a silver strand of hair left on his head. His singed eyebrows drew together, and his neck and torso were as black as his face. Jud gasped for a breath.

The man kneeling over Jud grabbed a scalpel from a leather bag.

Braun leaped for the man and grabbed his arm. "Stop! What are you doing?"

The man jerked Braun's arm away as if it were a mosquito and jabbed the blade into Jud's windpipe. He inserted a tube and put a Velcro wrap around Jud's neck to hold it in place.

Braun understood and nodded.

The camo guy handed the medic an oxygen tank and inserted a small green hose into the trach tube.

Jud mouthed, "Thanks," but no words came through the grimace. His ashen lips pinked up. Finally, he reached up to Braun, mouthing, "How's Rusty?"

Braun shook his head and squeezed Jud's hand. Braun removed his jacket and knelt next to Max. He tore off a sleeve, wadded it, and held it to Max's temple until blood soaked through it. Braun used the other sleeve and kept pressure over the wound. Max stirred, mumbled something, and lapsed back into unconsciousness as an ambulance siren wailed to a stop, and the paramedics took over.

Braun dreaded the call, but his job was to inform their wives—the sooner, the better. His cell phone was nothing but a melted brick. Glancing at his wedding ring through blurry eyes, he noticed a red stone. Cordy had texted an urgent message sometime during this fiasco. He hesitated, knowing he should contact Cordy ASAP, but what could be more important than getting care for his men? The least he could do was let her know he got her signal. He turned his ring in a full circle to his palm and back to face him. The stone turned from red to clear as a diamond, indicating he got the warning. He'd check Cordy's text message later when he had time. His team had more urgent matters.

Tears splashed as Braun blinked and grabbed the team's Satphone. "Hello, Britney?" The words tumbled among sobs. Later, he couldn't recall what he had said and remembered only the gut-wrenching horror of spilling the news, followed by silence on the line. He felt numb. Movement in the haze finally registered. An EMT shoved Rusty into a body bag.

Braun snapped, "That man is my friend! A soldier. Honor him. He doesn't deserve to be shoved around." Grief and regret ran through to his core. He clenched the Satphone so tightly that one of the numbered keys popped off. "He's my friend…" Braun's chest burned and tightened all the way to his throat. No more words would come.

"You're right," the EMT said and straightened the body, ensuring the zipper didn't catch on Rusty's clothes. "I'm sorry for your loss."

A paramedic took the phone from Braun's hand. "Agent Hastings, your team is waiting for you."

Braun scooped up what was left of his jacket, removed a tie-tack from the collar, and after pocketing the item, he allowed the lad to lead him to the ambulance. Rusty's image refused to leave his brain. He felt like he was in Afghanistan all over again, but this time, it was his fault—his responsibility to keep these men safe. He'd failed miserably.

Back To Bunker

Sept. 11 — 4:02 a.m. EDT, Washington, D.C./
2:02 a.m. MDT, Fort Collins, CO

President Spendorf was abruptly escorted out of the Oval Office following a sudden breach in the government's network system, which shut down the national defense program, leaving only Zac's computer operational. En route to the Bunker, a startling report of a drone sighting at the White House added to the sudden turn of events. Zac barely reached the Bunker before the entire structure was engulfed in violent tremors. The Bunker was thrown into disarray as cabinets swayed, books tumbled from shelves, and pens, files, and phones vibrated off desks, crashing onto the floor. The Bunker shook so violently that a mirror was ripped from the wall and shattered upon impact with the cement floor. Amidst the chaos, people screamed and sought refuge under desks, heightening the chaos and confusion.

The bulbs flickered and grew dimmer, casting shadows in the faint light. As Zac's legs wobbled, his bodyguard, Marv, rushed to steady him. Zac's voice quivered, "What's going on now?"

Within moments, other Secret Service agents surrounded Zac, their presence providing a sense of security. They listened closely to their earpieces as they worked to protect him and reassured his senior staff members who had gathered nearby. Their actions aimed to create a feeling of safety amid the chaos.

It wasn't clear what the agents had heard, but Marv quickly ushered Zac further down the hallway and toward the reception area. As the rumbling subsided and the shaking stopped, a hush fell over the Bunker. "Wait here, Mr. President," Marv said. "I'm sending in a security team to search your office and the Situation Room before you enter those areas."

"Do you think the Bunker is about to collapse?" Zac tried to peer over those closing in around him but was blocked at every angle by another agent. Instead, he studied the agents' faces, some wide-eyed and bewildered, others stone-faced and ready for action. None appeared calm. "I want to know what's going on. Did someone fire a missile? Are we under another attack?"

"Kyle's looking into it." Marv stepped back from Zac, still blocking his path. "Are you all right?" He brushed dust and debris off Zac's shoulder and patted him down. "Any injuries?"

Zac stilled Marv's hands. "I'm fine. Tell me what is going on! Do we know who is behind this?"

Marv slid from his grasp. "It's too early to know."

Stressing a sense of urgency, a shrill voice pierced the air, demanding immediate action. "It's early, but we must provide the press with something. The entire world is watching. We need to demonstrate strength.'" The crisis exuded fear, and the decision weighed heavily on all those present."

Zac glanced around the room, hoping to find answers, and saw Winston heading his way. "Mr. President, I'll call the press secretary."

Zac nodded and asked, "Do we know what caused the Bunker to shake?"

"We're checking on that." Marv lifted Zac's arms. "I need to know you're unharmed. I won't let anything happen to you like the last time."

One look at Marv's determined face convinced Zac to submit to inspection. He held out his jacket and turned in a full circle to make it obvious his body was intact. "I was just a little shaky during the tremor. I'm fine now."

"Good." Marv gathered a few files and a phone from the floor and placed them on the nearest desk. He straightened, put his fingers to the side of his head, and listened to his earpiece again. "Thanks. I'll pass along the information." He turned toward the agents and senior advisors. "Kyle says the tremor was an earthquake. It's the first one since 2011 and not a missile attack. You can return to work, but we may have aftershocks, so beware."

Marv cleared a path and moved Zac to a chair in the reception area. "We sent Vice President Tom Harris and his wife to Camp

David to make sure the second in command also remains safe. Have a seat while I check the current status of your office." A moment later, he replied, "Still checking the Situation Room, but your Bunker office is all clear, Mr. President."

It didn't take long for the noise level to go up a few decibels as advisors returned to what they were doing before the quake. Senior staff members regrouped to give unsolicited advice, suggesting what to do next—many were confused and shouted over one another to be heard.

The chaos in the room was overwhelming, a cacophony of voices and ringing phones that threatened to drown out Zac's thoughts. He had to focus—nearly impossible with officials barking orders to their teams, phones ringing, and text messages piling up for his review.

Chief of Staff Winston Willoughby held out a phone. "Mr. President, it's the Chairman of the Joint Chiefs of Staff. He says it's urgent and wants to talk to you immediately."

Zac rolled his eyes. Whatever General Shyler had to say wouldn't be good, and he didn't want to talk to the man, but it was his duty, and he never shirked his responsibilities. He took a deep breath, absently twisted his wedding band, and his military training took over. As usual, increased obligations aroused within him a corresponding measure of strength. But beneath the facade of composure, a storm of conflicting emotions raged. "All right, but just this one call."

General Shyler must have heard and didn't even wait for Zac's greeting. "It's about time I got through to you. The generals are heading to the Pentagon, and I got word that the U.N. is in an emergency session. Countries across the globe are calling in, each denying responsibility for the drone attack, but who can you believe? You have your code for the nuclear football, right?"

Zac's shoulders caved. "Of course, but—"

"I knew you would," Shyler cut in. "We want you to know we'll support you. All military bases are on full alert, ready for counterattacks. Battleships are stationed in the Persian Gulf and are preparing for launch. Calls are coming in from NATO—"

"Let's not get ahead of ourselves," Zac warned. "We don't need a nuclear solution. We need good common sense to prevail."

"The generals are all in agreement," Shyler persisted. "That's why we—"

"I know," Zac said under his breath. "You're advising the country to go to war."

"Yes," Shyler snapped as if he had just clicked his heels, stood at attention, and saluted. "The U.S. must show strength to keep the peace."

"Really? To maintain peace, we must go to war? I don't think so. We don't even know who our enemies are."

"With all due respect, sir," Shyler said, "this attack was massive, well-planned, and precise. If we don't show force, the world will see our weakness as an opportunity to swoop in and conquer. We must act first."

"I'm sure you believe that, and it must have taken months to plan such an assault. How did they keep this a secret, without a trace or hint of their actions before this strike? How did it get past your keen eyes and ears undetected, General? It's your responsibility to prevent such an attack."

"It was the Russians. They were behind the shipment of uranium to Iran's nuclear plant," he paused when Zac didn't immediately agree. "I don't think it's the Iranians."

Zac heaved a sigh. "You can't prove it was either. General, first, we need to find out who is behind these terrorist attacks. We have to get this right if we ask families to give up their sons' and daughters' lives. I need 100% proof before we declare war on anyone."

"I have the authority to—"

Zac fumed, "No, you don't. You report directly to me. I have the authority, and I say we wait!"

Shyler yelled over Zac's words. "We've been attacked. What more do you—"

Zac ended the call despite Shyler's protests, relieved that the Generals hadn't joined him in the Bunker. He needed to stay composed and diffuse the growing tension before losing his temper. "Everyone, please try to stay calm—" Voices continued to rise, and it seemed like panic was spreading. Zac attempted once more to get everyone's attention.

Winston stepped in front of Zac and rapped on the edge of the desk. "Hey, I need everyone to be quiet! President Spendorf has something to say." It was so unusual for Winston to raise his voice that the crowd fell silent, and all eyes turned to him.

Zac folded his hands and bowed his head—silence at last. "Please, let's take a moment to honor those who have lost their lives today." Thirty seconds flew by before he added, "Thanks, team. I'm counting on you to do what you do best. I want a full debriefing, but I need to touch base with the Secretaries of Defense and Homeland Security before meeting in the Situation Room. In the meantime, you have plenty to do, so go back to work."

Winston patted Zac on the shoulder and said, "We're here for you. Remember that." He left the area briefly and returned with a steaming cup of tea. "Sorry about Shyler. I should have held the call."

Zac took the offered cup. "Don't sweat it. At least I know where my generals stand."

Winston leaned close to Zac and whispered, "We're setting up a secure communication center for the briefing. I'm concerned that staff members are talking to their teams, and I don't know what's being shared."

"Good point." Zac raised his voice to be heard over the din. "Everyone, I want to make this perfectly clear. Until we know more, nobody talks to any press member or outside agency officer. Nothing leaves this room without clearance. This is not a threat. Your job is on the line."

Winston turned to Zac. "I saw Carl a moment ago, and he's ready to meet. He had a glazed look in his eyes but waved off my concern. I guess he's had a rough morning." Winston turned to go, and then paused. "Your press secretary called, and she's working with your speechwriters. They'll get your approval before holding a press conference. Anything else, sir?"

Zac sipped his tea and glanced around—*back to this blasted place.* A stuffy, windowless Presidential Emergency Operations Center, it was better known as "the Bunker." He heaved another deep breath, trying to sift through what happened over the last ten minutes—*I was talking to Cordy one moment and whisked away here the next. What did I tell her?*

"Oh yes, book Cordy the earliest flight from Fort Collins and fly her to D.C. ASAP." Zac glanced at his senior advisors, shuddered, and whispered to Winston, "Let's get the debriefing over with before we have another earthquake. If terrorists aren't enough, we must deal with Mother Nature, too."

Winston nodded. "Guy's on his way."

Zac met Guy Weimer from Homeland Security standing outside the Situation Room, talking to a woman colleague over his speakerphone. Zac whispered, "Is there any damage from the earthquake?"

Guy held up a finger and straightened his gray tie as he barked orders over his phone. "...rope off the debris. Install TSA equipment at the entry point. No one comes in or out of the crime perimeter without an ID and send up drones with bomb sniffers. Check for any biologicals, too." He glanced back toward Zac and added, "Do you see any damage from the earthquake?"

"No, and I haven't heard of any reports yet, but it's still early," she said. "Anything else?"

"Scan all license plates on every car parked within a five-block radius. Catalog everything—date, time, and location. Move quickly to secure the site."

Before Guy could say another word, "Yes, sir, but this was an airstrike." came from his cell phone. "Why log the cars?"

"Just do it. If any registration comes up on the watchlist, send in forensics and tear the car apart." Guy glanced up.

Zac whispered, "I'm ready."

Guy nodded. "I'll be right there, Mr. President."

"Get the latest info from your team, but hurry." Zac reached for the door and paused when Marv held up a hand.

"Let me double-check for clearance." Marv went into the Situation Room while talking over his wrist mic.

Guy pulled a vibrating phone from his pocket, opened his text app, and punched in a message while still speaking on the first phone.

A moment later, Marv reappeared. "All clear. Carl's already here, and I'll stand guard inside the room."

Zac tapped Guy on the shoulder. "Make it quick and update me."

"That's all for now, Janet, I'm meeting with the president and will get back to you." Carl pocketed both phones and followed the president into the Situation Room.

Zac joined his Secretary of Defense, who was watching a large screen TV, replaying the downtown attack over the news. "Morning, Carl." When Carl didn't reply, Zac set his cup on the table and moved closer for a better view.

Guy walked up to Zac. "President Spendorf, people are panicking with the recent assault on D.C. and the drones attacking the White House. They need to hear from you soon."

"I know." Zac motioned for Guy to have a seat. "My speechwriters should have something for me shortly. It's not an easy task. They have less than an hour to put together the right words to reassure the world. Calls are coming in from every country with their condolences, and I need my Secretary of State. What are you doing to find Mo?"

Guy glanced at his watch. "He's been missing for less than three hours, and we've had no demand for ransom."

Zac slammed his fist on the table. "I'm not waiting for a ransom demand. So, what are your teams doing to find him?"

Carl didn't even flinch, still staring at the TV screen.

Guy glanced at the floor. "We ran into a problem with the security tapes. The tech analysis shows they are old and on a continuous loop. Perhaps the photo of Mo entering the lot happened days ago."

"Are you telling me our equipment is outdated, or did someone hack into that system, too?" Zac shook his head in disbelief.

"It wouldn't be hard to do." Guy held up his hands as if in surrender. "I know that's not what you wanted to hear."

Zac glared. "Get better surveillance! Find him! And I told you to keep Mo's disappearance a media lockdown. Our chances of finding him are better if reporters don't blow it out of proportion, but somehow word got out."

"Yes, and once it was on the news, we couldn't keep a lid on it." Guy had the decency to blush with embarrassment.

Zac asked, "Who leaked the information?"

"I honestly don't know." Guy bowed his head.

Zac's voice got louder. "Someone in the White House is trying to undermine this administration. I'm counting on you, Guy. Find out who is leaking vital information."

"Yes, sir." Guy turned to face the news when Carl turned up the volume on the TV. Sirens wailed in the background. "Hey, Carl. What's going on?"

Carl remained sitting, still as a statue, and didn't glance away from the TV.

"Carl?" Guy frowned when he did not receive a reply and turned toward Zac. "Is Carl okay?"

Zac shrugged and studied Carl, who seemed fixated on the TV set up in multi-screen mode, getting reports from four different newscasts. Zac stepped closer to see what Carl was watching. His left hand covered his mouth as everything unfolded over the broadcasts.

A female reporter from MSNBC stood in the dark against a burning building in the upper left-hand corner of the screen. "Our nation's capital has been gripped by professional anarchists. Violent mobs, arsonists, looters, rioters, and others have taken advantage of the power outage that has left more than 5 million customers without electricity. Officials have 22 suspects in custody so far, and SWAT teams are still clearing the area."

To her right was a newsman from CNN reporting, "…twelve police officers, four firefighters, and two SWAT members were killed in the line of duty."

FOX News was on the lower left of the screen reporting, "…the city mourns after the most devastating terrorist attack in twenty years. Washington authorities confirm 192 dead and 310 injured after this morning's train wreck followed by an assault on fleeing passengers…" On the lower left of the screen, a camera panned the downtown area, showing fire engines and police cruisers lining the streets. Their red and blue lights blinked an eerie glow as looters ran off with stolen goods through cluttered streets filled with smoke and debris. "Arsonists are breaking into buildings with torches, and flames are engulfing downtown. Unrest is causing skirmishes with police…" Then, all four news stations replayed the drone attack on the White House. It was the first time Zac had actual eyes on the episode. "No one has come forward to claim responsibility for these attacks. Washington's Joint Terrorism Task Force is coordinating with the FBI to track down these terrorists."

Large chunks of debris cluttered Pennsylvania Avenue with downed sections of the security fence in front of the White House. The front gate was lying on the North Lawn. "Is all that debris from the drone attack or the earthquake?"

"Maybe a little of both," Guy said.

Zac's heart sank when he saw the damage to the beloved evergreen known as the National Christmas Tree. Several branches lay scattered throughout the northeast corner of the Ellipse near the White House. A vivid memory of his late wife, Theresa, flooded through him as he again twisted the gold wedding band he refused to take off his finger after her death. It reminded him of her secret message etched inside the band—"Love Eternally, Theresa." He remembered how much she loved the holiday season and anxiously watched every year as bright lights were hung around that evergreen.

When Zac became president, she made snow angels next to the tree on that first Christmas Eve. They stood in awe of the beautiful decorations, and she sang "Silent Night." Her sweet voice gave him tremendous healing power during times of stress. He missed her terribly, but he was glad she wasn't here to see the destruction. Cancer had taken her away so quickly. Zac swiped away the dust that must have gotten in his eyes.

Guy shook his head. "I know. It's bad."

Zac nodded. "If I left it up to the generals, we would have already declared war."

Guy's brow furrowed. "Against who?"

"I don't know, but I doubt it would matter to them. So, thanks for keeping them away from the Bunker. I have enough to deal with, and I prefer they stay in the Pentagon."

"They'll be knocking on your door soon," Guy said.

"True." Zac stared at Guy. "Why didn't they discover the attackers' plans before this happened? I was completely in the dark, hustled from the Oval Office to the Bunker—like a sack of potatoes, and now forced into a rushed press conference to assure our citizens when we don't even know who's behind this attack. No, I must have facts, so the press conference must wait until after our briefing. As much as I hate to admit it, we must conference with General Shyler and our senior staff to determine who our enemies are and what to do in response."

"The sooner, the better," Guy said. "The media is all over this—Congress, too. You know Justuso is ready to use this against you, especially after he lost the last election to you. He'll try for an impeachment—"

"Justuso is a pain, but he's not our enemy at the moment. Someone's leaking information to the press. I want to know who." Zac rubbed his chin. "I hate being back in the Bunker. It's like I'm hiding in a dungeon."

Guy tugged at his tie again as if it were choking him and cleared his throat. "Yes, but we had to act fast." He glanced over at the Secretary of Defense. "Carl's in another world." Guy swallowed. "Seems to be haunted by what's happened this morning."

"You're right." Zac stood still as if he wanted to be anywhere but there. "Let's have our briefing and make it brief. After the meeting, I'll deliver a message and let the nation know we'll hunt down these terrorists." Zac pressed an intercom button. "Winston, do you have any word from the Press Secretary?"

"Yes, Mr. President," Winston said. "She sent over the speech for your approval and says she will hold the press conference when you're ready. I also booked an 8:50 flight from Fort Collins. Cordy should be here early afternoon."

"Thank you," Zac said. "Great job—always two steps ahead of me."

Guy's cell phone rang. "It's the general again. Since Winston refused to forward him to you, Shyler tried me next. I think I've told you everything I know so far. If it's all right with you, sir, I'll take this call."

Zac managed not to moan under his breath. "Okay, I overheard your earlier call to your team, so I'll get an update from Carl, and then we'll call in the rest of the advisors."

Guy answered the call and grimaced. "The general says he has the enemy in his sights."

Zac shook his head. "Make it clear to this warmonger that we're not bombing anything without a full investigation. The last thing we need is to start World War III! Maintain surveillance and keep me informed."

Wounded

Sept. 11 – 4:22 a.m. EDT, Washington, D.C.

Carl Wyller glanced up from the conference table as if he'd only now noticed someone else was in the Situation Room. "Zac, while Guy's on the phone, I need a word with you in private." The Defense Secretary held his right arm at an odd angle in front of his torso, then leaned onto the tabletop with his left elbow and stood.

"One moment." Zac's jaw dropped as he watched the latest news, a live feed showing the city going up in smoke. Dizziness nearly rocked him off his feet. He reached for a chair, glued in place, watching the city burn. Imagining the pungent odor of sulfur mixed with the dense smoke made his eyes water and his nose sting as if he were inside those burning buildings. He jolted when Carl tapped his shoulder.

"Sir, we need to talk now—in private. I'm not sure the Situation Room is secure. Even Marv is worried about electronic surveillance in this room." Carl's concern was evident as he walked toward the door, paused, and spoke over his shoulder, "It can't wait. I believe our intelligence has been compromised, and we have an inside mole."

Marv moved between the two men. He was broad-shouldered and, at 6'3", towered over Zac by five inches. Although the room was only 62° F, a bit chilly for Zac's liking, Marv stood with his suit jacket open, hands free, like the trained guard he was, ready for action if needed.

Zac dragged his eyes away from the screen. "It's okay, Marv. Carl's not the mole." Zac left the room and entered an empty office down the hall. Carl followed. Before closing the door, Zac leaned toward Marv. "Stand outside, and don't let anyone else enter."

"Yes, sir." Marv checked out the room, "All clear." He exited, reached behind him, and closed the door as he faced the hallway.

Zac asked Carl, "How could this happen? It was on my watch. Our citizens are rioting in the streets, and downtown is burning.

Someone hacked into government computer systems, sent drones to attack the White House, and then an earthquake topped off the morning. Give me an update on the damages."

"No direct damage to the White House that I'm aware of, but downtown's a mess. The drones did attack, and Avenger shot them down over Pennsylvania Avenue. There is a lot of debris on the street." Carl grimaced. "And there's more you don't know. Not only did someone gain access to our computer system. Someone hacked our security system, knocked out the surrounding lasers, and shut down our missile defense system. If Cordy hadn't gotten Avenger back up in time, that missile would have hit the White House. I'm sure of it. As you saw on the news, assassins, looters, and arsonists have overrun D.C. Chief Polack is asking for more SWAT teams." The potential danger to the White House was a stark reality, making the need for protection even more urgent.

"Send him everything he asks for," Zac said. "What else haven't you told me?" The demand for more SWAT teams clearly indicated the scale of the threat and the need for reinforcements.

Carl coughed, inhaled, and coughed again before continuing, "Potomac Power believes someone tampered with the power grid, but they haven't released anything to the public yet. And we're keeping information about the White House hack quiet, too. I wanted to keep the drone strike a secret, but the news broadcast the attack. And that's not even the worst of it."

"There's more?" Zac's voice raised a notch.

"I'm afraid an inside mole is working with a terrorist group. With Mo missing, my suspicions are running even higher. Everything is happening without any warning, and so fast I haven't been able to update you on the latest findings."

"We've been standing together for the last ten minutes. Why didn't you say something?"

Carl peered over each shoulder and whispered, "I'm telling you now. We moved quickly to keep you safe." Carl winced as he moved closer. He coughed again. A dry, hacking coughed this time, and there was a soft popping sound. Carl paused to catch his breath. "No time. Needed to protect you—"

"Protect me from what?" Zac's eyes narrowed, giving that familiar glare. "You're not the first to suspect an inside enemy. Who's the mole?" The sense of betrayal was noted in his voice.

"Don't have proof. Laptop missing…" Carl gulped as he swallowed and refused to make eye contact. He kept holding his right arm tightly across his chest.

"Carl?" Zac watched him closely. Something was definitely wrong with the way he moved. *The laptop is a crucial piece of the puzzle, an it's gone.* "Whose laptop?"

"Zinmansky's. Reported…before rushing you to Bunker." There was no blush of embarrassment. In fact, Carl seemed pale. Sweat beaded his forehead, and he leaned against a chair. A rush of air escaped his lips, along with a groan and that popping sound again.

"Are you okay?" Zac raised an eyebrow.

Carl nodded and rushed on, "Einar Zinmansky. Civilian intelligence analyst…highly classified…reports to Chet." Carl paused and took a few shallow breaths. "He's rarely on Hill…" Carl shook his head. "Stay alert…"

"I am alert." Zac studied Carl. "Are you all right?"

"What? Not you," Carl rubbed the sweat from his brow with the back of his left hand and staggered. He quickly braced himself against a chair.

"Carl! Are you okay?" Zac felt a gnawing gut feeling that something was wrong, but he couldn't quite figure out what it was. When Carl didn't respond, Zac asked more questions. "Did Zinmansky sell government secrets? Or is someone trying to take over our national intelligence? Is that why I'm down here? Who are our enemies this time? What are the damages?" Zac paused. "You're beginning to worry me." When Carl still didn't answer, Zac grabbed Carl's shoulder. "Carl, answer me."

Carl flinched. "Ow!" His jacket fell open, revealing blood seeping through the front of his shirt and the right sleeve of his suit coat.

"What happened? You're bleeding! Why didn't you say something?" Zac spun to open the door and whispered to his guard, "Marv, call the medical unit! Carl's—" There was a loud thud behind him. When Zac turned back, Carl had collapsed onto the floor.

"Carl?" Zac tried to push past Marv, planning to grab the well-stocked emergency cart kept in the Bunker.

"No, you need to stay here." Marv was President Spendorf's security guard and wasn't taking any chances. He would protect Zac with his life. Blocking the door, Marv moved Zac away from the small glass office window and closed the door. Recalling his military days as a medic, he spoke over his wrist mic, "Need White House Trauma team to Bunker, STAT!"

The radio hissed back a tinny voice, "Trauma Services are on their way."

"Are you hurt?" Marv began patting Zac down once again, checking for injuries.

"I told you before. I'm fine," Zac said in disgust. "Take care of Carl."

"He was injured protecting you. I meant it when I said, 'I'm not losing you like the last time you were in the Bunker.' You nearly died, so stay down." Marv grabbed Zac's arm and led him further away from the door. Kneeling, Marv peeled back Carl's shirt and jacket.

Zac saw the pool of blood bubbling from Carl's chest. "Medics better get here quick."

Marv stuffed a clean handkerchief over the wound and held pressure. "When were you stabbed?"

"Don't know." Carl's eyelids fluttered. His voice slurred, "Felt sting…no time…got Zac to safety." His words came in bursts, and he gasped between short phrases.

"When did you feel the sting?" Marv asked.

"Passage…before Bunker." Carl took a shallow breath. "Never saw…it coming—everyone talking…shoving." Carl coughed, and his chest gurgled.

Not wanting to panic other agents, Marv didn't speak into his wrist mic. Instead, he pulled a radio from his pocket, directly linked to his boss, and hit the communication button. "Kyle, has anyone reported any injuries?"

"No, why?" Kyle asked.

"Secretary Wyller's been stabbed." Marv took control. "Lockdown the House. No one leaves or enters. Check the passageway to the Bunker for a weapon. Need to know only. Keep us informed."

"And get me, Zinmansky," Zac said. "I want him in my office within the hour."

"Who?" Marv asked.

"He reports to Chet Yelson." Zac continued, "Carl mentioned the contractor is rarely on the Hill. Send the FBI if needed. And get me his laptop."

"Drone leader," Carl said with a wheeze. "New firm."

Marv relayed the message to Kyle.

Drone leader? New firm? Zac couldn't believe the Defense Department had been so lax.

"My wife." Carl's eyes grew wider. "Police...4th Division." He leaned on his left elbow, gasping. "Can't breathe." A whistling sound came from his chest with each breath.

"Hang on, Carl." Zac threw open the door. "Winston, get me Peggy Wyller, Metro Police. I need to talk to her immediately."

"I'll find her." Winston grabbed the Integrated Service Telephone, or IST, his most reliable underground communication system.

"Trauma team cleared security and are heading your way," came across Marv's radio as two men in white lab coats covering navy scrubs sprinted down the hall into the Bunker's central area. A dark-haired man scanned the room with piercing brown eyes and nodded toward a small cove with a large, red Craftsman cabinet on wheels. "Toby, grab that crash cart." He halted at Winston's desk with a security pass in hand. "Where do you need us?"

"In here," Marv called out, "but first, I need to see your credentials. Then you can tend to Secretary Wyller. He's bleeding."

The man in scrubs moved in four confident strides and paused just inside the office, holding the pass for Marv to see with one hand and peeling off his backpack with the other. "I'm Dr. Petronowsky, Doc Pete for short." He turned to the younger man pushing the crash cart into the room. "And this is my PA, Toby."

Marv nodded but kept pressure on the wound while also keeping an eye on Zac.

Doc Pete asked, "Mr. President, do you have any injuries?"

"No." Zac stepped aside.

"I've already cleared the president," Marv said. "It's Carl. Chest wound. He's rapidly losing blood and having trouble breathing."

"Okay. Carl, I need to examine you."

Carl nodded. "Can't breathe."

"We're here to help make you more comfortable." Doc Pete removed two towels from his backpack, knelt next to Marv, and handed him one towel. "Use this to dry off your hands and then clear that desk. I want to move Carl to have a better look."

"Thanks." Marv grabbed the towel and scooted aside while wiping blood from his fingers. Then he cleared the desk of all paperwork, pens, and the phone with one sweep of his hands.

Toby didn't wait for orders. He broke the seals on the cart and started oxygen. He attached the cardiac monitor to Carl's chest. "Sinus tach at 110 per minute, B/P 90 over 50, and respirations 30 and shallow."

Doc Pete quickly slipped on latex gloves and a mask. "Carl, this may be uncomfortable, so bear with me." He used a second towel to remove excess blood from the wound and took a quick assessment. "We need a sandbag. Start an IV of Ringer's Lactate, and then we'll move him."

Toby handed Pete the sandbag, started the IV, and positioned himself at Carl's head. "Someone take his feet."

Marv grabbed Carl's ankles.

"On the count of three." While the men lifted him onto the desk, Pete held the sandbag tightly to Carl's chest.

Marv found a chair pad and placed it under Carl's head while Doc Pete listened to Carl's heart and lung sounds. The cardiac monitor showed Carl's heart rate was now up to 180 beats per minute. "Chest tube! STAT. Carl, do you have any allergies?"

Carl shook his head. "No."

"Give him Morphine 10 mg IV and prep him."

While Toby set up the equipment and prepped the patient for the procedure, Doc Pete motioned to the president to step aside. "Sorry, sir, but you and your agent need to leave the room. This is an emergency surgical procedure, and we must keep the room as sterile as possible. If we don't re-expand his lung immediately, he could die."

Zac nodded. "You're in good hands, Carl. We'll find your wife." Zac barked out orders as soon as he entered the hallway and saw Guy standing next to Winston's desk. "Track down FBI Director Sloan, find Zinmansky and that laptop, and update me on Homeland Security. I know your team already viewed the most recent videotapes covering the White House evacuation and the route to the Bunker, but I want them reviewed in greater detail. Find out who stabbed Carl. Connect them to the main conference room for my review, too."

"Yes, sir." Guy grabbed a Bunker phone from a vacant desk and headed down the hallway, giving orders.

Zac turned to Winston. "Delay the news conference until after I meet with my senior staff. This assault could start a war. Let the secretary know I'll address the nation at the press conference. Hand me the Press Secretary's notes for review."

"Too big a risk to meet with the press in person," Marv said. "Broadcast a message to the nation from the Bunker, and have Guy meet with the press to answer further questions."

"Maybe you're right." Zac placed the press secretary's notes on the table. "I'll inform the world that we're actively searching for the terrorists and won't rest until we find them. However, I want to review the security footage first. If there's a traitor among us, it's imperative that we identify them as soon as possible."

Marv moved closer. "It may even be someone who is already in the Bunker. Trust no one."

Fifteen minutes later, someone knocked on the Situation Room door. Marv opened it, and Toby stepped forward. "Mr. President, you can see Carl now. He's been sedated, so he may seem groggy, but his breathing is much improved."

"That's good news." Zac set aside the modified speech notes and turned to Marv, "I reviewed the security tape, but everyone was crowding around me, and I couldn't get a clear image of anyone stabbing Carl. Is this the only tape available? We need a closer image. Your team may need to view it frame by frame until they see what happened."

"I'll check with Kyle," Marv said.

"Send any other views to Homeland for review. I can't believe it…" Zac muttered something else under his breath as he left the room.

Winston caught him in the hallway. "Medivac enroute. ETA two minutes."

"Thanks." Zac followed Toby back to the secured office. Marv stayed close at hand and guarded the door.

Carl lay on his right side with a long tube inserted into his chest, taped to his torso. Bright red blood flowed through the tube into a clear plastic container sitting on the floor.

Zac knelt beside Carl. "You know you're family, and we'll get these bastards."

Carl's gaze was far off, but he nodded. "Yes, family."

Winston knocked at the door and entered. "I tracked down Officer Wyller. She says all hell's breaking loose out there, and it'll be at least half an hour before anyone can replace her, but she wants to talk to Carl and the doctor."

Carl's eyes widened, and he turned toward the phone. "Peg?"

"Carl, is that you?" came from the phone's speaker.

Zac recalled Peggy, a petite lady who was the fiercest woman he knew. She was an independent thinker and a problem-solver who made concise decisions and quickly acted upon them. She was a real spitfire. Carl was lucky to have her in his life.

"Yes, honey. It's me." Winston moved the phone closer to Carl's mouth. "Peggy, love, don't worry about me. I'm going to be just fine."

"Carl, thank God. I love you. Remember that." Peggy's voice was tense. "Let me talk to the doctor."

"Officer Wyller, I'm Doc Pete."

Peggy's words flew out in a rapid stream, "How's Carl? Is he really fine? Where are you? I need to see him."

"Try to stay calm," Doc Pete said. "Is there anyone who can take you to Walter Reed Hospital?"

"I'm fine to drive," Peggy said. "Walter Reed, I know exactly where that is. Give me the facts. I must know what I'm dealing with."

"I appreciate that. Your husband needs immediate exploratory surgery," Doc Pete said. "There's a stab wound to his chest. His right, so we inserted a chest tube to re-expand the lung and remove the blood pooling in the area. We won't know what else we'll find until we get him into the OR."

"Stab wound?" Peggy gasped. "Who? Have they caught him yet?"

"We'll find him, Peggy," Zac said. "You can count on it."

"Today's been a nightmare, and it's not even 5 a.m." Peggy sounded distraught.

"Medivac's landing," came over Winston's radio.

"I'm going with Carl. Meet me in the OR waiting room." Doc Pete wrapped his stethoscope back around his neck. "I'll leave word to page me as soon as you arrive."

"Thank you," Peggy said. "Carl, are you there?"

"He's sedated, but he can hear you," Doc Pete said.

Peggy's voice still sounded stressed, but she swallowed and said, "I love you. I'll be there when you wake up. I promise. Then I'm going to track down the vulture who stabbed you."

Inner Sanction

As officials in Washington, D.C., scrambled to assess the aftermath of the drone attack, Cordy, a seasoned intelligence analyst, found herself in a race against time in Colorado—trying to locate her missing lead analyst, Quint, who was crucial to their current operation.

"There's no sign of Quint," Perry's voice crackled over the intercom from the forensic lab, Quint's office. "He's vanished without a trace. I can't make sense of it."

"He left in a rush," Cordy mused, her finger tapping her lower lip in deep contemplation. "I spoke with him less than ten minutes ago, and now he's missing."

"And he took his laptop with him—it's missing, too," Perry said. "His screen is still lit up, and he flipped on his gadgety watch before disappearing. It's giving a direct link for us to track, and it's encrypted."

"His Wizmotch?" Cordy felt another wave of fear crashing over her. "He'd only do that if he's in—"

"He's in deep trouble. I know it," Perry finished her sentence.

"Right." Cordy knew the feeling and tapped Quint's Wizmotch GPS. She didn't need any more stress and worry today. She hadn't heard from Braun either, but at least she knew he had received her text that Zac needed him ASAP. His wedding ring alert had been verified. The stone had turned red and back to clear. *Perhaps, Zac reached him directly.*

Perry interrupted her thoughts. "I already called security. Quint didn't log out, and no one saw him leave."

"That's impossible. Surely, the cameras caught his departure." Cordy waited for a signal. "Quint's cell phone is sending a link. He's near the light rail station heading southbound. Oops, I just lost his cell's signal. He probably switched to his burner phone so no one can follow him, but Satchip is still tracking."

"Where do you think he's going?" Perry asked.

Cordy now wondered the same thing. *He's headed away from the vault. What's near the station in that direction?* Nothing came to mind. "I'm not sure. Keep him in your sight. Have security deliver all video feeds to the conference room, and keep me posted. Did he leave anything else in his office?"

"The screen shows that Quint logged into an Iranian virtual private network," Perry said.

"I see. Quint left me a short text message. 'Iranian bots behind hidden code are attached to government emails and have attacked the Pentagon's security systems. We're tracking their VPN exit nodes—'"

Perry interrupted. "There's a sticky note on his desk. Says, 'Check trapdoor. Dealing with both Iranian and Russian hacks.'"

Cordy asked, "The sticky says, 'Check trapdoor?'"

"Yup."

That's the same message as the guy at the GPS site. In the past, U.S. intelligence had verified that Russia paid bounties to Taliban fighters to attack U.S. soldiers and coalition troops in Afghanistan. Russia and Iran worked together then—it could be happening again. "Continue to quarantine the code." Cordy was already programming a search to review the system's inquiry and security logs. *Fortunately, the vault's backup accounts were still working. Anyone who managed to disable the laser or Avenger systems would require a high-level clearance. It had to be an inside job, but I want to know who would jeopardize our government and why their clearances were approved. All employees have a digital fingerprint and encrypted password entry modified every thirty minutes. The logs are monitored around the clock, so we should have a record of who has been in those systems.* Last week, she upgraded every program with the latest generations of firewall protection—antivirus software, intrusion detection, and many crypto-processors. *Maybe Quint is on another mission—tracking down the culprit. Why didn't he say something before leaving? How did he slip past the guard? What's going on?*

"Can you send Svetlana down here?" Perry asked. "I need help isolating this code."

Cordy rubbed her aching forehead. "Yes, and keep trying to reach Quint."

"I'm on my way." Svetlana grabbed two water bottles from the fridge and left the office.

Cordy, her heart heavy with the weight of the drone attack she couldn't prevent, struggled to push aside her desire to lead the search for her missing lead analyst. She had to trust Quint and the group of young adults, who had become her family, left orphaned after the tragic death of their parents. The lights went out in her office, but her backup power system kept her computers running. The room was bathed in a dim, eerie light, the only source of illumination being the computer screens, casting unsettling shadows on the walls. The darkness added to her dreary feeling, unsure of what direction to take next.

A message alert buzzed from her watch. Quint had sent her a text, "At 0035 EDT, someone shut down DoD's security system for five minutes, allowing access to the Maven II Project long enough to insert a virus and add some weapons to the drones during that timeframe. One system was delivered to Aberdeen Proving Grounds for testing." Quint sent the message at 0208 MDT, and it was now 0226. *Eighteen minutes ago. Why did it take so long to get the message to me?* The delay was nerve-wracking, each minute adding to the potential danger, the threat becoming more evident with every passing second. The danger was real, the suspense thick in the air, making every moment more intense.

If Quint detected Iranian and Russian hacks, what else is at stake, especially if they accessed our security systems? Someone inside the government must be working with them—my worst nightmare, a betrayal of the highest order. The potential betrayal was like a cold shock, shaking Cordy to her very core, leaving her in disbelief and uncertainty.

Still worrying about her husband, Braun, Cordy opened another special app she had created to keep him safe. The program was attached to a tie-tack that Braun always wore on his jacket's collar. Cordy had written the specs, but it was Quint, her trusted partner, who had brought the tie-tack to life, including a tiny camera eye and recording device built to her specifications.

As usual, Quint had enhanced her original specs. In the center of the tie-tack was a clear-studded crystal. The gem turned colors based on exposure to various dangers. She had expected to find a green or clear alert when she logged in. Any other color would have given her an alarm. The tie-tack had warned her in the past and saved his life more than once. To her dismay, the stone color had turned dark red, then black, and at 0422, it wasn't communicating anything more. *What does that mean? Quint never mentioned those colors and isn't here to ask what they mean.*

Why had she hesitated to talk to Braun in person, instead of just a text? All Cordy craved at that moment was to hear his reassuring voice saying, "We'll figure everything out together." She longed for a return to normalcy. No more undercover assignments. No more secret missions. No more separations. Her gut twisted with anxiety. *Surely, Braun was alive. But was he? She should know, shouldn't she?* The knot in her stomach tightened—a physical manifestation of her helplessness. The ripple in her abdomen told her that even their babies sensed that Daddy was in trouble.

Reporting In

Sept. 11 — 4:30 a.m. EDT, Rock Creek Park/
2:30 a.m. MDT, Fort Collins, Colorado

Farzad Zahair heard helicopters circling overhead and knew the CIA, FBI, and Homeland Security were hot on his trail. The thirty-seven-year-old Iranian felt genuine fear grip him for the first time in over a decade. He needed more time. His mission was to create chaos in Washington, D.C., attack the White House, and steal the blueprint for a highly sophisticated weapon system. The success of his job depended on completing each task. Ultimately, the plan was to weaken the U.S. defense organization through massive cyberattacks. He had activated sleeper cells with deadly plots. The most devastating strike was yet to come—an air assault using modified Maven II drones during the World Series, just after President Spendorf's ceremonial pitch.

Zahair had thought he had lucked out when he met Amir, a member of the Iranian Revolutionary Guard, who had links to Russian agents working undercover within the federal government. So far, with Amir's help, Zahair had accomplished most of his goals. The power outage, Metro train wreck, and planting weapons on the Maven II drone went as planned. However, joining the Russians for the first drone attack on the White House had failed. Someone spotted Amir before the launch and got the Avenger system back online to avert the strike.

After tracking the GPS signal, Zahair discovered that someone was in Fort Collins, Colorado. After more research, he knew it was the cybersecurity team. He realized he needed to neutralize them to carry out his planned attacks. This would start with targeting their leader, who was scheduled to fly to D.C. early the following day. However, time was running out, and Amir had presented him with an unexpected problem—what to do with the kidnapped Secretary of State Mo Hendrum and Nurse Sloan, who happened to be the wife of the FBI director.

Zahair fumed when he saw the unconscious man lying on a cot inside the dusty, rusty RV with faded flowers painted on the side. For now, it doubled as his headquarters, located far within Rock Creek Park. Frustrated, he slapped Amir across his already bruised and puffy left cheek. "You shot the Secretary of State in the chest and clubbed him over the head. How will he make a video demanding a ransom for his release? He can't even talk."

Amir was a proud, experienced, and highly motivated soldier dressed in an olive-green camouflage shirt and pants, combat boots, a helmet, and a Kevlar vest—the same as those used by the American Army. He continued to stand at attention, letting the blood drip from his cut upper lip onto the floor.

Zahair always harbored suspicions about the Russians associated with Amir despite being on the same team and reporting to the same commander. His frustration intensified when he found out he couldn't intimidate Amir, who responded with a nonchalant flick of his wrist to wipe his bleeding lip. This only added fresh blood to the dried stains already present on the left sleeve of his torn and tattered shirt. Zahair recognized the old stains from an earlier injury sustained during a scuffle at the subway station with a wily, weathered police officer, who Amir said, "fought like a leopard."

Amir returned to military attention, carrying an M-16 rifle in plain sight, unlike the 9-mm pistol tucked in the waistband at his back and a switchblade hidden in each boot.

"This is entirely your fault." Zahair glared at Amir. "Don't you have anything to say?"

Amir saluted, turned his head, and pointed to his other cheek. "Better slug this one, too, sir, if it makes you feel better, but I already told you I didn't injure the secretary."

Zahair took a step closer. "Explain."

"I used the security card that our IT genius mocked up for us." He pointed to Gregor, a tall, lanky lad busy typing on a laptop computer.

"It gave me access to the parking lot without any problems. I met with our contact. He verified the coin with the hidden chip of drone specs inside arrived in Iran, and he assured me everything was going as planned in Houston. He'll also wake up the sleeper cells in New York and California as you ordered. Then I drove around to locate the car with the plate number, as you instructed. When I passed by the first time, Secretary Hendrum was unlocking his car door, so I continued to drive to the end of the row, turned around, and planned to follow him out of the lot before ambushing him. But when I returned, he was fighting some thug who had just broken into a blue Subaru parked next to his. I'm not sure if the secretary was an innocent bystander who witnessed the break-in or the intended victim, but he was on his cell phone when a shot rang out. Hendrum fell to the ground. When the shooter saw me, he slammed the butt of his gun over the secretary's head, grabbed his wallet, and ran."

"That I don't believe." Zahair raised his fist but held it in check. "No one knew we were coming for him."

"Your contact, Zinmansky, did," Amir said, "but it wasn't him. This guy was muscular and built like a tank. After the shot was fired, two security guards ran from the entrance to investigate. I pulled the van behind his car, quickly scooped him up, and drove directly here. On my way, I called to warn you he was injured, and that's when you and Gregor followed the nurse home and kidnapped her."

Zahair rubbed his chin, annoyed at the world. "Nah, it couldn't be Zinmansky. He's too weak. He'd never plan this. Did you see anything else in the lot?"

"Muddy footprints and a combat boot tread in the blood," Amir pointed down the hall, "but my priority was him."

"More than one set of prints?" Zahair asked.

Amir shook his head and held up one finger.

Zahair clenched his fists. "You better come up with a better story for the chief commander. If the secretary dies, you'll bury him and dig your own grave next to his before I shoot you, too. What the hell were you thinking?"

"I followed orders," Amir said.

"Not mine," Zahair shouted.

Amir stood tall, still refusing to cower. "This plan was activated long before I met you, and I would never have allowed you to take charge if you hadn't agreed to kidnap the secretary. As for Nurse Sloan, that was all your doing. You spied on the FBI Director for a few days before kidnapping his wife. Admit it."

Zahair's fists clenched, but he didn't say anything. The silence was interrupted when the phone rang.

Gregor picked it up on the first ring. He sat at a table loaded with a laptop, server, printer, Satphones, radios, and various supplies to create false IDs and passports. Sweat beaded across his forehead. "General H.Q. is on the phone."

"What does he want?" Zahair asked.

Gregor shrugged. "He says he heads up a Quds Force of the Islamic Revolutionary Guard Corps. He's asking for you."

Zahair took a deep breath and scowled. "Now you've done it," he whispered to Amir. "This must be your boss. I'll handle this. Go outside and check on the men. Make sure that RCV is still operational after that tremor."

"Didn't you hear Gregor? If it's truly General H.Q., you should be shaking in your boots. Of course, he always disguises his voice, so it's hard to know who you're really talking to, but surely, you've heard of the general. He's everyone's boss. You'd be wise not to anger him. He will hold you responsible for any mistakes. So, beware. You have been warned." Amir gave a salute and left the RV.

Zahair stood straighter. He'd heard stories of the general's temper, but he was in Syria, not the U.S., and Zahair hated having his authority challenged. *What would General H.Q. want with me?* He grabbed the phone and greeted the general, "Salam Alykum."

The general didn't bother with a formal greeting and launched into a rant in his native Farsi. To Zahair's surprise, the general's voice wasn't disguised. "That drone attack on the White House failed. You can't trust Russian drones. We should have relied on our own. Did you plant the test weapons on Maven II as I ordered? It's essential. They don't know they're really testing Iran's malware."

"Done—but why didn't we test them? As you say, we should rely on our own." Zahair jotted a note to Gregor. "Are you recording this call? Voice is undisguised. Is it really H.Q.?"

Gregor nodded and scribbled, "I record all our calls."

The general continued, "It's one thing to launch rockets on the U.S. Embassy in Baghdad, but an attack on U.S. soil? That's a real coup, and with their own weapons. There is another issue of grave concern. I gave orders for a robust cyberattack, but you need to take care of certain analysts to ensure success. Do I make myself clear? That analyst and her team could muddy the water."

"Yes, General." Zahair had already made plans for the cybersecurity team's leader. He'd bide his time before wiping out the rest of the team. He planned to use their expertise yet in the near future, not that they would be aware of his plan. "Perfectly clear."

"Good." General H.Q. sounded pleased for the first time during this call. Then, his demeanor changed abruptly. "I repeat, our goal is cyberwarfare—and certainly not attacking the Secretary of State. Who ordered you to kidnap him?" H.Q. paused, but Zahair said nothing, so H.Q. added, "Never mind. We can use this to our advantage. The royal family in a certain country will be glad to hear of his capture. Maybe they'll even negotiate for decreased sanctions for his release or, better yet, pay a ransom. Yes, that could misdirect our involvement. Get as much as possible for his ransom. Make a video demanding $25 million. If you can't arrange a ransom as planned, I'm sure his wife will pay, but she'll expect to see him alive, so patch him up as best as possible and make the demand. Be sure he's still alive for the transfer."

"We can have the nurse speak on his behalf," Zahair said.

"That's another major mistake on your part!" H.Q. shouted so loudly that Zahair held the phone away from his ear and could still hear, "You're jeopardizing our operations. I ordered you to get a medic to remove the bullet. He would have been expendable, but you nabbed the Director of the FBI's wife!"

"I knew she was an ICU nurse," Farzad Zahair said in his defense, "and she removed the bullet. Without her help, the secretary would have died."

"I've heard of Agent Sloan," General said. "He won't negotiate, so don't even try. Do not let anyone capture his wife's face on video. I refuse to be associated with kidnapping her, and her demise falls on your shoulders. You will be marked as a traitor to our country. They'll hunt you down like a dog."

Zahair's temper snapped. "I do not take orders from you, General, and I doubt you are really General H.Q. He always disguises his voice. But if you are who you say you are, you'd know that I report directly to the Chief Commander of the Guardians."

"Idiot, he reports directly to me." H.Q.'s voice rose in pitch. "You can be replaced."

Zahair did know there were others, but none was his equal. "For your information, I'm the one responsible for waking three more secret cells within the U.S. over the past week starting with an attack on the Securities and Stock Exchange, disrupting the subway system causing riots in Washington, D.C, and a cell to launch next week in Texas. With that comes many risks, so do not bully me."

"I'm well aware of your actions. I ordered the cells to be activated, and I know the risks." The general's words clipped crisply over the speaker. "Focus on your own tasks. I'll take care of the rest."

Zahair seethed within. "I, too, have multiple assets—"

"Don't threaten me, you ungrateful fool!" The cursing coming from the other end of the phone nearly deafened Zahair. "Follow my orders!"

Zahair spoke over the general, "…contractors, inside investors, members of Congress—"

H.Q. dropped his voice to barely a whisper, forcing Zahair to listen carefully. "Better yet, you're on your own! I refuse to send a jet to bring you home. They'll track you down, and poof, you're history. You'll die just like General Qasem Soleimani." The line disconnected.

Zahair turned to Gregor, his eyes ablaze with determination. "To hell with him—he's only interested in the money and refuses to fly us back home. We'll get money my way and leave without his help. Work your magic and line up a jet for tomorrow between 2 and 4 a.m. It's about time someone challenged H.Q. He's a tyrant who has made many enemies, and he just rose to the top of my hit list."

Gregor's hands shook as he poised them over the keyboard. "How will you get the money?"

"I have a few people who will jump at the chance." Zahair speed-dialed JCJ300, his main contact, and waved Gregor away.

"Zahair, what may I do for you?" came across his cell phone.

"I have a great deal for you." Zahair made an offer and beamed with pride, his confidence radiating through the phone. "You place $50 million in a bank account in Cypress, and I'll give you complete plans for the greatest drone system on the planet. I know the royal family is vying for decreased sanctions and would appreciate better negotiations with the U.S. I already have the Secretary of State in custody, and we can negotiate a ransom deal for his release. The drone plans are secured."

"I'll need some evidence," his contact said.

"I can do that. The plans will arrive as soon as I confirm receipt of the funds. Where should I send my proof?" Zahair pulled a notepad from his jacket pocket and jotted down the address.

"Give me one hour," his contact said. "The boss must approve your money demand, but I'm sure we can work with you."

"I await your reply," Zahair said, his voice tinged with anticipation. "In the meantime, I'll forward the proof you've requested." He disconnected with a joyous bounce to his step. Then, turning to Gregor, he asked, "Where do we stand on the jet?"

"It'll take time to make arrangements with Ansin." Gregor rubbed his square chin, which protruded over his lanky body. Renowned for ignoring fashion, his gray-white jacket was too small, and his shirt too large with sleeves that hung low, nearly to his thumbs. It was covered with faint stains. His trousers were light-blue cotton and rode high above his bony ankles. Black socks and brown sandals completed his attire. Unlike his clothes, his personal grooming was pristine. He had black dyed hair that shone like raven's feathers, plucked eyebrows, and a hawk-like nose. "What are the real plans for the hostages?"

"The secretary's body is paid for—the woman, not so fortunate. I'm sure they'll find her over time." Zahair glanced around the small RV. He had sent four of his thugs out to survey the area. That left Rugar, who constantly asked questions and had become more of a pest than a soldier, to watch over the hostages in the northeast corner next to the toilet, far enough away that he couldn't eavesdrop on their conversation.

Gregor's long, slender fingers tapped across the keyboard. "I chartered a private jet, which is already booked for Toronto. We must eliminate the pilot and the original passengers, but I can fly it."

"How many passengers will it hold?" Zahair asked.

"Four max plus the pilot," Gregor said. "We can't take all of our team. Will that be a problem?"

Zahair answered, "No, only Amir and I will take the jet. You can fly it, but we'll say you will stay behind with Rugar. It'll be easier when we leave. The rest of the team can move to safe havens stateside."

Gregor glanced down the hallway. "And the secretary?"

"We'll need him to come as far as the jetway to appease Amir." *We have to move fast. It is time to leave the country.*

Gregor's cell phone vibrated, and he read the text message, "There's been a change of flight plans for that analyst in Colorado. She's coming here by private jet."

"Get me the details. I have a plan." Zahair placed a finger over his lips as he glanced toward the guards coming in from the cold. "Did you place the cameras?"

Amir, the guard's leader, nodded. "And one RCV."

Zahair wondered if H.Q. would also send a team to hunt him. "Are you sure one is enough?"

"A second can be activated as a backup." Amir motioned toward the large screen on the table. "You will connect to this, yes?"

Gregor nodded. "We will all be able to survey the area."

Zahair was disappointed that he couldn't witness the weaponized RCV and drone in action, but the testing site was 70 miles away at Aberdeen Proving Grounds, and he had other issues to address. He had to deal with the cybersecurity team, a group of the government's most trusted associates responsible for managing unforeseen circumstances and ensuring the success of aborting his mission. He took two notes from Gregor, jotted something to the bottom of one page, and attached them with a red paper clip. Then he stuffed them into a padded brown envelope. "Amir, I need you to take this evidence to a mutual friend. It's the same place you sent the previous message two days ago. The GPS coordinates and contact name is on your radio. Leave now and be back before 6 a.m."

"Roger." Amir took the envelope Zahair gave him. "What about the drone schematics and source code? That's our ticket out of the country."

"The coin should arrive in Tehran by midday. No one will suspect that the euro has a hidden chip inside. To be safe, take the motorcycle and cut through the woods. Then, hide the cycle when you return. We may need it later."

On The Run

Sept. 11 — 12:00 p.m. IRST, Tehran, Iran/
4:30 a.m. EDT, Washington, D.C.

Special Agent Usher Hastings heard the Islamic call to prayer over a mosque's minaret four blocks away from his dingy hotel room in the center of Tehran, Iran. The chanting echoed in the crowded streets. When Usher moved to close the window, he noticed a white pickup truck pull up in front of the building and park just below where he stood. For some reason, he felt goose bumps rise along his forearms, and the hair at the nape of his neck prickled.

Two Arabs yelled, "Yarkad! Naquil," as they darted from the truck, leaving both doors open. They frantically motioned for people to leave the area. Several men ran across the street, yelling and shooing people to move. A small girl scooped up a cat as she ran. A woman pulled a child behind her and ducked into an alleyway. A lumpy canvas was draped over the back end of the pickup.

Usher's senses were on high alert as he recognized the scene unfolding before him. "Explosives!" He grabbed his cell phone, yanked his backpack from the lumpy bed, and threw it over one shoulder. Darting out of his room, he weaved around a maid's cart and yelled, "Ian, danger!" as he reached the other end of the hallway. He banged on a door. "Jump out of the window." He didn't wait for an answer and kicked in the door.

Officer Ian McMurchein, a foreign intelligence spy for the UK, MI-6, lowered his pistol and stuffed it into his waistband when he saw Usher. With a Highland lilt in his voice, he muttered under his breath, "I could have killed ye. What's the rush?"

"Move! Jump now! Bombs!" Usher grabbed Ian's duffle bag and nearly threw the Scotsman over his shoulder as he dragged him onto the window's ledge. He dropped the duffle and backpack onto the ground below.

Ian cursed as the hotel shook. Furniture flew through the air, and windows shattered.

A geyser of black smoke, splintered wood, and cement fragments showered overhead. A burst of hot air blasted through the room, and Usher was thrown mid-air before the sound of the detonation hit his ears. The shock of the explosion was alarming, and Usher's landing on the hard-packed earth amongst debris was painful as he dropped and rolled.

"Oof!" Ian landed sprawled on top of Usher. Although the Scotsman was tall and lanky, he knocked the wind from Usher's lungs. The relief of surviving the blast was evident in their shared breathless moment.

Ian rolled to his side, dusted off his pants, held out a hand to Usher, and shouted, "Your not exactly a comfy cushion, are ye? But thanks for saving me life."

Perhaps Ian didn't shout, but Usher's ears still rang from the loud blast. He raised his own voice to be heard. "I think you broke my ribs." Usher panted in short breaths and moaned. He refrained from taking Ian's hand and crouched on his hands and knees. His shirt was blackened and torn, and blood oozed from his scraped elbows and chin. Finally, he stood hunched over, but at six-foot-four, he still stood a good head taller than Ian. Injuries, be damned—there was no time to waste.

Ash and smoke filled the air. The stench of charred wood, metal, and burning flesh overpowered their nostrils. The hotel was gone. Only debris filled the space. A tornado couldn't have done more damage. Bystanders began pawing through the rubble, searching for survivors and any treasures.

Usher found his backpack under debris from the explosion. He needed to get away fast. "Where's the car?"

"Not far." Ian picked up his duffle and moved further into the alley. "Do ye think that attack was for us?"

"I don't know, but I just returned from meeting our Russian contact." Usher glanced at his watch. "I better call Dr. Ping. He doesn't like surprises, and we need more backup."

Ian's water-blue eyes glanced up, "Not now. Machine guns at 4 o'clock!" He darted right and leapt behind a building.

Usher caught a glance of two men carrying AK-47s and followed Ian. They darted down another alley and turned a corner.

Ian paused. "Do you trust this Russian?"

Usher adjusted his backpack. "A friend of mine highly recommends him. I hope he's safe because whoever followed me could be hunting him, too."

"I thought the Russians were Syria's allies." Ian sounded hesitant.

"Allies to Iran and some Syrians, yes," Usher kept moving, "but not if it means smuggling Iranian missiles to the IRGC. Imagine what havoc the Islamic revolutionaries can create."

They rounded a second corner and found their mid-sized truck had been vandalized—slashed tires, dented doors, and a missing windshield. The glove compartment door lay open with nothing inside. "Ye were right! I should have taken the Satphone with me, but I only planned to be away for fifteen minutes. What's plan B?"

An older man in a white turban with a full gray beard drove a battered, dust-encrusted sedan and pulled up alongside the damaged truck. "Need taxi? Gustof, send me."

"We should probably go to the American Embassy," Ian said.

"No, I no go there." The driver pushed the floor's shift stick into first gear. "I know safe place. Get in quick."

Ian backed away from the car. "Do you know this, Gustof?"

"Yes, he's my Russian contact." Usher turned to the driver. "Roll down your windows."

The driver followed the request.

Usher searched the car's back seat. "How do you know Gustof?"

"Quick, get in," the driver said. "We not safe. Police coming."

Usher scanned the area. Two police officers ran toward them, waving their arms in the air and shouting.

The driver stepped on the gas, and the car lurched forward, but Usher hung on to the door. "Stop!"

The driver slammed on his brakes. "Get in!"

Usher opened the passenger door. "Okay, we go, but wait for my friend."

Ian threw his duffle bag through the open rear window, lifted the door latch, and climbed in. Usher took the front passenger's seat. "Hurry—"

They were moving, wheels screeching, before Usher had the door closed as a police officer leapt for the rear bumper. He missed and landed on the ground in a swirl of dust.

"That was close. We go to someplace safe, where no one will find you," the driver said.

People hustled through fragmented alleyways branching off Tehran's network of wider streets. When they got to the main road, traffic was backed up by the bomb blast. Honking and bleating came from a block away, car brakes squealed, and a small car, two vehicles ahead, nearly hit goats milling on the road. The car swung to the left to miss the herd and ran directly into an oncoming truck causing a domino effect of car crashes.

The herder rushed forward, shouting and waving his arms. "My goats, my goats, you hit my goats!"

Now, all traffic stopped, and drivers got out of their cars, arguing with the herder. People gathered in the street. Many headed from makeshift stalls of fruits and vegetables, spices and herbs, and various other goods to tell their side of the story. More horns honked as motorcycles and bicycles wove between the stalled cars and trucks.

"Patrol here soon." The nervous taxi driver's hands shook as he turned into an alley and stopped. "Get out, quick! You never see me."

Usher look up and saw Gustof sitting across the street in a military Jeep, his eyes intent on them. Usher paid the driver and got out of the taxi. The men hopped into the Jeep as the taxi driver sped through the alleyway, disappearing into the chaos beyond.

Gustof's English had a thick Russian accent. He rolled his R's, th's sounded like a Z, and W's became V's. "Zat vas close." As the taxi driver disappeared in the distance, he addressed Usher, "You vere right about ze missiles. zere is enough firepower to blow up ze U.S. three times over. We must hurry. Zey are being transferred to Syria tonight."

"Where are they?" Usher had heard Russian enough that he understood the accent. "Cracker mentioned you can take us there to retrieve—"

"Take you there? No." Gustof drove, crisscrossing through back alleys to a dirt road that looked more like a footpath. "They are in a guarded missile factory 70 feet below ground. We must use a freight elevator, but that just takes us to a tunnel. Missiles are behind three blast doors. The last one weighs ten tons and only opens from the inside."

Usher nearly choked on the dust kicked up from the road. He tried to roll down the canvas tarp to cover the car window, but the tied knot wouldn't budge.

"Here, put this over ye face." Ian handed Usher a frayed scarf.

"Thanks," Usher said, wrapping the scarf around his neck and pulling it over his nose. "If the doors only open from the inside, how do we get access?"

"We aren't going after the missiles while they're underground." Gustof cut across a field, and his voice trembled with every bump.

"Then how do we prevent their transfer to Syria," Usher asked.

"They will be moved from their hiding place," Gustof said, "but believe me, they will be surrounded by armed militia."

"How many missiles?" Usher asked.

"I don't know how many have been made, but Iran is only delivering three to Syria." Gustof drove through a field of waist-high weeds.

"Only three?" Usher asked. "That's three too many."

"Are you sure ye trust this Russian," Ian asked with a hint of fear in his voice. "That taxi driver was right. No one will find us here."

"Good point." Usher asked, "So, where are you taking us? Are we planning to hide out in the grass?"

Gustof chuckled without answering as the Jeep bumped along the uneven ground. He stopped a few feet from an old clapboard shed that had been whitewashed many years ago. The door stood ajar. The front windows were missing, and the window sashes sloped toward the ground.

Ian asked, "Where are we?"

"We're where no one will find us." Gustof turned off the engine, opened the door, and climbed from the truck. He grinned from ear to ear. "Like you say in America, home sweet home, yes?"

Usher wondered how well Cracker knew Gustof. Was he trustworthy? It was a little late to wonder about that now. He wished he had known that answer before he got into this Jeep. He pulled off the scarf, handed it back to Ian, and stepped to the ground, which looked like truck-matted grass and stretched. A moan escaped his lips when a lower rib popped. In the distance lay a silhouetted mountain peak. "Is that where they keep the missiles?"

Gustof nodded. "We only have four hours before we do the impossible. Let's get started."

What Went Wrong?

***Sept. 11 — 5:28 a.m. EDT, Chairman of the Joint Chiefs
of Staff, General Shyler's Office, Washington, D.C.***

Braun wasn't in any mood to report to General Shyler. The special ops weapons test had been a royal disaster. Rusty was dead, two of his teammates were in ICU, and air traffic control had rerouted his flight plan, so he was running late. Frustrated and pissed off, he pushed through the office door expecting a long wait.

To his surprise, the receptionist greeted him with a warm smile. "Good morning." Concern etched her brow. "What happened to you?"

Braun swallowed back his anger. "Miss Ward, you're a nice surprise. What brings you out so early this morning?"

She seemed confused. "Code Q called us from a sound sleep nearly two and a half hours ago, but I'm worried about you. You're bleeding."

"I'm fine. It's my men I'm worried about. You mentioned a Code Q?" *Surely, I would have been notified.* Braun reached into his back pocket to pull out his cell. All he found was a tie-tack—a wedding gift from Cordy. She insisted that he always be prepared for unexpected situations. The clear stone nestled in the middle of the tack was now black, destroyed when he'd tried to save Rusty's life. Neither had survived—his friend's loss left a hollow void in his soul. His mind seemed sluggish, and then he remembered he had been looking for his phone, which had melted during the fiasco at Aberdeen Proving Grounds. *Code Q. That explains why my flight plan was initially denied. It must have been called while I was at the testing site.*

"Miss Ward pushed back her chair. Would you care for a cup of coffee?"

Drained of adrenaline and feeling bone-tired, Braun refused to admit his fatigue. "No coffee, but thanks for asking." He glanced down at the incinerated tie-tack still in his hand. That's when he noticed the dried blood caked in the creases of his palm, knuckles, and nail beds.

"You look like you had a rough morning." Miss Ward checked her watch. "It's 5:30 a.m. The general can see you now." She pressed the intercom button. "Agent Braun Hastings, Commander of Special Ops, is here to see you, General Shyler, although he looks like he should be reporting to sickbay."

Feeling grungy and unfit to see Shyler, he said, "One moment, I should wash up before meeting the general."

Miss Ward reached in her desk drawer and pulled out a few disinfectant wipes left over from the recent Virus X pandemic. "There's also blood on your face, and that soiled shirt belongs in the ragbag, but the general needs to see you as you are." Using the tips of two fingers, she handed the wipes to Braun.

"Thanks." Gratefully, Braun took the wipes in one hand, while sliding the tie-tack into his back pocket with his other. He avoided using the charred and holey shirt pockets. He had no jacket—he'd used it to stanch the blood from Max's temple, but crispy bits of the taffeta lining still stuck to his shirt. Sticky splotches covered his pant legs, stiffening in varying shades of dried blood. He scrubbed at the traces of debris on his hands and face.

"You missed a spot on your right cheek," Miss Ward said.

Braun swiped at his face again, but the blood continued to ooze from the gash.

"Put pressure on the wound." She pressed the intercom button again. "I wouldn't keep him waiting if I were you, General Shyler."

There was a grunt from her intercom.

Miss Ward walked to the general's door and opened it.

With one look at Braun saluting in the doorway, Shyler said, "At ease. Just as I figured, testing didn't go as you planned, but be proud, son. You made history. The Maven II drones will see action soon."

Braun's anger flared, "You know it didn't go as planned!" He entered the office and slammed the door. "What's going on, sir?

Our assignment was to do a final test. Obviously, you scheduled it prematurely."

"No. Everything went supremely smoothly. After the attack on the White House, we need this weapon ASAP." Shyler crossed his arms. "I hear the drone's photos are sharp and clear, and the RCV responded on target."

Braun couldn't believe the general's comment. "What? The test failed miserably. The drone exploded without any warning."

"That RCV and drone," Shyler bit his lip and swallowed hard, "are required for nuclear and biological weapons, and they have passed all testing thus far. Fortunately, today, they had no load at the time of the explosion."

"That's not true," Braun said. "The drone was weaponized, and you didn't inform us."

"No, this was only a prototype. It couldn't possibly be loaded." Shyler glanced briefly at Braun. Then, his gaze drifted back to a pile of papers on his desk. "Certainly not with live ammunition, but it will be soon."

Braun already knew the general was a real S.O.B., but he wouldn't let the man get away with a lie. "It was loaded and fired on my men. What I want to know is who set it off? It wasn't any of us." Braun glared at the highly decorated general. "I nearly lost my entire team out there today."

Shyler's head jerked up. "Who was injured?"

"Two teammates were transported to Walter Reed with massive injuries. My second in command, Admiral Jud L. Browning, has burns to 30% of his body—mostly head, neck, and torso, and he's on a ventilator. Ranger Max Ruthmyer has a head injury and is in a coma. Rusty died in what was supposed to be a mock drill. You sent a man to his death, and his wife is pregnant. It could have been prevented if we had known—"

"My condolences to your team," Shyler said calmly, "my heart grieves at the loss of any of my men."

Braun heard the words but felt little empathy coming from the general. "Why did the drone attack?"

"It didn't exactly attack, did it? It is supposed to seek out targeted missiles, and that's what it did. Think hard about it. Isn't that what really happened? It couldn't possibly have been loaded with live ammo."

Does he truly believe the drone was ammo-free? Braun shook his head and opened his mouth to speak.

Shyler leaned forward. "The problem is that only approved team members, who have received clearance and are in our system, can activate the weapon. You were not authorized, so the drone blew up instead of allowing an outsider to take control. There was no live load onboard. Unfortunately, your men were in the way when it went into self-destruction mode." He jotted a note into a file and signed it. "I have reported the mission as a complete success."

"Success?" Braun narrowed his eyes. "You planned for this to happen? Why didn't you provide any extra protection or warning?"

"What if the intruder had been an Al Qaeda cell set to attack Washington, D.C.?" Shyler asked. "We needed to know what would happen, and it couldn't have come at a more opportune time. We'll be at war soon."

Braun could barely hold back his anger. "So, you put my team in the path of an explosive device using high-grade military ammo?"

"I did no such thing." The general stared at him as if he couldn't understand why Braun was so upset. "You and your men knew this was a test weapon, and caution is required. I already told you the drone had no munitions."

"What type of explosive was used?" Braun leaned over the general's desk. "Were we exposed to nuclear? No, wait. You wouldn't have allowed me in here if that were the case." Braun backed away, afraid he might strike the general.

"The explosive was not nuclear, nor a bio-weapon." Shyler's Adam's apple bobbed up and down as he swallowed, the only indication that he felt threatened. His smile brightened. "It was a complete success."

Braun wouldn't back down. "So, it was loaded, and you planned for this to happen. I recommend a full investigation of this explosive material and the ammo used to determine my team's exposure. Who actually has access, and how do they get it? I want—no, I need to know the truth."

"Investigation?" Shyler seemed stunned by the comment. "Why? The drone wasn't loaded. It was a mock drill. We'd look like fools running such an investigation."

"No, sir," Braun said. "The drone was loaded, and I'm going to prove it."

"I'm warning you!" Shyler's gaze locked onto Braun's, his authority and imperious manner intending to deliver a threat. "You are bordering on insubordination."

Braun had seen that menacing look before.

Shyler's commanding voice left no hesitation. "I told you that drone you tested today was not weaponized. The RCV, combined with our Maven II drones, gives us the most advanced armed robotic system in the world. It ranks number one of our five top-secret weapons. My specs included no weapons, and if anything about this test appears in the news, I'll know that you were the one who placed munitions on that drone. There will be no further investigation by you or your team. Case closed. This is not for public discussion. If I hear one word negating the success of this test, you'll go down as a traitor to your country."

Braun clenched and unclenched his fists. "I need answers."

"Other factors that do not include you are involved, and I'm not at liberty to discuss them." Shyler stamped *approved* across the file folder and shoved it into the outbox. "So, I repeat. There will be no further investigation, soldier. Are we clear?"

Braun bit his tongue to hold in his disgust and stared back at the general.

Shyler flicked his wrist toward the office door. "You're dismissed."

"And if I don't agree?" Braun's neck veins throbbed as he gritted his teeth. "You had no right—"

"I'm sure I made myself perfectly clear, Agent Hastings. You are dismissed." Shyler didn't raise his tone but made his command abundantly clear.

"Yes," Braun bit back.

"Yes, what?" the general snapped.

"Yes, sir!" Braun's voice strained as he swallowed the cuss words flooding his brain. His gut raged with fire. Standing his full 6'4", he gave a brisk salute.

"We're done here. And give my regards to your fallen teammates. They are heroes." Shyler lifted the phone to his ear. "Get me the president."

"You have a call on line 1," his secretary said. "Do you want to put him on hold?"

"Who is it?" Shyler asked.

"It's hard to say," Miss Warner said. "It sounds like he's talking through a comb."

Still seething, Braun stepped away from Shyler. "You'll have my resignation on your desk by noon."

"What? Oh, never mind." Shyler said. "Patch in line 1."

Braun turned, mentally thanking Cordy for her preparations for all unexpected situations. Although the tie-tack had been fried, he still had one surprise left in his arsenal, and he used it.

While the general focused on his phone calls, Braun slapped his hand on the outer ridge of the jamb as he left the office and slammed the door, leaving behind one rice-sized object, an amazingly accurate camera centered directly at the general's desk. *Then I'm bringing in my own investigative FBI team.*

Slimeball Strikes Again

Sept. 11 — 5:43 a.m. EDT, Outside General Shyler's Office, Washington, D.C.

As Braun Hasting left the building after a failed debriefing with General Shyler, his immediate boss, FBI Director Loran Sloan, pulled up to the curb. The passenger door flew open. "Get in. We need to talk."

Braun hesitated at the door. "Who set us up?" Sloan wore blue jeans, a wrinkled tan short-sleeve shirt, and a navy blue cap with "FBI" embossed in gold across the front. Braun leaned into the opened door and stared, noting Sloan's swollen and bloodshot eyes. A frown creased his forehead. "What's wrong? It must be horrendous. I've never seen you in civvies."

"Get in! That's an order," Sloan said. "And I refuse to accept your resignation."

"My, news travels fast." Braun folded himself into the black hybrid Toyota Camry. "When are you going to drive a decent car? I hate this toaster on wheels."

"Good thing I'm driving then. Look, we have a major problem."

"And…" Braun spat out.

"Farzad Zahair is in the country," Sloan said as he shoved the gearshift into drive. "Close the door. You better buckle up. I'm in no mood for niceties." As soon as the door slammed, the tires spun. Sloan skidded through a stoplight, swerved to avoid a girl riding a bike, and kept going. The speedometer was at 70 mph and rising in a 50 mph zone. "I heard he's packing a dangerous explosive—maybe even planted it at an RCV test site. He probably hacked into the Maven II Project and took control of that drone."

Braun grabbed Sloan's arm. He was about to tell Sloan to slow down, but the fierce glare in Sloan's icy eyes made Braun think twice. "How did that slimeball get into this country? He's on everyone's terrorist list."

Sloan jerked his arm away and slowed down. "You aren't going to believe it. I'm the Director of the FBI, and this has been kept top secret from me, but I've seen him in person. Heads are going to roll over that mistake."

"When did you see him?" Braun asked.

"Early this morning." Sloan slid his cell from his pocket and tapped the photo gallery. "See for yourself." He tossed the phone to Braun, who grabbed it before it hit the floor.

Braun studied the photo. A tanned face peered out of the tinted window of a black SUV in total darkness at 2 a.m. "How can you tell? If this photo is evidence—"

"Yup. It is. And it's him," Sloan said. "Have Cordy enhance the image. I tracked his license plate—a rental car from D.C. He used the name Ingram Freeman."

Braun handed the phone back. "How long have you known this bastard was in the country?"

"He arrived ten days ago," Sloan said, "but I only found out in the wee hours of this morning."

Braun punched his fist on the dashboard, causing a six-inch crack. "And you just got around to telling me now? My team—"

Sloan glanced toward the damage and sucked in a breath. "Check your office phone. I tried to reach you on your cell, but you were indisposed. No one could contact you once you hit that two-hour window before your special ops mission."

"You should have demanded emergency access. That drone attacked my whole team." Braun lifted his fist again.

Sloan abruptly turned the corner and slammed on the brakes. "If you touch that dashboard again, I'm kicking you out in the middle of this slum. I'm trying to tell you something, and I want you to stay safe," he said. He sped up again, seemingly unaware of how fast he was going. "My instincts tell me there's more to this, and it will get ugly."

Braun squinted and grimaced in revulsion. A wave of raw agony constricted his chest. "Rusty's gone, my team…" He restrained his fury. "It's too late. I couldn't save them—"

"Then help me because that scumbag has my wife!" Sloan choked and could barely make the words form through clenched teeth. "Where do you think I got that photo?"

"Zahair has Emma?" Braun stared at his boss, understanding the rage that seethed beneath every breath. He wondered what he'd do if it had been Cordy. "When? How?"

Sloan drove over a railroad track toward an isolated area. "He kidnapped Emma early this morning, right outside my garage, when she came home after work. That image is from our security camera. It was as if he knew the camera was there because this is the only shot of him once Emma stepped out of her car. I need your help, and I can't go to the police. If this hits the news, he'll kill her. I'm livid, torn in too many directions, and could hardly wait until your return. Please, you've got to help find her. I can't lose her."

"Any ransom demand?"

"Not yet, but I'll be ready when he calls."

"If he calls." Braun rubbed his chin. "Sloan, you have to sit this out. You're too close to the situation. Cordy can enhance the photo, and we can—"

"No way!" Sloan shouted. "What if he kidnapped Cordy? Nothing would stop you from rescuing her. The same goes here. Emma is my wife."

"Yeah, I get it. Sorry, Sloan." They were on the same wavelength. An image of petite Emma flashed in Braun's mind—clear, alert brown eyes and long, silky blonde hair, probably wrapped into a bun as she got off her ICU shift. Braun heaved out a deep breath. "What do you have so far?"

"Evans gathered what he could for forensics—in secret."

"Are you sure Zahair isn't watching your house?" Braun asked.

"I'm sure that he is," Sloan said. "That's why I had to smuggle Evans in my trunk. Fortunately, I didn't do the same to you."

"As if you could, without my knowledge," Braun said. "Okay, I'll send the photo to Cordy. Does Emma have her cell phone?"

"Nope, Evans has it, or I should say, he has pieces of it." Sloan adjusted his rearview mirror to check on a car behind him. "I found it smashed on the driveway. I'm guessing Zahair deliberately ran over it. Evans says the phone's a hopeless case."

"Send it to Cordy. She can do wonders with damaged chips. And…" Braun paused and whispered, "Are we in a secure car? Did Evans check for bugs?"

"I'm not stupid," Sloan said. "He stole my wife! Everything has been checked out in my whole place: phone, computers, and garage door opener. We found two bugs in Emma's car, one in the garage, and one in our bedroom. For God's sake, what's that all about? Her car was also rigged to explode. She could have been killed or me if Evans hadn't warned me not to open the trunk. Don't worry. He defused it."

"What was Zahair up to for the past ten days?" Braun asked.

"I have the FBI looking into it." Sloan fidgeted in his seat. "A few hours ago, Evans tapped into Zahair's burner phone from the day he arrived and found out he entered the country with no difficulties. He has a contact person, but I don't know if they ever hooked up."

"Who's the contact?" Braun checked the outside mirror. "There is only one set of headlights, far in the distance."

Sloan had been watching for anything unusual, too. "I see it. Looks harmless. We haven't figured out how the two are linked." Zahair instamessaged a DoD contractor, Einar Zinmansky, who was cleared for top security.

"Instamessaged?" Braun asked. "How did you trace the call? It should have been erased."

"It was erased, but Zahair trashed the phone at the airport, and nothing overwrote the text." "Evans was able to pull it from memory." Sloan's eyes darted from the front windshield to the rearview mirror and back.

"How did he find the phone?" Braun asked.

"An astute teenager pulled it from the wastebasket and tried to use it." Sloan turned off the main highway to a side road. The car behind them continued straight. "When the kid couldn't figure out how to set up his account, he left the phone on a seat at the gate and boarded a plane. An FBI agent discovered that a security officer confiscated the phone and placed it in lost and found. We fingerprinted the phone, tracked down the teen, and deemed him innocent, just a curious bystander. We lost Zahair for the first five days, and then he appeared on a security camera at a Wells Fargo Bank in McLean, Virginia."

"That sounds like pure luck," Braun said. "What was he doing there?"

"We're still researching," Sloan said. "He's been in the country for ten days, and we've only been on this case for less than five hours since he kidnapped Emma. We're running through every security camera feed we can access using social media, and facial recognition runs through local, national, and foreign databases. We've searched banks, subways, taxis, hotels, and restaurants, hoping to get a hit. We're also checking warehouses, arms dealers, biological, and biochemical corporations for purchasing or stealing weapons, ammunition, or explosives. Evans suspected a hit on biochemicals, but so far—nothing."

"Do you think Zahair was behind this morning's riot in D.C.?" Braun asked.

"We're checking on that, too. We don't know who made the bombing attempt at the Metro station." Sloan drummed his fingers on the steering wheel. "I don't see how any of this ties into kidnapping Emma."

"No, but Metro might have been a dry run," Braun said. "What if the real target is the White House?"

"They won't succeed." Sloan had reached open country when blinding headlights flashed directly in front of him. "That car's in the wrong lane." He blasted his horn.

Braun spotted a red flicker over the middle of Sloan's forehead. He yanked his boss toward him as the front windshield exploded. The headrest flew into the air, pulverized by a bullet.

A black SUV swerved at the last minute and sped past them while taking the corner on two wheels. A rifle retracted into the back seat as the car disappeared.

Braun yanked the steering wheel allowing the car to crash into a speed limit sign and come to a halt. The airbags deployed, nearly breaking his nose.

Sloan punched at the bag screaming, "Why did you crash my car?"

"It's perfect." Braun unbuckled his seat belt. "I have an idea. Let the shooter think he killed you. We'll publicize your death, go undercover, and track down the assassin. Call Evans and have him bring the forensic mock kit."

National Security Briefing

Sept. 11 — 5:45 a.m. EDT, Washington, D.C.

When President Zac Spendorf arrived, the Situation Room was filled with the National Security Team and several top generals on video feeds. A new policy was instituted after the Pegasus virus fiasco earlier in the year, where private cell phones could be secretly rigged to record and transmit conversations without the owner's knowledge, threatening operational security. Now, a vigilant Secret Service agent stood at the door, collecting all cell phones as they entered.

Guy Weimer followed Zac to the door, glanced around the room, and asked the Secret Service agent standing guard, "Where's your boss? I spoke to Kyle ten minutes ago. He was heading to the meeting before me but is not here yet."

The agent motioned for Guy to talk to him outside the room and closed the door.

Zac couldn't hear the reply and strode toward his team.

The Joint Chiefs of Staff Chairman, General Shyler, attended the meeting virtually and greeted him, "Good morning, Mr. President."

"No, this is not a good morning," Zac said angrily, ready to fight. Who better to spar with than the general who was so eager to start a war? "What the hell's happening? Who launched a drone attack on the White House?" His fists clenched as he stepped up to the table. "Why weren't any of you on top of this situation? I hate being caught unaware. This is anything but a good morning."

Shyler's shoulders stiffened. "We averted the drone attack without damaging the White—"

Zac pointed with a shaky finger and faced Shyler with a fierce scowl. "You call that mess on Pennsylvania Avenue not damaging the White House? It's your job to keep our country safe. Why didn't you discover plans for this attack before it happened? We don't have the luxury of time for these failures."

"Mr. President, honestly, there were no early warning signs. No one saw this coming," Shyler said, refusing to cower under Zac's glare. "I'm proud to announce that this morning's RCV and Maven II drone tests gave us superior intelligence. I was amazed by the detailed clarity of the photos, even in sleet and poor weather conditions when using a night vision lens. The success of this mission couldn't have been better timed. We will have access to the highest-level military weaponry."

The newly promoted Director of National Intelligence, Dr. Nat Ping, vehemently shook his head. "Not so." Ping's brow furrowed.

"Did you see those photos?" Shyler's voice sounded odd, with a hint of a foreign accent, which was unusual for the man with distinct diction. He cleared his throat, and the accent disappeared. "You can see the enemy for miles in the distance, and that's a fact."

"Speaking of facts," Dr. Ping glared at Shyler's image on the screen, "I heard from a medic that today's test was a complete disaster!"

Shyler leaned forward. "A medic? Do you take the word of a medic over mine? What does he know about combat surveillance?"

"I heard the drone exploded and nearly wiped out the testing team, causing one fatality and severely wounding two others. They are in critical condition at Walter Reed's ICU," Ping said in a severe tone. "Isn't that true?"

Sweat beaded on Shyler's forehead. "The drone followed protocol. It refused access to—"

Ping put up a hand. "Whatever the reason, that's not something to gloat over, General."

No wonder Braun didn't return my call. Zac stepped closer to the screen. His heart raced, wondering if Braun was still alive. "Who was injured?"

"Agent Hastings did mention something about his team going to Walter Reed Hospital to get care…"

"Who?" Zac asked, fearing the worst. *What happened to Braun?*

"The drone captured photos of everything, which was our major objective," Shyler pressed on. "Once we have the enemy in sight, our officers can make an immediate plan of attack. The RCV is specifically designed for undercover assignments—"

Nervous energy flowed through Zac, still waiting for an answer. "General Shyler, who was injured?"

Shyler took a deep breath. "Okay, we had some casualties, but this was a test. An ambulance was on the scene within seconds of their injuries."

Dr. Ping spoke up, "Some casualties? More like a major mishap. Admiral Jud Browning has burns to 30% of his body and is on a ventilator. Ranger Max Ruthmyer suffered a head injury and is in a coma. They are both in the ICU at Walter Reed Hospital. And with deep regret, U.S. Air Force Special Ops Officer Kip Kahooly perished during the test. We've sent two officers to give our heartfelt condolences to his wife and family. I understand that his wife is with child."

"So sad to hear." Zac lowered his head. "I'll be sure to give her a call." Relieved that Braun had survived the test and was well enough to report to Shyler, he bit back a swear word. "And I meant it when I said we are not going to war without knowing the facts."

"Mr. President, with all due respect, we need these weapons," Shyler insisted. "Our country has been attacked. Washington, D.C., was under siege before you sent in the National Guard. It took five hours to rein in the chaos, overwhelming the system. Firefighters are still putting out flames, and a drone attacked the White House."

"Are these events related?" Zac felt exhaustion flood through him. He pulled out a chair at the head of the table and nearly collapsed into it. This abruptly cut off the general's public dressing down. Zac turned back to Ping, "Thanks for the update on the drone test. Do you have anything more to report?"

Ping also ignored the general's concerns. "Yes, we're working closely with the UK and Germany. Both countries' drone systems were also hacked early this morning."

Guy and the Secret Serviceman slipped quietly into the room. The agent stood on guard inside the doorway.

Zac held up a finger. "One moment." He turned toward his Secretary of Homeland Security, who appeared quite concerned. "Guy, what's the latest news?"

Guy stopped his pacing. "Our threat analysis is ongoing, but I'll briefly explain what I know. Secret Service and Homeland Security are both searching the security tapes to see when Carl was stabbed. No one has been identified, and Carl showed no sign of being injured. I haven't seen the tapes yet, but I asked the team to enhance the images for a closer look. I plan to see the tapes after this meeting."

"What's going on downtown? We called in the National Guard," Zac said.

"Right. Carl was heading up that project. Let's see, I have an update on that." Guy patted his shirt pocket. "Where did I put it?" He searched his jacket and pulled out a memo pad. "Here it is. The mayor has placed Washington, D.C., under curfew until further notice. Metropolitan Police are rerouting traffic from the city until 7 a.m. This will give the mayor time to reassess the situation before most businesses are due to open. Park officers on the Ellipse are helping Capitol Police patrol the grounds and maintain surveillance surrounding the White House."

Guy paused again to check his notes and picked up where he left off. "After sifting through the drone debris, an investigative team member called Kyle Benson and an FBI field team to the scene. I'm waiting for a detailed report that should be available shortly."

Zac caught movement out of the corner of his eye as the Secret Service agent stationed at the front door shifted his weight, and his right hand cupped his ear. Alert eyes scanned the room. Squaring his shoulders, he leaned forward on the balls of his feet and spoke quietly into a wrist mic concealed in his shirt sleeve as he walked from the door into the room. He gently tapped Guy's shoulder and whispered loud enough for Zac to overhear, "Bomb threat. Kyle Benson needs you immediately."

Guy stiffened. "I'm sorry to disrupt this meeting again, but we have unforeseen circumstances—"

Zac nodded. "Go ahead. We'll come back to you when you return." Guy was already on his way out the door. Zac turned back to Dr. Ping. "Finish what you were saying before Guy's interruption."

Dr. Ping, a seasoned counterterrorism expert, jerked his eyes away from the closing door. Worry etched his face. "We had a cyberattack at the Pentagon around 2 a.m., and someone hacked into our Maven II drone program. One drone was sent to Aberdeen Proving Ground and exploded. I'm worried the test team's injuries were due to a hacked drone?"

"We have no proof," General Shyler cut in.

Zac, known for his intense and piercing glare, fixed his eyes on Shyler.

Ping leaned forward. "Something went terribly wrong, and more is happening overseas." He was about to continue when Guy threw open the door.

"Excuse me, Mr. President," Guy said urgently. "A K9 team has identified gunpowder and bomb materials in the trunk of a green sedan parked within the five-block radius of the White House. Forensics found a partial print on the driver's car door and ran it through Interpol. The print matches a well-known Iranian terrorist, Farzad Zahair." The resolution in Guy's voice reflected the undeniable need for immediate action.

"When and how did an Iranian terrorist get into our country?" The shock and disbelief in Zac's question hung in silence throughout the room.

Guy tugged at his necktie, cleared his throat, and finally spoke hesitantly, "Ah…he flew into Reagan International Airport." All eyes turned his way.

"When? How?" Zac asked.

"Ten days ago using an alias U.S. passport—Ingram Freeman." Guy bit his lower lip.

"Ten days ago? Didn't they fingerprint the man when he landed?" Zac asked.

Guy's face turned red. "It appears he never went through customs. Something happened on his flight from Tehran, and he was the first one off the plane. Then, he simply disappeared. Both the FBI and the CIA are searching for him."

Zac's anger was barely contained. "Find that man and bring him in for interrogation! I want him alive." The intensity of his words filled the room.

A loud rap on the door diverted Guy's attention once more. "I'm sorry, but things are unfolding as we speak."

Agent Kyle Benson popped his head around the door. "Guy, there's more."

Zac motioned with his hand. "Come in, Kyle. What's the latest?"

Kyle slid into the room and closed the door behind him. "We found a bomb inside a black SUV parked a block from the White House."

Zac twisted his wedding ring, trying to remain calm.

Kyle blew out a deep breath. "Don't worry. We defused it."

"Who owns the car?" Zac asked.

"The license plate was removed, but we tracked the VIN to a rental agency that leased the car to Ingram Freeman."

"Him again?" Zac's impatience took over, wondering if everyone around him was incompetent. "What else did they find—they did search the car after defusing the bomb, didn't they?"

"Yes, the investigative team stripped the vehicle and found a right index fingerprint on the SUV's rear door hatch, along with blood splotches. Making a positive ID took a while, but an FBI forensics analyst matched the print and blood type to Emma Sloan."

Zac crossed his arms over his chest. "Emma's no terrorist. She's FBI Director Sloan's wife. Why would they…wait, there's something you're not telling me."

"Her husband reported her missing around 2 a.m.," Dr. Ping said. "The FBI is searching for her, but the director wanted it kept private, away from the public's prying eyes. I agreed, but this changes things."

"Has anyone heard from Sloan lately?" Zac asked.

Murmurs went around the room, but no one knew where to find the FBI Director. Zac needed to move on. "FBI reports to you, Dr. Ping. Find Sloan!"

"Yes, I'll keep you posted." Dr. Ping jotted a note since cell phones were not allowed in the meeting.

Zac was about to say, 'Don't keep those kinds of secrets in the future,' then remembered how he wanted to keep Secretary of State Mo Hendrum's disappearance under wraps and bit back the comment.

Kyle added, "I reported our findings to the Washington, D.C., police, who issued a missing persons report. That's all we know for now."

Realizing his anger put a damper on the room, and his team may not reveal all facts if intimidated, he nodded. "Thanks. Good work, Kyle." Zac removed a handkerchief from his suit pocket and wiped his brow. "And keep me posted. Emma's life could be in danger!"

"Yes, sir," Kyle put his finger to his ear and listened. "Sorry. I'm needed out front," he said, leaving the room again.

"Anything else?" Zac asked.

Ping opened his mouth but was interrupted by Defense Deputy Director Chet Yelson, who took charge during Carl Wyller's recovery. "Yes, I'll fill in a few more details where Guy left off." Yelson pulled a notepad from his pocket and ran a finger down the page. "The terrorists picked a prime time to attack, and perhaps, Zahair's behind the downtown riots. Our SWAT teams found a bomb planted on the crashed train and another inside the Metro station. The mayor's last update reported that the death toll has risen to 183 fatalities and over 200 injuries from tonight's subway accident. Most passengers would have been safely tucked in bed if it hadn't been for the ballgame."

"Any further intel on Zahair's whereabouts now?" Zac asked.

"We're still searching, but we'll find him!" Yelson set down his coffee cup with more force than necessary, splashing coffee onto his shirt sleeve.

"What else can anyone tell me?" Zac glanced at his watch, hoping they could wrap up the meeting soon.

Dr. Ping cleared his throat. "Farzad Zahair. That explains a lot. I heard someone was waking up sleeper cells throughout the U.S., starting here in D.C. Zahair may have joined an undercover Iranian Revolutionary Guard leader named Amir. We're dealing with a high-level, very skilled, and dangerous man. The police force has been hunting Amir for months. But that's not our worst nightmare. As I started to say earlier, we've been working closely with the UK. They say that a Quds Force commander in Syria, who goes by General H.Q., sabotaged a weapons deal between the Russians and the Iranians. The Russians are furious."

Zac blew out a deep breath. "General H.Q. Number 4 on the 10 top terrorists' list."

"Right," Dr. Ping said. "This man sells arms to every failed state in the world. He has connections to the underworld, brutal mercenaries, and corrupt corporations. He's elusive as a butterfly. We have yet to capture a photo of the man, and he disguises his voice whenever he speaks."

A crease formed across Zac's brow. "What does this have to do with our problem here? Does Amir report to General H.Q.? Are these related or separate attacks on our country? I need more—maybe it has nothing to do with us, or does it? Does that mean that the Russians are hunting H.Q., too?"

"Is Russia facing hard times?" Shyler asked with a smirk. "It's about time."

"Hard times for all of us," Ping said. "According to our Intel, H.Q.'s financing a new class of hypersonic missiles and plans to smuggle them across the Syrian-Turkish border and from there into Iran."

Shyler paled. "Through Turkey? How will they get the missiles to Iran? I doubt they have the military backers for such a mission."

"Maybe not, but H.Q. has contacts." Ping turned toward Shyler's image, "Make no mistake about this. H.Q. may be the brains of the Quds Force, but the IRCG is the muscle behind every mission, and we have Zahair and Amir right here in our front yard—I believe both are IRCG."

"Well said." General Shyler sat up straighter as if to salute. "Our intel agrees with you. H.Q.'s the brains behind every one of their attacks."

Ping turned to Zac. "UK's Chief of Secret Intelligence sent a top MI-6 agent to Iran on an espionage mission. He discovered a rogue Chinese bioweapons engineer is helping the IRCG build an underground nuclear plant."

Zac glared at Ping. "Why am I just hearing about this now?"

Dr. Ping seemed confused. "I sent you a memo. That was four days ago."

"What the hell? I never received any memo." Zac's temper went up another notch.

Ping rubbed his chin. "I also gave you an update two days ago when I sent Special Ops Agent Usher Hastings to Iran to join the covert operation."

"You know that I answer my memos within 12 hours. I didn't get that update either." Zac's eyes narrowed into slits as a surge of anger pulsed through him.

"Take a breath, Zac. I know you always get back to me quickly," Dr. Ping said. He ran a hand through his silver-streaked hair, his brows drawing together. "I wondered why I hadn't heard from you, but I understand you've been pulled in many directions lately. We've worked together enough times that I had hoped for your trust, especially after working closely during last year's pandemic. I believed that you expected me to handle the problem, so I conducted business as usual. I apologize, Mr. President, for not getting back to you sooner."

Zac gnawed on his lower lip. "Someone is leaking information, and now they're blocking confidential memos. Are they also intercepting my emails and texts? Has anyone else sent me messages that I haven't responded to?"

"Carl mentioned something yesterday, but I don't have the details, and I've been in near direct contact with you for the past 48 hours." Guy checked his watch as if he, too, was impatient for the meeting to end.

Dr. Ping waited briefly, but no one else spoke up. He added, "What if Zahair is here to steal our Maven II drone specs and send them to Iran?"

General Shyler interrupted, "That's preposterous!" His ear tips turned bright red. "They are totally guarded. No one can access them!" Tension grew so thick in the room that it clogged the air, making it hard to breathe.

"But you admitted they had been hacked earlier today," Zac's jaw flexed, trying to relieve his rising tension.

Guy hopped to Zac's defense. "Maybe not accessed intentionally, General, but this recent cyberattack is quite sophisticated. They might have accessed the drones."

Zac suppressed his anger and let out a sigh. "Today's technology allows anyone with some computer skills to bring about an Apocalypse."

Dr. Ping continued to rub his chin thoughtfully. "That's very true, Zac. We need to stay ahead of our enemies. I spoke with Commander Usher Hastings earlier today. He has met with his contact in the UK, and they have discovered that a shipment of missiles is set to cross the Syrian border in the next 48 hours. Usher hopes to prevent this, but only two agents are available. As a result, a specialized team is on their way to the location to intercept the weapons before they cross the border."

Shyler leaned closer to the screen. "Why weren't the generals informed? We're here to serve in any way."

"This is a job for special ops," Ping said, "but thanks for your support."

Zac moved on without acknowledging Shyler. "So, no missiles have crossed the Syrian border yet?"

"Not that I know of, but we are waiting on news from the boots on the ground. I'll be sure to keep you informed," Pings said.

"I know I can count on you," Zac heaved a deep sigh. "In the meantime, I know the FBI and CIA are tracking down Zahair, but remember, I want him alive to answer questions. We can't let our drone specs get into the hands of any Axis of Terrorism groups. We need answers." Zac peered at the empty chair where the Secretary of State usually sat. "Give me an update on Mo Hendrum's disappearance."

Guy swallowed with a gulp. "We've searched Mo's phone, his computer, and emails. We found nothing out of the ordinary, but the FBI and CIA are actively searching security cameras throughout the metro area. They are assisting police in setting up new surveillance tools within a fifty-mile radius—posted along main highways and in abandoned warehouse areas. We've also interviewed several parking lot employees, family members, and key personnel. We hope something will give us a lead soon."

"Keep me posted." Zac's mind spun with ideas on who would be the best agent to find Mo and capture Zahair and Amir. *We have a traitor among us. I need someone I can trust.* Deep in thought, he again absently twisted his wedding ring. *I need to talk to Braun Hastings and soon.* He'd been mulling over an idea all morning, but Braun hadn't returned his call. It wasn't until Dr. Ping mentioned the weapon's test, reminding him that Braun was preoccupied at the time, *but the test was over. Braun would be perfect—*

"Mr. President?"

Jarred out of his thoughts, Zac wasn't ready to leave his plan yet.

"Mr. President," came a second time with more persistence.

Zac scanned the room when his eyes fell upon the red-faced Secretary of Transportation. "Yes, Nick." Zac wondered what was so urgent, then remembered he'd sent in the National Guard. "I understand downtown is still reeling. Give us an update."

Nick Chambers let out a deep breath. "It's total chaos, Mr. President. It actually started last Friday with the shutdown of DOJ computers. And if you recall, during our Cabinet meeting, the DOJ was investigating corporations selling their stocks short on the NYSE. On Friday, another stock sold short and disrupted the stock market again, driving the NYSE into a frenzy. Maybe it's a long shot and unrelated, but I believe it's worth investigating. Did someone shut down the network to prevent further research into their companies' activities?"

"The DOJ network is back up and operational," Zac said. "Let's concentrate on matters at hand."

"I agree," Nick said, "but I'm afraid something could get overlooked if we don't research the big picture."

Zac sighed. "Okay, enlighten us, but make it quick. People will be waking up soon to shocking news. I need to address the nation and calm their fears."

"Right," Nick said. "Our U.S. infrastructure is crumbling, and no city needs repairs at the moment more than right here in D.C. I just heard from the Director of WMATA—"

"Who?" Zac asked.

"Washington's Transit Authority. They discovered a flaw in Metro's new software program that allowed two trains to crash. The system was upgraded yesterday afternoon. All worked well until the power outage. The flaw was in the battery-operated backup system."

I'm confused, Zac said. "You mentioned something about the DOJ investigating corporations selling short, which happened again on Friday. Now you're talking about the transit system. Are they linked?"

"IYFTI is a company that bid to take over management of WMATA. Their stock went wild on Friday. Prices rose, then crashed. The owners and a few investors made a fortune, and then this morning, two subway trains collided without warning. As if that wasn't bad enough, a semi-truck crashed through a berm on the edge of the 14th Street Bridge and caused a head-on collision with a metro bus, resulting in a 23-car pile-up. The latest update on that accident was 18 fatalities, plus more than 200 died in the subway crash, and we still don't know how many were injured. The bridge is closed for massive repairs, but we don't know the full extent of the damage."

Zac shook his head. "My God, so many people have been killed." He rubbed his forehead. "You're right. This needs further examination."

Nick removed his silver wire-rim glasses and rubbed his bloodshot eyes. "We've called in civil engineers to assess the damages, but it's extensive. The bridge will be closed for a month or longer. We already know that Key and Memorial Bridges also need repairs. With the 14th Street Bridge closures, there will be massive traffic jams. More than 215,000 vehicles cross them on any given day."

Zac rubbed his neck. "The mayor declared a state of emergency, and the governor has asked for help from FEMA. I want to emphasize that the federal government will do everything it can to help. Any update on that earthquake?"

Nick shoved his glasses back in place. "The Potomac aquifer usually contains trillions of gallons of pressurized water. Unfortunately, the resource is being overused every day, drastically decreasing the pressure of the water. Yesterday, half a trillion gallons of treated wastewater were injected into the aquifer to replenish the system, but it may have been pumped too rapidly. So far, only minor quake damages have been reported, but it's too early for a full assessment."

"Who knew about the injected wastewater? Is it possible this, too, was a terrorist attack?" Zac asked. "We nearly lost the Washington Memorial during the last earthquake. Did it sustain additional damage today?"

Guy snapped to attention as if he'd just been aroused from a deep thought. "This quake was minor, only 3.9 on the Richter scale, although it could be felt for 60 miles. We'll have civil engineers check out the Memorial and the National Cathedral as both suffered damages during 2011."

"Keep me informed. We don't want another crisis." Zac turned when another knock interrupted the meeting.

The Press Secretary peered around the door. "They're ready for you to address the nation whenever you're available, Mr. President."

"Okay, there's no time like the present. Before you leave, does anyone here need to inform me of anything else?" Zac looked at every eye in the room.

No one spoke. Zac nodded to his advisors. "Good. This attack must have taken months to plan. Find a connection to Zahair. There has to be a link to H.Q. out there. Get to work and find it. We are up against the clock. When people wake up this morning, they will hear Washington, D.C., and their nation's White House have been attacked. On top of terrorist attacks, Mother Nature has given us an earthquake. The next few days will be crucial. I need you all to work together as a well-oiled machine—unyielding to fear—projecting strength. We'll reconvene as needed."

The Press Secretary approached Zac and whispered, "Sir, the press is already asking for details. Several reporters are calling in, asking if someone bugged your office. I've told them, 'Not that I've heard, but I'll get back to them later.'"

"Thanks." Zac blew out a deep breath—*another leak*. "From here on, we will assume all communication is compromised. Nothing goes out online. Communication will be limited to VidChat only. Make sure everything is encrypted. We'll address the reporters soon, but first, I'll address the nation."

Sept. 11 — 6:10 a.m. EDT, Situation Room of Bunker, Washington, D.C.

With his hands folded at his now uncluttered desk in the Bunker, Zac sat and gazed into the camera, waiting for his cue. He squared his shoulders, ready to address the burden of the country.

The Press Secretary announced, "And now, the president of the United States."

"Good morning." Zac's message was short and direct. "Our Cyber Crisis Agency, Joint Terrorism Task Force, and the FBI are pursuing suspects who were involved in today's attacks on Washington, D.C. After these terrible acts, a counterattack of the Avenger Missile system averted a drone launched on the White House. These acts fill me with terrible sadness and burning anger. Most of you have seen photos and live news coverage of the underground train wrecks, assaults on fleeing passengers, and downtown rioting, setting buildings on fire. Hundreds of lives were lost—numerous victims were college students, workers, moms, dads, children, friends, and neighbors. Some were police officers, firefighters, and emergency workers who died heroically while bringing safety to our city. I deeply mourn their loss, as does the entire country.

"The mayor has declared a state of emergency for Washington, D.C., and the National Guard and SWAT teams are regaining law and order. In addition to these attacks, we also had a minor earthquake. I have activated FEMA to provide food, shelter, and aid to victims of this disaster. We urge your patience and cooperation as we contain downtown fires and renovate the Blue Line Subway and transportation systems.

"Despite today's events, I ask for your prayers and want to reassure all Americans and our friends worldwide that our government will defend this great nation. We're fielding national and international calls, and our defense teams will hunt down these terrorists."

Zac glanced at his hands while twisting his wedding ring. Something clutched his soul. It felt like his wife was there beside him, giving him strength. "I am more determined than ever to keep peace in this country because that's the greatest responsibility we have in this life, to leave a safer and more peaceful world for our children. As a father and leader of this great nation, I will do everything I can to protect our people. To our front-line workers, we are grateful for your support. God bless you all, and above all, God bless the United States of America."

And with that, Zac stepped back two large paces while the press secretary wrapped up the session. He was sweating and exhausted from carrying more confidence than he felt. *Now, I must find Braun to hunt down Zahair, and we'll trap this White House snake.*

Shyler's Dilemma

Sept. 11 — 6:11 a.m. EDT, Situation Room of Bunker, Washington, D.C.

While President Spendorf addressed the nation, calming the fears of all who listened, General Shyler paced in his office. Somehow, Zahair had accessed the Pentagon during this morning's power outage and altered the Maven II specs. His overseas contact didn't mention anything about adding explosives, and the drone test wasn't supposed to injure anyone, much less take a life. *Could the drone have been weaponized?* Braun warned him of the devastating results, and now, Shyler had to think fast. *How did I get involved in this? No, it's not my fault. I refused to cooperate, yet here I am in the middle of this debacle.*

Shyler knew not to show fear, yet it gripped his gut and wouldn't let go. It felt like his mentor sat on his right shoulder, whispering into his ear, *Pull yourself together! Don't lose your temper. Admit nothing. Think clearly. Your integrity is on the line.* His little pep talk wasn't helping. The devil sat on his left, yelling, *Braun Hastings won't back down. He knows the drone was weaponized, and he is going to end your career if you don't act quickly.*

As if an answer to his prayer, the phone rang. His secretary's startled voice came across the intercom, "Someone is on the phone for you. He refuses to give me his name, and his voice is disguised. He says it's urgent. I'm sorry if I—"

"It's okay, Miss Ward. Put him through, and there's no need to record this call."

"But you said to be sure to record every phone call," Miss Ward reminded him.

"I'll take care of it this time," Shyler insisted. "In fact, it's been a long and unusual day. Go home and rest. You deserve some time off."

"Thank you, sir." Miss Ward put the call through.

Shyler waited a few moments until he heard her keys jingle and the office door open and close. "This is General Shyler. How may I help you?"

"I'll be brief, General," a baritone voice said, "I fear your testing team has a mole, Agent Braun Hastings."

"What?" Shyler was surprised anyone else had the same worries he was facing. "Who is this? Why disguise your voice?" Although he already knew who was calling.

"You can never be too careful," the baritone said. "Stay alert, and don't be fooled by his report. Agent Hastings seized the Maven II drone and RCV, and we're tracking an overseas account as a payoff. I'll send you an email as proof. He may be dealing with a higher bidder. Pull out all the stops to prevent that."

I knew it. "Yes, immediately," Shyler chuckled. It was the perfect answer to this dilemma. "How did you hear about the—"

"Later," the call disconnected.

Shyler knew what to do next. He placed an urgent call and triggered his well-kept secret backup plan.

Ransomware

Sept. 11 — 6:30 a.m. EDT, Washington, D.C./
4:30 a.m. MDT, Fort Collins, Colorado

Secretary Guy Weimer from Homeland Security agreed to hold a public Press Conference at 6:15 a.m. EDT at the National Arboretum, eight miles away from the White House, in a secured area. He would inform the reporters about the situation that had just unfolded in the highly secure Bunker, a central hub for sensitive government operations, and hoped to answer additional questions that erupted on numerous social media platforms after President Spendorf's earlier talk to the nation from the Bunker.

Authorities had locked down the White House, used crime scene tape to surround the drone and earthquake debris cluttering Pennsylvania Avenue, and installed a second outer non-scalable fence—no one got within five blocks of the building.

Screening of individuals attending the Press Conference was extensive, and only a limited number of reporters were allowed inside the area. A large display on either side of the podium enhanced the view so everyone could get a clearer picture.

The Press Secretary quieted the excited reporters, promising to provide answers to some, but probably not all, of their questions before they left. She addressed the train wreck, downtown arson, and drone attack on the White House. "We can confirm that this was an orchestrated terrorist attack, although, for security reasons, we can't tell you more about who is behind it yet. The emergency system was overwhelmed with many victims of last night's attacks. Hospitals are still being flooded with patients. The Washington, D.C., police have reported 229 fatalities and hundreds more injuries. This includes 27 critically injured police officers and firefighters wounded in the line of duty. We will release their names after notifying their families. We thank the citizens of this great city who have rallied to care for the injured, house the homeless, and feed those in need. They deserve our support. We will be scheduling regular updates to keep you informed. This is the first press conference since President Spendorf addressed the nation from the Emergency Command Center earlier this morning. I will turn over the mic to Secretary Guy Weimer to address any further questions you may have."

Guy cleared his throat and proceeded: "Thank you for the introduction. I assure you that President Spendorf is doing everything he can to track down who is responsible for this attack. He sent in the National Guard and SWAT teams and can easily communicate with the police to regain law and order. We must remain calm…"

Lights flashed, cameras whined and clicked as the chosen few from major networks, cable news, social media, and newspapers surrounded the podium. Questions erupted. Reporters started talking all at once. "Remain calm? Are you crazy? When we have thugs rioting in the streets and burning buildings?" "What about the power outage and the pile-up of subway trains?" "They attacked the White House. Have they attacked other cities?" "Who owned those drones?" "Who is behind this act of terror?"

As usual, Lisa Pagetti was on the scene covering the news. In contrast to her earlier newscast, every shoulder-length blonde hair was now in place. She sported a picture-perfect make-up job, complete with rosy cheeks and Ravishing Ruby lipstick. Her infamous red wool jacket and four-inch spiked, scarlet heels completed her attire. Shoving her microphone toward the podium, she demanded, "Is Russia behind this attack? Did they knock out the power grid? Is there a secret cell looting our city?"

"We have not verified anyone yet…" Guy had hoped for a short response to a few questions after President Spendorf covered the terrorist attacks. "But Russia is one country on our list of suspects. This is a rapidly evolving situation, and we'll brief you as we learn more in the coming hours." Guy opened his mouth to continue.

"The nation has been fighting cyber threats for years," a reporter from the Washington Post said. "Why didn't the government protect us from these attacks?"

"Why is President Spendorf sitting idly by while Russia continues to attack?" another reporter shouted.

"We haven't proven the attacks came from Russia." Guy's fists tightened. "The president's been busy non-stop—"

"What are we doing to retaliate?" a reporter from CNN asked.

"Will Spendorf place higher sanctions on Russia and China?" Washington Post reporter again. "What if they share stolen information with Iran?"

Rapid-fire questions kept coming as reporters inched closer. The tension built as security agents spoke over their wrist mics while moving through the crowd and surrounding the podium.

A man from MSNBC added, "Russia interfered with our elections. Now, are they hacking into Homeland Security? Are they stealing our military secrets? Was it one of our drones that attacked the White House? Where did it come from?"

"Talking about sanctions, where's the Secretary of State?" Lisa held her mic closer. "I have confirmed that we recently placed higher sanctions on Iran. Perhaps they are behind this chaos. As a recap, Mo Hendrum, husband of the newly appointed Justice Sophia Hendrum, has been missing since around 1 a.m., a little over five hours ago. I also learned that authorities had been alerted to Mo Hendrum's disappearance. They are treating this as a possible abduction."

The crowd was becoming a powder keg. Guy loosened his tie. "Homeland Security works closely with the FBI and CIA, and they are pursuing every avenue to find Secretary Hendrum. We won't stop until we do." He nearly mentioned possible Iranian missiles smuggling into Syria and the Maven II drone hack but caught himself in time.

"Then what will President Spendorf do?" Pagetti repeated. "Will he put higher sanctions on Russia? Or even higher ones on Iran?" Pagetti held her ground as a Secret Service agent moved closer. Her tenacity undaunted, she added, "Who's taking over our homeland security? I heard our Secretary of Defense was stabbed and is in the hospital with a collapsed lung. Is the president's life in peril? Are we going to war?"

This woman would be the spark to set off an explosion. Guy inhaled deeply, trying not to roll his eyes, and calmly said, "The president is safe, alive, and well. Secretary Wyller is recovering and expected to be back on duty soon." At least, he hoped that was true. "To our front-line workers, we are grateful for your support. God bless you all, and above all, God bless our great country."

Guy's phone gave a message alert. He dug into his pocket and found a text from DoD flashing, so he sent a return text, "Can't talk right now."

The Press Secretary took over the podium. "I'm sorry we have no more time for questions. I believe Secretary Weimer has been called back to the White House."

Guy, feeling the weight of the situation, stepped to the side but was still on the oversized screens. A large skull and crossbones lit up his cell. The camera zoomed in as a mechanical voice blared through the phone's speaker, "An alias virus has encrypted your data with an unbreakable algorithm. Purchase a…" Flustered, Guy fumbled to power off his cell phone, his heart pounding in his chest, and stared at the crowd. His throat tightened, barely able to say, "Press conference is over."

A Secret Service agent stepped in front of Guy. "Who called?"

Guy whispered to the agent. "Get me out of here!"

The agent radioed a 10-19 order to return to the Bunker. Secret Service agents surrounded Guy and escorted him to his car.

"What just happened?" Pagetti, a determined journalist known for her relentless pursuit of the truth, shouted in disgust, "The people demand the truth." She tried to corner the Press Secretary, but agents appeared from the crowd, preventing her from getting any closer. "We demand the truth."

The Press Secretary calmly picked up her notes from the podium. She repeated, "No comment," to several questions from reporters who shouted after her as agents whisked her safely away from the crowd.

Once inside the car, Guy mistakenly called the president using his infected cell phone to update him.

"Winston—" The skull and crossbones popped up on the cell screen, and the ransom demand message took over, leaving Guy with a sinking feeling of helplessness.

Guy tried to disconnect the phone, his mind racing with the possibilities. *Did I just infect the Bunker's network? Could this be the start of a major security breach?*

***

President Spendorf was on a conference call to an equally troubled Chancellor Huffenmeister, getting the latest details on Germany's drone system attack. Guy's news conference was on mute and played on a large overhead TV screen. Zac gulped tea and glanced up in time to see a skull and crossbones image on Guy's cell phone. "Sorry, Chancellor, something just came up. I'll call you back later. Let's keep in touch." He turned up the TV's volume, heard the mechanical voice, and bolted from the conference room.

His chief of staff, Winston, pulled the phone from his ear. "Homeland Security has been hacked. Listen to this."

The same robotic voice repeated, "…unbreakable algorithm. To obtain your data, purchase a decryption key or lose your files forever. Pay $500,000…" Red digits flashed on the screen, 23:58:28, 23:58:27, ticking down one second at a time. Click here and pay to obtain your untraceable link."

"We need Cordy here now!" Zac's voice echoed in the cement-walled chamber. "We're not paying any S.O.B., you hear me? Shut down all computers, phones, and network devices. Now! Better yet, isolate everything." He grabbed his VidChat phone. "This better not be infected. Get the FBI, and send Guy in here as soon as he arrives." Zac hit a special link and headed back to the conference room.

"Good to hear from you, sir," Cordy sounded winded, as if she had dashed down the hallway to get to the phone. "What's happening? Are you all right? Did you find Mo Hendrum?"

Zac spoke over her. "Not yet." He felt his temper rising, and he hated feeling out of control, yet he could not prevent what was happening around him. Now, someone had the gall to demand payment for their own software programs. "Homeland Security has been hacked. All data is locked up—some alien virus."

"Sounds like ransomware," Cordy said. "What link did you hit?"

"Not me, Cordy. It was Guy's cell phone. He called Winston to talk to me, and the Bunker's network is locked up, too. Someone shut down all White House computers before the drone attack. Now, we're shutting down everything except our defense systems." Zac paced as he spoke. "What the hell's going on? And where's Braun? I need him here. You, too."

"Shut down everything." Cordy felt overwhelmed and didn't want to leave her office. "You need to log out immediately. Consider all computers and every device connected to the network as infected. I have backup access to everything from here. VidChat is encrypted, so if an unauthorized person gains access, they won't be able to read the text messages or understand what we're saying."

The Bunker's conference room door flew open as Guy entered, spouting off as usual, "I'm not responsible for that virus, Zac. I think the hack originated in the Department of Defense. I got a text message from DoD. Like a fool, I didn't wait to answer and texted back that I couldn't talk."

"You don't have access to everything, Cordy," Zac said. "A civilian advisor and contractor to Deputy Director Yelson has been testing a few programs on one of DoD's laptops. It's missing, and I doubt you have any data backup."

"I can't believe anyone would be so careless. I constantly update antivirus software to keep our data safe." Cordy gasped, "Put Carl on the phone. I want a word with him."

"I can't," Zac said. "He's at Walter Reed—stabbed in the chest while escorting me to the Bunker. He's probably in surgery by now."

"Stabbed?" Cordy gasped as the news sunk in. "Who would make a murder attempt at the White House?"

"Hard to say. Homeland Security, FBI, and Secret Service are all looking into it," Zac paused his pacing. "In the meantime, Winston arranged for the earliest flight to D.C. We need you. Better yet, I'll arrange for a private jet. This is an emergency. Quint and your team can handle things from your end. And I need to send Braun on a special mission."

"When did you find out about the missing laptop?" Cordy asked. "We have rules. Set policies. No one's—"

"I know, and I have the FBI searching for the laptop, but this ransomware is falling in your lap. I swear, I'm not paying to get our own data. Add up paying for every infected computer, cell phone, and laptop, and it'll cost us millions. Not that the money is the issue. It's our security files. We'll be supporting a terrorist, and they can destroy our nation."

"I want a screen grab of Guy's phone." Cordy opened a new darknet file. "We're in luck. I rechecked, and we have a backup of all security and defense files. The bad news is we'll have to locate, isolate, and unencrypt the ransomware code. Then, we need to shut down the entire network, reload the latest backup taken before the ransomware onto a new uninfected network, and reboot the system. That will take at least two days."

"But who knows what's on that missing laptop?" Zac reminded her. "DoD's piloting new weapons, but only a handful of people are privy to that knowledge."

"Did the contractor have full access?" Cordy cringed when Zac admitted, "Probably. He headed up the project."

Cordy briefly closed her eyes and breathed deeply, trying to calm herself, but her babies were hyperactive. *Calm down, Katrina.* For some reason, the female name had popped into her mind. They still hadn't settled on a boy's name. Katrina didn't listen and became even more active, delivering an unexpected kick to Cordy's rib cage. Cordy placed a hand over her abdomen and gave three quick pants to relieve the pain.

"Did you hear me?" Zac asked. "We need you here."

"All right, I'll come to D.C., but I haven't heard from Braun, and I sent an urgent message to his Smart ring. He received it but didn't contact me. Do you have him off on another classified assignment I don't know about?"

"We'll find him." Zac sat down and jotted a note on a yellow sticky, hoping Ping had tracked down the FBI Director. "His boss will know where to find your husband, so get here ASAP. We have enough to handle with rioters attacking our city. Any cyberattacks and ransomware are your responsibility."

"While I wait on a jet, I'll have the team secure our data and track down the ransomware hacker," Cordy said. "Dig out the old flip phones. They don't have any smart chips. Use them until I get there."

"I'll line up a jet from Colorado," Zac said, "so you have no more than an hour to track this virus and catch that jet."

"It'll take longer than an hour to track." Cordy glanced at her watch. "My team will get right on it. They'll keep working while I'm heading to D.C.," Cordy hung up, her mind making mental additions and adjustments to her already long to-do list.

Binary Snippets

Sept. 11 — 4:35 a.m. MDT, Fort Collins, Colorado/
6:35 a.m. EDT, Washington, D.C.

Preparing for her trip to Washington, D.C., Cordy grabbed her prepacked bag and added a few last-minute accessories. Dry heaves had plagued her all morning. She kept munching on crackers, lost them twice, barely making it to the restroom. She plowed forward and refused to let it divert her. Glancing at her watch, she had only twenty minutes before heading to the airport. Her mind felt cluttered with last-minute details before leaving. *At least the electricity is back on. I better check on my team.* Leaning over her desk, she reached Perry via intercom and logged into the conference room screen. "Any word on Quint's whereabouts?"

"We've located him, and he's currently at the vault," Perry informed her but seemed stressed. "How long have these hackers had access to our data?"

"Why? Did you find an earlier breach?" Cordy asked.

"Someone shut down all White House computers except the president's. I'm still searching for who is responsible." Perry shoved his glasses back in place. "Hackers normally hit email systems first. What if they engineered a sophisticated phishing campaign to enter those computers? It's happened in the past."

Cordy was sure their latest update would prevent access. "Not with the cybersecurity team's software."

"Yes, but what if someone connected a personal laptop to the network?" Perry's tone was serious. "Probably not an intentional act, but it can happen, and the consequences could be severe." His words hung in the air, the weight of the potential disaster settling over them.

"We have protocols—"

"I know," Perry said, "but let's say, 'What if?' Once hackers gain entry, they can masquerade as legitimate users and participate in inside activities. Whoever shut down the White House computers had access to the entire network."

Cordy remembered that Zac mentioned there was a missing laptop. "Okay, that could happen, and I have more bad news. Ransomware hit DoD and Homeland Security. I'm sending you a screen grab copy of the demand. I found no data about it on the Internet or other sources and tried to trace the IP address. The hacker's signal piggybacked onto a TV satellite, hopped to multiple sites, and then routed to Russia and back through a NASA ground transmitter deep in the Mojave Desert, where I hit a roadblock."

"Should I retrace the address?" Perry asked, understanding the gravity of the situation and the need for caution.

"No, we don't have enough time. I have to leave for the airport shortly. I'm rechecking cybersecurity on all our internal equipment to ensure none are infected. Install new servers and upload the latest backed-up files before the ransomware hit. Replace the infected systems while I fly to Washington, D.C. I'll meet you in the conference room in a few minutes." Cordy finished a quick update on the Gnatcatcher to isolate the ransomware, encrypted the code so it wouldn't infect any more data, and grabbed her laptop.

The conference room felt chilly after Cordy had been in her office most of the early morning. She pulled on her navy sweater and buttoned it up to her neck. "Have you reached Vlad yet?"

"Not yet," Perry said, his voice tinged with concern. "I left him a message, but my cousin hasn't returned any texts. We need to reach him as soon as possible."

"Okay, then let's call Cracker," whose real name was Alyosha Krackovitz. "It's 2:30 p.m. in Russia." Cordy searched for the number and found his wife's, Rozalina's, phone number. They were both members of the FBI's International Program to combat terrorism originating in Russia. "Rozalina helped discover and isolate APT29, a Russian hacking unit behind the FireEye cyberattack on U.S. government contractors a few months ago. Maybe they can help us. Perry, take the lead on this."

"I will be his, ah, what's the word, sport?" Svetlana asked. "No. His support."

"You mean backup," Cordy smiled. "Yes, you need to be his backup and give him your support. I left a text message with the details for Quint, but you'll need to keep him updated. Nothing goes live until Quint approves."

"A lot is going on, and I wish he were here now," Svetlana said. "But we'll do our best and will keep him informed."

"Thanks. I'll make the call on VidChat to ensure we have a secure line." Cordy dialed the number. The call bounced off several cell towers and finally reached Moscow.

"I'll get it," as he answered the phone, followed by, "Rozalina, it's Cordy," Cracker said.

"Did I catch you at a bad time?" Cordy asked.

"No. She'll be here in a moment," Cracker said out of breath. "It's good to hear your voice. I just got off the phone with Usher. He's on a special assignment somewhere in the Middle East. I put him in touch with a mutual contact there, and Rozalina is taking care of a few last-minute details."

Cordy knew that Cracker deeply appreciated Usher—the man who freed him from a harsh prison sentence in the U.S. two years ago. Usher's intervention proved Cracker's innocence and allowed him to return home to his wife and children. Eternally grateful, Cracker would do anything for Usher, and his loyalty to the U.S. created deep trust within Cordy. "The last I heard, Usher and Zina were visiting her family in Ireland." Usher was Cordy's brother-in-law, and Zina was his wife.

Cordy wondered if Usher's special ops assignment had anything to do with today's events. She wished she could tell Cracker about the laser and Avenger system going down, but she needed higher authority to share that information. *Dr. Ping, our top cybersecurity expert, would probably approve, but he has other issues to deal with at the moment.*

Cracker cleared his throat. "I heard about the drone attack on the White House and the train wreck in Washington, D.C.,—dreadful business."

"Yes, that's one of the reasons I called." Cordy checked to be sure her phone link was secure. "I'm sorry to inconvenience you, but I've encrypted this call between our two lines for security, so you won't get any other phone calls while we're on this line."

"We understand," Cracker said.

Cordy opted to share what she could, "Someone hacked into our systems. Perry believes it has a Russian fingerprint, and the culprit logged off using the name Karl, with a K instead of a C. It reminds me of the hack the SVR used in the past but more complex."

"The drone attack might have been just a distraction for the real crisis yet to come." Cracker briefly hesitated. "Send us the encrypted, quarantined code. I'll show it to my wife. You know Rozalina is better at this than I am, and we'll help however we can."

"Thanks, but I'm calling about another threat—ransomware." Cordy connected her software to a signal scrambler, a device that disrupts communication signals, pulling up the ransomware code, a malicious software that blocks access to a computer system until a sum of money is paid. She shuddered, knowing that all defense programs were in jeopardy. "Unfortunately, 75% of all ransomware comes from Russia. Hackers break through our borders without ever leaving their country. This can devastate the defense department."

Cracker sighed. "Yes, Americans spent nearly half a billion dollars in ransom money to collect their own data last year, and 42% of organizations who do pay never received a decryption key to regain their data access."

"We aren't going to pay to access our own programs." Cordy uploaded two files. "I just sent you a screenshot and a recording of the demand for payment to get back our data. I'd like you to check on Russian cyber groups to see where this originated."

"I got the files. Let us study this a bit." There was a brief pause, and Cracker played the recording a few times in the background.

Cordy glanced at her watch. Ten minutes, and she had to leave—the time was going by too fast.

Rozalina said, "This may not have come from here. At first glance, the written message has no misspellings, which are common when translated from Russian, but I'll study this. I have a few leads to investigate. I want to see how the worm propagates. It may help to track down who infected the network. A sophisticated group, Darkside, comes to mind. They may be responsible. I have some links."

"Thanks," Cordy said. "I'm flying back to D.C. immediately, so Perry will be your contact."

"Okay," Cracker said. "Perry, give us a few hours to track down some leads, and we'll get back to you."

Rozalina cleared her throat. "One more thing before you go—are there any familiar binary snippets in the ransomware code that could override password protection during user log-in? Plus, this code may have been planted by covert terrorists in your own country. Is there any way to track new terrorists entering the U.S.? I mean, other than the normal customs check."

Cordy nearly dropped the call. "Oh, why didn't I think of that?" Her fingers were a blur on her laptop keyboard. "Binary snippets, and we need to create an algorithm for security cameras to hunt through Interpol surveillance cameras at key locations such as airport terminals, rental car agencies, and banks. I see two objectives here. Terrorists don't use their own names, but tagging fingerprints and facial, retinal, and ear images will give their true identity. We can scan ports of entry. Identify the person and gather info for future attacks. I wonder..."

Perry grasped the immediate need for action and said, "I can work on airport security camera updates after we handle the ransomware."

"Thanks." Cordy shook her head as if trying to clear it. "I'm sorry; I have to go. Rozalina, Cracker, keep us informed if you discover anything."

"We'll do that," Cracker said, but Cordy was already grabbing her laptop, letting Perry make their farewells.

"Have you heard from Vlad lately?" Perry sounded worried. "My cousin doesn't keep in touch."

"He's on a mission." Cracker paused. "I'll tell him that you want to speak to him, but he's away for a couple of weeks, so don't hold your breath as you say. Talk to you soon."

Perry disconnected Cracker and called to Cordy before she darted out the door. "Is there anything else you need from us while you're in D.C.? I saw that look and know ideas are floating through your head. We can help."

Cordy's mind clicked through her list as she thought out loud. "First, we need to shut down DoD's entire system to replace those files, but we can't without exposing our country to grave danger. We'd have no way to defend—"

"There has to be a better way." Perry placed a finger on the bridge of his glasses and shoved them back in place. "Maybe something like we did for the Justice Department?"

Cordy snapped her fingers. "Great idea! Split DoD's database into five segments, and put them on separate servers. Have Quint run everything through Gnatcatcher before going live."

Perry's brow furrowed. "Why divide the data?"

"It'll cut the backup time to six hours instead of two days, and Internet access will be quicker for the end-users, too." Cordy set down her laptop and jotted down a few more updates to her already long to-do list. "I have a code finder that matches snippets in a binary format and will track down any code that could bypass user authenticity. That will also speed up the process. And it may ID other security vulnerabilities."

"Can't we just reprogram the servers like we did earlier?" Perry asked.

"Not while the ransomware locks up the files." Cordy scooped up her laptop.

Perry nodded in understanding.

Svetlana hopped from her chair. "I'll get started."

"Maybe there's a similar known virus with matching binary codes," Cordy muttered and raced for her office. "We need an algorithm to hunt through Interpol…" Glancing at her watch, it was 5:25 a.m. She only had five minutes before she needed to leave the office to catch the jet to D.C. "I need more time."

As soon as she reached her desk, Cordy notified Guy with Homeland Security and Deputy Director Yelson, who was temporarily in charge during Carl's absence. "We're separating DoD's files into five segments."

Yelson asked, "How will that prevent the defense system from crashing?"

"It's already crashed," Cordy said. "The ransomware is not a file. It's a worm attached to the Dynamic-Link Library and hides under several layers of embedded encryption, making it harder to find."

"Cut the geek-speak," Guy said. "We've kept all the White House computers off since they went down without any warning. Only the president's computer refused to shut down. I'll need you to look into that when you get here."

"Okay, the ransomware won't let any programs function anyway, and we must replace the data with the latest uninfected backup ASAP." Cordy bit her lip. "Is that clear enough? I'm asking for your help, and expect your teams to be on the alert for any additional terrorist threats."

"What about Homeland Security?" Guy asked.

"Notify the Pentagon, the chiefs of staff, and we'll work as a joint team to keep the country safe." Something gnawed at her mind as if she were missing an important point. Then, like a flash of lightning, it hit. "We'll need to replace Homeland's servers with a total update of your files and replace a backup of the Bunker's phone system, too. That will be the safest and quickest way to return to business as usual, and hopefully, no one else becomes infected."

"How long do we have?" Guy asked.

"We've already begun replacing DoD's files by running through and isolating any questionable binary codes. Any discrepancies will be replaced with a clean backed-up version. The system will rotate through five servers—file by file. If an error occurs, the code will immediately abort the last order, shut down, and notify you, the Joint Chiefs of Staff, and the cybersecurity team. This process will continue until we replace all infected files."

"How long will that take?" Guy asked.

"Over 24 hours if we don't divide the system." Cordy entered a few numbers into her calculator. "By running five servers at the same time, it'll take less than six hours. In the meantime, Homeland Security data will all be backed up onto new servers as well. The programs should be up and running smoothly by mid-afternoon. I'll be heading to Washington, D.C., in two minutes, and you may be forced to go offline. If that happens, notify my team. They'll know what to do." She disconnected the call and intercommed Perry, "After updating the five new servers with DoD's data, how many more servers are available?"

Perry took inventory. "Four."

"Use them to upload all of Homeland's files and the Bunker's phone system while Svetlana works on DoD's update. Order ten new servers for future use, thoroughly scrub the old ones, and remember that nothing goes live until it's routed through our analysis program. Quint must sign off on all the updates. He will upload the servers as soon as the new ones are backed up and secured."

"Does Quint know?" Perry asked.

"I'm sending a message explaining our actions right now," Cordy said. "Do you have any questions?"

"No, I'm already setting up the first Homeland server." Perry's voice faded briefly over the speaker. "Svetlana just handed me a note. She is prioritizing DoD's programs based on the Cybersecurity Defense System we set up in March—nuclear and biological weapons defense first."

"Perfect." Cordy gathered up her notes. "Once you upload Homeland's data files, help Svetlana manage DoD's transfer. It has a higher potential for glitches."

"You can count on us," Perry said.

"Thanks, I'm leaving now." Cordy was getting off the elevator when her cell phone rang. "Quint, where are you? No, don't answer that until I know you're on a secure line. Call me—"

"01111001 01100101 01110011," Quint said and hung up.

Cordy paused, trying to understand what Quint had just communicated. She replayed the numbers in her mind. "Y. E. S? Yes, what?" *What had she just told Quint? "Call me on a secure line." He replied, "Yes." Why did he speak using binary code?*

Cordy's watch vibrated, and Quint's face popped up on her wrist screen. He was pale, sweat running down his cheeks. "Why use binary?" Cordy asked.

"Girlfriend, I needed to lighten my mood, and you sounded afraid the line may not have been secure," Quint said. "This has been a hectic morning."

"Now that sounds more like the Quint I know." Relief flowed through her, and Cordy laughed for the first time today.

Quint pulled off his backward ball cap and wiped his brow. "Vault hacked. I shut down every White House computer."

"It was **you** who shut down the computers?" Cordy asked. "Zac was afraid someone hacked into the network."

"Someone did hack into the network, and I hadn't reached the vault yet to troubleshoot the problem." Quint slapped his cap back onto his head. "That's why I shut them down, but I couldn't get access to President Spendorf's. I secured all other systems when I got here, but they need work."

"I'm glad you rushed over to our vault. However, I would have appreciated some notice." Cordy signed out at the security desk.

"The programs were flying off the shelf quicker than I could track them." Quint loaded his computer into his backpack. "I had to quarantine, encrypt, and abort any new code from entering the

White House network and our vault servers. Since they aren't on location, the only way to repair the reboot was to be on-site, and I took a couple of detours in case someone followed me. I couldn't find the security guard when I left, so I left a message on a sticky note and put it on his desk, then I tried to text you, but it wouldn't go through, so I scrambled for the next best solution."

"Thanks. I'm leaving the office now for D.C., and I need you here." Cordy raced to the parking lot. "Ransomware attacked both DoD and Homeland Security, and we're loading uninfected servers with updated data. Who hacked our vault?"

"Don't know, but I'll study the encrypted code when I return." Quint sounded out of breath. "I saw two distinct patterns—probably from Iran and Russia. Girlfriend, you be careful. You could be walking into a trap."

"You'll have my back, and we called Cracker. Rozalina doesn't think the ransomware is from Russia, but this morning's code is suspect." Cordy reached her car while still talking over her wrist link. "Why did you log off using Kuint instead of Quint?"

"I didn't do that, and Kuint was repeated in the vault hack, so it must be from the same source. The infected code is isolated on our bad boy account." Quint held up an e-notebook. "And I have a copy for a more detailed analysis."

"I want to check the vault code against the other hacks, but I'll be on a jet for four hours. Can you handle that?"

"Yup." Quint shoved the e-pad into his pack. "I'll be back within the hour. I tracked this morning's Maven II drone malware. The laser hack came from Russia, but entry into the Pentagon and the drone virus came from near the Golestan Palace complex in Tehran."

"Tehran?" Cordy unlocked her car door. "I wondered. The hack to the Avenger also came from multiple pings from a museum in Tehran. Two more attacks came from Ryazan, Russia, and one from the West Bank of Israel. However, it's different from the DoD ransomware IP address. That went around the globe and snagged somewhere over the NASA ground transmitter in the Mojave Desert. I'd search there first."

"You don't honestly think NASA's involved, do you?" Quint asked.

"I'm covering all our bases. I have some other ideas for later. Gotta go." Cordy opened her car door and was about to log off.

"Wait," Quint said. "We need to talk when you have a minute. I know now's not the best time, but a quick FYI. Did you hear from Braun? He tested a drone from the Maven II Project this morning. I know it's classified, but you need to reach him. The test didn't go well."

"Braun's not answering. Was he hurt?" Cordy snatched a breath and climbed into the driver's seat. "My gut's been screaming at me ever since I discovered the tie-tack stone turned black. What does that mean?"

"It can't be good," Quint said. "I never programmed it to go black, and there's not enough time to make another tie-tack. You better take along some other recording devices. See which one Braun prefers. Oh yes. Wear that flag pin so we can contact and trace each other, just in case of an emergency. And, Girlfriend, stay safe."

Cordy glanced at her watch. "I need to text Zac, and more bad news—DoD's missing a laptop." She opened her glove compartment, rummaged through a few bugging devices, found the flag pin, and shoved the pin and a couple more recorders into her bag.

"And remember to check out Zac's computer," Quint said. "I want to know why I couldn't shut it down. I was able to access all the others in the White House. Something is blocking our access."

"Will do." Cordy nearly disconnected, then added, "By the way, I programmed an SOS link between our contact numbers. Switch all communication to our vaulted private files. As you mentioned, you never can tell what we're going to encounter, but I should know more in a few hours." Cordy logged off and started the car's engine. She was already three minutes late heading to the airport.

Special Ops Mission

Special Ops Agent Usher Hastings scanned the overgrown pastureland, stared at the glassless window frames and broken door to the shabby shed, and knew it would give no shelter, *so why come here?* He guessed this would be their temporary headquarters and fished a cell phone from his filthy, tattered shirt pocket. His heart sank when he saw zero bars. "No cell service."

"What? You don't have a Satphone?" Gustof chuckled.

"I did, but it was in our vandalized vehicle," Usher said, "gone for good."

"Guess you'll have to relay your messages through me." Gustof slammed the Jeep's door, yanked away a wad of grass caught around the hinge and pocketed the keys.

A gust of wind blew grit across Usher's face. He ran a hand through his dark, overly long hair that reached his collar. Way too long for regulations, but he'd been on vacation, visiting the in-laws, when Dr. Ping assigned him to immediate duty. "Do you have phone service up here?"

"Phone service?" Gustof headed for the swinging front door. "Yes and no. There's no security in this country—any ground lines here are tapped unless you have connections. We send all sensitive issues by a private envoy or carrier pigeon. You'll be amazed at what we've done with the place."

Ian McMurchein, an MI-6 agent from the UK, dragged his duffle from the truck and scanned the area. "I can't wait to see it. Lead the way."

Gustof shoved the door to open wider, and it promptly fell off the one attached hinge. "No harm done. It was only in the way." He stepped across the threshold onto a dry, mud-packed floor and stopped next to a stone chimney on the right side of the room.

Usher shivered. "We could use the door to build a fire. It'll drop to freezing tonight."

"This isn't a fireplace—watch." Gustof lifted the grate, reached into an open hole, and switched on a light. A loud, clanking sound echoed in the room as a metal ladder unfolded and dropped to a cement floor below. "That's our headquarters. After you. I'll reset the alarm once we're safely inside."

Usher leaned over the narrow opening, dropped his pack, and his foot made contact with a ladder rung as he descended into a room filled with bright lights. Grabbing his backpack, he moved further inside the room and scanned the area. A metal rack filled with computer equipment and multiple server banks lined one wall. A printer and two mini-computers lined another. A long, narrow wooden desk with two open laptops sat in the middle of the room. He set his backpack on the floor to take a better look.

Ian dropped his duffle and promptly followed Usher. "Wow, what a setup."

Gustof followed, closed the trap door, and reset the alarm before joining the men in the cement-blocked room. "This is the main headquarters, but a tunnel opens into another bay where we store helicopters, weapons, and other vehicles. The exit is built into a burrow, and camouflaged hinged doors keep it well hidden."

"Not as posh as Pentagon headquarters, but it'll do." Usher studied a large overhead screen. "Is that a movie?" A man wearing a light-blue turban with the same colored tunic walked in the shadows of what appeared to be a cave.

"No, this is happening in real-time," Gustof picked up a remote control. "It wasn't easy, but we have hidden cameras inside that missile silo I spoke of earlier. Three covert agents are also working there, and they keep us informed."

Usher continued to watch the screen. The man's mouth moved, but there was no sound. "Turn up the volume."

Gustof unmuted the sound, and the man's graveled voice appeared over a set of speakers at the top of the screen. He spoke in accented Farsi.

Ian moved next to Usher. "It sounds like he's smoked all his life. Is he one of the covert agents?"

"Wait, I know that man." Usher leaned in for a closer look. "At first glance, I didn't recognize him with the gray beard and turban, but I know his voice. That's Rozalina's Uncle, Marshal Albert Chernyshevsky."

"Who?" Ian asked.

Gustof's eyes widened. "Yes, I'm surprised you know the man. He's a hero who retired from the Russian Federation as one of the highest-ranking commanders in our country. He now heads up a rebel army, but he doesn't want to draw attention to his last name, so he goes simply by Albert."

Usher moved toward the desk. "Are you recording him? I see lights blinking when he speaks."

"Yes." Gustof set down the remote and logged onto a computer. "Let's see what our enemies are planning for tonight."

"Did Albert bring his whole rebel army?" Usher hoped so.

"No, just his most experienced pilot, Dimitri, Lieutenant Colonel Leo, and an IT guru, Captain Vlad, who helped set up this equipment." Gustof entered a different code to access the laptop.

"How do you know this team?" Ian asked Usher. "Have you worked with them before?"

"They're the best. I met the rebel team in Russia last year." Still unsure if he could trust Gustof, Usher added, "But I didn't meet you. Did you join later?"

"Let's just say I get around." Gustof smiled wide enough for Usher to notice he was missing a molar beside his upper left eyetooth. That wasn't quite the answer Usher wanted. He'd watch his back a while longer.

Gustof tapped on the keyboard. "I'll open a decryption program to translate Albert's Farsi message into Russian and again into

English. Once we get an update, you can use this laptop to inform your boss."

"Is the line secure?" Usher asked.

"Yes, we use VidChat, too." Gustof entered his ID, letting Albert know they were online. "Let's see what's going on in the missile factory."

Albert stepped deeper into the shadows and ran his finger under a number imprinted on the side of a wooden crate. It read YBX27905-TEL.

"Is that some sort of code?" Usher asked.

Gustof frowned. "I'm not sure of the first few letters, but 27905-TEL means one missile is due to launch for Tel Aviv on September 27th, at 0500."

"YBX?" Ian ran a hand through his mahogany hair. "Could mean airdrop."

Gustof nodded and typed a message. "It's as good a guess as any."

Usher gave an audible gulp. "That's less than two weeks from now."

Albert entered the crate on the screen, moved to the far-right corner, and raised his left wrist to his lips.

"What's he doing?" Ian asked.

"He's talking into a communicator on his wrist, like this one." Usher pushed up his sleeve to reveal an identical device. "It was a gift from my sister-in-law, Cordy Hastings. Turn up the volume."

Gustof shook his head. "The volume should adjust when translated. I'll replay it in English since there are two of you, and I'm fairly fluent. Listen closely."

Albert spoke, "A Syrian Quds Force commander is scheduled to receive three hypersonic missiles. A five-vehicle convoy is transporting them. Soldiers will be loaded into the first and last tactical military trucks to protect the middle hypersonic glide vehicles. The convoy leaves at 1800 tonight and will head to an airfield outside the city. I'm sending aerial photos of the location." Albert tapped his communicator and turned toward the door.

"Are we supposed to attack the convoy?" Ian asked. "These are nuclear missiles."

Gustof put his finger to his lips. "Shh, we need to reach Albert for direct orders."

"Well, the missiles won't be loaded during transport." Usher held his arms tight around his lower chest and groaned when another rib popped back in place.

Gustof turned to Usher. "Let's stop guessing. Can you use your communicator to talk directly to Albert? I hope so because then we can keep constant communication during the attack."

"Is it safe to contact him?" Usher asked. "I know he's using his device, and only when the area is secure. What if I call him at an inopportune time? I don't want to jeopardize the mission."

"Good point. I'll check." Gustof texted a message to Albert using his computer.

Usher felt his wrist device vibrate. He entered a code and then spoke, "Usher here. We're awaiting orders."

Albert's voice could barely be heard, so Usher adjusted the volume. "You already heard that the convoy leaves here at 1800 sharp, right?"

"Yes, and the missiles are headed for the uploaded GPS site you sent."

Albert nodded. "At 1830, each missile and launcher will be loaded onto a cargo plane and smuggled into Syria through Turkish airspace to Beirut. From there, they will be transported by caravan into Syria."

"So, we need to attack before the missiles leave Iran?" Usher was already mentally making a list of the necessary gear for the mission and hoped Gustof had the supplies needed.

"Hopefully, before they arrive at the airfield," Albert whispered. "That gives us only a narrow window of opportunity. I have a small unit that will lead the attack." His voice became even softer. "Leo has been scouting the area. He met a trusted guide who has Intel of the region—knows every cave, every family within the city, and their alliances, and most importantly, he hates the IRCG as much as we do. But Leo's ground team can't do this alone."

"What do you need from us?" Usher asked.

Albert lifted his head from the wrist device and put his ear to the crate wall. "One moment. This area isn't secure." He moved to the door, opened it, and stepped outside the crate. The camera view shifted. Albert motioned to someone. "I heard something out here a moment ago."

Vlad, also disguised as an Arab, appeared from behind a rock. "It was just me. I'll signal if anyone comes this way."

Albert nodded, and the camera shifted back to inside the crate as he returned to the corner. "Here's the plan. I need someone to set up a diversion at the designated checkpoints on the aerial map. There are two locations, so we can't let the caravan go beyond the second if we miss the first attempt. Leo will call you for an airstrike when the convoy gets close. I typed in Leo's wristlink code."

"What type of airpower do you have?" Ian asked.

"An Apache AH-64," Albert said. "Don't ask where and how we came by such a treasure, but we've been planning this attack for a while. It wasn't easy to fly unnoticed into Iran, but we've had the helicopter hidden in that burrow for nearly a year, and it's fully loaded. Leo will call for a hit on each checkpoint as needed."

Gustof rubbed his hands together. "You can count on us."

"Oh, there's one more item. Leo just reported that Maven II drone specs were smuggled into Iran on a chip hidden inside a fake euro. I have a contact name and the GPS coordinates of the drop site. The coin will be transferred at 1515. I know that gives you less than half an hour to intercept, but you'll arrive in less than five minutes if you take our other helicopter. You'll need to hurry to get that coin."

"But do we have enough time and ammo for both missions?" Ian asked, his concern reflecting the potential risks of the operation.

"If that's all you can do, just get the coin, and create a diversion," Albert said. "Gustof will do the rest."

A gentle rap on the crate door made Albert pause. His hand flew to his left hip.

"He's going for his gun. He always carries it on his left." Usher tensed when the crate door opened.

Vlad stepped inside and dumped what appeared to be an armload of grain sacks into the crate. "Company's coming, two minutes."

Albert walked toward the door, whispering into the communicator, "We plan to attack the convoy before it reaches the first checkpoint at 1612. We'll need the first distraction by then. If all else fails, Dimitri will fly one cargo plane containing the missile scheduled to drop on Tel Aviv. He'll reroute the aircraft and destroy that missile, but the other two planes must not reach Syria! While the armed forces protect the caravan, Vlad and I will sabotage the missile factory. We need to shut down this plant. Over and out." A hand reached up and removed the camera. The picture turned dark, and Albert disconnected the direct link to Usher.

Gustof flipped the camera setting to another view. Albert and Vlad moved back into the cave and split ways. Albert greeted a younger Arab. "Is all going as planned?"

The young man nodded. "They're moving the missiles to ground level one at a time. We're a go for 1600."

"Well done," Albert said in Farsi. "Are you prepared?"

"Yes. I'm driving the first truck." The young man seemed proud as he smiled and walked away. The screen went black.

Usher moved closer to the desk. "Albert said he sent an aerial photo of the airfield. Let's take a look, discuss plans with Dr. Ping, and determine the best way to approach the convoy."

Gustof sat behind the laptop and brought up the aerial view. After studying the photos, he did some calculations on Google Maps. "If I take the Apache, I can intercept the convoy in ten minutes, but we'll need to fly in low, which will be dangerous."

"Okay, let's get Dr. Ping on the line," Usher said. "What radio frequency will you use during the attack? We'll need to block all others. And where will Albert and Vlad be during the raid?"

Gustof sent a message to Albert's communicator. "It may take a while for an answer."

"Scoot over." Usher took a seat, called Dr. Ping, and discussed their upcoming missions. Intercepting the coin would be Usher and Ian's priority.

"Destroy the coin," Ping said. "Melt it down to be sure the chip inside is useless. Once that's complete, disrupt the convoy by making the road impassable. Remember what happened in Afghanistan a few years back? We burned tires to create thick, black smoke. You couldn't see the road even with night vision goggles. Set the tires ablaze near the target sights. Plus, fires signal trouble and will bring in the militia. The IRCG smugglers don't want to be caught off guard, especially by U.S. allies."

"My guess is the IRCG will have units hidden away in caves, shuttered houses, and maybe even out in the open along the route to the airfield," Ping said.

"Albert agrees." Usher brushed a stray lock from his forehead. "We'll be backup for Leo's troops and help with airstrikes as needed." He signed off with Dr. Ping.

Gustof searched online. "There's a tire factory not far from the airstrip. I'll set a truckload of tires ablaze at 1600 while you intercept that euro. Albert sent the drop site GPS coordinates. It's not more than ten kilometers from here."

Usher pulled up the coordinates and researched the terrain. "Tell me about the second chopper."

"It's a Russian gunship helicopter with autocannons and machine guns, but we only have one anti-tank missile. Let's move into the tunnel." Gustof punched in a code, and part of a wall slid open. "You can see for yourself. While you and Ian retrieve the coin with the chip inside, I'll create the diversion at checkpoint one. Then you will be Leo's backup at checkpoint two."

Still cautious around Gustof, Usher asked, "Where will you be at that time?"

"I'm going to destroy the aircrafts scheduled to fly those missiles out of Iran." Gustof said. "Don't worry. Dimitri and I know what we're doing."

"Does Albert know of your plan?" Usher asked.

"Everything we do is with Albert's permission," Gustof said. "Have you flown this model before?"

"No, and we don't have much time to check it out, but I'm impressed."

Gustof beamed a bright smile. "The nose has high-definition tracking technology using infrared and lasers to detect a target. The image links directly to the pilot's helmet, so the gun aims in the same direction wherever I look. When we complete this mission, I'll let you both have a turn flying it. That is, if Albert agrees. He's quite possessive of this one."

"Have you flown a Russian chopper before?" Ian asked Usher.

"Yes, last year, and it allows for a high-speed attack, which we may need if facing gunfire from the ground." Usher quickly loaded gear into the second helicopter and took the pilot seat.

Ian sat in the co-pilot position, strapped himself in place, and adjusted his helmet and headphone. They familiarized themselves with the equipment, and after a brief discussion, Usher and Ian agreed on the best plan of attack.

"Okay, we're ready. See you shortly." Usher gave Gustof a sign to open the burrow door.

"Hit the blue button on the dashboard," Gustof said, "twice to open and once to close the double doors. Safe travels, and if all goes well, I'll see you in an hour. Our mission should be wrapping up."

Usher followed directions and coasted through the open burrow doors. Once outside, the nose lifted above the trees and glided smoothly into heavy storm clouds. The burrow opening completely vanished below. Usher contacted Albert's link. "Did you assign Gustof and Dimitri to destroy the aircrafts scheduled to fly those missiles out of Iran?"

"Dimitri mentioned it as a last resort, but I didn't make that an assignment," Albert said. "Why?"

"Gustof will set a truckload of tires on fire at checkpoint one. The thick smoke will make it difficult for the drivers to see to stay in formation, and they may even separate the convoy. The drivers will probably detour before reaching the second checkpoint. Then Gustof and Dimitri plan to demolish the carrier planes. Ian and I will retrieve the drone plans hidden in that fake euro and then head to checkpoint two as a backup for Leo's troop."

"That wasn't exactly the plan," Albert said. "Gustof is supposed to wipe out the convoy and return here to help destroy the plant. Sometimes, he can be a loose cannon, but that isn't a bad plan. Thanks for the information. I'll discuss Gustof's option, clarify orders, and get back to you. In the meantime, retrieve the drone specs. The last thing we need is for the Iranians to build lethal drones on top of these missiles."

"We're one minute out from our target," Usher said. "I see a military combat vehicle about a mile out and approaching a two-story cement building, and a second vehicle has already parked by the front door. We need to verify that this is our target and our enemy."

Albert whispered, "Can you get close enough to see any markings?"

"The truck has a Quds Force logo on the driver's door." Usher uploaded the image to Albert.

"Yes, and a gorilla force as backup," Albert said. "Those soldiers in the truck's rear have M4 Carbine assault rifles, probably smuggled from Iraq or Afghanistan—looks like that coin is well-protected. It may not be as easy to retrieve as I thought, but you have speed and surprise on your side."

Usher brought the chopper closer to the target.

As the moving combat vehicle braked, a cloud of dust blew into the air. A flurry of gunfire and flames erupted. A few deflected off the nose of the helicopter. Six soldiers piled out and took cover.

"We've been spotted. Man the autocannon." Usher banked the chopper sharply to the right.

Ian sent rapid-fire bursts that blew up the truck and four of the six men. Two others dove for a pile of rocks and took cover. They fired on the helicopter. One propped a rocket launcher on his shoulder, but Ian brought both men down with another round of gunfire.

Usher leveled the bird out of range and hovered over the building. "An officer is knocking on the front door." The door opened. "A man dressed in a black hoodie either handed over to or received something from the officer."

"Wait, the guy in the hoodie went back inside the house," Ian said.

"And it looks as if armed soldiers are surrounding the place." Usher kept a screen open for Albert to view the action and checked his options. "That officer has a Major General insignia."

"Take him and the civilian in the hoodie alive if possible," Albert said. "If it's Major General Kybuhrych, he's armed and dangerous and tops our watchlist for transnational organized crimes, illicit weapons, and drug trafficking. He has contacts in high positions, maybe as high as General H.Q. I want to know the final destination for those specs."

"We'll do our best to deliver." Usher noticed a soldier lighting a Molotov cocktail near the rear of the building. He tossed it on top of the porch roof. A gust of wind caught the flames, and sparks flew in every direction.

Ian shouted, "Soldiers are torching the place."

Nearly deafened by the comment, Usher jerked at his headset. The soldiers opened fire on the helicopter. Usher lifted the bird and flew out of their range. "Gotta go, over and out."

The soldiers piled into their truck and drove a few feet before Ian blasted it with another round from the autocannon. "Albert won't be happy. I didn't spare the officer's life, but we'll bring his body to headquarters. It didn't go far if he has that coin on him."

The building was engulfed in flames when the man in the black hoodie climbed from a front, upper-floor window onto the ledge, stopped, and propped a Satphone between his right shoulder and ear. He appeared to be frantically searching for a way down to the ground.

"Drop me down on a rope," Ian said, "and I'll rescue him."

"I doubt he'll come with you willingly," Usher said.

"He won't have a choice," Ian held up a Taser and a syringe half-filled with a clear liquid. "Sleeping juice."

"He'll fall if you Tase him," Usher said. "I saw ropes with the gear. Do you know how to lasso?"

"Aye, me father owns Highland cows," Ian chuckled. "I guess ye'd call them Red Angus, but I've done me share of round-ups."

Brothers Thru Thick & Thin

Sept. 11 — 6:57 a.m. EDT, Washington, D.C./
2:27 p.m. IRST, Tehran, Iran

Congressman Conrad Justuso held his cell phone to his ear. "Hang on one moment until I get outside." The huge dome of the U.S. Capitol's Rotunda loomed overhead, but Conrad barely noticed the paintings and heroes in the form of statues that surrounded him as he raced through the roped pathway to the main exit.

"Hey, bro, are you still there?" came from Conrad's phone.

"Keep holding." Conrad cupped the phone to his ear, cautiously stepped outside, and paused. Wisps of vapor curled from his mouth with every breath. Fear sent his heart racing. Three sets of fresh footprints stood out in the newly fallen snow, two made by heavy boots and the third by a pair of dainty spiked heels, but no one was in sight at the moment. *Let's get this over with.* "José, my cockroach of a brother, what have you done now?"

"Calm down. You'll have a heart attack before you turn forty-six." José's smooth, baritone voice dripped with sarcasm.

How his brother loved to goad him. Conrad reflected, *well, I made it to Congress, and it's up to me to stop this maniac even if he's my own blood.* The thought burned a path from his gut to his throat, *and before anyone else learns the truth. He'll ruin my future.* Conrad whispered a prayer.

José chuckled. "Oh, quit your whining and pleading with the Almighty."

Conrad breathed and stood in awe of the bright apricot and pinkish glow of sunrise behind the white marble columns of the Supreme Court building. It felt like God was saluting from the heavens. *Yes, I'm in the right.*

A rustling sound came from José's phone. "They're early…H.Q. said I had an hour…" He muttered something else in the background.

"Who are you talking to?" Conrad waited for a second, but there was no reply. "Why would you betray me? Who did you tell about our little arrangement? Now someone's hunting me."

It sounded like José was walking as he spoke. "I never told anyone about those little fund transfers." José's voice got louder. "Oops, I know who. My old Zeta partner, Ernesto—we didn't leave on peaceful terms, and he has access to my financial records. What did he want, besides my cabeza en una bandeja."

"No, more like, 'My head on a platter,' and I'm rather fond of it. How much does he know? Why didn't you keep your records secure? How much should I fear him?"

José chuckled. "He probably knows everything about the transfer of funds but not what you used them for. He can't do much damage since he had his little accident. His leg gives him fits, and he can't walk without a limp."

"I spoke to Dad, and he says you're in more trouble now than ever—so you've moved on from the drug cartels to Iranian missiles?" Conrad whispered, "Why?"

"Oh, I'm still peddling cocaine, just not with Ernesto. Now I'm evening the playing field. Let hell take you devils by storm." José sounded proud of his actions. A loud knock came over José's phone. "Sorry, bro. It's your turn to hold. One moment, I'm coming. Don't break down the door."

It sounded like metal keys jangling, and something like a door creaked over the phone. There were voices in the background, and Conrad thought he heard a door slam. Rapid gunfire could be heard in the distance.

"Where are you?" Conrad wondered if he should return to his car or get another ride. He didn't want anyone tailing him, and he recalled Ansin's last words, 'Leave the car, and walk away.' But for how long? The Congressman hurried down the Capitol steps, torn between going home and hunting down José. "Are you still there? I can hear your heavy breathing."

"What's up? Gotta leave in five minutes."

"We need to talk," Conrad said louder than he planned. "How many missiles?"

"Doesn't matter," José whispered. "These aren't the common ballistic cruisers. I'm more sophisticated these days."

"You always loved those big words," Conrad huffed.

"Ever heard of hypersonic glide rockets?" José asked. "Fast speeds. You can't see them. Then boom! They hit the U.S. before you know you're being attacked. So, little brother, be careful. You may think of me as a pest, but this cockroach has a master disguise, hidden in plain sight, and I breed weapons prolifically."

"Santo Dios." Conrad made the sign of the cross. "Now, where are you?"

"In Tehran. That's in Iran, for you ignorant Americanos, but you'll never find me."

"Tehran?" Conrad gulped. "Why the hell are you in Iran?"

"Important meeting," José sounded out of breath.

"Listen, don't go to this meeting." Conrad headed for the West Executive Avenue parking lot, hoping to find his car and drive safely home, but then where should he go? Iran?

"Too late," José said.

"Too late for what?" Conrad asked.

"I already traded the magic euro."

Unlike his brother, Conrad hated talking in code. "Magic euro? What are you talking about?"

José chuckled. "This euro is worth millions. It paid for the missiles, and they are being delivered as we speak. My Syrian contact just sealed the deal—something's brewing outside. I hear gunfire. Gotta go."

"Gunfire?" Conrad gasped. "Wait, I'll catch a flight. You're my brother. You can't do this."

"Catch a flight?" Loud footsteps sounded, and José blew out a deep breath. "And what? Meet me for drinks—" A hint of fear entered José's voice. A rustling sound came from José's phone. "Shit!"

"What's happening?" Conrad asked.

"That dirty double-crosser!" José grunted, and a scraping noise erupted.

"Who? Ernesto?" Conrad asked. "What's going on?"

José breathed heavily. "Roof. Gotta get to the roof." Breath ragged, he shouted. "Gotta go!" José sounded distracted.

"Wait!" A flash of guilt raced through Conrad. He'd heard rumors while in his office. "Listen, I got word that a special ops force will be there soon—"

"Thanks for the warning." A series of loud claps like thunder sounded over the phone. "Too little, too late. As usual! The whole building is on fire!"

Popping noises like fireworks combined with a whirring sound of helicopter blades sounded louder in the distance. "Drop the gun!" Conrad heard more bullets fire. He counted four more shots before José cursed in frustration.

"He's out of bullets. Drop a wee bit lower. Gonna grab his foot," a man with a Scottish accent shouted. "Good, I have him in me sites. Just a tad lower."

"Shut off lights. Can't see. Stop." José's voice trembled. "Stay away. Get away from me."

"Who are you talking to?" Conrad asked.

The helicopter roared, its rotor blades screaming in the phone. It was close enough that Conrad heard little but ear-bleeding engine noises and a high-pitched whistling. Something hit the phone.

"Ouch! Let me go!" José shouted. "Get that rope off my ankle!" There was a loud pop, and José yelped!

"José? Talk to me. What's going on?" Conrad waited with no reply.

"Got him." The man with the brogue shouted, "Sweet dreams. Bring us up and land so we can load the Major General's body. He must have the euro."

"If we find that euro, don't destroy the specs," a deeper voiced man said. "I'll send them to Cordy."

There was rustling over the phone, a clunk, and the call disconnected.

"What just happened?" The Congressman made it to the parking lot in record time, but his blue Subaru was on a tow truck being hauled away. The front windshield had a massive hole punched through it. A spiderweb of fractured glass with long cracks radiated out from it. A crumpled rear fender and a flat tire also greeted him. He wouldn't be driving away anywhere soon. Nearly paralyzed with fear of what might happen to him and worried sick about his brother, he allowed anger to sweep him into action. His trembling hand motioned to a car parked near the security gate. "Taxi!" He nearly tripped as he ran for the yellow cab. *I must get out of town ASAP via an untraceable route!*

Game Plan

"Loran, it's time to go undercover," Braun Hastings shouted as he punched at the deployed airbag. "You're my boss, but right now, you are a target. How much convincing do you need, for God's sake? The windshield is shattered, the headrest is torn to shreds, and you have a deep gash over your temple, but for luck, a nanosecond slower, you would be dead with a slug between your eyes."

Loran shook his head, trying to dislodge the windshield splinters. Blood splattered the front dash and windows. Fortunately, his glasses protected his eyes, although the impact of the airbag bent the frames out of shape.

Debris covered their shirts and laps. However, most of Braun's wounds were leftover from the earlier explosion at the testing site.

"Lean your cheek onto what's left of the headrest," Braun said. "Make sure there's plenty of your blood on the steering wheel, too."

Sloan also let the blood drip onto the car seat.

Braun held out his hand. "I need your cell phone."

"No, I'm calling Evans." Sloan dialed with one hand as he fished under his seat with the other. "But I always carry a spare." He passed a burner phone to Braun. "It needs to be activated."

"Agent Evans," came across Sloan's cell speaker.

"Glad I caught you," Sloan said. "I need another favor, and this time, you can drive and put me in the trunk, but I'd prefer a van. Turnaround is fair play, don't you think? Somehow, we need to fake my death."

"We who?" Evans asked.

"Agent Braun Hastings," Sloan said. "Some dork used a rifle to blast out my windshield. Braun saved my life."

"Is he still with you?" Evans asked.

"Yes. He'll call 911 after you get me into an ME van," Sloan said.

"Take me off speaker." Evans' voice was barely a whisper.

"You can say whatever you need to in front of both of us." Sloan was matter-of-fact. "Braun has saved my life more than once, and he's like a brother to me."

"Okay, but you're not going to like this," Evans said. "Zahair ditched the SUV, and we ran forensics on the vehicle. I used infrared photography and found evidence of blood. Three droplets blotted and probably presumed cleaned up with bleach, but further testing proved the blood was type B and Rh-negative—matches Emma's blood type."

"She's still alive. I'd know in my gut if she were dead. We have to step up our search." Sloan threw open the car door. "Screw faking my death. Get me out of here, now!"

"No, you were the target," Braun shouted as he darted around the front of the car after Sloan. "We need to let Zahair think he succeeded, or we'll be dodging his next attempts."

"Braun's right. I tracked your GPS coordinates," Evans said. "Did you get a license plate number?"

"No, I missed that." Sloan frowned and rolled his eyes. "Black SUV is all I caught."

"Okay," Evans said. "Believe me, we'll find your wife and track down Zahair. I'll grab my gear and meet you at the scene shortly." The call disconnected.

"Zahair's in our crosshairs." Braun jotted a note and shoved it into his pocket. "My guess is he furnished the explosives used by the drone and could have launched the drone attack on the White House. We need to call Cordy." After two attempts, there was no answer. It didn't surprise him that she didn't pick up. She wouldn't recognize the burner phone number. Braun left messages on both her cell and the office phones. "My wedding ring indicated you sent a text, but my phone is history, so I didn't get it. Call me ASAP."

Sloan tried calling from his phone, also no result. "Probably busy tracking down the White House attack."

The streets were still deserted when Evans arrived. He was dressed like a medical examiner and drove up in a white van.

Braun waited for Evans to work his magic—applying moulage for fake bruises, a gunshot wound to Sloan's forehead, and fake blood splattered along the back of his head and neck.

Sloan studied his reflection in a mirror, made a few minor touchups, and then climbed into a black body bag lying on a gurney at the rear of the ME van. "Okay, I'm dead. Do your stuff."

Braun made a 911 call. "Hurry—someone just killed my boss! Shot while driving…"

Two minutes later, the roadside was a zoo. News reporters, two police cars, an ambulance, and the medical examiner's van surrounded Sloan's shot-up and crashed Toyota. Flashing lights lit up the scene as patrol deputies canvassed the area taking measurements, photos, and jotting notes of their findings.

A lanky officer with a blond crew cut strode up to Braun. "I'm Officer Packer. What happened here?"

"My boss is dead!" Braun sounded out of breath. "I can't believe it. Some jackass drove straight at us, driving in the wrong lane. Their headlights blinded us, then the car swerved, and someone shot at us."

"Slow down." Packer jotted the time onto a form on a clipboard. "What's your boss's name?"

"FBI Director Loran Sloan." Braun paced in front of the car. "The medical examiner just loaded his body into that van. You'll need to get the details from him."

"Who was driving?" Packer asked.

"He was." Braun pointed to the van. "I was talking to him one minute, and the windshield exploded the next. He was dead before I could do anything."

Packer scribbled a few lines on the form and called out, "Wait up, Examiner, I need to see the body."

Evans pulled open the rear double doors, revealing a black body bag secured on a gurney in the back of the vehicle. It was zipped up around Sloan's chin, and the top flap remained open.

"Time of death?" Packer asked.

Evans glanced down at a long, probed gage. "Body temperature 97.6° F. TOD within the hour—more like fifteen minutes ago."

Packer hopped into the back of the van. "Cause of death?"

"Gunshot wound to the head." Evans also climbed into the rear of the van. "Execution style, mid-forehead, right between the eyes—he didn't know what hit him."

"I need to verify." Packer bent over the body.

"Sure." Evans pulled the unzipped body bag lower, exposing all of Sloan's face. There was a large black spot in the middle of his brow. Blood saturated a terrycloth towel that lay under Sloan's head. "He didn't have a chance."

Packer's face paled. Gagging noises came from the back of his throat.

"Is this your first gunshot victim?" Evans asked.

Packer nodded and turned away from the body. He nearly fell as he hopped from the rear of the van and puked on the road next to the rear tire.

"Anything else?" Evans asked.

Packer wiped his mouth with the cuff of his sleeve and was already walking from the van. "No. He's dead."

"I'll finish the paperwork and send it to your department after the autopsy," Evans called after him. "Am I free to go?"

Packer nodded. Moisture blossomed over his face, and his lips were white as chalk. His wobbly knees led him to his patrol car parked next to the van, where he leaned against the door.

"Mind if I ride along with you?" Braun asked Evans. "Sloan's car will be impounded, so I have no way of getting home."

"I guess there's room." Evans dropped to the ground and closed the rear double doors.

Packer faced Braun. "I'm sorry for your loss."

"Thanks." Braun closed his eyes. "Now what?"

"You have a few nasty cuts on your face," Officer Packer said. "Best have the paramedics get you cleaned up and bandaged."

Evans called out, "I'll take care of his wounds. Get in. The FBI will also want to process the scene."

Packer stood staring as if he was unable to make a decision.

Braun handed Packer his card. "Thanks, Officer. If you have any more questions, you can reach me at this number, anytime." Braun didn't wait for a reply and climbed into the van's passenger seat. "Let's go."

Evans climbed into the van, made a U-turn, and headed for town. "I'll notify President Spendorf."

Braun buckled up. "That should prove Sloan's death to Zahair. It'll be all over the news."

Just before reaching the city limits, Evans' cell phone rang. He pulled over to take the call. "Yes…Are you sure? Have you already discussed this with the FBI?"

Whoever called said something that Braun couldn't hear.

Evans bit his lower lip and shook his head. "Sloan's not going to like that!"

"Who's on the line?" Braun whispered.

Evans muted the phone. "General Shyler wants the FBI to track you down and bring you in. He just ordered me to confiscate your computers, cell phone, and wants me to look into any emails or text messages."

"I know you're talking to someone. Is it Agent Hastings or Sloan?" Shyler's voice came across loud and clear. "The evidence against Hastings is irrefutable. He sabotaged today's test and vows the drone was weaponized. Only he would know that. The unit left the Pentagon unarmed. He blew up the drone and contaminated the scene before we could investigate the explosion."

"He's shouting loud enough, I can hear every word, and what he's saying is not true," Braun said.

Shyler continued to rant. "I know he's a traitor, and I'll make sure he gets the death penalty. He's accused of conspiracy and treason. I know Sloan met Hastings after our meeting, but where are they now?

Better get with your boss and bring him in before someone else hunts him down.”

“What proof does he have?” Braun whispered. “Someone’s setting me up.”

Evans appeared confused. “He thinks you weaponized those drones. He says you’re a traitor. Is it true?”

“No.” Braun raised his hands in surrender. “I swear, someone is setting me up.”

Evans shook his head. “Shyler says you had access to the Maven II drone specs. Did you sell them?”

“Never,” Braun said. “I’d never betray my country.”

Evans clenched the steering wheel as if debating what to do. “I know Sloan trusts you, but give me one good reason why I should believe you.”

“Because if we don’t find out who really is behind the attack, what will they do next?” Braun lowered his hands. “Rusty’s dead. Do you honestly believe I’d allow that to happen? He was my best friend in the whole world.”

“The Braun Hastings that I think I know would never jeopardize his team.” Evans leaned closer. “The general needs a fall guy for the failed test, and I have a plan.” He turned off the mute button and spoke into the cell phone. “You’re in luck. Braun is in the van with me.” He mouthed to Braun, “Tell me to get away from you.”

Braun caught on quickly and played along. “What the hell? Get away from me.”

Evans grabbed a pair of handcuffs from his pocket and jingled them, then slammed his fist against the car seat.

“Hey, back off!” Braun shouted. “Get these cuffs off me.”

After both men swore at each other, smacked the dashboard a few times, and groaned, Evans blew out another deep breath. “General, it wasn’t easy, but I have him in custody. I’m bringing him in.”

Evans disconnected the call. “Sorry, Braun. Something’s going down, and you’re in the middle of this. Nice acting, but you need protection from a higher power.”

The van's rear doors opened and slammed shut. Sloan darted to the passenger's side. "Braun, scoot over." Sloan climbed aboard. "I heard everything. This isn't going to fly. You need protection, and we're taking you in for real. It's the best way to keep you safe."

"But I didn't do anything," Braun said.

"The feds have evidence," Sloan said. "They know you have access to the Maven II specs, flight plans, and RCV schematics. You're up to your ass in alligators, and it's going to take more than the FBI to keep you safe."

"You have to believe me," Braun said. "Someone set me up."

"I know that, and Evans knows that, but look, Braun, Shyler, and the top brass don't care what you say," Sloan said. "They believe you're guilty, no matter what you tell them. You're in a shitload of trouble. Jeez, Shyler of all people, hunting you down."

Braun's heart raced. First, Rusty's death, then his team was completely knocked out of commission, and now someone was after him. Whoever was behind this wanted the whole test team silenced.

Sloan took control as usual. "We need help from the top. Evans, call Winston to arrange for a meeting with the president, somewhere other than the Bunker." He turned toward Braun. "We can't be seen by the staff, and you'll need a disguise. Good thing Evans still has his make-up kit."

High Treason

Cordy's mood grew testier with each passing minute as she drove to the private airstrip in Fort Collins, Colorado. She parked, unloaded her gear, and checked in. Once on the tarmac, she watched a familiar pilot descend from a larger jet than the usual Gulfstream 450. *Why hasn't Braun called?* She couldn't get the fear for her husband out of her mind. Quint had said the weapons test didn't go well. *What could be keeping him from returning my call?*

For some reason, the pilot's "Hi, gorgeous" greeting irritated her.

Cordy gave a curt, "Hello, Buckley. I see you're flying a different jet today."

"Yeah, a Citation X—the fastest private jet available. Not bad on such short notice. President Trump used to ride in one of these babies. Set your bags down, and I'll load them." A breeze stirred Buckley's sandy blond hair as he grabbed her luggage, waited for her to board, and followed her up the steps. "You'll want full access to the internet, live TV, and phones, as usual, right?"

"Yes, and a direct line to President Spendorf." Cordy reached the top step and paused.

Buckley stepped around her and led the way. "You can use the mini-office." He stowed her bag and gear, and returned. "Equipment is much like the one aboard the Gulfstream: complete with two secured computers and a hub to connect to your laptop. You can network everything to the large monitor at the front of the plane, and it accommodates up to nine smaller images and the latest news without tapping into your internet."

Cordy checked out the desk and computer system. The desk held three phones—one was labeled "secured" and another marked "direct line to president." Cordy pointed to the red phone. "What's that?"

"It's linked to STRATCOM, but it will only ring if the pilot needs your input," Buckley said. "The mainline is in the cockpit. We're on high alert and may need to divert from our original route. They will keep us informed. For now, the pilot wants you to buckle up and prepare for flight."

Cordy took a seat behind the desk. "Aren't you the pilot?"

Buckley hesitated. "No. It surprised me, too, but I'm co-pilot today since I'm not as familiar with this aircraft. Can I get you anything? Some food or water?"

"Just water, thanks. I'll be busy the whole flight, and food isn't sitting well with me at the moment."

Buckley handed her a sealed bottle of water. "How far along are you on Braun's little project?" He smiled and nodded toward her baby bump.

Braun had proudly bought her a new wardrobe of maternity clothes. Early on, she couldn't wait to fit into the oversized blouses, spandex-waist pants, and new unmentionables. She was now dressed for comfort, unlike a few weeks ago, when she barely fit into her jeans with the zipper open. Lacy bras were optional in the past, and now she nearly overflowed a size C-cup and couldn't even button most of her fitted blouses. She seemed to have outgrown them overnight.

"Thirty-two weeks." Cordy couldn't help but return his smile as she sat behind the desk, adjusting the seatbelt around her. "They can't wait to hear Daddy's voice again, and neither can I."

"Is he on another classified mission?" Buckley asked as he moved toward the cockpit.

She nodded.

"Buzz if you need anything." Buckley disappeared around a red velvet curtain separating the cockpit from the cabin, and the jet's engines roared to life.

Cordy put on her noise-canceling headphones to ensure private communication, logged into one of the computers provided on the aircraft, and placed a thumb drive into the USB port. She started her analysis program to ensure everything she entered remained secure.

Anxious to check on Braun, she called Loran Sloan directly. The call went to voice mail. She tried his private line, but no one answered. It didn't even forward or give an option to leave a message. *That's weird.* Desperate for answers, her hand shook as she entered his number into her GPS, logged into his car tracking device, and found the Toyota parked along the side of a back road. It had been there since 6:38 a.m. EDT. Nothing made any sense.

Once the jet was at altitude, she opened an internet TV broadcast to get the latest news. "…fatal shooting…FBI Director Loran Sloan was pronounced dead at the scene. JSOC Commander Braun Hastings survived the crash…." Cordy's breath hitched. A cold shiver ran through her. *I feel like I'm in a tsunami. Complex problems wash me out to sea. The harder I swim, the deeper in water I find myself. When I launch a solution, and before I get ashore, another problem rushes toward me, hoping to bury me.*

The jet's nose took a dive, jolted, and knocked her water bottle onto the floor. The screen went black as the plane rose again and then leveled out. "No! What now?" Frantic to reconnect, she tried to reboot the system with no success. Determined, Cordy threw off her seatbelt and fought against gravity to stand upright. Checking the connections, she struggled to trace each port back to the screen—still no response. All of her programs had shut down. *It's time to find answers.* Cordy returned to the desk, buckled up, and pressed the intercom button. "Buckley, what's happening?"

Buckley didn't answer, so she added, "I need to reroute this jet. Get me to Aberdeen, Maryland, ASAP."

"We have our orders, Director Hastings," a strange man's voice came across the intercom. "You are to meet with the president as soon as we land."

"Sloan's dead. Braun was with him at the time, and I don't know if he's injured, taken to the hospital, or—" Her mind raced with more what-if scenarios.

"Braun's in custody." The man's voice came across as abrupt and uncaring. "His attorney will meet you soon."

"What? There must be some mistake. Why would Braun need an attorney?" When Cordy received no answer, she tried to reach President Zac on his direct line, but her call wouldn't go through. *I can't just sit here and pretend this will blow over because it won't. Keeping the country safe is one thing, but now I need to save my husband.* Thinking fast, she was glad that Quint had suggested she bring a few bugging devices to replace Braun's tie-tack. They were tiny, barely the size of a paper clip. She reached into her backpack, dug them out, and pocketed them. Then she plugged in a tiny earbud that communicated directly to Quint and punched the SOS warning.

Quint's voice came across the bud, "Going dark."

A flash of anger overpowered her fear. Cordy unbuckled her seatbelt and nearly tripped over the water bottle still lying on the floor. Scooping it up, she slammed it on the desk, marched to the cockpit, and yanked back the curtain. She didn't recognize the pilot, a dark-skinned man with a closely cropped crew cut, but that didn't surprise her since Buckley had already told her there was another pilot.

In the past, the jet pilots wore navy slacks and a matching wool jacket over a light-blue, button-down shirt. However, the man's two-piece, olive green service uniform caught her off guard. She scanned the cockpit. "Where's Buckley? I talked to him earlier."

The pilot jerked as if startled and glanced up from reading a book. "Buckley's not here."

"Where is he?" She couldn't read the pilot's name tag, and when he didn't answer, she asked, "What's going on?" panic swirled low in her gut.

The pilot frowned. "To assure security, we're taking a different route."

"This is crazy! I want to talk with Captain Buckley. I am here at the president's personal request."

"Didn't Buckley tell you? He was called away at the last minute and is not on the plane," the pilot said.

"When did he leave?" Cordy scanned the cockpit and backed into the cabin to check the passenger area. "What's your name? I haven't met you before."

"Name's Stone, but you'll need to return to your seat for now."

"No. I need to talk to President Spendorf." Cordy held her ground and glared at the pilot. "You must have access in here."

"Our connectivity has been breached," Stone waved his hand toward the control panel, "as you can see. You can talk to the president after we land."

"Breached?" Cordy peered at the controls, hoping for clues to what was happening. "Does that include the jet?" She realized Stone wasn't at the controls. "We must be on autopilot. Where are we landing?"

The pilot sounded robotic, with no emotion in his words, almost like he was reading to a group of strangers. "We're heading for a pre-determined area, away from the Bunker, where it's safer for all involved. This was not my idea."

"Did orders come from STRATCOM?" Cordy felt herself hyperventilating but couldn't slow her breathing. "I didn't hear the phone ring." Then she remembered she was wearing her noise-canceling headphones.

The pilot didn't give any indication that it wasn't STRATCOM, but she remained on alert. *Why would Buckley leave the plane without telling me? How does the pilot know about Braun? Who's in charge?*

Cordy's knees wobbled. "Sorry, I'm feeling a bit faint." She leaned against the curved window frame on the pilot's side while attaching a voice-activated recording device and camera that would go directly to her team. The camera eye could see both the cockpit and the front of the cabin when the curtain was open.

"Do you need help getting back to your seat?" the pilot asked.

Still feeling light-headed, Cordy sighed and lied. "No, just give me a moment." She widened her stance to keep her balance, slowed her breathing, and took a few deep breaths while counting to thirty. "Okay, I'm feeling better."

The pilot pressed an intercom button and then turned back to Cordy. "Be sure to buckle up."

An unfamiliar man moved up the aisle, paused at her desk with his back to her, then turned and entered the cockpit. "So you are the renowned cybersecurity analyst, Cordy Hastings. I'm pleased to meet you. Carl Wyller speaks highly of you. Join me for some hot tea at your desk? I have a few IT concerns to discuss with you, starting with the ransomware that's holding our Department of Defense hostage."

Cordy eyed him—mid-thirties, 6-foot, plus, and muscular with light brown hair under a navy blue baseball cap. *He knows about the ransomware?* She glanced back at the pilot to see if any trouble brewed between the two men but found none. "Who are you?"

Without hesitation, the man said, "I report to Secretary Wyller. No doubt you heard of his injury."

Cordy refused to show her rising temper, which went against her half-Irish heritage. Something was wrong. She could not access the computer or the Internet or reach the president, and it felt like she had gone back to the Stone Age. "Do you have any ID?"

The man nodded, removed his wallet, and held out his credentials, which read, "Casper Grest." At least his uniform was the typical navy blue instead of green, although the ball cap was not official. Cordy scrutinized his ID—it appeared authentic. A business card slid from behind the ID. JCJ300 was scribbled on the back of the card.

Cordy made a mental note, but it didn't mean anything to her, so she didn't mention it when he shoved it back into his wallet. "Okay, Casper, I had a brief dizzy spell a moment ago. Mind lending me your arm?"

"Gladly." Casper held out his arm like a wing and paused to wait for her.

Cordy forced a smile and gently placed her hand around the crook of his elbow while dropping a recording pen in his suit pocket. Her mouth felt dry. When she reached the desk, she guzzled down half of the bottled water sitting next to her computer. It was warm and tasted stale, so she set it down. *This man knows too much. Is he trying to pick my brain? Why is he asking so many questions?* When in doubt, she refused to trust anyone, but it wouldn't hurt to do a little investigating of her own. "Do you have any updates on the ransomware?"

"No, I hoped you could enlighten me," Casper said. "First, some tea. I'll be right back."

"I don't want any tea, but we do need to talk." Cordy buckled up. As soon as Casper walked away, she tried her phone again—still dead. *A cell jammer?* She checked around her desk, found a small device under her seat, and removed it. Casper's back was turned toward her, so she dropped the device to the floor, crushed the bug with her foot, and stuffed the remains into her pocket.

If Quint had gone dark, Cordy could reboot her computer after fifteen minutes, unless he used the safety mode, which could lock down her data for five hours. In the meantime, everything was secure but unavailable until she entered her access code. She had to remember which code to use to gain access, and things weren't adding up, so she would wait another few minutes.

Stifling a yawn, she shook her head to clear it. *What's going on? It's been a long day, and I got up early, but that's nothing new.* Her fuzzy mind and roaring headache made her nauseous. Glancing at the water bottle, she didn't remember breaking the seal. It had tasted odd, or was it drugged? She headed for the toilet and leaned against the door. It was locked.

Quint's voice sounded in her ear. "Cordy, what's wrong?"

"Tired, drug…" Cordy's vision blurred as she dropped a mini-pin recorder and slid to the floor.

Casper's voice echoed from a distance. "Ma'am? Are you okay?"

I hope Quint got my message. Cordy drifted into blackness.

***

It had taken Quint longer than planned to return to his Forensic Lab in Fort Collins. He had barely settled back into his office chair when he got her SOS warning. He hardly had time to switch Cordy's computers and cell phone to their safety net account before they automatically went offline, which would cause a five-hour delay unless they were rebooted. Cordy would need to enter the code and he would verify it before anyone could access her data.

Svetlana intercommed Quint, "Can you join us in the conference room? Cordy just buggered the jet, and you need to see this."

Perry chuckled. "She means Cordy planted a bug."

"I'm on my way." Quint grabbed his e-tab, cell phone, and hit the door's keypad. Svetlana rewound the recording. The multi-screen showed Cordy walking up the jet's aisle to the restroom as he entered the conference room. She pushed on the door, but it didn't open. Her hand slid into her jacket pocket.

"Cordy, what's wrong?" Hoping her earbud was activated, Quint put her on the conference room's speaker.

"Tired, drug," her whispered voice slurred.

A second screen lit up as she dropped a mini-pin recorder, which slid from her hand to the floor outside the bathroom door.

"Cordy?" Quint frowned when she didn't respond.

"She acts like she's been drugged." Svetlana hopped from her seat. "I'll replay the recordings for Homeland Security."

Quint dialed President Spendorf on SatVid's direct line.

"Winston Will—"

"This is Quint. Cordy's in trouble, and I need someone to meet her jet ASAP. Let me talk to the president while you make those arrangements."

"Last I heard, which was only twenty minutes ago, the jet is still in Fort Collins, waiting for Cordy to arrive," Winston said. "We've tried every phone number we have, but there's no answer. We even called you, but—"

"Sorry, I went dark." Quint asked, "Are you sure it's still in Fort Collins?"

"I'll check the log." Winston paused for a moment. "Yup, it's still at Christman Airfield. The Pilot's cell phone number is…"

Quint's fingers flew over the control keyboard, hoping to track Cordy's flag pin, but it hadn't been activated. "Perry, bring up the bug's GPS. We need to locate Cordy."

Quint pointed to Svetlana, "Lockdown her laptop and electronic devices again just to be safe. Check her cell for any messages. Winston, get me the president, Homeland Security, and Braun."

There was static on the phone then a familiar voice came through loud and clear, "President Spendorf. What's going on, Quint? Where's Cordy?"

Perry slid a note to Quint. "GPS shows Cordy's aboard a jet, flying over Washington, D.C."

Quint relayed the message to the president. "Someone already met Cordy in Fort Collins and is flying over D.C. right now. If it's not the feds—who has Cordy? She appeared unconscious in our latest recording. Where are they landing?"

An image popped up in the Fort Collins conference room as a man lifted Cordy and buckled her into her seat.

"President Spendorf, I'm patching Homeland Security into our Vidfeeds." Quint typed in his code. "Cordy has bugged the jet, and we're picking up distinct images and one audio feed. According to the jet's GPS, they're crossing open water, and it looks like the Potomac River."

Svetlana checked Cordy's phone. "Six unopened messages on her cell—three from the Bunker, two from an unknown number, and one from Agent Sloan."

"Sloan died in a car crash," Zac said. "Braun survived the accident."

Svetlana looked puzzled. "According to the last message, Sloan's alive, having faked his death, and Braun's wanted for treason. They have both gone underground and plan to notify you shortly, Mr. President."

"I look forward to their call," Zac said. "Send me the messages. I'll review them."

Quint's breath hitched. "The jet is dropping altitude. Please, find Cordy."

"Guy got your video feed and is standing beside me," Zac said. "He's already briefing a SWAT team."

A third screen popped up in the Fort Collins Conference room. "Wait, we have something coming from the jet's cockpit," Quint said.

Aboard Jet

Sept. 11 — 12:27 p.m. EDT, Washington, D.C./
10:27 a.m. MDT, Fort Collins, Colorado

Cordy was still unconscious aboard a jet, purportedly taking her to Washington, D.C., to meet with President Spendorf. Half of that was true. The plane reached Washington, D.C. However, neither Pilot Stone nor Casper had any intention of taking her to the White House. Stone had been instructed to bring the cybersecurity expert to D.C., and Casper would deliver her wherever as ordered. *Where?* The boss wasn't one to share unnecessary details, and neither knew until the time was right.

Pilot Stone monitored the jet's altitude as it began its descent. The sophisticated navigation system had taken over mid-flight with an altered flight plan. He had no idea where they would land until now. "We're crossing the Potomac River."

Casper sat in the co-pilot seat. "So we're in D.C. after all. I thought STRATCOM would land us at Offutt Air Force Base in Nebraska. I wonder where they're taking her."

"It's not up to us to question," Stone said. "We follow orders, and this is where they brought the analyst. Is she all right?"

"Yeah, she's sleeping peacefully," Casper said. "I strapped her into her seat so she is safe. Did you know the lady's pregnant?"

"I noticed, but we'll deliver as ordered." Pilot Stone watched the jet fly over the Washington Monument and land in a green field of National Park.

"I hope the drug I added to her water doesn't hurt the baby," Casper said.

Stone asked, "Did you get access to her computer?"

"No—I guess it got fried when our connectivity switched to auto-pilot. It won't even boot up," Casper said. "Does President Spendorf know she missed her original flight?"

"Not our concern." Stone flexed the index finger of his left hand to form a quotation sign. "STRATCOM's orders." He made an end quotation sign with his right hand. "They can deal with the president."

"Somehow, I doubt STRATCOM has anything to do with this mission." Casper pulled his cell from his pocket.

"You and I both know STRATCOM is a code for H.Q.," Stone said.

"H.Q.?" Casper shivered with fear, "I better make contact."

Stone watched three dark SUVs pull up alongside the jet. "Do not bother. They are already here."

"What should we do with Captain Buckley?" Casper asked.

"Leave him tied up," Stone said. "Someone will find him when they clean the head."

"I'm in disguise, but he saw your face," Casper unbuckled his seatbelt. "It's not smart to leave loose ends."

"We both falsified our passports and flew under a fictitious name, and I didn't sign up for killing anyone." Stone made his usual log entries as if he'd been flying all along according to his plan instead of being under an autopilot route he had no control over. "And neither did you. Better yet, you aren't even on the flight's logs, so open the hatch and deliver the girl. We will leave the country as soon as we have refueled as planned."

The Wait

Sept. 11 – 1:10 p.m. EDT, Walter Reed ICU, Washington, D.C.

"This makes no sense." Officer Peggy Wyller paced from one side of Carl's ICU bed, around the foot, and back to the other side. A medical trauma team treated the Secretary of Defense for a collapsed lung and airlifted him to Walter Reed Hospital for open-chest surgery. Time dragged on—it had been six hours since her husband moved out of the recovery room into ICU. She'd never expected that his being Secretary of Defense could land her husband in the hospital with a collapsed lung after a stabbing while vacating President Spendorf from the White House. As a police officer, her job was supposed to be the dangerous one.

Peggy thought she would go crazy while waiting for Carl to wake up. Unable to set her thoughts into an orderly fashion, her emotions ran from wild with fear for Carl to anger at the chaos around her, especially with the new metro police chief, who refused to let her be involved in tracking down her husband's attacker. It was time for action, not sitting around, but Carl hadn't been lucid enough to tell her what happened during the escape from the Oval Office to the Bunker.

Mindy, his nurse, flitted around the room. "Sit down and relax. He needs to rest." Unable to obey her own advice, she took Carl's vital signs, adjusted his IV, and pulled back the covers to check the dressing. A faint pink-tinged fluid oozed through the gauze. She put on sterile gloves, cleaned, and re-bandaged the wound.

Carl moved his head but still didn't open his eyes. His cardiac monitor showed a rapid pulse at 110 per minute. His B/P was 102 over 54, low for his normally hypertensive state. The monitor above his bed showed his pulse ox, which should have been running above 95%, frequently dipped below 90% even while on the ventilator. The third unit of blood dripped into his vein, and his skin was still chalky white.

"I'm here." Peggy gripped his cold, clammy fingers. "Who did this to you?"

When Carl didn't respond, she turned toward Mindy. "Doc Pete said the laceration was with a narrow-bladed knife. Was it serrated or straight-edged?"

"According to the surgeon's notes, the wound was a clean cut. He suspected it was made by a retractable scalpel—not more than 6 mm wide."

"A retractable scalpel!" Peggy jotted an entry into her cell phone. "All the perp had to do was place the blade's handle to his chest and pop the retraction button twice—once to plunge the blade through Carl's skin and then again to retract it. No wonder all he felt was a sting. It was like being jabbed with a sharp needle."

"Pretty much," Mindy admitted, "but the damage beneath the skin was devastating."

"What do you mean?" Peggy asked. "Don't spare the details. I want the facts. All of them."

Mindy nodded. "The blade punctured the sac that protects his right lung and nicked the organ. The chest cavity filled with blood, so he couldn't take a deep breath. Without enough oxygen, his heart raced to send more blood, which continued to pool."

"That was his lung, but why is he still sleeping?" Peggy asked.

"It's complicated." Mindy paused from her duties.

Peggy stopped pacing and glared at the nurse. "Please, I need to know."

"Okay." Mindy put up a hand as if in surrender. "Lack of oxygen caused a high level of carbon dioxide. That caused swelling of his brain tissue. His lung was damaged, but it's his brain that's most in danger. That's why he's taking so long to wake up. We won't know the full extent of damage until he regains consciousness."

Peggy rubbed Carl's hand and fingers. Tears brimmed and threatened to fall. "But you will wake up. I can't live without you. Please give me a sign that you hear me."

She waited anxiously, but Carl gave no sign. There was no squeeze of her hand, no movement, not even a deep sigh—just an intermittent whooshing sound of the ventilator.

"I need some air." Peggy bent over Carl and kissed him on the cheek. "I'll be right back, honey. You rest." Tears splashed as she blinked. She rubbed them away with a quick swipe of her hand and dashed from the room. A blurry figure stood in front of the nurses' station. "Dad? What are you doing here?"

Her father, the recently retired chief of police, turned with a grave expression. "President Spendorf called. How's Carl?" He stepped toward her and opened his arms.

Peggy felt relief just from that simple, comforting gesture—a bear hug she could melt into. He didn't even flinch, although he had a fractured rib from his earlier fight with Amir. She wished she were a child again and that Daddy could fix everything now that he was here. But no, her world was more complex, and that wasn't why he'd come. There was something more, she could see it in his eyes. She moved out of his embrace. The concern on his face made her cringe. "What's wrong?"

Dad's smile dipped. His jaw and cracked lip were still bruised and swollen. He pulled Peggy aside and whispered, "Zac also said, 'Carl logged in and shut down the Avenger Missile System, protecting the White House airspace just before two drones attacked.' Even I know treason when I hear it—but it wasn't Carl. I'm sure of it. He's being blamed for something he didn't do."

"It's ridiculous." Peggy clenched her fists. "Carl had to have been framed, but he's in no position to fight the accusation. And the new chief of police won't let me anywhere near the investigation. Dad, I need your help."

"Zac made it clear that we are on the brink of war," Dad said, "but we don't know who our real enemy is. Carl may have been our first casualty, but he won't be the last."

"This has to be a mistake," Peggy said in disbelief. "I know Carl is not a traitor. He loves our country and would never put us in jeopardy."

"I agree." Dad put his hand on Peggy's shoulder. "But you know, when faced with a national disaster, it's easier to paste every suspect's name onto a board, throw a dart, and see who it lands on. Carl may have been at the wrong place at the wrong time and needs us to clear his name, but you're exhausted. You worked the evening shift, were up all night, and my guess is, you haven't eaten for hours. Why don't you go home, eat, shower, and take a nap? I'll stay here with Carl until you return. While you're sleeping, I'll make a few calls. There are many people who owe me favors. And when you return, we will investigate this together."

Peggy knew she could count on his word. "Thanks, Dad. I'll do that."

Ransom Demand

Sept. 11 – 2:00 p.m. EDT, Supreme Court Chambers, Washington, D.C.

The Supreme Court was normally closed over the weekends, and it was almost unheard of for the Supreme Court to hold sessions on a Sunday, but the Justice Department had to close early Friday morning due to downed software systems. It took until late Saturday to reverse the hack, so to make up for lost time, the Supreme Court met this morning to hear the Zogster case. Even with the latest threat to the government or maybe because of the drone attack, the Justice Department refused to postpone the hearing another day. Something suspicious was happening at Zogster, and the court dug deep to get to the root of the matter.

Congressman Conrad Justuso was in the middle of his testimony when a female aide quietly made her way into the chambers, tapped Justice Sophia Hendrum's shoulder and whispered, "I'm sorry, but there's a man out in the lobby who demands to speak to you. He went through the scanner without incident, and he says it's urgent—something about your husband. The security guard is tending to an urgent matter, so I'll take you to him if you wish."

"This is about my husband?" Her heart beat double-time as she checked the young brunette's name tag that read, "Lindsey."

The aide nodded. "He's adamant about giving you the message."

Sophia scooted back her chair, raised a shaky hand, and was permitted to speak. "Excuse me for a moment. There is an urgent matter I must attend to, and I'd like to speak to the Chief Justice in private."

After a brief discussion, the Chief Justice called a temporary recess.

Sophia turned toward the aide. "Show me the way."

Although the Supreme Court is open Monday through Friday from 9 a.m. to 4:30 p.m., this was a Sunday. Normally, the building would be closed to any visitors, so Sophia was surprised to see a man dressed in a navy pin-striped suit, standing at the reception desk with one hand in his pocket and the other wrapped around a paper cup. The brew wafted steam into the air. As Lindsey warned her, there was no security guard at the desk.

The man bolted toward Sophia when he saw her, splashing coffee onto the floor, but he didn't seem aware of the splotched carpet. "Thanks for seeing me on short notice. This is about your husband." He pulled a slip of paper from his pocket and shoved it into her hand. The note said, "For Justice Sophia Hendrum only. Deliver immediately."

Out of nowhere, the security guard, ever vigilant, sprang into action when the man thrust the note toward her. "Keep your hands where we can see them," he commanded. His presence reassured her in the face of uncertainty.

Sophia, taken aback, almost dropped the note. "Where did you get this?" she managed to ask, her voice trembling with shock.

"Some man slipped it onto my coffee tray," the man said.

"Who was this man," the guard asked. "Did you know him?"

"No, I've never seen him before in my life," the man said, his eyes darting between Sophia and the guard.

Sophia plucked the paper by the corner, opened it, and held it up to read: "If you want to see your husband alive, deposit $25 million in the following bank account by midnight tonight. No police, no publicity." Her gut clenched. *Where can I get that kind of money?*

The guard pointed to the paper. "Shouldn't we bag that note as evidence? It may have the abductor's fingerprints."

Sophia sucked in a deep breath. "You're right. This is evidence."

The guard motioned toward Lindsey. "Get a bag from the security desk."

Lindsey returned shortly and held up a zip-lock plastic bag.

Sophia slipped the note inside. "Hold it up for a moment." She tapped the camera icon on her cell, took a photo, and then leaned against the wall, barely able to breathe. Her heart raced as if she were running a marathon. Blackness fringed her eyesight. *Oh God, is this how Mo felt last year when he found out I was kidnapped? Stop. You have to stay calm.* "How do I know that he's still alive? Even if I came up with that much money, I won't pay unless I know for sure."

The guard turned toward the aide. "Lindsey, find a room for Justice Sophia, so we can talk to this man."

"No! I have to leave," the man backed away with his hands up. "I'm just delivering a message. I don't know who gave this to me. As I said, it was on my coffee tray. The ransom demand was attached to a $10 bill." He fished in his pocket and pulled out a crumpled ten with a red paper clip attached. "Here, bag this, too." He dropped the money into the guard's hand.

"What's your name?" the guard asked, his tone firm.

"I feel like James Bond," The man nervously laughed, his unease evident as he continued to back toward the door.

"Not his real name," Lindsey said. "He signed in as Tom Olson. He works at the Metro Station's Bank of America. I have the phone number and his home address at my desk."

"Thanks, I'll need a copy of that data." The officer found another zip-lock bag and sealed the money inside.

"May I go now?" Tom asked.

Ignoring his protests, the guard held onto his left arm and led him to an interview room. "We have many questions left unanswered."

Sophia's mind raced. She reached for her cell and speed-dialed Chief Jackson. He barely had time to answer when she gushed, "This is Sophia. Mo's been kidnapped. I just got a ransom note for $25 million. I don't know what to do. They are demanding money I don't have. I don't even know if Mo is alive, and it says no police!"

"I'll be right there. Are you at the courthouse?" The chief's calm voice felt like a blanket of warmth.

"Yes, I have to go back into the chamber," Sophia said. "I'll need to excuse myself and meet you in the lobby. How long before you get here?"

"Half-an-hour tops," Chief said. "Did you properly secure the chain of evidence?"

"Yes. Security has it and a $10 bill that was with the note. They are currently questioning the man. I'll ask the guard to send over his notes for your review. Hurry!" She headed for the courtroom as she disconnected the call.

Five minutes later, she was pacing the lobby, checking her phone and watch, and she even tried calling her bank for a loan, but then remembered it was Sunday, and they wouldn't loan her that much anyway.

A guard handed her a bottle of water. "You look pale. Shouldn't you sit down for a while? I'll let the chief know where to find you."

"Thanks." Sophia took the water bottle but didn't open it. She was afraid she'd vomit if she consumed anything, but she did take a seat. Her hand wrapped over her mouth as fear crept up her spine. Her knees twitched, her heel tapped, and her mind spun with thoughts. *If only I had let Mo walk me to my sedan. Maybe the thugs would have already been gone when he made it back to his car. This is a nightmare. Did I tell him that I love him?*

It felt like hours before Chief Jackson came through the door. "Sophia, I'm here." He scooped her into a bear hug. "Let's get out of here."

"Thanks for coming." Sophia grabbed his arm and blindly followed him out into the cold air. She barely remembered the walk, but when he led her to the Supreme Court Cafeteria, she remembered her last meal with Mo. "No, I can't go in there. Let's go to my place."

"Sure, I know the way." They walked to his car and headed to her home.

"Now, who would want to hurt Mo?" Sophia's gut twisted. "Oh, wait. He mentioned something odd, but I didn't think anything of it at the time—he mentioned calling Iranian royal family members with the news of additional sanctions, and he added, 'They say I'll soon regret these actions.' How soon is soon? He'd barely gotten off the call at midnight and was ambushed before 2 a.m." She turned toward Jackson. "I'm serious, Chief. Could the Iranians be behind the ambush?"

Chief turned somber. "Iranians threatened him? That seems like a good lead, and we need to tell the FBI."

As if she hadn't heard a word Chief said, she added, "And where will I get that kind of money?"

Chief Jackson placed his hand on her shoulder to get her full attention. "Sophia, paying this ransom could guarantee he gets killed. I've dealt with many hostage situations, and it would help if you pleaded your case on the news—CNN, MSNBC, and even Fox News. Get the word out."

"I was told no police and no publicity." She pulled out her phone and showed him the photo of the ransom note.

"No one would hand over money without proof he's alive," Chief said.

"No, I can't risk it!" Sophia bit her lip, trying to remain calm.

"I think it's your best recourse." Chief pulled his cell phone from his pocket. "At least, you may get some proof that he's alive. We need to involve the FBI to get their cooperation and ask for federal funding for the ransom money. I'll call and line up interviews for the five o'clock news. You stay calm and be ready to communicate with the abductor. Think of what you want to say during the broadcast."

Being a former FBI agent, Chief Jackson was quickly granted a meeting with the Deputy Director, Neil Gray, who was in charge during Director Loran Sloan's undercover assignment.

"I know what to do," Gray said. "Once Sophia goes public on tonight's news, we'll have a hotline available to take any calls. If a call comes in, one of us will answer and get as much information as possible. If the caller makes any demands, we may ask you to speak, but remember to stay calm. Ask to speak with your husband. See if you can get them to prove he is alive. We'll make arrangements for any ransom drop and pick-up. Do you understand?"

"Yes," Sophia's voice sounded shaky. She repeated with more conviction. "Yes. I understand completely. Thank you, but I'm still worried about going on the news after they warned me not to involve the police."

"Make it perfectly clear that you must know he's alive before paying." Gray convinced her.

Sophia wrung her hands, still doubtful, but finally agreed.

"Okay, next, we need an interview with the media," Gray said. "Choose a public place where the newscasters can convene at the same time for a larger audience."

"No!" Chief shook his head. "I want a recorded message first to prevent any breakdowns."

"A breakdown is sometimes better," Gray said.

"We're talking about a Justice of the Supreme Court," Chief said. "No, chances for the public to—"

"I get it." Gray held up a hand in surrender. "Okay, let's make this happen."

Clocked

Sept. 11 – 2:58 p.m. EDT, Building Near
National Park, Washington, D.C.

Cordy gradually regained consciousness, stirred, and could not move—her wrists bound in front of her. Upon further exploration, she discovered a rope ran under her arms and around a ladder-backed chair. Duct tape secured her ankles to the wooden legs. Her mouth felt dry as desert sand. Unable to figure out where she was or why she was here, she kept her eyes closed and breathed deeply to get her bearings amid the darkness. There was no way Cordy would become a victim. She had her children to protect. She found within her inner spirit a calm refusal to admit defeat, and the stealth to never give up—like a tigress, she would fight!

Sounds and smells spoke to her—a clock's rhythmic ticking, persistently refusing to fade into the background. She imagined a pendulum swinging to the insistent tick-tock, tick-tock. A cold shiver raced up her spine when it played the opening bars to Fur Elise, followed by three bongs. Three o'clock. The chime echoed—*hard-surfaced walls and little furniture—still no light, probably a windowless room*. Sniffing the air, she noted a hint of cigar smoke and peppermint. Her fingers flexed to ease the numbness.

A click of a door heightened her awareness. A whispered voice said, "Cordy? Are you awake?" It sounded like Buckley, but how was that possible? She inhaled sharply when someone grabbed her arm.

"Shh," Buckley said. "It was hard to find you in the dark."

Cordy chanced a peek but only saw his shadow. "How did you get here? Pilot Stone said you left the plane."

"He lied, and that red phone didn't connect to STRATCOM." Buckley untied the rope holding her to the chair and then worked to free her wrists and ankles, pausing a few times to listen. "When that phone rang, I leaned over to answer, but it was out of reach, so I unbuckled my seatbelt. Someone with a thick Arabic accent spoke,

'Orders from General H.Q. Change of plans' and hung up. The jet's controls locked in a dive. I stumbled, hit my head, and woke up here, duct-taped to a chair."

Cordy noticed a bruise over Buckley's left temple. "Are you okay?"

He nodded and winced.

She remained concerned about his condition as she rubbed her unrestrained wrists and flexed her ankles. "Thanks. How did you get away?"

Buckley went back to the door to listen. "I struggled, bounced around, and finally tipped the chair. It broke, leaving a jagged edge."

Cordy crept up behind him and whispered, "Where is H.Q.?"

"Don't know, but Stone is a pawn, and he works for the general."

Voices in the hallway grew louder. "Buckley's gone." A male with a heavy accent said, "Spread out and find him. Kill him if you must, but bring me the woman—alive."

Buckley grabbed the knob and locked the door. "They're coming. Find a weapon."

Cordy backed away. Her mind raced as she assessed her options while inching her way along the wall, feeling for anything she could use to protect herself. Tick-tock, the clock sounded from across the room. Nothing in reach but that clock—a tiny seed became rooted in her mind, growing with each passing second.

Buckley grabbed the chair Cordy had been tied to and held it over his head. "I'll stand by the door. They'll have to go through me to get to you."

Rage flowed through Cordy's veins, and a kick of protest surged through her abdomen. *How dare anyone threaten my children?* She grabbed the clock and ducked behind a desk.

A noise came from the other side of the door. "It's locked," a man said. Keys jingled as someone opened the door.

Buckley slammed the chair over the first man's head, knocking a gun from his hand as he fell to the ground, but the hallway light revealed two more men.

A shot rang out. Buckley yelped—blood dripped from his left shirt sleeve. He dove for the pistol, rolled, and fired through the open door. He was on his feet in an instant.

A second man dropped, but not before another round blasted cement fragments from the floor, catching Buckley in the leg. The pistol flew from Buckley's hand as he landed on the floor, whacked his right temple against a raised metal doorstop, and lay still. Blood dripped down his face.

Cordy thought Buckley was unconscious, and his weapon was several feet away. *Can I reach it in time?*

The third man spoke into a radio. "Buckley's down, but the girl's missing."

"She has to be in the room," an accented voice said. "The door was locked, and there's no sign of her escaping on the security tape."

The clock seemed to tick louder and vibrated in Cordy's sweaty hand. Afraid her rapid breathing would give her away, she inhaled a calm, slow, deep breath and held it, exhaling through her mouth while moving slowly along the wall in the dark, hoping to get closer.

Light from the hallway shone on the third man, who was muscular and dressed in combat gear. He stepped farther into the room, moving sleek as a cougar, and aimed his gun at Buckley's head. Mirrored aviator glasses reflected Buckley's grim face.

Behind those shades, Cordy was sure the man's beady eyes stared directly at her friend like a hawk ready to pounce on a hare. Moving away from the wall, she threw the clock at the gunman's head and swept up the pistol. She fired, but he had spun away from Buckley. Not sure if Buckley was still alive, she wasn't going to let this thug execute her friend without a fight.

Blood dripped from the gunman's temple, and he staggered against the doorframe. "I knew you were in here." His gun pointed at her. "Drop it."

"No, you need me alive." Cordy stayed in the shadows and noticed Buckley moving toward one of the downed men. She had to divert the gunman's attention. "Take me to your boss. That's why you're here. I heard him give you that order before you opened the door."

The man came closer. The weapon never strayed from her chest.

Buckley tried to move without drawing any attention, inching his way toward the downed man's ornate left boot bulging with a knife. Buckley pulled free the weapon, and in one fluid motion, he threw it straight at the gunman's neck.

A warm, bloody spray hit Cordy as the standing gunman fell forward, collapsing on her. She brushed away debris, shoved the barrel of the gun into his chest, and was ready to fire, but he fell to the floor, staring up at her with dead eyes.

Rapid gunfire came from down the hall. "Clear."

Buckley grabbed the dead man's gun with his good hand and was at the door in a flash. Blood caked his left arm, which hung loosely at his side. "Hurry, let's get out of here." He limped into the hallway.

"FBI. Drop the gun."

"Don't shoot." Buckley lowered his pistol and placed it on the floor. "I'm Captain Frank Buckley."

"Where's Dr. Cordelia-Hastings?"

Cordy faced four men dressed in combat gear, "FBI SWAT" emblazoned on their vests. "I'm Cordy." She felt dizzy, weaving a bit.

Buckley grabbed her arm before she fell. She leaned on him, or maybe he leaned on her, but they were both shaking as the adrenaline drained from their systems.

"How did you find us?" Buckley asked.

"Quint called, right?" Cordy asked. "I knew I could count on him."

"Our orders came from the president." An FBI agent held up his ID.

"Who were we dealing with?" Buckley asked. "They also said President Spendorf sent them."

"We're working on that," the agent said. "We have one man in custody, and he says he was under STRATCOM's orders, but I doubt it, and he's not pulling the strings."

"Did you find my phone, laptop, and luggage?" Cordy asked.

"They're safe," the agent said. "We'll return everything after we run forensics."

"I'll need them ASAP. The president is waiting to see me," Cordy said. "I want to interview the schmuck you have in custody, but I'll have to do that later."

"Check in with the paramedics first," the agent said. "Then we'll take you to meet the president."

"Thanks. You guys are my heroes." Cordy turned toward Buckley. "And especially you, my friend, you risked your life to save me." She glanced at the FBI agents. "Treat him well." She stepped closer when Buckley faltered. "How's your arm and leg?"

"Been better, but I'll live." Buckley supported his left arm at the elbow and stared at his wound, then back up at Cordy. "I'm glad you're unharmed. Braun would never forgive me if anything happened to you or the twins."

Two paramedics came forward and triaged the extent of their injuries.

"I'm fine," Cordy said, "but Buckley needs medical care."

They loaded Buckley onto a gurney. One paramedic said, "You can ride along to the hospital and get a more thorough exam if you like."

Cordy declined. Before they loaded Buckley into the ambulance, she squeezed his hand. "If I can, I'll check in with you later, and thanks."

"I'll be good as new in no time," Buckley said. "And Cordy, we're going to get these bastards."

"You can count on it." She waved as Buckley was lifted into the rear of the ambulance and then turned toward the FBI agent. "Let's go. We have a lot of work to do."

Sophia's Plea

The afternoon flew by way too fast. Justice Sophia Hendrum stood in the wings of a news control room, preparing to address those who kidnapped her husband, Mo. The studio felt huge and overwhelming. People darted from place to place, setting up small booths, cameras, and lighting. Phones rang, lights flashed, and people with headsets spoke softly, giving orders. Camera crews pushed large booms across one stage to another. Feeling her nerves tingling, she asked, "Where do I go?"

Chief Jackson motioned her to a smaller studio.

Two men moved two navy chairs slanted at an angle on either side of a corner table. They placed a large gold vase filled with red roses on the table.

A woman directed from off stage. "Too high—it'll draw attention away from the speakers."

They replaced the vase with a crystal bowl of candy. "Perfect." She turned toward Sophia. "Sit on the left chair so you're to the right of the interviewer. I'll have a make-up artist freshen you up a bit, run a comb through your hair, and you'll be all set. Do you know what you want to say?"

"Yes," Sophia ran a hand over her hair as if the woman's comments had blown it out of place.

"Just relax. Cross your legs at the ankles if you must, but not your knees." The woman motioned to a man heading their way with a small black bag and hairbrush in hand. The woman said, "Not too many touch-ups. I want her to appear natural. Cool, calm, and professional."

"Understood." The man took Sophia's elbow. "Sit with your head slightly tipped and look directly at me. No one else matters at the moment. Only you." He opened his bag, fussed and brushed, fluffed, and padded on rouge, eye shadow, and rolled on lip gloss.

"Smack your lips together. That's it." He held up his hands as if taking a photo. "To perfection." He briefly held up a mirror. "Don't you agree?"

Sophia barely saw her reflection. It didn't matter—her mind was a hundred miles from here.

The woman clipped a microphone onto Sophia's light blue suit lapel.

The news anchor introduced himself, "I'm Ted. Let's run a check. When the cameraman holds up three fingers, stay silent, two fingers, smile, and when he points one finger at you, say, 'This is a test.'" He adjusted a small earphone in his right ear and spoke so low that she couldn't hear what he said.

The cameraman nodded to Sophia and held up three fingers, two, and one.

Sophia smiled at the camera. "This is a test."

"That's perfect. We're ready to roll." The cameraman repeated his cues. Ted stared directly into the camera and began. "We are speaking tonight with Justice Sophia Hendrum. She has an important plea for those who kidnapped her husband, Secretary of State Mo Hendrum, early this morning. She has received a ransom demand from his captors." He turned toward Sophia. "Without wasting precious time, I'll turn it over to you."

Sophia took a deep breath. "Thank you, Ted. As the reporter mentioned, this message is for the people holding my husband. We have received your demand and are taking it very seriously. At this time, we are worried about his well-being and want to cooperate with you fully. To do so, we must have proof he's alive. He's a diabetic and needs his medicine. Please." She nearly choked on the words.

Ted rescued her. "The public supports you during this hour of uncertainty. Do you have anything else to say?"

"Yes," Sophia stared at the camera zooming in on her face. We must have an open channel of communication to work out the details. You can reach me at any time by contacting this hotline."

The director in the control room flashed up a message with a phone number.

"Please call if you have any additional information. I must know he's… he's alive." Sophia swallowed with a loud gulp and blushed. "Let me be clear. Our primary concern is for the well-being of Secretary Hendrum, and we will do whatever it takes to ensure his safe return. Thank you."

Ted said, "I know this must be horrific for you, Justice Hendrum. If there was a way your husband could see this, what would you like to say directly to him?"

This was unexpected. Sophia fidgeted, and hesitated. "Mo, you mean everything to me. I love you. I need you. I live, eat, and breathe…" She gasped a sob. "Please come home." Her throat closed up, and she couldn't say another word. Her eyes flicked from the camera to Ted and then locked onto Chief Jackson. "Get me out of here," she mouthed.

The camera had panned to Ted. "Thank you, Justice Hendrum. Our hearts and prayers are with you and your family. Remember to call the hotline number." The camera zoomed in on the phone number once more.

The director called, "Cut."

Sophia's whole body crumpled into a fetal position as she rocked herself. "I'm sorry. I thought I could do this. It's not what I expected!" She got up and fled the room. "I failed. I can't. I failed him."

Chief Jackson followed her out of the room. "It's all right, Sophia. Gather your composure, and we'll go back in and re-tape your message to Mo. This is important."

Sophia sat in an overstuffed chair somewhere away from cameras and news anchors, while panting and trying to calm her nerves. She felt light-headed.

"Slow down your breathing," Chief said. "Do you need a paper bag?"

"No." Sophia blew out a breath and inhaled deeply, holding it for a count of ten. Recalling her yoga training, she slowly exhaled and counted again to ten. In…hold, and out…hold. After five cycles, she felt more in control. "I never knew this would hit me so hard, and to think Mo faced this only a year ago. How did he survive? I feel like I've died ten times over. It was much easier being kidnapped and figuring a way out of captivity than worrying about a loved one."

"That's true," Chief said. "I've been in your shoes more than once, but we'll tackle this together. You practice your yoga. Breathe, admit you're feeling anxious, and relax."

"Anxious?" Sophia asked. "I'm not anxious. I'm petrified, and I'm furious!"

"Yes, use that anger," Chief Jackson said. "Take a breather, freshen up, and let's say what you want to say. Rehearse it until it comes as natural as brushing your teeth."

Sophia gradually opened her clenched fists and closed her eyes. Sophia's eyes popped open, and she sat up straighter when Ted entered the room and brought a glass of water. "Feeling better?"

She took the glass offered. "Yes, I can do this. Should I take it from the top?"

Ted shook his head. "Fortunately, we recorded your interview, and it didn't go live. Don't worry. We can edit and splice all day to get the message just right. We do it all the time. How long do you need?"

Sophia sipped her water. "Is there a place to freshen up? I'm sure my mascara could use a touch-up." She forced herself to smile, not wanting to frighten the reporter away.

He pointed down the hallway. "The lady's room is the second door on your right. I'll be in the studio when you're ready. We'll replay the clip, and you can decide what to cut and what to save. Then we'll record a new segment and plug it in as needed."

"Thanks." Sophia headed for the restroom.

By 5:05 p.m., her pleas were heard across the nation. "Now to wait." She felt drained, knowing it would be a long night. They waited all evening for a phone call that never came.

Back On Task

In the twenty minutes that it took for the paramedics to examine, treat, and release Cordy, the SWAT team had handed over Pilot Stone and two of his minions to the FBI. An agent also swabbed down her phone, laptop, and all of her personal belongings, but Cordy was none the wiser about who was behind the kidnapping. The FBI assured her it was definitely not STRATCOM. Finally, an agent escorted Cordy to meet President Spendorf.

Chief of Staff Winston Willoughby met her when she arrived at the Bunker. "President Spendorf is expecting you, but he isn't here at the moment."

"Where is he?" Cordy adjusted her backpack.

"Secret Service escorted him to a private meeting," Winston whispered.

Cordy scanned the Bunker, filled with aides, Secret Service agents, and other personnel. She knew Zac kept all of his private affairs secure from roaming ears and eyes. "So when and where should I meet him?"

"I'll text him." Winston motioned for her to follow him down the hallway.

"In the meantime, maybe I could talk to Guy, or is Homeland Security also meeting with Zac?"

Winston cleared his throat when an aide came within earshot. "Not here."

Cordy was confused and whispered, "Guy's not here? Or we can't talk about it here."

"You're quick." Winston winked and motioned to an empty office two doors to the right. "You can set up in there. I'll see you shortly."

Cordy took the hint, went into the office, and shut the door. The windowless room sent a chill through her. Although the Bunker had adequate circulation, the dry air seemed stale. She knew Zac hated it down here, and she understood why. A metal desk, a leather rolling chair, and a computer monitor filled the small room. *I hope this isn't my assigned space while I'm here.*

Winston reappeared shortly, entered the office, and closed the door. "Now we can talk. Zac's at the Pentagon, quelling the lion. General Shyler wants to launch an airstrike against Russia. Not only that, but the general swears your husband is a traitor, a Russian double agent—"

"No!" Cordy hopped up from her chair. "My husband is not a traitor or a double agent! How could anyone think that?"

Winston winced while shaking his head. "Shyler believes Braun deliberately sabotaged the weapons test."

Cordy clenched her hands into a fist and headed for the door. "I'll set Zac straight. Where is he now?"

Winston put his hand on her shoulder. "Calm down. Zac agrees that Braun's no traitor and plans to prove it."

"Is he on another special ops mission?" Cordy whispered.

Winston ran his thumb and pointer finger over his lips as if to zip them closed. "I can't say. You'll have to ask the president for the details, but there's a little matter of tracking down an international terrorist, Farzad Zahair, that is at the top of Zac's list."

Cordy had heard of Zahair, and she wondered if he had anything to do with the drone attack.

"The president is still at the Pentagon, so give me a minute to arrange a meeting. I'm sure he'll be glad you arrived safely." Winston left the office, once again closing the door behind him.

After dusting for fingerprints, the FBI had left Cordy's phone, laptop, and keyboard covered with a faint residue. She used a soft rag to remove the debris and made a note to check with forensics for the results. Setting up her laptop came next. It wouldn't boot up, which was good news. That meant anyone who tried to steal information couldn't open any programs. Quint said he was going dark. She plugged in her access drive with the ISO file, entered the bios setting, logged on using her special code to reboot, and watched nervously, trying to hurry along the process until the computer lit up.

Quint had added an extra layer of protection. It would notify him when Cordy or anyone else logged on. A second code was required to open the special vault backup data he'd rescued earlier that day.

"You okay, Girlfriend? Why didn't you activate the flag pin? I could have tracked you once you left the jet," popped up as text on the screen—in typical Quint fashion.

Cordy shook her head. She had scooped up the flag pin and her other recording devices and became so busy that she forgot to wear it. She dug through her bag, found the tracking pin, and tacked it to the left collar of her blouse, and continued to read Quint's message.

"I'm available on VidChat when you have a minute. Your cockpit bug gave some interesting info, and the FBI has Pilot Stone in custody. That isn't his real name: surprise, surprise. Stone flew from Iran to Toronto and crossed the Canadian border illegally using a fake passport, probably by private jet, and he planned to return to Toronto. Talk to you soon."

Cordy logged on VidChat to reach Quint. "What about the co-pilot? He went by the name Casper Grest. He told me he's working with Secretary Carl Wyller, but I doubt it."

"The only co-pilot listed on board was Buckley," Quint said. "Sorry, that's all I know."

"That's one of the reasons we need to build a program to track terrorists at all entry points and link it to Interpol's list," Cordy said as Winston opened the door.

Upon seeing her equipment spread across the tiny desk, his bushy eyebrows rose above his silver wire-rimmed glasses. "I forgot this room was so Spartan. Oops," he pointed to her phone and mouthed, "Sorry."

"Winston is here, and I hope to meet with President Spendorf shortly. More details later." Cordy disconnected the call to Quint.

Winston apologized again. "You'll want to set up in the technical room. I'll arrange that while you meet with the president. He's moved to Carl's office, and Braun and Evans are briefing him at the moment."

Cordy felt relief flow through her. "So you've seen Braun?"

Winston's smile reached his bloodshot eyes.

She wondered how long it had been since his last peaceful night's rest.

Winston remained steadfast during emergencies. Everyone could lean on him, and yet he stayed invisible as his usual demeanor. "Braun's a bit tattered after this morning's activities. I even lent him a shirt, but he's eager to see you."

"Who is Evans?" Cordy asked. "Is he new to the team?"

"FBI forensics."

"Perfect. I need a forensics expert." Cordy typed a message to Quint, "Give me half an hour."

"Follow me." Winston stepped into the hallway. "Bring your gear."

Cordy stuffed her laptop into her backpack and slipped one strap over her shoulder. "Ready."

Winston showed her where to go by leading her past a conference center, three occupied offices, and an interview room. She admired his calm command of the vast anthill of activities around them.

She peeked inside the technical room as they continued down the hallway. It was the first time she'd seen the space, which was impressive—computers, printers, screens, phones, and more. It wasn't her home office, but it had all the amenities.

Cordy rubbed her lower back and stretched. Her entire body felt stiff and sluggish. Whatever drug she'd been given wasn't totally out of her system, but she had work to do and fought the side effects.

"Are you okay?" Winston asked. "We're going to Carl's office via the underground system. It's quite a hike, and in your condition…" His eyes glanced at her midsection, where the occupants moved around vigorously. "I mean," he stammered.

"I'm fine," Cordy cut him off and picked up her pace, then realized she had been rude. "Thanks for your concern, though. I get snippy when my blood sugar crashes. You know, starving one moment and nauseated the next. Most women get over their nausea after three months, but not me. I guess with twins, I got a double dose of those hormones creating morning sickness—by the way, that's a myth. It comes and goes all day long." With one look at Winston, she realized she'd said too much.

Winston blushed so much that his face was red as a radish. "I should have offered you a sandwich or some fruit. I remember when my wife was…aah…preg…umm…expect…, I mean with child. Anyway, all she could keep down were crackers."

"Pretty much," Cordy agreed. "I brought my own. Why are we meeting there?"

Winston said, "The office is vacant while Carl's in the hospital."

Cordy asked, "Is Zac safe there?"

"Yes, Homeland Security checked out the space," Winston said. "Marv won't leave his side, and several other Secret Service agents surround him."

Race Against Time

***Sept. 11 – 4:18 p.m. EDT, Carl's Office, Washington, D.C./
2:18 p.m. MDT, Fort Collins, Colorado***

Cordy followed President Spendorf's Chief of Staff Winston Willoughby through the tunnel to Carl's office, which was at least five degrees cooler than the Bunker. She wrapped her jacket tighter, still shivering, unsure of the cause—temperature or her nerves.

Once they reached the building's entrance, Cordy went through security again. She pulled her laptop and an external hard drive from the backpack, removed her cell phone and keys from her pockets, and removed two thumb drives from her purse. "Clear," the guard said.

Turning to Winston, she asked, "How did you get through so quickly?"

"They see me at odd hours, day and night, so I usually show my badge and enter my code, but since we're on high alert, they waved a wand over me, and I'm in."

"It must be nice." Cordy hated the inconvenience, but she was also a stickler for security.

Winston patiently waited as she replaced items into her backpack, purse, and pockets. "If it makes you feel any better, that's the last scan until we reach the White House."

Cordy laughed. "And I get to do this for the fourth time today."

Winston led her through a narrow hallway and up the stairs. As they approached, an agent stood guard outside Carl's office door and spoke into his wrist radio.

Marv, the president's Secret Service agent, opened the door and announced, "Dr. Cordelia Hastings has arrived."

"Come in." Zac set down his teacup and motioned them inside, beckoning with his left hand. "You, too, Winston."

"Yes, sir," Winston walked inside Carl's office and stood at the door to await further orders.

Once the door closed, Zac continued talking to two men at a round conference table, "…not the first time he's been accused of treason. I remember another incident barely a year ago, during the pandemic. Braun proved himself then, and I know he'll do the same now. I want Zahair captured alive. It'll be risky, but Braun's good at his job, and we must keep Emma safe during her rescue. Get the best SWAT team as a backup."

The room was spacious, with a computer in the corner of an L-shaped desk. A screen sat on each side of the centered keyboard, and a printer was to the right. The round table was to the left of another door, which Cordy thought probably led to a break room.

Cordy waited until the president finished speaking to the two men sitting around the table. At his signal and with a tired, welcoming smile, she thanked Winston for escorting her and spoke, "Good afternoon, gentlemen. You must be Evans…" She stumbled when she saw Loran. "You're alive!" She patted her chest. "How? The news said…." Her throat felt tight. "You know…how did you survive?"

"Not my time yet," Loran smiled. His eyes were red and bloodshot.

His behavior confused her. "What am I missing?"

"Loran's wife was also kidnapped earlier today, and we are formulating a strategy to rescue her while protecting certain agents, but enough about that." Zac stood ramrod straight. "I heard about your trip, and I'm glad you made it here safely." His worry seemed well hidden behind a firm grip as he pumped her hand and turned toward the men in the room, but Cordy noticed he gnawed on his bottom lip and twisted his wedding ring—both were habits when Zac felt stressed.

She scanned the room. "Where's Braun?"

"Over here." She hadn't recognized him until he spoke. She wouldn't have known him on the street as her competent, handsome, efficient husband. A freshly scabbed-over wound split the skin across his left temple, and a more healed, puckered, jagged scar ran across his right cheek. Borrowed, stained, and tattered clothes helped to give him a rakish, piratical look. He wore dark-brown contacts over his gray eyes, had a reddish mustache and goatee, and his blond hair was dyed auburn. He winked at her, his familiar crooked smile flooding her with warmth, heating her soul. He was alive and okay! Holding up his brew, he asked, "Do you want a cup?"

"No thanks, but a glass of water would be appreciated." Just seeing Braun brought a bounce to Cordy's step—a zest for life manifesting within her and joy knowing her husband was alive. She wanted to run into his open arms, but after one glance at the president's eyes filled with seriousness, she said instead, "Fill me in on everything." She peered back into the break room, where Braun fetched her drink. "Shouldn't Guy be here? This is a matter of Homeland Security."

Zac sat back in his chair. "Now that you're here, we'll shift gears." He jotted a note and turned to Winston. "Give this to Guy. Tell him it's top secret and not open to discussion. As discussed earlier, inform him about Braun and Loran's new assignments. They're under my protection and are not to be arrested."

Cordy's breath hitched, "Arrested?"

Zac waved his hand as if to calm her. "We'll address that later, too," and turned back to Winston. "Guy has privileged information. I know he's busy, but he needs to be here, even if via video communication." Zac asked Cordy, "You can do that, right?"

"I'll link him into VidChat." Cordy set up her computer.

"Thanks, and get Quint on the call, too, if you need him, but let's keep this all contained as much as possible." Zac turned toward Winston. "If anyone else asks about Braun, you haven't seen him in over a month."

"Security comes first, as always." Winston opened the door to leave.

Zac paused, then called out to Winston once more, "Wait a moment. Find out if Guy has cleared the White House for my return. If I don't need to go back to that safe house, it's fine by me. Thanks. That'll be all for now."

Winston nodded, and the door clicked shut as he left Carl's office.

Loran moved his cup and relocated to a chair across from Cordy—absently tapping his fingers against the table.

"Loran, I know you want to be out searching for your wife," Zac said, "and I have a hundred things to do, so we'll make this a quick briefing. I want to know who endangered Carl's life. A man, a potential killer, is in a private secure tunnel, and no one knows who he is or how he got there. We need to find that person and plug security breaches. I want answers, and everyone must be on the same page."

Four minutes later, Zac greeted Guy and Quint in their virtual presence and added, "I jotted down a list of things we know so far. A security breach at the heart of this government is my primary concern, and there are a few more bullets under each heading. We need to dig deeper as a team. Each knows different pieces of this puzzle."

Evans stood beside a large whiteboard on the opposite wall to take notes. "I'll add more items as we discuss each topic." He pointed to the first item on the board:

1. Drone attack on White House
    - Software hacks—Perimeter lasers and Avenger system down
    - ? Who's behind the attacks—Iran, Russia, Syria, North Korea, others?
    - ? Who's involved? Inside mole? DoD contractor—Einar Zinmansky, other?
    - ? Who & why stab Carl? Was it meant for the president?

Zac raised a finger. "Before we get started, we need to follow up on who hijacked Cordy's flight and why. Is someone trying to infiltrate our government, overthrow democracy, create panic in the markets, or chaos in our international standing?"

"Or worse, steal our military secrets?" Cordy felt her stomach lurch to her throat. *Blasted nausea. No, not here. Not now.* She quieted her mind, trying to control her stomach from its rebellion. She slid a package of crackers from her backpack, nibbled a few, and refocused on the meeting. "Evans, can you follow up with the FBI forensic results run on my laptop and phone? I understand that Pilot Stone's in custody, but I'm afraid the co-pilot, Casper Grest, got away. Not their real names, but maybe we can get accurate IDs."

"Yes." Evans added to the list, "ID who hijacked Cordy's jet?"

Zac leaned forward. "Not just who hijacked her jet. How did a hostile, random plane fly clear across the country and land near the White House without anyone stopping them? Where was air traffic control? Why didn't we know about this? We had no communication."

Cordy said, "Buckley mentioned receiving a phone call while on that jet. It came from someone called H.Q."

"H.Q. again," Zac said. "He won't be easy to track down. He has many minions working under him—Zahair and Amir, for starters. Rumor has it that H.Q. has hypersonic missiles in Iran and plans to send them to Syria. We're still waiting on communication from Usher. Dr. Ping sent him to Iran."

"Usher's in Iran?" Cordy asked. "Cracker mentioned he was on special ops, but he didn't exactly say where. Oh, I almost forgot. Talking about communication…" Cordy dug into her pocket, pulled out what remained of the blocking device she found on the jet, and handed it to Evans. "Bag this, too. Maybe you can find a print. If not, I'd like to know what kind of signal jammer this is."

"Good luck with that," Evans said. "It's pretty mangled."

"I know. I smashed it with my foot." Cordy swallowed a mouthful of crackers and washed them down with a full glass of water—her bladder was already complaining, and she needed a restroom soon.

Evans pointed to the next item on the whiteboard:

- Software hacks—Perimeter lasers and Avenger system down

Cordy leaned forward. "The cybersecurity team barely quarantined the hacks on the lasers and the Avenger system in time to foil the drone attack on the White House."

Guy cleared his throat. "You cut it awfully close, and we couldn't reboot the system."

"That's because the last person to access Avenger was Karl Wyller, that's Karl with a K, and he shut it down. Of course, Carl knows how to spell his own name, so what happened?"

Zac asked, "What did happen?"

"I have no clue," Cordy said. "Everything failed so fast that I had no time to research how it got into the code. I had to work around the problem ASAP."

"How do you know that?" Guy asked.

"As I just mentioned, it's in the code using Karl, obviously a misspelling of Carl, but it suspiciously included his assigned signature code. I spoke with Carl earlier today, and he denied shutting down Avenger. I'm sure he's innocent, but who did it? I need to talk to him again—not about the code shutting down our defense systems, but I would like to hear what he thinks went wrong. I want to know why Zinmansky had access to that computer. I need more facts." Cordy scanned the office. "Better yet, I want to inspect Carl's computer. What if someone used it to shut down the systems?"

"Something's fishy, and I can't believe Carl shut down Avenger either," Guy said. "That's treason!"

"Yes, it is, and this information stays here. It will not be shared with anyone outside of this room." Zac glared at Cordy. "No matter what that code says, someone else will have to fight a potential treason charge because Carl was with me and got stabbed while escorting me through the secret passage to the Bunker."

Cordy agreed. "To be honest, I think whoever logged in was trying to frame him, and I hope to prove that."

Zac bit at his lip. "Cordy, are you sure you're feeling okay? You're a bit pale and have been nibbling those crackers since you entered the room."

"I'm fine. But thanks for asking." *I know they're worried about me, but I have work to do.* Cordy pushed away the crackers and dug through her backpack for supplies. Multitasking was her specialty, but this was getting out of hand. "Don't mind me—I'll just sit here and collect samples from Carl's computer."

Guy cleared his throat. "You know that Homeland already searched—"

Cordy paused. *Oh great, I'm stepping on his toes again.* She slowed her speech and explained what she was doing above and beyond a normal Homeland search. "I know you've done counter surveillance and swept this room for bugs, so I'll just run a deep search on this computer, brush for fingerprints inside the machine, and give the samples over to Evans to submit for forensic testing. I'll be sure you get a copy of all reports."

"Thanks," Evans said. "I'll contact my team."

Zac added, "Someone kidnapped Mo, and stabbed Carl, in the Bunker of all places, then tried to murder you, Loran. I want to know how that happened. Carl's condition is critical, and the real question is, who would attempt an assassination in the White House? And the people around me are falling like flies. Another attempt could happen again. What can we do to prevent this in the future."

"We checked the security tapes and located the exact moment when Carl was stabbed," Guy said.

"I want to see that tape again," Zac said, pointing toward Guy's image on the screen. "Everything happened so fast. Maybe now that we have a moment, we'll notice something we overlooked."

"I'll replay the video, but I have no idea how the man slipped through security, much less with a weapon. One of our greatest threats is that President Spendorf might have been the real target, and Carl accidentally got in the way."

Cordy set to work dusting Carl's keyboard and inside the computer. As a precaution, she also dusted the desk and chair for prints. *Perhaps that is a bit much, but Guy seems preoccupied, and since I'm here, I don't want to miss anything.*

Guy cued the tape and hit play. A long hallway appeared on the screen, presumed to be the secret passage to the Bunker. The whole area was crowded, but the camera zoomed in on three people clustered around the president as they headed for the Bunker, including Carl and the Press Secretary. "Watch for someone in a light gray suit." Guy's brows wrinkled over the bridge of his narrow nose in disgust. "It happens quickly, and all I saw was a sleeve, so don't blink."

The video blurred as the man's hand slid between Carl and the president. Something briefly glinted as Carl nudged Zac toward the outer corridor. The glint grazed Carl's suit coat, and a split second later, the man's gray sleeve bumped against Carl's chest. Carl grunted but shoved Zac forward with barely a flinch. The man's blurred hand became clear.

"Pause it right there." Cordy pointed at the screen. "Is that blood? Zoom in."

The image became larger. Guy frowned. "That could be blood on his sleeve, but we didn't find any splotches in the passageway. Nor did we see a knife, gun, or any other weapon. My team has reviewed this tape repeatedly."

The image piqued her interest, and Cordy leaned in for a closer look. "Who is that man?"

"We've searched the daily visitor logs at every security checkpoint, including all camera feeds," Guy said. "According to the Visitor and Worker Entry System, fifty-three people signed in but hadn't logged out of the White House. At that hour, most were Secret Service agents, household, and operations staff. Fifty-four people evacuated during the crisis, including President Spendorf. We accounted for everyone, and only three men wore light gray suit jackets."

"Who were the three men?" Cordy asked.

"DoD's Undersecretary, an NSA cybersecurity analyst, and the Secretary of Internal Affairs." Guy held up his fingers, ticking each off as he spoke. "We've interviewed all of them and everyone else who left the building at that hour. No suspects, no bloody sleeves."

"What times did each of them arrive?" Cordy jotted a note, her mind turning over possibilities. "What about the unofficial WAVE? Some administrative personnel, such as the president, Vice President Harris, and his wife, don't sign in routinely. We have discussed this in the past." She turned toward Zac. "Did you recognize the man in the gray suit?"

Zac shrugged his shoulders. "To be honest, people were rushing to get out of the building to the Bunker. I was bumped, jostled, and herded from my office without much ceremony. We had to cross from the West Wing all the way to the East. I didn't know Carl had been stabbed until we were down in the Bunker, and I think it even surprised him."

"I'd like to send the complete roster with arrival and departure times, a copy of the security recordings, and this image to Quint and my team." Cordy turned toward the two men on her screen. "Enlarge it, check other tapes in the room to see if any captured the man's face, and run it through several databases. Match check-in times with the names that hadn't logged out before evacuation."

Guy reacted as if she were challenging his work. "Don't you think we've already done that? We only captured the man's arm on camera, and it's as if he knew he was in a blind spot."

Zac's voice remained calm. "I'm sure you have, Guy, but why not put a few more eyes on the problem? Send over the tapes and logs."

"Yes, sir," Guy said.

I'm always dealing with fragile male egos. Cordy finished bagging and labeling samples from Carl's office space, including inside the computer, and then passed them to Evans. "Give me a complete list of prints when they are ready."

"Will do," Evans took the bagged samples.

Cordy made a few more notes, booted up the computer, and inserted a thumb drive to start an analysis program. "Quint, I need the team to track all of Carl's entries in the last twenty-four hours. Assign them to Perry. He already saw the hacked code earlier today."

Quint said in an overly cheerful voice, "Okay if you say so."

Cordy immediately noticed his exaggerated response, ignored the comment, and returned to Carl's computer.

"Now, have you cleared the White House?" Zac asked, hopefully.

"Aah." Guy swallowed as if his mouth had gone bone-dry.

"Why did you hesitate?" Zac asked Guy.

"We searched everywhere and found something in the Oval Office—I'd feel better if Cordy analyzes your workstation."

"Okay, I'll do that after this meeting." Cordy worked quietly on Carl's computer using her systems analyst software. As she tapped the keys, something didn't feel right, so she started taking apart the keyboard while still listening to the conversation.

"Did you only search the Oval Office," Zac asked, "or the whole suite?"

When Guy tugged at his tie, Zac asked, "What else did you find?"

"Two bugs—one under Winston's desk and another in a ceiling light over yours. We also found a tiny camera attached to your wife's photo sitting in the center of your credenza."

"Aha, and here's another bug!" Cordy sat next to a disassembled keyboard—holding a pair of forceps clamped around a small chip. "I found it embedded under the Shift key."

Evans held out a plastic evidence bag. "I'll take that and dust it for fingerprints."

"Thanks." Cordy dropped the bug into the bag. "Can you label that while I dust inside the keyboard?"

Evans nodded and held the bag up to the light. "Wow, I've never seen a low-frequency KeySweeper up close. It's smaller than I imagined."

"A what?" Zac asked.

"It's a digital recording device," Cordy said. "It doesn't track human voices, so they weren't eavesdropping on our conversation. This little bug listens for keyboard taps. Each key makes a unique sound. The right software records every keystroke typed, decodes, and then sends it to a private Ethernet account or wireless device. I'm sure I can trace the path."

"How did we miss it?" Guy asked. "I had Carl's office checked for bugs before Zac decided to meet here today. And I know Carl runs routine security sweeps."

"Even I nearly missed it," Cordy pointed out. "We don't usually take apart the equipment when testing its security. This little device avoids detection from external sensors, but I noticed it seemed sluggish whenever I capitalized a letter."

"So, whoever planted it wasn't eavesdropping on our conversation." Zac leaned forward, his frown deepening.

"That's right," Cordy agreed. "They were listening for keyboard taps."

"Doesn't everyone type differently?" Zac asked. "Winston can type 110 words a minute, while most of my typing is hunt and peck."

"It's not how fast or slow one types," Cordy said. "A bug like this would bypass most secure software protocol, and no typed password would be safe."

Evans held another plastic bag for Cordy to place the inner keyboard samples. "Last year, you told us our passwords were protected. Are they, or aren't they secure?"

"They are safe down to the last minute," Cordy said. "DoD uses secure IDs, and all passwords regenerate authentication every minute. However, this bug records five hours of data and then blasts the collected information over five seconds using only the latest password generated. I'm beginning to see how someone could tap into your office and this network."

"So, someone has access to DoD's passwords and data. What do they plan to do with it?" Evans asked.

"Better search every computer, laptop, and inside the keyboards." Zac's index finger pointed toward the corner desk. "If someone has access to inside Carl's computer, there may be others. Maybe even in my office. Guy said they already found a bug."

Marv, the president's Secret Service agent, moved from the front door while speaking into his wrist radio. "Sorry to interrupt, sir, but I have orders to move you back to the Bunker ASAP. Kyle's on his way here."

"What happened now?" Zac's voice remained calm, but Cordy noticed he gnawed on his lower lip.

"One of our agents found a body in a West Wing bathroom near the Oval Office—the small one next to the Roosevelt Room. We have no log of him entering the White House. The unidentified man has a dark beard and mustache. Even more mysterious is that he's wearing a light gray suit coat like the man who stabbed Carl, and there's blood on the right sleeve. He also has a dark area over his left eyebrow, maybe a bruise. It's not much of a description, but we don't know how he got into the building undetected so far."

"How did he die?" Zac asked. "Any sign of a struggle?"

"I don't have any details yet, sir." Marv moved closer. "Your safety is my primary concern right now."

"Why wasn't I notified?" Guy asked.

"Check your messages," Marv said. "They just found the body, and it wasn't there twenty minutes ago. Kyle says the medical examiner is on her way, and he's checking with the agents assigned to the front entrance to see how this man got past the checkpoint undetected."

Cordy frequently used mnemonic devices to jar her memory, and for some reason, the comment, *The body found in the bathroom near the Roosevelt Room has a dark area over the left eye,* popped into her mind—*like FDR.* She wanted to check out the body, too, but Marv whisked Zac away so fast that she didn't have time to ask questions.

Zac noticed her concern and asked, "Is there a room at the Bunker, where we can continue our meeting?"

"I can't go to the Bunker," Braun said. "I'm undercover, and Loran's dead, remember?"

"That does create a problem." Zac rubbed his chin. "You're to remain in Loran's custody. Your undercover work won't be easy— no one can find out you are both in the street. Get out of here, fly low, and free Emma from Zahair's clutches. Report your findings through Cordy since she will be working with you from here. My wingspan only goes so far. Catch this bastard, and I want him alive. Hopefully, he can lead us to H.Q., who I believe is the mastermind of these attacks." Zac turned to Cordy. "In the meantime, resume your duties, and let me know as soon as you clear the Oval Office."

Agent Kyle, Head of the Secret Service, rapped on Carl's office door and entered. "Ready? Our agents are anxious to move. We cleared the tunnel and hallway."

Zac stood. "Cordy, let Winston know if you need anything. Evans, assist her."

"This is a team effort." Cordy glanced up from Carl's keyboard as she reassembled it. "We'll keep you updated, and Zac, stay safe."

Marv gathered Zac's papers with one brisk swipe of his left hand. His right hand hovered over his pistol, "Time to go."

Several Secret Service agents surrounded Zac, who hastened to follow Kyle out of the office. Rapid footsteps echoed in the hallway and faded. Marv stayed glued to Zac's back.

Watching them marching away in lockstep, Cordy thought, *No one will get a second chance at Zac's life if Marv has anything to do with it. They will have to go through him first.* She made a quick pit stop and called Carl at the hospital for a few minutes. He was still on a ventilator, but his wife, Officer Peggy Wyller, was at his side. Cordy needed to get some answers directly from Carl, but she would have to wait until he could talk coherently enough to communicate.

Cordy had Peggy transfer her call to the hospital operator and spoke briefly with her usual pilot, Buckley, who had undergone surgery for the removal of bullets to his left arm and leg. "The doctor said I have a concussion, but I'll be discharged in the morning, and a few bullets won't stop me from flying you again soon."

"Thanks for everything and take care," Cordy said. "I'll see you soon."

Teams Unite

Sept. 11 – 4:42 p.m. EDT, Carl's Office, Washington, D.C./
2:42 p.m. MDT, Fort Collins, Colorado

After President Spendorf left the office, a heavy silence filled the space behind him. The room became stuffy. Even Quint, back in Colorado, waited, wondering where to begin. Cordy felt every nerve fiber spark—on active duty, ready to bolt into battle. It was time to get some answers and move forward.

Cordy wanted to assume control immediately but faced multiple issues and did not want to step on any more toes. She asked, "Guy, can you have your team go back and search all offices? If more computers are infected, notify me."

"We'll start immediately," Guy said, "but I need to follow up on that body, and I want you to check the Oval Office."

"Okay, I will, but Zac is safe for now, and we need more information." Cordy checked her list. "Did the FBI locate Zinmansky's laptop?"

"No," Loran said, his forehead resting in the palm of his hand. "But surely he doesn't have clearance to classified DoD data, and the person would be pretty stupid not to disguise the name on his files if he planned to steal any documents."

Guy asked, "If he did steal classified information, where would he hide the metadata files?"

"The cache, and if I know Carl, he'd surely have a link to that laptop. Let me take a look." Cordy tapped away on the keyboard to open all linked files. "Quint, I found something. It's definitely an ini file for the RCV that Braun tested this morning, but where are the schematics and software for the drones? I found a file on the network, but all local links are missing. There are only headers left. All the data has been transferred, but to whom or where?"

"If Zinmansky has already sold the data, we're racing against time. We need to secure everything without causing any panic," Quint said.

"This contractor has a DoD laptop loaded with our most sensitive intel," Cordy felt her temper rise. "Why would anyone inside our defense system allow that? I want to talk directly to Carl, but he's still on the ventilator, so I'll need to speak to the Deputy Director."

"You mentioned Zinmansky has sensitive intel," Guy said. "Concerning what?"

Cordy's fingers continued to fly across the keys. "I can see here that he has info on the Maven II drones and RCV, for starters."

"The FBI has already downloaded a profile on him," Evans said. "I'll send over what we have."

"We must find that software while we still can," Cordy insisted. "We need to leave no stone unturned. Start searching for potential buyers by probing any cell phones, emails, credit cards, or landline calls, as well as Zinmansky's search history. I'm giving Quint access to continue the search, but the best criminals rarely leave trails."

Quint asked, "Does any of the laptop's data link into DoD's criminal data list? It could give us potential buyers."

"That's a good idea, Quint." Cordy opened a few files. "I'm sending you all of his latest links. Let me know if you find any connections."

"Thanks," Quint made a notation on his to-do list. "Once we compile the data, I'll have Perry and Svetlana review all the contacts and narrow it down to potential buyers."

"What kind of contractor is Zinmansky?" Cordy peered directly at Guy, who was fussing with his tie, which appeared to need straightening. "You said he heads up a new firm—weapons, software development, aerospace? Does anyone know him?"

Guy's face paled. "He's researching drones, and I believe he's heading up the modified Maven II drone project. Carl will know for sure."

"This situation is even worse than I expected," Loran continued, tapping his fingers against the tabletop. "He must have had access to that test drone that exploded."

Evans walked over and placed his hand over Loran's drumming fingers. "Enough. I know you want to search for your wife. We're getting bogged down in too many details, and I think we've already moved into the second item on the board. Cordy, keep working on your end, and let's quickly move on."

Cordy glanced at the board:

2. Attack during RCV/drone test
    - Who activated the drone attack? Zinmansky? Zahair?
    - What type of explosive?
    - What kind of ordinance was used in the drone, who planted it, and where did it come from?

Loran caught Braun's attention. "You have a real hardass after your hide. General Shyler will send you and your team to hell if he can. He won't hold himself responsible—especially after Rusty's death."

The words on the board blurred as tears pooled in Cordy's eyes. "Oh, Braun, Rusty's dead? What happened? How horrible." Her breath caught in her throat in a silent sob. She could say no more. *Poor Brit. They haven't even been married for a year. I have to get to the bottom of this.*

Braun grabbed her trembling hand to still it and whispered, "It was my worst nightmare… I'll tell you later."

Quint asked, "Shyler? Why is he involved?"

"General Shyler." Braun's gray eyes darkened with anger. "He's responsible for the DoD test that nearly wiped out my team this morning, and he's accusing me of treason."

"That doesn't make any sense." Cordy tapped Shyler's name into Carl's computer, searching for any information. She already knew he was a four-star general, a Desert Storm hero, and well-respected, even though he was known for his temper. Whatever he ordered was followed to the letter. Several emails popped up. She skimmed the top two and hopped from her chair. "Oh, no! Braun. I may have a clue as to why he is accusing you of treason."

"What is it?" Braun's heart thudded so fast that Cordy could see his carotid artery throb with each beat.

Like the jigsaw puzzles she loved, she snapped pieces together in her mind. Every loop, tab, and slot shifted, enlarging the image. *General Shyler is responsible for testing the RCV and Maven II drone. Did he mastermind the test failure this morning? I'm missing some vital pieces, but the whole picture will unquestionably emerge in time.* "I just ran across an email."

"What do you mean?" Braun's left eyebrow lifted.

"The White House was attacked, President Spendorf's life threatened, the Secretary of State is missing, Carl was stabbed, and your whole crew nearly wiped out. You're the only one who walked away virtually unharmed, and I just learned that at 6:10 this morning, $10 million was transferred to an offshore account—in your name."

Braun nearly choked with anger. "Are you out of your mind? I don't know anything about an offshore account. You know I never would take a bribe."

A flash crossed Cordy's mind. *Was the money placed in a foreign account to divert blame to Braun? Who would do such a thing, and why target him?* "We need to discover who is behind this and fast because once the media gets wind of it, you will be fired, arrested, and charged with treason. I know that you're innocent, but this looks like a big payoff was sent to you."

Braun's voice rose in pitch. "Who sent that lie to Shyler? I certainly wouldn't harm my team. I'd give my life for this country. I've put it on the line more than once."

Cordy placed her hand over his clenched fists. "Calm down. We'll get to the bottom of this."

Braun returned a squeeze of her fingers, let go, then turned toward Loran. "Someone's trying to set me up."

Cordy drilled down further. "It appears the money was sent from three different accounts and pooled together—one from Wells Fargo in the U.S., which should be easy to track, another came from Tehran, Iran, and the last one from Ryazan, Russia. The return address on the email is blocked. I need to contact Cracker and Rozalina again. Maybe they can track the account from Russia, but it will be hard to trace funds from Iran."

Braun turned toward Guy. "How do the modified drones fit into our defense system? They aren't safe."

"Project Maven II is top secret because of the possible implications." Guy seemed to gloat over Homeland Security's knowledge of this detail when the FBI remained in the dark.

"That's what General Shyler hinted at," Braun said, "but there's more he's not telling me." He turned to Loran again. "What do you know?"

Loran's brow furrowed. "One thing is for sure. You don't know anything about the money, do you? I was worried that this might be a setup from the start."

"You knew about the money?" Braun asked. "Is that why you ambushed me as I left General Shyler's office?"

"No," Loran nearly shouted, then muttered, "I hadn't heard about the money, just that the test went poorly, the drone was weaponized without our knowledge, and you threatened to resign. That I refused to let happen."

Guy added, "To be safe, this stays in the room. DoD plans to replace its entire fleet of unmanned vehicles with the RCV and modified drones you tested this morning. If any of this, lands in the wrong hands, every drone we currently have in the air will be grounded, and those weapons could turn on us—extremely deadly."

Braun grimaced. "What should we do?"

"It appears that your hands are tied at the moment," Cordy said. "I'll work invisibly for a time—until we can prove your innocence."

"My hands may be tied," Braun said, "but I placed a bugging device on the door jamb to Shyler's office. We can watch what's going on behind the scenes, and hopefully, I can protect myself from these charges."

"You placed a bug? Was it one of mine?" Cordy asked. When Braun nodded, she turned and asked, "Quint, did anything pop up on your screen?"

"No, what frequency?" Quint asked. "I'll put a search on the GPS coordinates."

"Ten megahertz," Braun said. "I haven't had time to track it, but everything should be recording."

Quint pulled out an electronic pad, typed in the GPS coordinates, and hit search. "I'll track the recording and update you."

"Thanks," Cordy said.

"We're undercover for a reason," Loran said. "I suspect Zahair may have something to do with this. Remember, he sent a transaction from Wells Fargo Bank. Maybe it's part of the bribe, but we haven't yet figured out where it was sent."

"I'll find out what I can." Cordy typed an encrypted message to Cracker.

Guy wrung his hands. "Also, track down where the other funds originated and from whom. We'll need to get access, and that may take some time. I know someone who can help us track funds from Iran, but we need more information."

Quint gave a shrill whistle. "I found it! Listen to this. It's from that little bug Braun planted in Shyler's office. I'll start the recording from the beginning." There was brief static then, and the secretary's voice came across the bug, "Someone is on the phone for you, General." She sounded scared. "He refuses to give me his name, and his voice is disguised. He says it's urgent. I'm sorry if I—"

"It's okay, Miss Ward. Put him through, and there's no need to record the call."

"But you said to be sure to record every phone call," Miss Ward reminded him.

"I'll take care of it this time," Shyler insisted. "In fact, it's been a long and unusual day. Go home and rest. You deserve some time off."

"Thank you, sir." Miss Ward put the call through.

Shyler waited a few moments before answering, "This is General Shyler. How may I help you?"

"I'll be brief, General," a baritone voice said, "I fear your testing team has a mole, Agent Braun Hastings."

"What?" Shyler sounded surprised. "Who is this? Why disguise your voice?"

"You can never be too careful," the baritone said. "Stay alert, and don't be fooled by his report. Agent Hastings seized the Maven II drone and RCV, and we're tracking an overseas account as a payoff. I'll send you an email as proof. He may be dealing with a higher bidder. Pull out all the stops to prevent that."

"Yes, immediately," Shyler chuckled. "How did you hear about the—"

"Later," the call disconnected.

Braun interrupted, "So someone other than Shyler is pulling the strings. Go to real time. We can listen to the rest later."

Quint went to live recording to capture a disguised male voice, "Tell me what the hell's happening! You promised to ship the equipment at 10 p.m. tomorrow night. Is that still happening?"

"There's too much heat in D.C. right now," Shyler whispered. "I told you from the beginning I don't want any part of this, and why didn't you call on your burner phone?"

"Listen, those weapons ship no matter what," the voice said. "Our investors already paid. Cancel delivery, and you'll face hell."

"No way, and lower your voice," Shyler said.

"What do you suggest we do with $50 million worth of firepower that doesn't exist?" the voice asked. "H.Q. will have our heads. We need it by Thursday to make adaptations. It makes its debut in Houston a week from Friday."

"More than your heads—I'll have your hides," a second, lower bass-disguised voice shouted. "Shut your mouth. Both of you—Now!"

"Sorry," the first voice squeaked.

"Shh, your office can have ears," the bass voice said.

"Highly unlikely," Shyler said. "I do a sweep every morning."

"In that case," the first voice said, "Do as you promised or pay the price with your life."

The bass voice added, "Clean house, or I will!"

Shyler must have had second thoughts. There was a high-pitched squeal. Shyler swore. It sounded like he slammed his fist on the desk and cursed again. "What? A bug, and I just let that rotten scumbag of a traitor walk away this morning. Give me all the proof you have on Agent Hastings. I'll deliver and be sure he pays—with his life." Then, there was nothing but static.

"He found your bug," Cordy gasped. "Braun, you can't be seen by anyone. General Shyler is a very powerful man."

Quint rubbed his chin. "I wonder who he was talking to. Could it have been Zinmansky?"

"Or maybe Zahair," Loran said. "Either way, Shyler's involved, and he believes you're a traitor."

"I'm not the traitor! He is, and I bet the second disguised voice was H.Q. It sounded like the guy on the first call taken by the secretary." Braun's fingers clenched into fists, "Whoever he is, I'm going to find him. Shyler thinks I'm a mole. Does he actually think I killed Rusty and injured my team? Is it a wonder he's after me?" Braun got up from the chair and started pacing. "Somehow, $10 million shows up in an overseas account in my name? How did that happen? Now I'm a terrorist against my own country, and how does he know H.Q.?"

"And why does Shyler have a burner as a direct line to a terrorist?" Cordy asked. "We'll monitor him closely. Quint, see what else was recorded. Hopefully, we captured more incriminating evidence. See if you can track that burner phone Shyler mentioned. Maybe we can collect more data."

Braun paused his pacing. His brows narrowed, eyes glared, and fists clenched. "Weapons are to be delivered tomorrow night. I don't know where, but we know when. If it's a mole he wants, then I will be that mole and track down the real terrorist."

Cordy grabbed his clenched fist. "Braun, what are you going to do? I've seen that look before and don't want you to do anything rash. Please, let us help you."

"There may be a better way," Loran said. "We'll work as a team. We've done it before. Braun, don't shut us out."

Braun pulled out his chair and sat down. "I'm already undercover, and if I can't find the real mole, I'll make sure he finds me. I want the FBI to put an agent on Shyler. Watch his every move. If he sneezes, I want to hear about it."

"Okay, that's better," Loran shifted his weight. "I'll contact Gray. He'll have to make the call since I'm still dead, and he'll have to contact DoD. Shyler would fall under their department."

"No, let this fall under Homeland," Guy said, "or better yet, let me call Dr. Ping. Gray is busy finding Mo, and it can't come from Loran. He believes you're dead, and Braun's a traitor." Guy called Dr. Ping, replayed the bug's recording, and listened in on the cell's speaker as Ping responded.

"I'll take care of this," Dr. Ping phoned General Shyler. The call went to Shyler's voice mail, "I am currently unavailable. Please leave a message, and I'll return your call."

Ping replied, "General Shyler, this is Dr. Ping. We have an urgent matter we must discuss ASAP. This is regarding the recent Maven II drone test at Aberdeen Proving Grounds. I fear someone was involved in covert activities, and your life may be endangered. I'm sending over two Secret Service agents ASAP for your protection. They will escort you to my office to discuss our concerns." Ping disconnected Shyler's call and said to Guy, "I'll keep you posted."

"Thanks." Guy had barely signed off when his cell phone rang. He checked the caller ID, "It's the ME." Guy answered and listened briefly. "What? They found Novichok in the president's teapot. I'll be right there!" Guy glanced toward Cordy. "I gotta go." He logged off and raced out the door.

"Did Guy say Novichok?" Loran asked. "That's a Russian poison that kills off spies, right?"

Braun nodded. "Guy has his hands full, so this is up to us. I have a real concern about the explosives and ammo used by the drone attack. They could be the weapons Shyler talked about." He removed a metal bullet and a few shards from his pocket. "I took these from Rusty's wounds. As you can see, the bullet is undamaged even though it went through his Kevlar vest and hit bone. It appears to be made of hardened polymer. See the red tip? I bet you could reload it, and it would fire like new."

Evans examined the bagged bullets and fragments. "That's armor-piercing and illegal."

Braun handed the evidence bag of metal debris to Evans for analysis. "These are the only breadcrumbs I have to lead us to our enemy. Whoever framed me made this look like I activated the weapons. Help me find the real terrorist."

Evans reexamined the bullets. "These are definitely military-grade—probably not hollow-tipped as there are no damages on impact. It was not made in America. It could be from Syria or Iran. We have government contracts allowing us to tap into secure databases."

Braun turned toward Cordy. "I want your team to analyze the weapon's program code. Just work behind the scenes. Quint can help and get back to you."

Evans added, "Cordy, I'll give you and the team access so you can do more research."

"Thanks," she nodded toward the board. "Okay, Quint, take the lead on analyzing the program code, but your to-do list is growing too long. Prioritize the list and bring in our CrowdStrike team. Ask Alysha to coordinate like she did last year."

"Should we add her to this call?" Quint asked.

Evans shook his head. "Too many classified tasks."

"I'll be glad to prioritize and run the list by Cordy before making assignments." Quint typed another note on his e-list.

Cordy heaved a sigh. "Having CrowdStrike's help takes a load off my mind. We can move on."

Evans lit the third item with his laser pointer. "That brings us to another dilemma. We know Farzad Zahair is back in the country. He may not be behind all of this, but we have solid evidence that he kidnapped Loran's wife and attempted to kill Loran." The board read:

3. Farzad Zahair – alias Ingram Freeman
    - Emma Sloan – kidnapped

Cordy held up a finger. "And don't forget another kidnapping, the Secretary of State. Could it have also been Zahair?"

"Perhaps," Loran said. "Our Deputy Director is working with Chief Jackson and Mo's wife, Sophia. I hope we can narrow down his location and hear from the hostage-taker soon. If it was Zahair, we'll find Emma and the secretary."

Evans added these to the board and moved on to the next item:

- Drive-by shooting targeting Loran Sloan and Braun Hastings (coincidence?)

"We'll start with Emma's kidnapping first," Evans said to Loran. "Tell us what happened to your wife. What do we know?"

Loran launched with a vengeance and explained that he had faked his death so he could go undercover to find his wife. He showed the photo of Emma's kidnapping from his security camera.

Evans added, "We found a partial left index print on Emma's trunk. It was Zahair's. He left a bomb inside, but I defused it."

"We now know he used a different rental car to run us off the road before shooting out my windshield," Loran said.

Braun recounted being shot at and run off the road. Between Evans, Loran, and Braun, the car accident scene became etched vividly into Cordy's mind.

Loran said, "I can understand me being a target, but why Emma?"

"Speaking of Emma, were you able to find her cell phone?" Cordy asked.

"Zahair drove over it. I sent it to forensics, but they couldn't find any data. Braun suggested I pass it over to you." Evans pointed to his backpack. "I'll give it to you after the briefing."

Cordy jotted "check Emma's phone" to her list.

"Were you able to match that strange, mossy substance on my driveway?" Loran asked. "It came from the SUV's tire treads."

Braun leaned forward. "Where would the tires pick up moss?"

Evans added: "Strange moss" on the board. "The FBI lab is researching the components. We haven't found the source, but it must be from somewhere in the vicinity since the odometer logged only sixty miles since Zahair leased the car."

Loran agreed. "He would want to stay close if he were involved in any of the terrorist attacks."

Cordy's head snapped in his direction. "Do you mean the cyberattack on Avenger or launching the missiles over the White House?"

"Launching the missiles? Maybe, but I meant the bomb threat and subway collision at the Metro Station earlier this morning. People were trapped underground for over an hour. Emma had to stay after her shift to treat the casualties."

"So, he kidnapped her after creating chaos in D.C.?" Cordy clarified. "I was so focused on the cyberattack that I didn't realize it was far worse." Cordy made another note. "What time was the accident at the Metro station? Did it happen at the same time as the attack on the White House?"

Evans shook his head. "No, it happened around midnight. Potomac Electric had a faulty transmission line in Southern Maryland. There were rolling outages. Terrorists took advantage of the dark and looted the subway and downtown area. Power to the White House didn't go down until 1:30 a.m."

Cordy asked, "Were the defense systems deactivated at any time during the outage?" In her notes, she underlined Evans' reply:

"Defense programs stayed operational and on battery power until the electricity returned around 2:08 a.m. I'm not sure when they got access to the drone."

"That's probably why we had no warning at headquarters." Cordy turned to Quint. "We need to remedy this in the future. We should be notified immediately when any device goes on to backup battery power."

Evans added another note to the whiteboard: "And the White House generators failed during the outage."

"We better add that to our programs, too," Quint said. "By the way, I've been thinking about that moss you mentioned earlier. Was it Dicranum? It thrives on old granite."

Evans pulled out his notes. "Yes, that and lichen, but where would a pile of granite stone—"

"Granite? Somewhere within sixty miles? Hmm. What about Rock Creek Park?" Cordy smiled at the memory of her father taking her there on a field trip. "It's only a mile from the Capitol building. Hundreds of sandstone, marble, and some carved granite statues were removed from the White House during the 1958 renovation. Mamie Eisenhower oversaw the project but had no authority to sell the old stone, so it was gathered and piled behind a maintenance shed hidden alongside an unmarked trail."

"So, how do you know about this place?" Evans asked.

"Dad brought me there once when I was a kid." Cordy pulled up a D.C. map. "I loved all the ornate pieces, but it was overgrown and abandoned even then." Locating the park, she tapped the area a few times. "It would be an ideal hiding place to take Emma."

Loran hopped from his chair and peered at the location over Cordy's shoulder. "What are we waiting for? Let's check it out!"

"Slow down, Loran," Evans motioned with his hands, palms out. "I know you're eager to find your wife, but let our departments help. You are dead, remember? You can't just jump in a car and drive to the park."

Braun agreed. "Send up aerial surveillance. Check the area for suspect activity."

"Emma's been missing for ten hours." Loran dropped into his chair and returned to drumming his fingers on the table. "We have to find her—89% of victims die within the first 24 hours." Loran twitched and crossed his right leg over his left knee one second, then switched back to his previous position the next. The man couldn't sit still. "I want to search right now. Not sit here in this blasted briefing."

"We already have two FBI divisions working on it, and you've called for a SWAT team," Evans reminded him. "Let them do their job."

Loran pulled out his cell phone. The man was haggard, desperation written all over his face. "I don't want us falling over ourselves in hysteria. That might get her killed. I want to get my wife back unharmed! I'm checking in with the SWAT team." He pushed back his chair and stood. "Sorry to leave you, but Zac's not here, and I have to find Emma."

Braun motioned to Loran. "Wait, I'll go with you."

Evans nodded and informed the group that Carl's office had long-range base radios. He suggested that each of them take one and log in, and then Cordy and he would take on the lead roles. "Since none of the other team members know about your undercover operation, we'll need to maintain open communication throughout the mission." Evans acknowledged, "It won't be easy for Cordy, who is already pulled in ten different directions."

"We can do this with the team's help." Cordy opened a cabinet near Carl's desk. She assigned a radio to each man, Braun, Loran, and Evans, and then took one for herself. They linked up to Evans' radio frequency for a test. Cordy started packing up her gear. "I guess we're adjourned. Let's get moving."

Braun pushed back his chair and stood. "Zahair may have answers as to who weaponized those drones and why I've been set up to take the fall for the failed weapons test this morning."

Cordy said. "In the meantime, I need to check in with Guy. The medical examiner should have briefed him on that body by now and keep us posted."

"Got it," Braun said, turning to Loran. "Before you leave, have Gray order a background check on Shyler. Ensure Dr. Ping assembles the best team to set up the trap."

Loran turned to Braun, "I know you want to lead this, but you must let it go for tonight. I need your help to free Emma. I'm not waiting until tomorrow to rescue her." Loran grabbed the radio. "So, I'm also sending a federal team to backup Ping as recon ops. If Shyler's shipping weapons overseas, they'll find them. The general won't know what hit him."

"If I can't take the lead, at least keep me in the loop." Braun kissed Cordy and then gave Loran his full attention. "I need to change for combat duty. We'll take the back way to the supply room and get our gear. This won't be a cakewalk."

Loran quickly called Agent Gray and relayed his messages about Shyler and tracking down Zahair. "Contact Dr. Ping to coordinate our effort, but be sure Shyler doesn't leave their sight." Loran nodded in response to something Gray said, disconnected the call, and headed for the door as he updated Braun. "The FBI will send helicopters over the park to narrow our search. Once we've located Emma, we'll send in the SWAT team."

"We'll need a vehicle with traction in this weather," Braun said. "I'll line up a Humvee, large enough to load our equipment. Once we go live with the SWAT team, we must patch them into Cordy." He paused in the doorway and turned. "Will that work for you?"

"I'll check out the Oval Office in the meantime," Cordy said. "Stay safe."

Braun met Loran in the hallway as he left the office with renewed energy.

Cordy's mind raced while ticking through items—her list growing. She signed off with Quint and turned toward Evans. "Get me the names of anyone's fingerprints you find, and let me have what's left of Emma's cell phone. I'll examine the chip as soon as possible, but I must check the Oval Office's computers first. By then, we'll need to be on task with Braun, Loran, and the SWAT team."

"I'll drop off these evidence bags with our team and meet you at the Oval Office in five minutes." Evans gathered up his things and left ahead of Cordy. Before doing anything else, she followed up with Guy and then used the restroom.

When Cordy returned to Carl's office, she met a familiar face, Secret Service Agent Trudo, standing outside the door. He held up his ID for her to verify. "Rumor has it, there's an unknown internal mole."

"Surely, I'm safe among my colleagues," Cordy said.

"You've been kidnapped once, and Guy's not taking any chances. He sent me to escort you to the Oval Office."

"Thanks, I appreciate your concern."

H.Q.'s Secret

Sept. 11 – 5:08 p.m. EDT, Shyler's office, Washington, D.C.

General Shyler couldn't believe someone had bugged his office. *How and when did it happen? It had to have been Braun Hastings. No one else would dare to be so bold. Braun left my office at 6:22 a.m., and I didn't discover the device until after 5 p.m. That means I've been exposed for over 10 hours.*

Shyler reviewed his day to see how safe he was to stay in his office or if he should move to his secret headquarters. He had arrived at 2:50 a.m., ten minutes after the Code Q alarm, recalling how his mind flew in a dozen directions. *What caused the Code Q? As Chairman of the Joint Chief of Staff, I should know what caused the alarm.*

He'd met with foreign heads of state worldwide, set up meetings for senior diplomats, and traveled overseas to attend conferences, even as a keynote speaker last month in Germany. *Surely, none of those activities would lead to a Code Q.*

He had checked his security camera as he did every time he entered his office, scanned for any surveillance devices, and sighed in relief when he found no evidence of spying. *Today could be challenging—I promised the impossible to H.Q. and sent a dignitary's brother on an unknown mission in Iran; I heard that Zahair had delivered the drone and RCV specs hidden in a magic euro, but I have no real proof, only H.Q.'s word. Is that what triggered the Code Q?* Sweat broke out across his brow. *No, I covered all my tracks, although Braun came close to the truth.*

Shyler bolted upright when a call came in from Dr. Ping. He waited for his secretary to answer, and then, too late, he remembered he had sent her home early since she, too, had arrived in the wee hours of the morning. By the time he reached for the phone, voice mail had been triggered, "General Shyler, this is Dr. Ping. We have an urgent matter we must discuss ASAP. This is regarding the recent Maven II drone test at Aberdeen Proving Grounds. I fear someone was involved in covert activities, and your life may be endangered. I'm sending over two Secret Service agents ASAP for your protection. They will escort you to my office to discuss our concerns."

Shyler felt his blood boil and didn't wait for another second. His mind raced through several scenarios of what Dr. Ping really wanted to discuss. He felt numb, his legs wobbly, and his hand shook as he grabbed his briefcase. Glancing around his office, he had to think. *Did Ping know about H.Q.? What will they be looking for?* He stuffed three top-secret files, a government-issued cell, and a burner phone inside the case, and locked it. Eyeing the small duffle he kept packed for rare occasions, he snatched it, too, and left the building—the remains of Braun's crushed bug in his pants pocket. On his way to the parking lot, he ducked into the men's room and changed into civilian clothes.

Knowing he had a target on his back, the general stayed out of the line of the security cameras, he set the briefcase on the back seat of his car, slammed the door, and calmly sliced his finger. He dripped several drops of blood onto the ground by the front car door, smeared the key fob, and tossed the keys under a nearby vehicle. He checked to see that all was clear. Satisfied that no one was around, he attached an IED to the underside of his car and walked away. Shyler was already at the end of Hayes Street Pedestrian Tunnel, turning onto Navy Drive, when the blast sounded—imagining his car in flames.

He stopped at the Pentagon City Mall, picked up another cell phone and a few other items, boarded the Yellow Line at Pentagon Station, headed to Huntington, Virginia, and called JCJ300 for protection. He was surprised to hear the call forwarded to the usual encrypted voice and then instructed to enter an unfamiliar code. *Why the change?* He'd proceed with caution, making his own backup plan just in case of any snafus.

Continuing The Search

Justice Sophia Hendrum hated to sit idly, killing time while waiting to answer the silent FBI hostage line. All she could think about was her fear for her husband, Mo. She had no appetite, couldn't sleep, and her heart raced every time Chief Jackson reached for his cell phone. It was never a call to the hotline. That phone sat on the conference room table—dead enough that it should have been placed in a tomb. Her head throbbed, and her mouth was dry as cotton. She took a sip of water and tapped her fingers on the edge of the chair's armrest.

"Relax." Chief Jackson put his hand over hers and gave it a gentle squeeze. "We're not giving up until we find him."

Sophia nodded. "Let's be honest. I nearly froze today in that newsroom."

"You're under a lot of stress," Chief said. "No one expects—"

"Stop." Sophia placed a finger over her lips until he quit speaking. "I may have hesitated, but I've been following my instincts for a long time now in the courtroom, and I think we're searching in the wrong places."

"Where should we be looking?" FBI's Deputy Director Neil Gray asked as he walked into the Conference Room with a steaming cup of coffee. Sophia and Chief had declined an offer of any refreshments.

Sophia stood and walked closer to Gray. "Who will benefit from keeping Mo silenced?"

Gray thought for a moment. "Many countries face increased sanctions—Iran, Russia, and Syria, to name a few."

"Yes, but removing the Secretary of State will not alter that." Sophia took a jagged breath. These thoughts had been haunting her mind all day. It felt good to talk about them. "A demand for ransom from me doesn't make any sense either. It's a desperate plea. Ransom may be paid for Mo's death by one of those country's leaders, but again, the result could increase the risk of hardships and even war. No, I've thought this over. Whoever took Mo plans to kill him."

"If that was the plan all along, they could have murdered him in the parking lot and left the body without going to the effort of capturing him." Chief Jackson lowered his voice and continued, "Sophia, we can't give up hope."

Sophia clasped her trembling hands and turned to Agent Gray. "How did they get access inside the secured parking area?"

"That's hard to determine." Gray set his coffee cup on the table. "No electricity meant the scanners were down, and the backup generator failed. Once they opened the gates, the security agents monitored the area best as they could under the circumstances. Still, I'm afraid someone slipped through without cameras, badge readers, and proper staff levels to survey the area. It shouldn't have happened, and we must improve our emergency protocols."

"I don't believe this was a random act. It was too perfectly timed." Sophia paced. "A power outage at the same time as Mo's capture, and the backup generator failure wasn't an accident. Someone had to control the system—watching and waiting for an opportune time."

"Do you feel like someone is watching you?" Chief Jackson ran his hand through the silver hair at his right temple. Sophia knew he frequently slicked back his hair when mulling ideas through his head. Chief continued, "You had a late-night snack at a closed cafeteria. Anyone who might have noticed? Was it written in your appointment book? Or do you think someone listened in on your phone calls? How would anyone know when you were leaving?"

Sophia tapped a finger against her chin and replayed thoughts of her early morning when she left her office. "The rendezvous was unplanned, so, no, I didn't have it on my appointment log. I called Mo, and he later texted me." Sophia closed her eyes to get a clearer picture. "I don't remember seeing anyone following me. Wait!" Her eyes flew open. "I did meet a short man in a soaked trench coat."

"Did he talk to you?" She felt the force of that whiskey-colored stare as he looked through her.

"I didn't get a good view of the man. A black umbrella hid his face, which I thought was odd since he was walking in the tunnel at the time, but he was drenched and may have just come out of the rain. He asked, 'Where is the White House entrance?' I stopped and gave him directions, and he went back outside. I never saw him again."

"Was there anything threatening about the man?" Gray asked, sitting down at the table and sipping coffee.

Sophia paused her pacing. "No, not that I noticed then, but if he was an employee, wouldn't he already know how to enter the White House? I know the Hill is confusing, but he wasn't even in the right tunnel." She dropped into a chair between Gray and Chief Jackson. "I want answers."

Gray reached for his radio.

"Who are you contacting?" Chief asked.

"Head of Secret Service, he'll know who was assigned to the House employee entrance early this morning," Gray said. "He may even know who this man is and if he ever arrived."

"Agent Kyle Benson, how may I help you?" came from the radio.

"Kyle, this is Neil Gray. Were you on duty during the late night/ early morning shift?"

"Yes, and what a night," Kyle said.

"Who was stationed at the House employee entrance between 11 p.m. and 2 a.m.?" Gray asked.

Kyle gave him a couple of names. "Why do you ask?"

Gray explained, "We wondered if a man with a black umbrella—"

Kyle's phone rang. "One moment, I have another call." There was a pause. "It's Guy. I need to take this. Can you hold or call back? It might be a while."

"Thanks. We'll try these agents first. I'll call back if I need more information," Gray said. Kyle had already disconnected, so Gray made a few calls, finally tracking down the young agent on duty. Gray spoke over the phone and described what he needed, "Did a short man with a black umbrella arrive at the White House while you were on duty at the front entrance?"

Sophia whispered, "Put him on speaker. I want to hear what he says."

Gray nodded and hit the speaker button.

"Who did you say is calling?" the agent asked. His voice cracked with surprise when he heard Gray was with the FBI. "Oh, this is worse than I thought. Am I in deep trouble? I know I screwed up. Kyle has already written me up, and I don't want to lose my job. I promise it won't happen again, sir."

"So, you did see this man," Gray clarified.

"Yes. Well, the man was short, and I guess his suit jacket was light gray. It was hard to tell with it being so dark, and I really hadn't noticed the color until Kyle called asking what color suit the man was wearing. I know he wore a soaked beige raincoat and carried a black umbrella."

"Yes," Sophia nodded. "That's the man."

"That's when I made a mistake," the agent said. "The power had gone out, and I couldn't find the paper ledger. The man, I don't recall his name, but he jotted it down on a sticky. Unfortunately, I had misplaced the note by the time the electricity returned."

"Think hard," Gray said. "Is there anything else you remember about the man?"

"Yes." The agent sounded more confident. "He was holding a black umbrella with an ivory handle."

"You're right," Sophia said. "Was the handle in the shape of a snakehead?"

"Yep, and it had an odd curve to it." The agent became more excited. "Wait, I took a photo with my cell phone and sent it by email to Agent Trudo. I forgot to tell that to Kyle when he called. He woke me from a sound sleep. Check with Agent Trudo. He was on duty, too, and was there at the same time when the man checked in."

"Thanks, I'll do that. You've been very helpful." Gray disconnected and called the office to speak with Agent Trudo.

"This is Agent Masters. Trudo's not on duty tonight."

Gray thanked Masters and finally caught Agent Trudo at home. He asked the same questions.

"I remember the man," Trudo said. "He became quite upset when the lad delayed his entry into the White House. Let's see. The man had a blue ID with two gold asterisks."

"So, he has top clearance." Gray made a few notes. "Was he an employee, aide, or contractor?"

"I didn't ask," Trudo paused. "I guess I should have checked. Wait, Carl Wyller was also there and said the man was a contractor. I can't remember the man's full name, but his last name sounded sort of Polish or maybe Russian—Hemsky, no, Manski, mmm, that's not quite it either, but close. I heard the agent lost the sticky note the man signed before entering his info into the log. Sorry, I can't be more helpful."

"Can you verify the time?" Sophia asked.

"I didn't catch that," Trudo said. "The phone cut out."

"The time, can you verify the time this man with the black umbrella arrived?" she repeated louder.

"Yes, close to 1:45, maybe 1:50 a.m."

"Think back," she added as if she were back on the bench asking questions. "What did the man look like? What was he wearing?"

Trudo hesitated and added, "He was a heavyset man wearing a beige raincoat. The coat was soaked and muddy along the front. His pants also were smeared with dirt, but he brushed away most of the muck. I don't know if that helps. I heard that he passed the wand test and headed for the West-Wing, while I returned to the main office. Oh yes. The lad used his cell phone and took a photo. He said he sent it to me by email, but all our computers have been shut down until the network has been cleared by the cybersecurity team. I'm sure the photo will be on file when the computers go live, but I don't know the man's name."

"Wait a moment." Gray moved to a secured computer on the corner of the table and pulled up a list of all employees and contractors with last names ending in sky or ski. "Do any of these names sound familiar? Dabrowski, Kaminski, Kowalsky, Petronowsky, Polinsky, Symanski, Truenwski, Zinmansky, Ziplinski…"

"Back up one," Trudo said. "Zinmansky sounds familiar. Yes, Einar Zinmansky, that's the name."

"Thanks for your help," Gray said. "I have a home address and one for his business. I'll send agents to bring him in for questioning. Call me if you think of anything else."

Trudo agreed and disconnected the call.

Gray contacted one of his agents to pick up Zinmansky and was surprised to hear, "We've been searching for this man and his laptop for several hours. You should have received a memo from Homeland Security on this."

"I probably did get one, but I've been in and out of the office working on other crisis issues." Gray searched his e-mails and nodded. "I was notified several hours ago, but Evans took the lead, so I glossed over the message."

The agent continued, "We've been to Zinmansky's apartment, his temporary office at the White House, and the listed business address. He wasn't at any of the locations, but he left muddy footprints in his office, and it looks like he cleaned out his apartment."

"Have you checked if he recently left town? Did he book any flights, cruise lines, or other means of transportation?" Gray asked.

The FBI agent blew out a deep breath. "We checked—none made under that name, and no activity on his passport ID. We're not the only ones searching for this man, and they may have found him, but not the laptop."

"What do you mean?" Gray asked.

"An agent found a body in the Roosevelt bathroom. The man remains unidentified, but he was wearing a light gray suit jacket, and it had blood on the right sleeve. I heard a forensic team is running DNA tests on the man and his clothes."

Sophia wrung her hands. "I hadn't heard about a body. Oh, no. If he did kidnap Mo, we'll never be able to ask for details. Who was he, and how did he die?"

"The ME hasn't released a statement yet," the agent said, "I'll let you know if I hear anything more."

There was a knock on the door, and Agent Gray got up to answer. An aide allowed a female police officer to enter. "Agent Gray, I'm Officer Peggy Wyller, Carl's wife." She glanced around the room. "I'm sorry. Am I interrupting something? I have a one-track mind lately, and I need your help."

Sophia now stood behind Gray and offered her hand. "Officer Wyller, I'm Justice Hendrum, but you can call me Sophia. I'm glad to meet you." Sophia motioned to her left. "This is Chief Jackson, and he's working with me to find Mo."

Jackson shook Peggy's hand. "Officer Wyller, I'm sorry to hear about Carl."

"Please, call me, Peggy." She turned toward Sophia, "I'm also sorry to hear about your husband. I watched your news interview. Have you heard anything yet?"

"No, and I doubt I will." Sophia gave a jagged breath.

Gray's eyes darted between Peggy and Sophia before he asked, "How may I help you?"

Peggy stepped closer to Gray. "I'm here about my husband, Carl. No one is telling me anything, so I came to you for some answers and straight talk. I know I'm his wife, and the new chief and my whole team refuse to let me get involved, but this is my specialty. Dad retired from being the chief of police last year, so we've been searching on our own. We've discovered some important facts, and since my team won't give us the time of day, I'm bringing the info to you, hoping that you will listen."

"To be honest, I'd have to agree with your police chief," Gray said, "but if you have something new to add to the investigation, we need to hear it."

Peggy swallowed. Her eyes narrowed. "I'll share our data, but Dad has had to pull in many favors to get this information. I want to know if we're on the right track."

"I'm listening," Agent Gray said.

"Originally, Carl didn't even realize he had been injured," Peggy said, "but he was seriously wounded. I want to know who stabbed my husband. At first, Homeland Security would only share their security tapes with Chief Polack. He viewed one tape and didn't see Carl's attacker. Frankly, Polack's so busy with the D.C. riots, I don't think he's taken much time to investigate Carl's case, so Dad got involved."

"Did your dad see the tapes?" Agent Gray asked.

"Yes, but it wasn't until after seeing the security video three times, each version zoomed in closer to Carl than the last, that Dad noticed a close encounter with someone in a light gray suit jacket. All he saw was a gray sleeve. Security agents surrounded President Spendorf and Carl, so whoever stabbed him simply reached between the two men and plunged a sharp object into Carl's chest. The person must have been close to the wall as if hiding from the camera's view. Dad never saw a body, much less the face of the attacker."

"Someone in a light gray suit?" Sophia asked.

"Right, and according to Guy, there were only three men wearing that color suit jacket who were in the White House at that time. Guy had interviewed everyone, including those three men, before allowing anyone to leave, and security cleared all of them. Then an agent discovered a body in the Roosevelt bathroom—a fourth man wearing a gray suit jacket."

"We just heard about the body," Sophia said. "I heard it might be a defense contractor, Einar Zinmansky."

Peggy added, "Yes, since no one seemed to recognize the body, Kyle tracked down the agent who was stationed at the front entrance and discovered he had allowed someone into the White House during the power outage. That person was also wearing a light gray suit jacket. However, the agent couldn't remember the man's name. It's taken a while to ID the body, but a forensic analyst discovered several discrepancies. Einar Zinmansky's DNA was on the suit collar, and Carl's blood was on the sleeve."

"So, did Zinmansky stab Carl?" Sophia asked.

"That's what Dad thought at first, but he had no clue why the man would do such a thing," Peggy said. "This also baffled me, so I went by the ME's office to get an update. Dad's worked closely with her in the past, and now I have more questions than answers."

"What kind of questions," Sophia asked.

"The body is not Zinmansky's, and the FBI is still running tests to ID the man." Peggy rubbed her temples as if she had a headache. "Although both are blue-eyed Caucasian males, the dead man's body is 5-foot-10, weighs 212 pounds, and may not even be Russian. According to a recent medical record, Zinmansky is 5-foot-6 and weighed 308 on his last physical exam."

"That's quite a discrepancy," Chief said. "How did anyone mistake the body for Zinmansky?"

Peggy shrugged. "I think it was the suit jacket. And, the ME found a yellow sticky and a plastic scalpel handle in the suit jacket's right pocket."

"Was there a blade in the scalpel?" Chief asked.

"No," Peggy said, "but Einar Zinmansky's signature was written on the sticky along with a date and time. It also had an initial at the bottom of the memo."

"The missing yellow sticky." Gray made a note. "Zinmansky must have pocketed the paper after signing in—it's no wonder the agent couldn't find it."

Peggy nodded. "That's what I thought, too. Anyway, I have two main questions. The first one is, did Zinmansky stab Carl, or was it the man dressed in Zinmansky's suit jacket? And the second question is, was it Carl they meant to stab, or was President Spendorf the real target? I can't imagine why anyone would target Carl. Either way, I have a lead on Zinmansky. I told Chief Polack, but he's not interested, so my father is checking it out while I came here to get your help."

"It appears we're both looking for the same person," Sophia said. "Maybe we can help each other. I need to focus on something—anything to keep me sane."

"I agree." Peggy placed her hand on Sophia's shoulder. "Fill me in on the latest updates."

"Give me more details on this lead you have," Gray said. "If it's legit, we need to keep the police chief informed."

"I believe Zinmansky booked a private jet to fly him out of the country scheduled for tomorrow at 4 a.m.," Peggy said. "My dad's investigating a private firm as we speak. I want to prevent him from catching the flight, and I need your help."

Gray updated Officer Peggy Wyller, including details on Mo's hostage situation, the tie-in with Einar Zinmansky, and what he knew about the body wearing Zinmansky's jacket with Carl's blood on the sleeve.

Sophia added, "We don't know when the light gray jacket was switched—before or after the stabbing."

Chief Jackson asked, "Did the ME get an ID on the body?"

Peggy shook her head. "The fingerprints have been chemically removed. Perhaps the left index finger has enough ridges, but she hasn't found any matches. She's also checking the DNA against international records. No ID yet, but she said the cause of death was the deadly poison that Russians frequently use—Novichok."

"Was it injected?" Sophia asked.

"No. Based on the stomach contents, the Novichok was ingested in tea. They found traces of the poison in Spendorf's favorite teapot and feared that the president may have been the target. Thank God he didn't drink any of that poison." Peggy stopped pacing and sat down. "The ME also mentioned someone altered the jacket, but it was still two sizes too short for the body and much wider. So, after viewing the security camera's recording, I think someone switched the coat after the stabbing, or else the coat sleeve would appear way above the stabber's wrist, which was not on the video, but I don't know that for sure."

Gray glanced down at his notes. "I understand Zinmansky had cleaned out his apartment before disappearing."

"Along with his laptop." Peggy sounded irritated. "President Spendorf and the cybersecurity team are more interested in that stupid laptop Carl loaned to the contractor than they are about Carl." She swiped a tear from her cheek. "Oh, I know it's unfair to say, but Cordy Hastings called. She did ask about Carl, but then she launched into questioning Carl's reason for handing over DoD access to a foreign contractor without clearing it with the cybersecurity team first. She's afraid Zinmansky has stolen the specs for some drone her husband tested earlier this morning. I didn't get all the details, but she insisted Carl should have notified her team."

"Carl didn't clear it?" Chief asked and then reworded his question. "I mean, surely he cleared it. Cordy must have been under a lot of stress after everything that's happened today. I heard the drone testing was a real fiasco."

"How well do you know her?" Peggy asked.

"We go back a long way. Her father mentored me when we both worked FBI, then I became a private investigator and became Cordy's boss," Chief said. "When she turned twenty-three, I helped her apply to the FBI. She and her team know IT and security better than anyone in the field."

Peggy licked her lips. "Well, Carl didn't indicate if he did or didn't clear the laptop. He's still on the ventilator and under the influence of painkillers."

"What's on the computer?" Sophia asked.

"Zinmansky's heading up the Maven II drone project," Peggy said. "Carl nodded through his drugged haze when I asked, but he couldn't give me any details. You know what it's like being married to a secret holder."

Sophia let out a groan. "And I have to keep secrets from my husband, too, as I don't doubt you have to at times. It's hard to open that door even a crack to peek inside when your spouse is facing life and death."

Peggy smiled. "I couldn't have said it better." She turned toward Agent Gray, "So, please peek into that crack because you have clearance, and I don't. Can you help track down Zinmansky and ID that body? I want to determine if whoever stabbed Carl really meant to kill the president, and Carl got in the way. Either way, I want to know if either man is guilty or if I need to continue searching for the real assassin. Dad should have more information on that possible flight soon. We must ensure Zinmansky doesn't leave the country."

"Did your dad contact the new police chief with his latest findings?" Gray asked.

"He will when he has more proof of his theories," Peggy said. "He's been in the chief's shoes and knows how important it is to be fully informed."

Gray's phone rang. Before he could answer, an exciting agent yelled, "There's been an explosion at the Pentagon car park. Defense Deputy Director Chet says to meet him at the scene. You can't miss it, he thinks General Shyler's car was bombed. See you there."

"Was General Shyler at the scene?" Gray asked, but the agent had hastily disconnected.

Gray left the room, saying, "Sorry, ladies. We'll talk again later. I have a critical situation and need to go."

Rock Creek Park

***Sept. 11 – 6:22 p.m. EDT, Southeast Rock
Creek Park, Washington, D.C.***

Braun never knew what would transpire during a SWAT team raid. Each one progressed differently, even on a clear day, but he could barely see through the ice crystals accumulating on the BATT's windshield tonight. "Weather's getting worse." He upped the defrost to high and the windshield wipers to full speed, but he still had trouble keeping up with the sleet.

Loran ran his gloved hand over the fogged window to clear it. "The search will get more dangerous after dark."

Questions raced through Braun's mind as he walked through the options and outcomes of the coming raid. He was good at his profession because he was prepared and anticipated unlikely scenarios. *Is Zahair the ringleader? Does he report to a higher power? How many enemies will we encounter? Will we have time to prepare, or do we need to act in the blink of an eye? Will they negotiate or fight to the death?* "I'm glad that SWAT will back us up, especially since we don't know what trouble we might face."

Loran's mind must have been on the same wavelength. "I briefly profiled Farzad Zahair after Emma's capture. He lives in two worlds. In one, Zahair is mild-mannered, polite, and even generous—silent in demeanor, with a 'live and let live' attitude. In the other, he's a monster—relentless when he doesn't get what he wants—nimble as a cat, stealthy as a tiger, and sly as a fox."

Braun nodded. "Today, Zahair will be the latter."

"If that bastard so much as breaks Emma's fingernail, I'll make sure he never touches anyone again." Loran enlarged the map. "I've heard of Rock Creek Park, but I still don't see a trail. It's a good thing the chopper's pilot gave us GPS coordinates."

Braun continued to drive the tactical Humvee closer to the park. "Turns out the target is about 200 yards southeast of the horse stables. Looked like an abandoned motor home or RV. I doubt they moved to a new location in the last hour. It wouldn't be an easy task. We'll send up two drones, with night vision and infrared, to survey the area and update their status before going in on foot."

"Who manages the area?" Loran asked.

"No one." Braun turned left onto a gravel road and still slowed even though they were going at a snail's pace.

Loran refolded the map. "Someone must oversee the site."

"I checked," Braun said, "not the Architect of the Capitol or the National State Park Service, and it's not a well-known region. I wonder how the foreign agents knew to use it. Pretty smart of them—ETA three minutes."

Static hissed over the encrypted broadcast radio, and Loran hit the decryption key.

"What's the message say?" Braun asked.

"SWAT team leader Russ Bracken here. We're pulling into Rock Creek Park Horse Center. What's your E.T.A.?"

"We're close enough to breathe in your exhaust fumes," Braun said. "Russ, how did you get to D.C.? I thought you were stationed out of Colorado."

Russ replied, "The team's here for training. D.C.'s SWAT teams are running ragged, so we volunteered. See you soon."

"Do you know the team?" Loran asked Braun.

"Yes." Braun nodded. "Cordy used to date Russ, and she says he's the best SWAT team leader she knows—experienced, dedicated, and persistent. He's a former Navy Seal Explosive Breacher who later served in Afghanistan." Braun pulled up behind the black-armored tactical transport.

Loran opened his door to pelting rain. "Better make a run for it."

"I'm right behind you," Braun shouted, although he could barely hear his own words through a crack of thunder. He had parked only two car lengths from Russ's BATT, yet Braun was drenched by the time he gathered his gear and joined the SWAT team.

Russ held open the door, "Miserable weather." He handed Braun and Loran towels to dry their faces. "I see that you're incognito again. Not bad. I wouldn't have recognized you if I hadn't heard your voice. I've never seen you with hair this color, but don't you think that goatee is a bit much?" Russ gave the familiar low, rumbling chuckle that came from deep within his chest. "Nice job on those scars."

"The cheek wounds are mostly real." Braun gently dabbed his face.

Russ collected the used towels. "Are you sure we've tracked down Zahair?"

"Sure hope so." Braun formally introduced his boss. "This is Agent Loran Sloan, head of the FBI. We believe Zahair kidnapped his wife earlier this morning."

"Sorry to hear about your wife." Russ shook Loran's hand. "Let me introduce you. I'm proud to say my team is homegrown. You won't find a better group of men. I was their platoon sergeant in Afghanistan. Since then, we have spent five years working SWAT in Fort Collins. Last year, we moved up to Federal Protective Forces. To my right is Poncho. He's second in command. Not long on words, but when he does speak, we listen."

Poncho stepped forward and offered his beefy paw to Loran, "Nice to meet you." Turning, Poncho clasped Braun's hand. "Glad to see you again."

Although Braun stood a good head taller than the dark-haired man, he saw Poncho's muscles ripple across his arms and shoulders. The handshake left no doubt about his strength, and Braun was glad they were on the same side.

Russ nodded toward an agile man already checking out his gear. "Chico is always alert and on duty, as you can see."

Chico glanced up and gave a robust laugh. "Nice night for a hunt." He wore a black tank top exposing a white scar running from his left wrist to his elbow as he strapped on a Kevlar vest and slipped into a camo jacket. Even fully geared up, he was a good twenty pounds lighter than Poncho. His step was quick and seemed to glide across the room.

Braun went over and patted Chico on the back. "He saved Cordy's life last year when she delivered the vaccine during the pandemic. Thanks, you are my hero. I never got to say that earlier."

Chico's face reddened with embarrassment. He cleared his throat. "Glad I was there."

"Our other SWAT members are Officer Kayman and two bomb experts, Sergeants Foley and Desmond." Russ moved toward his laptop. "Give us the details."

A photo of Emma and Zahair popped onto the screen. "We believe Farzad Zahair followed Emma home from the hospital and kidnapped her after she pulled into our driveway," Loran said. "She was still wearing her teal scrubs and a white lab coat. I have no idea why he targeted my wife."

"Maybe he needed a nurse," Poncho said.

Loran's jaw dropped. "Everything has been running through my brain, and I hadn't thought of that."

"Gather round," Russ said, "we'll make plans to rescue Mrs. Sloan."

"Emma," Loran said. "Russ, it's good to have you here, and my wife, Emma, would be proud to have her rescuers know her by her first name. She's the least formal person I know in D.C."

"Okay, Emma it is." Russ chuckled again.

"Thanks," Loran said. "We're glad to have your help."

Russ pulled up several photos on his screen. "About an hour ago, the FBI sent a helicopter overhead with infrared cameras. We can see six heat signatures varying in size, temperature, and shape. One is smaller than the others, in the southeast corner of the RV, and it may be Emma's image. The others move around in the space, but not this one."

"So, you think we're dealing with at least five perps?" Loran moved closer to study the screen.

"At least five," Russ popped a stick of gum into his mouth—a habit he'd developed since he stopped smoking. "Okay, let's discuss our approach."

"We brought two drones equipped with infrared and night vision cameras," Braun said.

"I'll connect them to our screen, which links to our goggles." Russ typed on the keyboard, and two smaller windows popped up. "Do the cameras also have speaker capability?"

Loran nodded. "The video has sound, but the rain may muffle any noises."

"How quiet are the drones?" Poncho's dark eyes turned toward Braun. "We don't want to give away our location."

Poncho had a powerful stare that seemed to peer right through to one's soul.

Braun could see that no one would question his authority when locked in that gaze. "These drones have been specked for low noise, and as Loran mentioned, the storm may help mask the sound."

"We'll send the drones in a one-mile radius from the GPS center point, gradually narrowing the range," Russ said. "Chico and Foley, you're with me. Desmond, join Poncho and Kayman. Loran, are you familiar with these electronics and computers? We need someone to stay here and monitor all activities on the screen, keep us informed, and provide additional backup if needed."

"Not me. I'm searching for Emma," Loran said. "We hoped to patch this over to Cordy. Agent Evans is with her and between the two of them—"

"Yeah, I guess that will work," Russ said. "She's done this for us in the past."

Braun called Cordy's cell to let her know they were preparing to launch the drones.

"I'm still in the Oval Office making a final sweep of the president's computer network," Cordy said. "I need to move to the Bunker's technical room before you make your move. That way, I can multi-task, and Evans will join us. Give me ten minutes. I'll text you when I'm ready. Wait—put me on speaker."

Braun turned to Russ. "Cordy says, 'Ten minutes.' Will that work? She's on speaker and wants to talk to you."

Russ smiled. "We're glad you have our backs, Cordy. It'll take that long to prepare on our end."

"Do you have a medic with your team?" she asked.

"No, not this time," Russ said, "but we've all done medic duty in the past, and EMS is on standby."

"Be careful." Cordy's voice warmed Braun's soul, although she sounded tired. "I'll call Guy and head for the Bunker. You should get a text shortly."

Russ linked their earphones and the main radio to Cordy's frequency, masking the signal so that if intercepted by an outside source, it would notify her.

When Cordy disconnected the call, Braun felt more alert. Completing this mission would bring him one step closer to closing this case and being with her—and their family. He gave a silent prayer. *Keep us safe.* He strapped on his helmet. "The drones are in the trailer behind the Humvee."

Russ completed the final checklist, waiting to hand over surveillance to Cordy. "Okay, gear up and prep the drones. We need to locate each person in that RV. Braun, go with Poncho and set up the second drone. Loran, you're with me. Stop tapping your fingers against your leg. If you can't quell that nervous energy, stay here. We'll get Emma."

"That's not going to happen." Loran glared at Russ but made an effort to stop his fidgeting. "This isn't my first rodeo. I'll have your back."

"That's more like it," Russ said. "We'll prep the first drone and wait until Cordy texts us before launching. Chico, link the drones to our screen and then pair it up with hers."

Before making it out the door, the SWAT radio spewed static, and then an unknown voice erupted, "This is Metro—"

Russ grabbed the radio. "10-11. 10-12."

Braun frowned. "He should know enough to use an untraceable frequency and be discreet."

"10-4. Switching." Police Polack flashed across the decrypted screen, followed by a typed message, "Agent Gray informed us about your assignment to bring in Farzad Zahair. This is our jurisdiction."

Russ typed. "Call me on a secure line!"

Seconds later, Polack fumed over the phone. "Zahair is a threat to national security and is suspected of criminal activity within D.C., so this is a JOINT effort. Department of Justice agrees you're to hand Zahair over upon capture. You can gather intelligence once he's in our custody."

Russ rolled his eyes. "Roger, Chief Polack, a joint effort only after takedown, and we process the case—FBI will handle the details—over and out." Russ disconnected before Polack could object.

Secrets

Cordy was about to leave the Oval Office when she ran across a recovery partition on Zac's computer. After further inspection, she also discovered a hidden drive requiring a backdoor code and password to gain access. Intrigued, she immediately quarantined the drive and texted Zac, "Do you have any secret files or a hidden drive on your workstation that I should know about?"

Zac returned her text immediately, "No, I wouldn't have a clue how to enter one, but if you find any, check them out."

With time closing in around her, Cordy saved and encrypted the drive, then sent the encryption to Quint along with a message, "I believe this hidden drive is spying on the president. See if you can open it and send the data through our analysis program. Zac denies any knowledge of the drive's existence. He definitely can't open it, nor could I get more details in the short amount of time I have, but it's on his operating system and utility program. Keep this highly classified. Find out what's on it and get back to me."

Cordy jolted when Quint called. "Sorry, I can't talk! Braun's team is waiting for me."

Quint kept talking. "Listen. I know you're in a hurry, but this is important. Since you're already in Zac's office, take a sec. to check all USB ports for a mirror drive. It could capture data via the web camera."

"A mirror drive?" She could hardly breathe. *That could copy and update the whole network to the cloud for easy access anywhere.*

Quint spoke so fast, that she barely caught, "I know someone hacked into the network, and I couldn't shut down the president's computer. I want to know why."

"Glad you mentioned that." Cordy turned Zac's computer so the back faced her and ran her hand along the USB ports. She didn't see anything, but her fingers felt a small nub over the middle port. "Got it. It's so small, I missed it." She knew what to do. "As soon as I send everything to VeraCrypt for encoding, I'll send you the files. Open them and block any other access to the drive."

"Will do, Girlfriend," Quint continued, "wait, give me another moment."

Cordy felt pressured. "Okay, but hurry." She needed to move to the Bunker's technical room in the next five minutes and log on with the SWAT team, but she couldn't brush aside the gnawing feeling telling her to continue her search. Someone had bugged Zac's office, and it terrified her. *Think of the impact a leak could have on the entire free world.*

"A drive like this was on the black market two weeks ago, purchased by a darknet holder, CJ42, and forwarded to a JCJ300." Quint sounded excited. "I have no idea how this drive found its way to President Spendorf's computer, but I'm copying it onto a darknet backup account. It's probably written in JSON or JavaScript. It will take a while to crack, but how did a spy get into the Oval Office? Even a harder task, how did anyone manage to get into his computer?"

"It wouldn't be easy." Cordy felt her heart race. *For some reason, JCJ300 sounds familiar. Where did I see that number?*

Quint asked, "Are you still there? You were so quiet I can almost hear your mind turning."

"That's scary," Cordy paused, "but Zac says there's a mole among his team, and Guy has a theory."

Quint nodded. "I'm listening."

"Could this morning's attacks on the Washington Metro transit systems be linked to the assaults on the White House?"

"Why do you ask?" Quint asked.

"Here's what I learned," Cordy said. "The Potomac Power Plant went down around midnight, and the subway trains crashed eleven minutes later. By 12:30 a.m., D.C. was in total chaos, and the president called in the National Guard. At 1:30 a.m., the lights went out at President's Park. While the Secret Service agents maintained surveillance for the 38-minute power outage, someone managed to hack into our defense systems. It wasn't until 2:40 a.m., when the laser and strobe light system shut down, that a Code Q alert was triggered. By 3:20 a.m., we all scrambled to get the systems back online, barely in time for someone to shut down the Avenger system. At 3:36 a.m., all White House computers went down. Ten minutes later, at 3:46 a.m., someone launched a drone strike on the White House."

"I can't believe all that happened, and we had no warning," Quint sounded angry.

"And it's just the beginning," Cordy said. "During that initial golden hour without any electrical power, someone kidnapped the Secretary of State, while a Maven II drone was sabotaged, resulting in sending a weaponized drone to Aberdeen for testing, and it nearly wiped out the team. Moments later, there was a murder attempt while moving President Spendorf to the Bunker. Carl was stabbed, Emma Sloan was kidnapped in her driveway as she returned home from working at the hospital, and someone tried to kill FBI Director Loran Sloan. I think Guy's right. This was perfectly planned."

Quint agreed. "The timing of each event suggests this was a coordinated attack, well planned, and executed to create the most chaos."

"Our job is to find the people behind these attacks and stop their next steps before anything else happens. And the more I think about it, the attacks could have started on Friday with the shut down of DOJ's network."

"That reminds me, Cordy." Quint's voice sounded strained. "We got a request from the Securities and Exchange Commission a few hours ago to look into Friday's NYSE activities, but I haven't had time to seriously research everything. I do know, as with most terrorists, to follow the money."

Cordy glanced at her watch. *Two minutes before I need to be at the Bunker.* She powered off her computer.

"I'll check into the transit system, but how would that tie into the U.S. government?" Quint asked as he typed in the background, already fired up to find answers.

Cordy felt overwhelmed. "Haven't a clue at the moment, but there's something on that hidden drive. I know it. And if we follow the money as you say, someone profited. Determine who is behind the riots and who placed those subway bombs, and we will be a step closer to hunting down our terrorists."

Quint let out a shrill whistle that nearly split her eardrum. "You're onto something big. I just Google-searched Washington's metro area transit system, and it is bleeding cash. The WMATA announced it needs $800 million in loans, federal grants, and private funding to stay solvent. I wonder what is on that hard drive."

Cordy groaned. "Another mystery." Cordy felt exhausted. "What does this have to do with President Spendorf?"

"Maybe nothing. Have you heard of IYFTI?" Quint asked. "Intercity Future Transport, Inc. just made a bid to take over D.C.'s Transit System."

"Yes, the company's offer was all over the news on Friday as I flew back home," Cordy said. "It sent the New York Stock Exchange into a tizzy. The stock soared to four times the initial stock price."

"Initially, that's true," Quint said, "but look at this! According to CNN, the owners sold 10% of their stock as allowed by their bylaws, making a great profit, but when they reached their limit, the CEO went even further and borrowed security at a much lower offer. By mid-day, their stock sold short in huge volumes. One hedge fund, SkyUrsis Capital, made a fortune when the stock plummeted. I think this has all the hallmarks of insider trading."

Cordy was on overload. "Insider trading? Not Zac. He would have no part of that. Look, I'm afraid there's more to this hard drive, and Zac truly believes someone is spying on him." Cordy rechecked her watch—*I'm running late, but I can't drop this lead.*

"I've been reviewing the data, and it also has something to do with IYFTI stock sales—a buyout of corporate shares by SkyUrsis, and more. I haven't had time to get into the details, but something's not right."

"And?" Cordy knew Quint was usually spot-on when concerned. She had to listen.

"I need a network engineer at the stock market that I can trust— and I mean trust like 100%. If this is what I think it is, we need to report it to the FBI and CIA if they're dealing with foreign funds." Quint paused.

"Who is IYFTI's CEO?" Cordy asked.

"One moment." Quint tapped on his keyboard. "Her name is Azinnea M. Krysin, and SkyUrsis has numerous investors through their hedge fund. One of their largest investors is Ansin Associates & Securities."

"I've never heard of the CEO, and I've already shut down my laptop. Send me the spelling of her name. I'll see if anyone here has heard of her or SkyUrsis Capital. In the meantime, do some more research."

"Will do," Quint said. "I'll have the team check out hedge fund managers and major investors and get back to you. I know you're busy, and we'll keep you posted, but my gut says there's a lot more to this. I suspect malware. A remote access Trojan."

"A RAT? You think someone accessed through a backdoor and set the prices?" Cordy worried the team's workload was already overwhelming.

"We don't have access to the stock market records. That's why I need help, but I'd like to research this a bit more?" Quint added, "I'm worried about—"

"Embezzlement?" Cordy cut in to save time. "How do these two incidents connect? Would the D.C.'s transit system be so desperate that they would commit fraud to obtain funds?" *And how does that help solve our current terrorist attacks?*

"If someone is skilled enough to create a RAT and download a payload of stock prices, they could also have shut down the Justice Department's network, especially since the DOJ was investigating corporations and hedge funds that sold short on the stock market." Quint cleared his throat and dropped his voice to barely a whisper. "I can't talk now. I'll send a text when I know more."

Taking on this task definitely meant the list for her team was too much. She added, "I'll ask Loran for permission to include CrowdStrike on this task, too. I'll text you when I get his approval. Then, have Alysha's team check into IYFTI's activities. List the dates of purchases and the price, dates of sales and the price, plus the net profit/loss of each employee and member of the hedge fund."

Evans rapped on the office door, impatient as ever. "Ready? We better get to the Bunker. My team's been busy, and I have a lot of forensic data to share."

"Thanks, Quint. Gotta run." Cordy felt torn in too many directions.

"Wait," Quint said, "Breaking news just reported a car bomb went off at the Pentagon. They think it was General Shyler's car. I know you gotta run, so I'll look more into this, too, and talk to you soon." He clicked off.

Shyler's car blew up? Was he in the car when it exploded? Braun's team was nearly wiped out, and now Shyler, the man who ordered the drone and RCV testing, may have been murdered. Cordy's head spun with the news as she scooped the remaining gear into her backpack and followed Evans using the back way to the Bunker's technical room. It wasn't easy, but she had to switch gears.

Entering the hallway to the Bunker, she tried to imagine her location based on the earlier surveillance tapes. "Is this where Carl was stabbed?"

Evans scanned the area. "It's nearby."

Cordy moved close to the wall and dropped to the tile floor, sighting at eye level, first in one direction and then the other.

Evans nearly ran into her. "What are you doing?"

"I'm looking for something. I don't know what it is yet, just a feeling, but I don't see anything." She placed her hand on the wall to brace herself as she stood. "Ouch!" She jerked herself toward the middle of the hallway and grabbed her right wrist, blotting at something warm oozing onto her jacket's sleeve. The palm of her right hand stung. "Something cut me." She pointed at the bloody streak on the wall.

Evans shone his flashlight. A well-hidden, chalky blade was wedged within the grout, but once Cordy brushed off the powdery dust, the metal glinted in the light. Evans pulled out a pair of latex gloves from his pocket, took his pen, and pried out a narrow object, sharp as a razor blade.

"Do you think Carl was stabbed with that blade?" Cordy rummaged through her pack with her left hand and found a tissue, antiseptic gel, and a small dressing. She brushed against a plastic evidence bag and grabbed that, too.

"We'll take the blade to the lab and run it through forensics." Evans dropped the object into the bag and labeled it. "Do you need help bandaging your hand?"

"No, I can manage." Cordy wiped away the excess blood, washed it with the gel, wiped it dry, and slapped the dressing tightly across the wound. She looped the backpack over her arm, held her throbbing palm in her left hand, and glanced down at her watch. "It's been twenty minutes since I spoke to Braun."

"Ready?" When Cordy nodded, Evans took her by the arm and led her along the dimly lit hallway to the Bunker. "This way—let's hurry."

Daily Grind

***Sept. 11 – 5:31 p.m. MDT, Cybersecurity team
headquarters, Fort Collins, Colorado***

Quint's mind spun after talking to Cordy. *Did H.Q. follow through with his threat to kill Shyler? If the general wasn't in the car, was he kidnapped, or did Shyler plan this to escape? Is Shyler involved in the drone test caper?* These questions raced through his mind, but he knew he had to refocus. He was on a mission of utmost importance. *The DOJ network had been investigating corporations that sold short on the stock market. Then, the Justice Department's network went down on Friday, just before the NYSE opened, where another stock went wild and ended up selling short. I need CrowdStrike's help to track down facts, and the fate of many could depend on it.*

And how long ago had the president's computer been compromised? Was it before or shortly after a coordinated attack in downtown D.C.? No doubt, to draw attention away from also hitting the government's network and defense programs and disabling Avenger before launching a drone attack on the White House. The timing suggests that the terrorists planned for all to hit simultaneously or at least in a domino effect to make it more challenging to discover who was behind the attacks. The complexity of the situation was staggering, and Quint knew he had his work cut out for him.

Quint closed his eyes and chastised himself. When on overload, his mind often went in ten different directions. "Get back to work!"

Cordy would be tied up for at least an hour, so he connected a password cracker to Zac's hidden encrypted drives, hoping to unlock them and gain total access soon. However, if the password cracker failed, he was confident he could still recover most of the data, but Quint wanted to track down the culprit who placed the secret drives, especially the mirror drive that could clone everything. For that, he needed the password.

As he waited for the software program to reveal the password, he checked on the data between Zinmansky's laptop and Carl's computer. His confidence was shattered and turned into shock. Someone had replaced Zinmansky's initial hard drive with an unencrypted main drive that was stealing and replacing defense data. Quint also found three additional files that caused him to break out in a sweat of panic. One had a detailed blueprint of Minute Maid Park in Houston, Texas. It labeled all security checkpoints and three emergency exit routes. The second folder marked NY mass transit, and another marked LAX remained a mystery—both empty. The mystery of the empty folders added to the intrigue and the need for answers, and that need for answers was pressing. The suspense was nearly unbearable. *Were the files erased or hidden?* Either way, Quint couldn't immediately access the data, so he texted Cordy.

Cordy texted back, "President Spendorf is scheduled to throw the ceremonial pitch at the World Series in Houston a week from Friday. Get FBI agents out there right now! God only knows the plot, and we must stop this before anything happens. Zac's life depends on it." Cordy added, "To be safe, also forward what data you have to Homeland Security, DoD, FBI, and the CIA."

Was the U.S. president's life in danger? It certainly seemed so. Quint felt the weight of the impending danger as he read Cordy's urgent message. Two tasks were completed, and three new ones were added. *This situation can't be allowed to persist.* He promptly forwarded the warnings as requested.

Quint scanned his to-do list and also added, "What happened to Zinmansky's encrypted drive?" *He headed up the drone project.* The weapon codes for the Maven II drone and the RCV popped to the top of his mind, but he needed some isolation to review those, and that wouldn't be forwarded to CrowdStrike. Braun's weapons test was over. The DoD wouldn't use them again until they completed their investigation. At least, he hoped not and moved on down the list.

Some items had a line through them, meaning they were handled. Others were in process. Feeling the mounting pressure and the need for quick action, he rapidly created a decision tree of his options. *Is this how Cordy feels when stressed?* His respect for her went up a notch.

As he reviewed the list one more time, he checked it against Cordy's. "Check bug in Shyler's office" was missing from his list. Quint again worried about Shyler. *Is he even alive? What happened?* He had logged into the frequency of Braun's bug placed in Shyler's office, but nothing new had come up on the screen once Shyler had received that email regarding an overseas account in Braun's name. *Why was that? Had Shyler disabled or even destroyed Braun's bug? Did he run a bug blocker in the background? Was there another way to track data from Shyler's office? I mean, legally? Maybe it would explain what happened to Shyler.* Quint ran a hand through his tousled hair. *I could tap his cell phone if it wasn't destroyed in the car, but better have Evans check into that.* Satisfied he had listed all the items, he divided the list into seven segments, made assignments, and posted them on the team's large to-do list screen in the conference room. It gave him a sense of some accomplishment.

Help From CrowdStrike

***Sept. 11 – 6:03 p.m. MDT, Cybersecurity team
headquarters, Fort Collins, Colorado/5:03 p.m. PDT,
CrowdStrike headquarters, Sunnyvale, California***

Quint enjoyed immersing himself in research. The more deeply he delved into a problem, the better the solution. However, today, he felt overwhelmed. He disliked asking for help, especially from Perry, but Cordy expected him to collaborate with the Russian expert, and he truly needed the assistance. In this intense situation, he realized he needed CrowdStrike's help, too.

He excused his teammates because they were already ensconced in their vital assignments to revive DoD and Homeland Security systems after the ransomware attack. Quint called the program coordinator at CrowdStrike via VidChat. He explained the crucial need for additional help tracking down the D.C. and White House terrorists, who are suspected to be involved in a series of cyberattacks and financial frauds that pose a significant threat to national security. He emphasized the importance of the audience's role in this mission.

"I have a twelve-person team," Alysha said. "Can we help with other tasks? You vetted them last year, and they've maintained clearance."

Quint sipped his Coke. "Everything goes through you, then directly to me," He said to Alysha. His cell phone vibrated. Quint checked the time—5:34 p.m. "One moment, I have a text message from Cordy." It read, "Loran Sloan gave permission to have CrowdStrike look into IYFTI. Get back to me at 10 p.m. EDT, 8 p.m. your time. Text me if you need anything."

"Sorry for the interruption, Alysha, but I have another urgent task for you and your team. I know you help both the FBI and CIA at intervals, and normally, Loran Sloan would deal with this, but he's bogged down on another mission. Cordy got his permission for you to work on his behalf." Quint relayed the request from the Securities and Commission Office to investigate Friday's NYSE activities. "Have you heard of IYFTI?"

"No, they must be a new corporation." Alysha typed in the background. "I see Intercity Future Transport, Inc. was taken public six months ago. Azinnea M. Krysin is the CEO. That's an interesting name. What do you suspect?"

Quint doodled on his tablet. "This is bare bones at best, but here is what I know so far. Metro and a few states that currently fund WMATA are desperate for money. According to the Transit Board, they need funding like yesterday—over $800 million to avoid bankruptcy. They have increased fares, state taxes, and received government subsidies as a stopgap, but it's not enough. After nearly a year of debates, Congress has finally approved outside funding. IYFTI made WMATA an offer to take over management of Washington, D.C.,'s transit system, including the subway, cross-country and metro bus routes, airport transportation, and taxi services. So far, IYFTI has succeeded in raising half the money. It's enough to breathe some life into their contract agreement, and WMATA is holding a board meeting this Wednesday to consider signing."

"That's a lot of money for a start-up." Alysha continued browsing the Internet. "How can they raise that much?"

Quint ran his hand again through his already tousled chestnut hair, as he often did when confronted with a complex problem. He was determined to get to the bottom of this. In fact, he had spent more time researching than he should have, but too many irons were already poker hot. "I discovered that SkyUrsis Capital sold short several airline, freight, and transit stocks four days ago. IYFTI also bought and immediately sold these shares—huge volumes of money exchanged hands."

"So we need to research transactions that occurred before Friday leading up to this event." Alysha leaned closer to the computer screen and squinted. "How much money are you talking about?"

Quint set his Coke aside and scanned his notes. "Half a billion went to SkyUrsis members over the past three days. Sixty percent of that was added Friday when IYFTI stocks also sold short. The CEO and President own 70% of the corporation, and they sold a tenth of their shares, which their bylaws allowed, doubling their initial investment. Then the CEO borrowed additional shares to sell short."

"I don't see anything illegal in their transactions," Alysha said, "but our team will study this in more detail."

Quint turned the page on a notepad to doodle some more. It relaxed him, and frequently, new ideas would pop into his head. "During further research, I discovered SkyUrsis Capital wasn't the only hedge fund to make a huge profit. Two hours before closing, a private security contracting firm sold short a large volume of IYFTI's shares, netting $3.3 billion. This, too, has all the hallmarks of insider trading."

"Okay, and?" Alysha hesitated.

Quint hopped up from his chair. "Jeez, I've been worrying about an idea for a while now, and all points head in that direction! What if IYFTI or the contractor is responsible for crashing the two Metro trains underground and threatening to blow up the tunnels with well-placed bombs."

Alysha frowned and shook her head. "What?"

"I know." Quint sat back down. "It sounds far-fetched, but IYFTI is vying for a contract with WMATA to manage D.C.'s transport systems. No, wait, I see that look. You think I'm crazy but bear with me. What if IYFTI or even the private security firm planted the attacks, showing what happened without their help? It could be a terrorist plot. A secret cell launched to disrupt the financial system."

"The attack was massive." Alysha frowned. "Besides the subway train crash, four metro buses were set on fire, closing down I-95, I-395, and I-295 for hours. Rioting disrupted the airport hub, causing several flight delays. An accident on the 14th Street Bridge caused traffic across Washington, D.C., to come to a standstill, and on a Sunday when most members of Congress were due to return."

"And maybe IYFTI or the security contractor is making the point that this would never have happened if they had been overseeing the transit system," Quint added.

Alysha sighed. "Who is this security contractor?"

"That's the rub," Quint said. "The firm is Ansin Associates & Securities—a private security corporation that's been in business for seven years. Mierzany K. Ansin is the CEO and President, but I searched and can't find him in any national or international databases, including Interpol. No International Driver's License, green card, US or EU Social Security number—nada. We tracked tax data up until fifteen months ago, then it's as if he's disappeared off the planet or he doesn't exist at all! No photos, no newspaper clippings mention him, no magazine articles—he is the invisible man."

"How much did you say sold short on Friday?" Alysha asked.

"The NYSE closing auction trades an average of $18.9 billion/day, but Friday's trades came to $23.3 billion?" Quint said.

"All that extra cash would have triggered an automatic alert with the government," Alysha said. "And that's probably why you were called in to investigate."

"Yes, Ansin must have gotten a lot of attention from the Departments of Transportation and Commerce. Probably the DOJ, too, and Congress may also investigate, but we cannot wait for them to hold committee hearings. That could take years! No. Something is brewing, and it doesn't bode well for WMATA or our country."

"Where did the money go?" Alysha asked.

"Another mystery," Quint said. "Track down what you can."

"So Ansin is our target?" Alysha asked.

"Ansin sold IYFTI short, but we have insufficient evidence for any accusations. Ansin is only one piece of the puzzle."

"What else do you need from us?" Alysha asked.

"First, we need to track down the insider that leaked the tip." Quint was getting more involved and knew he couldn't hand the lead off to Alysha without being a part of the investigation. Glancing once more at the task board, he sighed. "I don't have enough time to check into IYFTI's CEO, so do what you can. Track down if any of these contacts know anything about hacking or software, and…"

Alysha madly took notes.

"How about meeting on VidChat with Cordy at 10 p.m. EDT? She'll want an update and should be freed up for a few moments by that hour."

"I'll get right on it. Talk to you then." Alysha disconnected the call.

Quint checked on his team's progress on removing the ransomware from the Defense and Homeland Security databases. Svetlana was listening to music through her wireless earbuds, and he poked her shoulder to get her attention. "Any glitches?"

"A few, but I figured out a workaround. I'm over halfway through the update." Svetlana entered code on her main laptop while the servers continued to hum along smoothly in the background.

Quint studied the code she entered. "What are you working on?"

"I'm creating a CyberVaccine to ward off another virus attack." Svetlana scooted forward in her chair.

Quint noted how fast her thoughts jolted from her brain to her fingertips. "Sorry to bother you while you're in the zone."

"No problem." She gnawed at her lip and paused. "This AI code will automatically alter software to block infections. It operates like a vaccine in that it educates the immune system to fight against a new bug."

Her insight sparked Quint's interest. "That's a great idea, but I need you to work on the posted list. Then when we've wrapped up this nightmare, you're free to build your vaccine. In fact, let me know if you need any help."

"I will once I finish the program." She snuck a peek at him, but her fingers never left the keyboard. "It'll take months, maybe even a year, but I work on it when I can."

"Sorry, Svetlana, but for now, I must abort the programming," Quint really did admire her innovative mind, but not now.

"Okay, but I'd like your help to brainstorm how to break the code, create a strong patch, and repeat the process until nothing can interrupt the system."

"Hot Mama!" Quint winked.

"Stop that," Svetlana's voice rose. "You call Cordy, Girlfriend, and me Hot Mama? I'm half your age. Think up something I can live with."

"What would you like me to call you?" Quint asked.

"My Queen will do." Svetlana laughed.

"Okay, My Queen." Quint smiled, amused at her request. "Cordy found some concerns at the White House and needs help. Check all Department of Defense entries, including access to files, e-mails, web searches, and updates for the past 72 hours. That includes any links to outside contractors."

"I rather like being called Queen." Svetlana held up her hand for a high-five. "I recognize that look. It means get back to work. You're a real taskmaster and a golf ball."

"That's goofball," Perry said from across the room. "English is tricky, My Queen."

She ignored his remark. "Grapes sake, does Cordy want to check on every DoD employee?" She typed a few last thoughts and then turned to a different desktop computer.

"Yes, and contractors, too." Quint chuckled. "I think you meant cripes sake, but your way is cuter."

She shrugged. "Does she only want the last 72 hours?" Svetlana raised her head in question. Her ice-blue eyes sparkled, probably in anticipation of starting a new task. "It won't take any longer to write the code for the last 30 days to be safe."

Quint rubbed his chin. "That will collect a lot more data."

"More data is a breeze for you," she half-suppressed a giggle. "I saw you read the entire War and Peace novel again over lunch break yesterday, so it shouldn't be a problem."

Quint let out a "pfft" sound and briefly covered his mouth. "I wish. When you're done loading the new servers, notify me. We'll review each and reboot the system. Then, I'll show you how to reconnect the Internet using the secured accounts protocol we created last week. I should have uploaded the program to all servers instead of just the teams. It may have prevented the hack."

Svetlana logged onto the desktop and glanced to her right. "How are you doing, Perry?"

Perry stood holding his Coke bottle lens glasses in his right hand and rubbed his eyes with his left. "I just finished Homeland Security's files. Can I take a break and put in my contacts while you check the servers? These glasses refuse to stay in place, and everything is blurring."

"Please do. It'll make you look less like a geek." Quint moved to Perry's station to check his work.

Perry teased back, "You would know."

Quint didn't like Perry, but he appreciated his sense of humor. "When you return, I have a few more things to check off the list."

"I saw your assignments pop up on the screen a while ago. I can handle the extra load. Let me know if you need anything else." Perry left the room.

Quint wondered what Cordy was doing. She rarely got flustered, even though her day blossomed with multi-task items. But today, she was back working with the SWAT team. It suited her to a tee. Something exciting, being in control and not knowing what would happen next, keeping her alert—her mind leaping from one scenario to another. At times like this, he envied her ability to work so well with others. Sometimes, his total lack of social skills and inability to say two words without making them into a whole paragraph got in the way of communication.

Svetlana pulled up the DoD list. "Do you want all the contractors? There are over 464,000 firms, and they come and go, like a revolving door."

"Run only contractors hired on within the last two years," Quint said. "That should narrow the list—be sure that Einar Zinmansky is one of them."

"Will do." Svetlana got back to work.

Quint hadn't eaten all day. Perry always had food inside his desk. Quint wondered how that kid could eat so much and stay so skinny. He opened Perry's desk drawer, hoping to find a Power Bar or a Snickers. No food. Instead, he found a postcard from Vlad, Perry's cousin living in Moscow, Russia. The card had a crude, large, bold print using red ink and written in English, "Beware, Cozy Bear is back."

"Did I pass inspection?" Perry asked Quint as he walked into the conference room, but his focus was on Svetlana.

"What's Vlad talking about?" Quint held up the postcard. "Cozy Bear? Really, as in APT29, backed by Russian Intelligence? Did you know about this hack? If you had warned us, we could have been on the alert and prevented it."

Perry paled. "I've never seen that card, and I don't know what that warning means. I've been calling Vlad for several days, but he doesn't answer."

"But you do know Cozy Bear is another name for APT29, don't you?" Quint got up and stood over Perry. "They're an organized Russian hacking group. If Cordy hears that you had a warning of this hack before it happened, she will fire you! And good riddance!"

"But... I've never seen that card before now. Where did you find it?" Perry took a step backward. "Besides, I thought their nickname was Fancy Bear."

"Yeah, Fancy Bear, Cozy Bear, APT29, Tsar Team, Sednit—they all are the same group of hackers." Quint shook the card in his hand toward Perry. "Don't play dumb with me. I'm sure you researched Cozy Bear when you got this card."

Perry put his hands on his hips. "I didn't—"

Svetlana hopped from her chair and jumped into the space between the two men. "Stop this right now! He didn't put that card in his desk drawer. I did. It came late last night in an envelope addressed to our team. I opened it and saw it was from Vlad, so I slipped it into his desk. With all the commotion going on this morning, I forgot to tell him about it. I'm the one to blame. I have to admit, I read the note and didn't tie the two together either. I just slipped it into his desk drawer because he had gone home for the night."

"If Vlad believed we were in imminent danger, he would have texted me," Perry said. "When we talked with Cracker earlier today, he said Vlad is on a black ops mission with the Rebel Army. I don't know how to reach him to clarify this message."

Quint slammed the card back on Perry's desk. "Wait until Cordy hears of this!"

"She has enough to handle at the moment," Svetlana said. "Why do the two of you always fight? I'm sick of it. Be open and honest with each other. No more snipering."

"Sniping," Perry corrected her.

"Whatever." Svetlana rolled her eyes. "If you made a mistake, fix it. We are a team, and sometimes I feel like I am a empire."

"An Umpire," Quint said, "and I think you really mean referee." He hated being chastised, but she was probably right. He did find little things about Perry to pick at, but this was serious.

"Boys, I'm sure you're both going back to work quietly now, so I can finish this task." She added something in Russian under her breath.

***

Perry smirked at the comment, knowing Quint had no idea that she'd called him a bossy old man, and kept walking, side-stepped Quint, and sat at his station. "So, am I good to go here? We need to get Homeland Security's system back up and running."

"No, I'm taking it from here." Quint tapped Perry on the shoulder and pointed for him to move. "Go over there and call Cracker. Get the latest updates from Russia, and see if they know anything about Cozy Bear."

Perry agreed wholeheartedly with Svetlana's comment but refused to let Quint upset him. "Roger." Perry grabbed the card and headed for the main conference table to place his call. He read the scrawled letters and checked the date but then remembered that she said the card was inside an envelope. "Svetlana, do you still have the outer envelope?"

"No, I threw it in yesterday's rubbish." She checked her wastebasket. "It's not here."

"Did it have big red letters like the card?" Perry asked.

"No, it was typed and addressed to the cybersecurity team. There was no return address, but it was postmarked two days ago."

"It must have been airmailed to get here in two days," Perry said. "It usually takes four. I wish you had saved the envelope. We could have fingerprinted it."

"Then fingerprint the postcard. It's the next best thing." Svetlana checked the main trash container by the refreshment stand. "It's not here either. I don't remember which one I threw the envelope in."

"Anything else inside?" Perry asked.

Svetlana returned to her desk. "Wait, a red paper clip fell out with the card. It should be here somewhere." She searched and found a red plastic-covered clip. "It wasn't attached to the card. Sorry, I should have put this in your drawer, too."

Perry barely acknowledged her apology as his mind leapt through several questions. *A separate paper clip? It meant unity during World War II, but would Vlad know that? Why red? Why is Vlad's writing so distorted? He always had great penmanship. Was this really from Vlad? Who else would it be from?*

Perry pulled out his cell phone and texted Vlad one more time. "Received your postcard and paper clip, must talk ASAP." Holding the card up to the light, he noticed something in black behind the red letters. *Maybe the clip meant attachment included.*

Spying a magnifying glass on a credenza next to him, he slid the card under it for a better image. Code 7-4912 became clear under the red letters. The code didn't jar any memory cells. He was about to call Cracker when he decided to research the number. *Is it a Zip*

Code? Cruz Verde, Nuevo Leon came up. He searched for a Postal code—Codigo, Mexico.

Google also brought up product numbers, biochemical numbers, and policy numbers, but none made any sense. Then, he experimented with phone numbers. He entered code 7-4912, and Ryazan, the largest city and administrative center in Western Russia, popped up. Country code = 7. Area code = 4912. *This has to be a clue to something, but what? And if it is a clue, what does it mean?* Perry speed-dialed Cracker's number.

Ready, Set, Go!

Cordy set up in the Bunker's technical room, linked into the SWAT's surveillance command center, and brought up a mirrored image of their data, including audio and video views on a large screen divided into several smaller displays. Each team member wore a helmet with an internal night vision screen that accessed the drone images, allowing Cordy to view what they saw. Each helmet had a built-in two-way radio linked to the onsite Command Center and Cordy's master radio. She also had two larger screens—one view for each of the two drones that could switch between infrared or night vision images. Cordy opened two more monitors, ready to capture any radio or infrared visuals of the enemy.

She was twenty minutes late after setting up her space and linked to the SWAT team leader, Russ Bracken.

Russ was prowling around in the rain, reexamining the drone links, checking camera settings, and adjusting the infrared sensors. Cordy was glad to be in a dry room of the Bunker rather than the cold drizzle that she had experienced with the team in the past. She made contact via VidChat.

Russ answered as soon as he heard the ringtone, his voice dripping with irritation and tension: "It's about time! Emma's life is at stake. We need to find her before it's too late."

Cordy knew he was ticked. "Sorry I'm late, and what I'm going to ask next will make you downright angry, but it's not the first time, nor will it be the last. I see Loran's with you, and I want to run something past him for approval."

Loran's fists clenched. "Can't it wait?"

"No. The Securities and Exchange Commission wants us to investigate Friday's NYSE transactions, especially stocks that sold short. We may have another reason to track the huge profits that day, too."

"Is this really important? Cut to the chase." Loran paced.

"Okay…" She quickly explained her concern regarding IYFTI and SkyUrsis Capital. "We're all bogged down with the terrorist attacks, and I want CrowdStrike to check into this."

"Sure, just take care of it," Loran said. "My priority is Emma, and I don't want to wait another minute."

"I'll text Quint." Cordy entered a message as she spoke, feeling the testosterone building within the team. Quint was already on VidChat with CrowdStrike when she texted.

Russ snapped into his 'let's do this' attitude. "Both drones are ready. Are they connected on your end?"

"Yes, I can see the display on the helmet cameras," Cordy said. "I'm also connected to the drones and your radios."

"Fill me in on your plan to launch." Evans sat by a laptop, ready to type notes. "While Cordy has worked with you in the past, I'm new to this."

"Roger," Russ's voice sounded clipped. "I'll lead team 1. Poncho is second in command and will lead team 2. Poncho, Chico, Kayman, and Sergeant Foley fought alongside me in Afghanistan, and we're like brothers."

Braun piped up, "One of the best SWAT teams I know."

Cordy was glad to see that Braun had changed clothes and was now in combat gear. Knowing that Russ was close by, she felt better about the mission.

"Thanks," Russ said. "We adopted Desmond a few years back. Foley and Desmond are our two bomb experts. Enough introductions—let's get to work. Foley and Chico, you're with me."

Loran asked, "Which team am I on?"

"Come with me," Russ said. "Braun, join Poncho's team along with Desmond and Kayman."

"Okay, thanks for the introductions," Evans said. "Now, can you share your plan of attack and let me know what is expected of me?"

Russ explained, "Each drone has a night vision lens and thermal sensors. There's also a multi-weapon detector to identify guns, bombs, and explosives and a bug detector. The latest feature searches for hidden cameras. Cordy will show you what to do."

Evans seemed oblivious to Russ's impatience and scooted closer to the screen. "Does it have a light intensifier, or will we only see shadows in red and green?"

"There is some enhancement, but mostly green and black from the night vision lens and bluish-green to reddish-yellow from the infrared." Russ moved toward the first drone. "I'll relay orders as we go. It's time to get these in the air. The sleet is letting up. It's the perfect time to move."

"Drone 1 ready for settings," Chico announced.

Russ pulled on his gloves. "Circle once going east in a one-mile radius from the GPS point. On the second loop, narrow to half a mile radius for the first 180° and then fly directly over the RV and return to base. Check if RV is equipped with surveillance cameras watching out for us. If so, block their access."

Cordy made adjustments on her end. "Ready."

Chico set the parameters. "Launching in three, two, one," and the first drone lifted, making a soft whirring sound.

Cordy saw tall, soggy weeds appear and then several stables and fields. As the drone continued to fly its path, dozens of horses were inside, plus a few smaller critters among the trees.

Russ turned toward Poncho and Desmond. "The second drone will go west, but set the initial radius to half a mile, then cut to a quarter-mile on the second loop for 180°. Fly over the RV and back to headquarters. Based on what they capture, we'll determine the next steps."

Poncho adjusted the settings. "Launching drone 2."

Russ adjusted his goggles. "Let's move inside and watch on the large monitor."

They barely got situated inside headquarters when Cordy warned, "There's something at drone 1's three-o'clock position, just in front of the granite pile." Cordy zoomed in on the object. A dark, lumpy plastic bag appeared, resembling a heap of trash and scrap metal. A few meters away, the thermal detector sent an image emanating heat. "Someone is out there, and I think he's planting IEDs in those trash bags. Get the drone closer and see if—"

"Good eye," Russ said. "The weapon sensor just alerted, and I marked the GPS coordinates."

"There are three trail cameras, set ten yards apart in trees near the trash bags, and a bug on top of the granite pile. I bet they have a screen inside the RV surveying the area. I'll let them get a good image and lock it in place so they don't see you coming."

"How close is drone 2 from the RV?" Braun asked.

"Thirty meters." Cordy zoomed in on drone 2. "I see eight heat images inside the RV, plus the one captured on drone 1 makes nine. Someone is lying down in the northeast corner, and another person is standing over him or her."

"Drone 2 just located another two cameras outside the RV," Russ said.

"And as I surmised, a screen, six radios, and surveillance software set up inside the RV." Cordy locked onto the coordinates and ran a frequency detector. "I have access to the enemy's channel."

"Patch us in." Russ waved to his men to stay silent.

Cordy plugged in, and they listened to a man with a deep, gravelly voice, "…move out in the morning, but what we do with ze woman, Mr. Zahair?"

"No witnesses, Rugar," a man said in perfect English. He clipped his words with a commanding voice. Cordy heard no hint of Farsi, and it sounded like the same brusque voice she had heard from the rooftop across the street from the White House before the drone strike. *Was it Zahair who launched that drone?* Cordy knew Zahair was Iranian, but you'd never know it by listening to him.

"But, Misure Zahair, ze work hard save secretary like you ask," Rugar said. "Ze make meals, do as you say."

"Spoils of war," Zahair said. "You know that. You live that. It must be done."

"And ze man, he not well," Rugar said. "We keel him, too?"

"No!" Zahair's voice boomed. "Mr. Secretary is our ticket out of the country. We have a contact who paid $3 million for his capture—that's half a million apiece. We need him alive, at least until our jet arrives. Once we're safe, dispose of him. You still get a big reward."

"You get reward if I stay," Rugar said in alarm. "They keel me, too? I no like plan."

"Gregor will be with you," Zahair said. "He's a whiz with technology. He'll make a new ID and passport for you."

Russ spoke over Cordy's radio to prevent the enemy from hearing. "Six males are sitting in a circle in the southwest corner." Russ stared at the monitor as if it would talk back to him. "What jet is Zahair talking about? Sounds like he's holding Secretary Hendrum and Emma. Right?"

"Sure sounds like it," Cordy said. "Better plan on two hostages."

"Hover drone 2 closer to the RV," Loran drummed his fingers against his leg, "I want to see if Emma is inside."

Cordy took control of drone 2. "The infrared thermal imaging shows a female standing in the southeast corner."

"Wait, there's a fast-moving thermal object on the right of the screen." Braun pointed at the image. "Maybe the man we saw earlier is heading back to the RV."

Russ added, "Or setting up more booby traps."

Loran took a step forward as if to pace, but the crowded tactical unit, filled with men built like tanks, made that impossible. "I'm ready to raid the place."

Russ pulled up a map of the area. "Hold on. We'll free your wife, but let's get the drones back to headquarters and load them with live ammo first. Once they're in the air, team 1 will go right. Team 2, go to the left. We'll stay 3 meters apart."

"Shouldn't we defuse the IED first?" Team 2's explosives expert, Desmond, asked. "Foley and I can do the job."

"Yes—and there may be additional booby traps, tripwires, Punji sticks, or landmines." Russ scooted behind Loran, moving toward the door. "Drone 1 is heading our way. Move out and intercept. Drone 2 is just past the RV in the woods. ETA is two minutes."

"So, there are nine total, counting Emma if she's the female inside the RV. If one is Hendrum, there are seven enemies," Cordy confirmed. "Your team has eight. You've faced worse odds."

Drone 2 picked up voices coming from the woods. "Check your radios for interference."

Suddenly, the four radios muted. *Have we been detected?* Cordy quickly checked the frequency blocker, hoping the men were just maintaining silence. She would if it were her. She paused drone 2 near the granite heap and turned up the communicator's volume. One of the men in the woods whispered, "…Rugar says we each get half a million for this guy, but I know that's a lie. Zahair got $50 million."

"How do you know this?" a man with a higher-pitched voice asked.

"I saw it in an email. It's a covert bank account that converts to cryptocurrency. Money was sent to Cypriots in Cyprus. And that note you dropped off at the coffee shop for his all-powerful wife, the judge? That was for another $25 million. She went to the news. We'll never see that money, but Zahair's playing with dynamite. Watch your backs, boys."

The high-pitched voice warned, "Quick, turn your radios back on and say nothing. Zahair just texted. We need to report as ordered. I'll stand guard out here." The men scattered, and Cordy sent drone 2 back to the SWAT team.

Russ adjusted his gear. "These men are killers. Hit hard and fast. Stay safe and rescue both hostages unharmed. Immobilize Zahair if you must, but keep him alive. We need answers."

Cordy watched her screen intently but couldn't sit still any longer. Her bladder was about to burst, so she turned her radio over to Evans. "I'll be right back," and then rushed to the restroom.

Cozy Bear Alert

Perry took a quick look at the postcard found in his desk drawer, which had a message written in rough handwriting, saying, "…be careful, Cozy Bear is back." This made Perry wonder what it meant. *Was it sent by Vlad? If not, who could it be from? Was it a warning about the recent hack into the government's defense system?*

Quint's cruel words still echoed in Perry's ears, "If Cordy hears that you had a warning of this hack before it happened, she will fire you! And good riddance!" Perry's nose wrinkled in disgust as Quint took over the assignment Perry had worked on all morning and brought Homeland Security's data back online. *The mighty Quint can't get me fired without a fight.* Perry entered his user ID and password into another computer and opened the backdoor to log off the one he had been using.

"What the hell?" Quint shouted as Perry's old desktop turned black.

"Didn't you log in using your own ID?" Perry smirked. "You would have yelled at me if I did that."

"Never mind," Quint said beneath his breath and tapped in his ID so hard that Perry thought he would pop a key from the board.

I'll show him who's best at his job! Perry chuckled and logged on to a VidChat conference call with their Russian contacts, Cracker and Rozalina. The call would ping every thirty seconds to a different server across the globe to ensure a secure line. The signal bounced off servers in Utah, California, Paris, the Hawaiian Islands, Singapore, and finally, Russia.

"Cracker, here." The call was crystal clear even though they were nearly 5,500 miles apart. "Rozalina, it's Perry. Come join us."

Perry greeted his old friends and explained about the postcard. "It's signed by Vlad using crude red letters, and there's a hidden code written behind the letters, along with a red paper clip. I know you've been researching who downloaded the ransomware. Was it from Cozy Bear? If so, I need proof of this alleged group's activity—video, audio, or a written statement to verify their actions."

"No luck linking the ransomware to Cozy Bear, ATP29, or any of their aliases on our end," Cracker said.

"However, I tracked Darkside out of Eastern Europe, which could be from Russia, but there are similar groups from China, North Korea, Syria, and Iran. I also found suspicious money flowing in and out of these countries," Rozalina said. "At first, I passed over the information, but then I saw a wire transfer from Wells Fargo Bank in Washington, D.C. It was like the transfer reached out and grabbed me, so I kept searching. Where do you want the files sent?"

Perry set up a new folder and forwarded a link. "How much money are you talking about?"

"Over half a billion U.S. dollars in twenty-three accounts, mostly from Russia, two from Iran, one from Syria, and the highest single transaction was for $250 million from Wells Fargo in D.C." Rozalina downloaded several files. "Although Russian authorities cooperate with the FBI here in Moscow to fight terrorism and criminal activity that affects both the Russian Federation and the U.S., at times, there's a thin line that we must not cross. Since we're speaking over an encrypted phone, I can admit that I'm dancing close to that line. It could be dangerous if I get caught. I had to reroute my entry and data access several times, but it led me to a small group of high-powered hackers laundering their money through an International Bank. I wouldn't doubt they are also linked to Cozy Bear and or Darkside, but I have no proof of that yet."

"I need to know how an account got opened in Braun's name. Who at Wells Fargo would allow that?" Perry asked.

"I don't know who set it up in the U.S.," Rozalina admitted, "but the Russian banker's name is Olga H. I've tracked her before, and this woman meets with clients regularly. I suspect her of setting up tax scams, bogus funds for hedge funds, and other activities, but she has excellent lawyers and somehow stays one step ahead of the authorities."

Perry typed a message. "Thanks. I'm going to find out the name of the banker who set up the U.S. account at Wells Fargo."

"We've attached tracers to each of the accounts," Rozalina said. "They will send every new transaction to our server. I added a camera and audio to three primary hackers and tried to tag the Wells Fargo account, but I couldn't break through their firewall. Whoever built it, knew what they were doing. Maybe Cordy or your team can break through."

"Thanks. I built that firewall last year. It's quite a compliment coming from someone as skilled as you are," Perry said. "It was made to prevent anyone from getting access, but I know how to get inside the system. I'm sure I can nab whoever is behind the transfers."

Cracker cleared his throat. "I don't think we want to do that. It's better to know your enemies and let them think they have power over you, but build a better firewall and reroute their activities. Set up a temp file for the hackers to implode."

"Won't they catch on?" Perry asked.

"Not before we siphon their funds," Rozalina said. "It's the money that they want, not the notoriety."

"For those paying the money? Now that's a different story," Cracker said. "They want to destroy the U.S. security system, and that's who you want to track down and charge with cybercrimes."

"Monitor where the money originates," Rozalina said. "As I mentioned, most of the money came from Ryazan, Russia, but I found sources from Tehran, Iran, Damascus, Syria, and another from Washington, D.C. Focus on them first. I highlighted their transactions, which diverted to four locations before the final destination. I'm sure there will be more money transfers, and I'll track those originating in Russia. It will be easier for me since I'm already in the country. Oh, yes. I also found cryptocurrency used on two occasions."

"I'm not very familiar with that whole process of dealing with money. Did they use Bitcoin or some other form?" Perry asked.

Rozalina checked her notes. "They used Ethereum, which can route more than 1.5 million transactions per day and is expected to get even more."

"Wow, Bitcoin can only process 900 in that time frame!" Perry said. "What about the ransomware?" Perry entered several notes into his computer as they talked.

"Still working on that," Cracker said. "Did you find another solution?"

"We were able to get access to our data without paying, but we want the people responsible for the attack."

"We'll do our best to track them down." Cracker's brow furrowed. "You mentioned the postcard was from Vlad. I doubt he sent it. He's on a mission in Siberia, and postal departments are rare in that area. I can't even reach him by phone. There is no cell service, and the clock is ticking. From there, he's transferring to Iran, but I'm unsure where or when, and I couldn't reach him even if I needed to."

"Then who would have sent the note?" Perry noticed the room had gone quiet. No one was typing, and Svetlana had left the room. He glanced over at Quint, who was staring at him. *He's watching my every move like a hawk, ready to pounce. Show no fear.* Perry continued to stare until Quint's gaze flitted away.

"Did you find any fingerprints?" Cracker asked.

Perry's attention was pulled back to the conference call. "The outside envelope was trashed."

"Trashed?" Rozalina sounded confused.

"Put in the rubbish bin," Perry clarified. "I don't have it anymore, but we did bag the postcard for evidence, and I'll run it for fingerprints after this call. Do you know anyone from Ryazan?"

"I know an oil engineer from there," Cracker said, "but I doubt he'd be much help tracking down hackers. However, he's been known to have connections with some shady characters in the past."

Rozalina was typing in the background. "Ryazan is also known for its aviation museum, which displays mainly World War II planes." The tapping sound paused. "Wait, I may have discovered something. You referred to a red paper clip sent along with the postcard. Did you ever hear of a man in Canada who, about fifteen years ago, traded a red paper clip for a house online?"

"No, I never heard that story," Perry said.

Rozalina laughed. "Someone in Ryazan recently opened a website. They refuse to use money as payment and only barter for items."

Perry waited for the punch line, but none came. "Why is that important?"

"My gut just flipped when you mentioned the red paper clip, so I shared it," Rozalina paused as disappointment hung in the air. "I don't know why I even mentioned it. Then again, there was an Operation Paperclip, where Nazi scientists were recruited to the United States after World War II, to provide covert information and launch future technology to forge ahead in aerospace, medicine, and chemical warfare, especially during the cold war. What if Russia, better known as the Red Army, created a similar program partnering with Syria, Iran, and maybe even China, signified by a red paper clip?"

Cracker patted his wife on the back. "Honey, you know your gut has saved us more than once. Keep searching." His affectionate tone for Rozalina revealed their close relationship.

A high-pitched ding sounded from Rozalina's computer. "I just got notice of another account transaction. Give me a moment." Rozalina took ten seconds. Perry could hear her gasp. "Check this out. The account transfer came from Rappic Leperd in Ryazan at the Central Bank. I did an Internet search, and Leperd means cunning or sly fox."

Perry typed the name into his program connected to Interpol, Europol, and numerous other searches. "The name Leperd comes up twenty-eight times, but no Rappic. That's an unusual name."

"Is there an R. Leperd?" Rozalina asked.

"Two hits as R. Leperd, a fifty-three-year-old, and another man, who is quite young—in his early twenties." Perry drilled down deeper into his system. "They are father and son. The older man is the new CEO of a major oil firm in Iran, and his son has a criminal history—arrested for hacking into a Franco-German defense system while in the military. Daddy got him out of jail with a small fine and a rap on the knuckles. The son now specializes in drone architecture."

"Drones?" Rozalina stifled a yawn. "Sorry, it's past our bedtime, but we may have found your hacker. Whoever sent this also used Ethereum. Now, let's see where this money ends up. We'll keep you posted."

"Thanks, great job," Perry disconnected the call and glanced around the room.

Quint was now sitting next to Svetlana, showing her how to connect their updated security system to the Internet.

Perry texted the latest info to Cordy directly and didn't bother to cc Quint. *If the jerk wants to know what transpired on the call, he'll have to ask for the details.* Perry set to work to break through the Wells Fargo firewall he'd created last year to track the account sent from the Washington, D.C., Bank. Then he'd follow up and lock in R. Leperd's hacking activities as proof to send to Cordy to forward to the CIA. He'd used a similar trap while working at Red Panda. *This could clear Braun from being charged with treason.*

Perry wasn't sure if swabbing the postcard for fingerprints would generate any leads, but he couldn't contain his excitement when he hit a match. "That postcard has a right thumb and index fingerprint that matches Farzad Zahair. There are several other prints that aren't in the database, so I don't know who actually sent this."

Quint hopped from his chair. "Are you sure? How does Zahair even know about us?" Quint turned to Svetlana. "Are you sure this arrived last night?"

"Yes, why are you so upset?" Svetlana asked.

"Whoever sent this knows Zahair, or he sent it himself, but why? I'll text Cordy."

"She's working with the SWAT team, so this will have to wait," Svetlana said. "What did you find out from Cracker?"

Perry shared his conversation with the team, but he didn't mention the trap he'd placed into the Wells Fargo system. That information would go directly to Cordy.

Rock Creek Raid

Sept. 11 – 7:56 p.m. EDT, Southeast Rock Creek Park, Washington, D.C.

When Cordy returned from the restroom, Evans was gone, but he'd left a sticky note on the desk: "Briefly called away. Be back ASAP."

Cordy scooted her chair next to the large screen located in the massive technology room deep within the Bunker. The room was filled with the latest AV, audio, and computer systems, but Cordy preferred the comfort and familiarity of her own office in Fort Collins. The subdivided screen displayed images of the SWAT team, two drones, images from six cameras, and audio speakers connected to the SWAT team's radio signal. She listened for the terrorist's frequency as she fine-tuned a second set of speakers. "Gotcha!" She locked onto the rival's signal as a graveled voice came across in Farsi.

Her belly prevented Cordy from sitting close to the desk where she accessed her private laptop and a government-issued desktop. One hand rested over the baby bump, trying to quiet the twins, who were performing calisthenics at this late hour. *Katrina doesn't like all that coffee I've been gulping.* The thought made her smile. *I'll have to come up with a name for our son soon.* Braun had refused to call him Junior, *so what is your name, little one?*

She startled when Russ spoke through the radio, "Cordy, are you back with us? Evans got an urgent call, and we're ready to move."

She had muted her end of the terrorist's radio frequency but continued to monitor their conversation through her translator program, "Ready for action."

A shrill voice came from outside the RV. The man sounded alarmed and out of breath. "We've been spotted! I saw flashing lights...horse ranch...not far from here. Get in position."

From inside the RV, Gregor said, "I don't see anything unusual on the cameras."

"Maybe they blocked them. You three, outside with Amir," Zahair ordered. "Gregor, stay with surveillance and reset the cameras. Rugar, guard the hostages."

Cordy heard chairs scoot across the floor, footsteps rustling, and a door slammed. The graveled voice she recognized as Rugar's said, "Baleh." "Yes" in Farsi.

Russ, too, was moving his men in position. After loading and launching the drones, he motioned Sergeant Foley forward and fell in behind him. "We'll head for the IED site first. You and Desmond disarm the explosives. Watch for tripwires."

Agent Evans must have run back to the Bunker's technical room as he arrived out of breath, his shoulders heaving with the effort. He had an armful with two manila files, both six inches thick. "I thought you might want to browse through the research we have on Farzad Zahair in your spare time."

"You left to get those folders?" Cordy huffed and pointed to the stack.

"No, I had another urgent matter, but I grabbed them before leaving the office." Evans set the folders on the desk. "The top one is from the FBI—the other from the CIA. Zahair's only 37—he must have started early to produce this much info."

"I'll digest that later." Cordy shoved the worn folders to one side of her desk. "Can you stay? The team is moving." Cordy's full attention was on the SWAT team, staying one step ahead of the enemy surveillance cameras and blocking each as they rotated. They reset twice while under her watch. Finally, she said, "If you're available, I need you to watch and reset these cameras as needed. I'm monitoring the drones, and I'd appreciate your help."

"Okay. Let's do this." Evans pulled up a stool. "Are they saying anything over the radio?"

"Sorry, I muted yours." She tapped a button to unmute, and Evans nodded. "Okay, they're in the woods."

Cordy watched Sergeant Foley, in the lead, creep through the thick forest covered in heavy sleet, yet his boots never made a sound.

His breath came out in fluffy puffs of vapor as the temperature dipped to near freezing. He motioned to Russ, whose bulky form paused. They both dropped to one knee.

"Tripwire," Russ warned over the radio.

Desmond was three feet to Foley's left, followed by Poncho. "Clear here. There's a wire tied to the evergreen to your left."

Cordy heard the whine of a small drone as it came into view. "Enemy drone, ten o'clock."

Poncho's silenced shot knocked it from the air even before she had finished her sentence, "Neutralized."

Russ tensed. "That could have had an explosive."

Poncho shrugged. "Our drone would have warned us."

Desmond checked the downed drone. "Night vision camera only, but they now know our position."

"You're safe. I blocked it," Cordy said.

Foley cut the tripwire and lowered an overhead explosive to the ground. He defused the IED. "That was more complex than what I expected."

Cordy sent drone 2 to hover over the enemy's headquarters. "Three men are heading your way. They're armed."

"Can you tell if any of them is Zahair?" Russ asked. "I want him alive."

"I can't tell them apart," Cordy said, "but I think Zahair stayed inside the RV."

"Team 2, go left, and intercept," Russ ordered. "Foley, find those trash bags and defuse explosives."

"Roger" came through the radio as a duet.

Russ scanned the area, "Cordy, redirect drone 1 to the trash site. Check for thermal images."

She rerouted drone 1 and sent it to the trash's GPS coordinates, but the plastic bags had disappeared. Instead, an unmanned robotic vehicle activated and advanced toward team 1. "Russ, RCV 800 meters at 2 o'clock moving at—"

"I see it." Russ hit the dirt and belly-crawled behind the evergreen.

A splash of mud blew into Foley's face as he dove to his left behind Russ.

Chico was on one knee, the RCV in his sites. His automatic assault rifle blasted a full round, but a robotic arm rapidly set up shields to protect against the assault. Bullets pinged off the metal without any damage.

It gave Russ enough time to load an anti-tank missile launcher. "This will get its attention." The robot blew into the air and exploded before the team even heard the missile launch.

"They got our robot," came from the radio inside the RV.

Cordy wondered how the enemy knew the RCV was shot down. "Reset the camera blocker. He shouldn't have seen the hit."

"Sorry," Evans lurched forward to do as she said.

"Then send in its replacement," Zahair said.

"There's another one, seven hundred meters to your right." Cordy counted down as the RCV moved closer, "Six hundred fifty meters, six..."

The vehicle came to a stop, and a robotic arm emerged, aiming at the evergreen guarding Russ. With a loud crack, the tree splintered, showering team 1 in debris in a thunderous explosion. "Fall back!" Russ ordered.

Cordy watched the RCV advance once more. She had to intervene. "Evans, do you recognize that weapon? It's smaller than the first."

"XM1216." Evans pulled up the specs. "It's ours. Four men with assault rifles can't stop that, and Russ probably didn't bring a second missile launcher."

"Check on team 2." Cordy grabbed the spec requirement for drone 1, searching for the code. "Russ, what weapons are on drone 1?"

"Best bet is the 40 mm grenade," Russ said.

Drone 1 dove toward the robotic arm and dropped the grenade before Russ could give further orders.

"Area cleared." Cordy beamed a bright smile.

"Do you see any more RCVs?" Russ asked.

"No," Cordy did another search to be sure, "but I didn't see these either until a few moments ago. I will send the drone ahead to circle the area within a quarter-mile radius. Where's Loran? Isn't he with your team?"

Russ pulled splinters from his knee. His trousers were like porcupine quills. "Poncho, is Loran with you?"

"Negative," Poncho radioed, "and we're pinned down."

"I'll find him." Cordy adjusted drone 2.

Poncho gave an update, but it was hard to hear through the shelling in the distance, which echoed over the radio. "Desmond defused…tripwire and… Kayman twenty paces…RV rear…under attack. Two enemies down, two more outside. Drone 2 shows three men inside an RV with a female and probably Hendrum, sustained no injuries so far. Braun and I are—" There was nothing but static.

"Poncho, repeat. You cut out." Russ waved team 1 forward. His gun extended as he half-crouched and scurried behind Foley. His night vision goggles showed a hazy green image of the woodland. Poncho didn't reply.

Chico crept forward and nearly landed into a line of punji sticks. "Stay clear." He went around.

Cordy's voice came out high-pitched, "Drone 2 shows Loran outside the rear window of the northeast corner of the RV. At least, I think it's him."

"Loran, fall back," Russ said. "That's an order. Wait for backup."

"I see Emma," Loran whispered with excitement. "She's tied to a chair next to a cot, and I think that's Mo Hendrum lying down. He has his arm in a sling, and he's either sleeping or unconscious."

"I said: 'Fall back now,'" Russ snapped.

"I didn't see anyone else inside the RV, but Poncho and Braun need backup. Desmond is defusing another trap." Loran lifted his hand to rap on the window.

"Get down!" Kayman grabbed Loran's raised hand and yanked him to the ground away from the RV. "Tripwire!" A tiny thread the size of a spider's web ran across the edge of the window.

"Jeez, I nearly got everyone killed," Loran said.

"That's not all," Kayman brushed aside a pile of leaves, exposing a punji stick not more than two inches from where Loran had been standing a moment before. The sharp bamboo stake would have sliced his leg in two or worse if triggered.

"Okay, I'll wait for backup," Loran said. "Where's Desmond? We need to disarm this tripwire."

"I'm busy at the moment," Desmond said over several popping sounds like firecrackers.

A bearded man, dressed in a tunic and wide trousers fastened at the ankle, ran past the RV and around the left, past one of his colleagues. Words exchanged, and Cordy recognized the gravelly-voiced man in the tunic as Rugar. He raised a hand, tossed down his rifle, and ran toward Poncho. The man screamed and flew forward through the air, followed by the sound of a gunshot. He landed with a thud.

Cordy gasped, "Did the enemy just shoot one of their own, or was he a hostage?"

Poncho knelt in the high grass, crab-walking toward the downed man. "I don't recognize him, but he has a pulse, and—"

There was a flurry of activity. Two snipers opened fire, pinning down team 2, while a man carrying Hendrum over his shoulder dashed from the RV and loaded him into a black SUV. A second man raced behind him, carrying Emma, and loaded her into the back. The car engine roared to life.

Team 1 reached the scene as Poncho darted behind a tree, but he wasn't fast enough. He flew sideways and collapsed onto the ground, his left leg unable to support him.

Braun threw a grenade at the two snipers and headed toward Poncho. The grenade was a direct hit, downing both.

Desmond dashed toward his team leader. "Poncho's been hit! Left groin and losing a lot of blood—may be an artery. Braun's strapping his belt around the wound to form a tourniquet."

Cordy's fingers shook as she dialed 911, "SWAT Officer down, Rock Creek Park." She gave the GPS coordinates, "Hurry."

Russ and team 1 made it to the RV.

"They're getting away," Evans said. "Loran, Kayman, go around to your right, Russ and Chico, to your left."

Kayman came around in a flash and shot a hole in the front and rear tires on the passenger's side of the SUV.

"FBI, get out of the car!" Loran shouted out of habit, although the enemy already knew they were under attack.

The driver flashed his brights and drove forward on the flat tires, threatening to run Loran down.

The windshield shattered when Loran fired two shots, and the car came to a halt. Loran pulled open the door, and the unrestrained driver, crouched by the door to avoid being shot, fell from the vehicle. Shattered glass covered the man, who stared up at Loran and swore in Farsi.

"Say nothing, Gregor!" Zahair shouted.

Kayman grabbed Gregor's gun, yanked him upright, and frisked him. He removed a knife strapped to Gregor's thigh and handcuffed him.

At the same time, Russ yanked the side door open, and his gun pointed at Zahair's head. "Get out, or I'll shoot."

Zahair tossed his gun to the ground, raised his hands, and eased himself from the car. "Don't shoot. I never harmed her."

Russ handcuffed the man and handed him over to Chico.

"How are the hostages?" Cordy asked.

Russ went around to the driver's side door, yanked it open, and caught Secretary of State Mo Hendrum as his head flopped to the side and his body slumped toward the door. Russ slid his fingers over Mo's carotid artery. "He has a thready pulse."

Emma called from the back of the SUV, "He's been shot. I removed a bullet from his shoulder over twelve hours ago, and he has a severe concussion. Maybe even a cerebral bleed. He needs medical attention."

"Emma!" Loran shouted and flung open the rear door. He uncuffed her wrists and pulled her to him in a gentle embrace. "Did he hurt you?"

"No," Emma said, but she didn't let go.

Desmond from team 2 radioed. "Weren't there two bodies after the explosion?"

"Yes, two bodies, why?" Braun asked as he continued holding pressure on Poncho's groin.

"There's only one, and he's dead," Desmond said, "the second man must have feigned his death and got away in the commotion. Wait, I see footprints among the trees." There was a pause, "The prints disappeared after forty yards."

Russ radioed Cordy, "Send drone 1 up to check for a heat sensor in the woods."

Desmond spoke again, "I found a radio, backpack, and a blood-splotched camo jacket lying by a fence. A pouch inside the pack held two thumb drives, a hard drive, and an e-tablet. We'll hand them over to the FBI for review. There are fresh motorcycle tracks on the sleet-covered ground, but they, too, disappeared in the woods. The man was definitely wounded and maybe dead by now. Should we continue our search?"

"Cordy, any sign of life out there?" Russ asked.

"I don't see any heat signatures except for a few rodents in the surrounding area," Cordy confirmed. "I just got word that the ambulance is on its way to your location, and I'd like our team to also review the hard and thumb drives. Perhaps it's the missing drive from Zinmansky's laptop computer."

"That's up to the FBI," Russ said. "We'll get medical attention for the wounded and hand over those we've captured. Notify hospitals and clinics to be on the lookout for a man in his thirties presenting with a gunshot wound to the leg and powder burns to the face and hands."

"I think the man's name was Amir," Cordy said. "He's not among the captured."

Foley radioed, "The guy in the tunic is still breathing, but he can't move his legs. His pulse is weak—probably spinal shock. I'll disarm the tripwire at the rear of the RV." A few minutes later, he went around to the front to join the rest of the team as sirens grew louder.

Russ followed Foley into the RV. "Clear!" They gathered up the equipment, including a DoD laptop. Russ handed it over to Loran.

"Bet it's Zinmansky's missing laptop, but how did Zahair get a hold of it?" Cordy reminded the team, "Loran, if it is, I want access to that computer."

"After it's processed by the FBI," Loran said, "then you can analyze it." He held onto Emma's hand as he called an additional response team, the crime scene investigators, the M.E., and the Washington, D.C., police.

Kayman and Chico escorted Zahair and Gregor to the SWAT vehicle and strapped them to a seat in the rear as the ambulance arrived. EMTs and paramedics treated the injured. A paramedic examined Emma while Russ, Braun, and Loran briefly interviewed Zahair, but he wasn't talking.

During the interview, Cordy was also on speaker but had signed off when Russ contacted FBI Agent Gray to update him.

"Chief of Police Polack is demanding a transfer of Zahair," Gray said. "We've agreed to allow a joint investigation, and they have already arranged to meet you at the park's entrance. Anyone requiring medical services will also be transferred to their custody."

"Isn't that Loran Sloan's call?" Russ asked. "He's with our SWAT team."

"The Department of Justice made the call," Gray said. "He'll need to check with the Attorney General to get an override."

Loran shook his head. "No need. Emma's safe, and we can work with the police chief."

Russ turned to his team. "You heard the order. A police squad is on their way and will meet us at the entrance to the park. Let's help

Loran and Braun load the drones and make the transfer before we call it a day."

The paramedic cleared Emma, and the medical attendants loaded Poncho, Rugar, and Hendrum onto gurneys and radioed ahead to the hospital.

Before the ambulances headed out, Loran pulled Braun aside. "Once we get to our vehicles, I'll ride with Emma. You can go to Blair House tonight and stay with Cordy. I'll see you in the morning. Be sure to stay undercover. Russ is heading for the hospital with Poncho, and the team knows to keep your identity a secret."

Braun agreed. "We'll interrogate Zahair and the others in the morning." He thanked Russ and the SWAT team members for their help, then grabbed his gear and headed for the Humvee. He waited for Loran and his wife and then radioed Cordy, "I'll meet you soon at Blair House."

"Don't wait up. I still have to meet with my team," Cordy said, but her heart felt lighter, knowing he was safe.

Not wanting to put it off until tomorrow, she called President Zac Spendorf and gave an update on the rescue. "Two dead, three injured, one got away, and the team captured Zahair and his IT guru alive. The FBI will I.D. all and question those who survived in the morning."

"That's good news," Zac said. "And Loran called. I heard you rescued Emma Sloan and Mo Hendrum."

"Yes, the SWAT team freed the Secretary of State. One of Zahair's thugs had captured him in the parking lot. The thug claims Mo was already shot and had a head injury before he hauled Mo away. Zahair was afraid his key hostage would die, so he kidnapped Emma since she was an ICU nurse. Emma managed to dig the bullet from Mo's shoulder, but he's still unconscious."

"Why did they ambush him in the first place?" Zac asked.

"Zahair's not talking, but one of his men, Rugar, says there was a big reward for Hendrum's hide," Cordy said.

"Reward paid by Russia, Syria, or Iran?" Zac asked.

"Rugar's only a pawn in this scheme," Cordy said. "He doesn't know who was behind the payout."

"Mo told me those sanctions were a bad idea, but I backed it anyway. I'll call his wife, Sophia, and have an agent take her to the hospital to be with him." Zac had regret in his voice. "Were there any injuries to the SWAT team members?"

"Poncho was shot in the leg. Braun thinks it's an arterial wound. They started a unit of blood, and he'll be in surgery most of the night. The surgeon expects him to recover." Cordy heaved a sigh of relief. "Bracken and Chico are at the hospital with him."

"Thanks for your help today," Zac said.

"Glad to be here. Did Homeland Security ID the body found in the White House?" Cordy asked.

"We thought we had an answer when the agent at the front entrance explained that Einar Zinmansky was wearing a light gray suit when he signed in during the power outage early this morning, but the body isn't Zinmansky. The suit jacket is, however, and it had a yellow sticky in the pocket signed by Zinmansky. It also has his DNA on the collar, and the blood on the sleeve matches Carl's. We're still researching that."

"What was the man's cause of death?" Cordy asked.

"The ME said he'd been poisoned with Novichok, probably put in his drink. They also found traces in my teapot. I'll think twice before drinking from that pot again. Luckily, Winston used the Bunker coffeepot to brew my tea, so I wasn't exposed. And before you ask, there's no sign of Zinmansky's laptop either."

"I think Loran found it inside the RV." Cordy checked her texts. "The FBI will encrypt, duplicate, and forward a copy of the hard drive to my team. They also fingerprinted the laptop. Quint sent a message that he'll run an exhaustive analysis on the drive. It appears the original one is missing, and there are some suspicious thumb drives and an e-tablet to review. Evans will get another crack at the disk in the morning. He says the FBI will hand that drive and other devices over to me once he finishes his analysis."

Zac thanked Cordy for all her work once again and signed off.

It was nearly 10 p.m., and there was still a mountain of urgent work left to do. She longed to see Braun, knowing he was still undercover, but he would be at the apartment waiting for her when she eventually got there. She couldn't wait, but first, she needed to check in with Quint. Sighing, she thought back to 24 hours ago and remembered her plan for a relaxing Sunday. Nothing could have been farther from the truth. *How had the day flown by so quickly?*

Chief Polack

The coal-black sky sent shivers down Braun's spine. It had been a perfect night for the raid, with the full moon hidden by heavy clouds. Through his torchlight, a thick quilt of mist drifted above the pile of discarded granite that, at one time, adorned the White House. In the wake of gunfire, the natural scent of pine mingled with cordite.

Two members of Russ's team trekked back to the horse ranch to retrieve the vehicles and parked them behind Zahair's shot-up black SUV. In the meantime, the captives were handcuffed and remained standing under guard while the injured were triaged and treated by medical personnel.

When the vehicles arrived, Braun and the SWAT team marched their fugitives, Farzad Zahair and his acolyte, Gregor, through the slippery, sleet-crusted grass to the rear of the BATT, buckled them into seatbelts and shackled their feet to the floor.

Once the drones were loaded and the injured taken away in ambulances, it took another ten minutes to reach the Rock Creek Park entrance, where two patrol cars and four motorcycles sat at the gate. Thanks to Polack's slip-up of speaking over a non-encrypted radio, news of the raid traveled fast. Reporters blocked access to and from the park and were already broadcasting live news from the location.

MSNBC gave a full report. "At approximately 1:45 this morning, Secretary Mo Hendrum was assaulted while leaving the West Executive Avenue parking lot. He was shot, beaten, and kidnapped. Shortly after 2 a.m., the wife of FBI Director Loran Sloan was also kidnapped from her home as she returned from a late-night shift at a local hospital. Now we have learned that an FBI SWAT team has tracked down the kidnappers and rescued both victims. Secretary Hendrum is in critical condition after suffering a head injury and a gunshot wound to his shoulder. An ambulance is transporting him to Walter Reed Hospital."

"Bringing in the press will give us some positive publicity. It'll be one hell of a story." Police Chief Polack moved closer to the media and spoke to his team in a voice loud enough to be overheard. "Zahair's our responsibility, so let's keep our heads up, men. We'll turn him over to a federal facility soon enough, but he's ours for now, and we don't know who else might be out there."

"Yes, sir," an officer said.

Fox News was unimpressed and reported, "Due to the inability of our president to maintain order, a hostage situation was created and nearly cost the lives of two government officials. We demand an investigation into the blundering and incompetence of everyone concerned. More later."

Lisa Pagetti's news nearly drowned out the reporter. "We have drama in D.C. tonight. An explosive gun battle erupted as the esteemed FBI SWAT team took down a deadly fugitive…"

Police Chief Polack stepped forward and interrupted, "We are awaiting the arrival of Farzad Zahair, an international terrorist charged with arms dealing, extortion, smuggling, kidnapping, and…"

Braun elbowed his way through the crowd and finally caught Polack's attention. "Where's your team? You wanted Zahair transferred to your custody, so come get him and Gregor."

Polack motioned six officers forward. "You two, move them to the patrol car."

Reporters surrounded the team.

Polack pointed to the other four officers. "Come on, we've saved the country and have our terrorists. Load them into the patrol car." Still in an ordering frenzy, and before the TV cameras while they were running, Polack saluted Braun and turned toward the SWAT team with a bright smile. "We'll take it from here. You boys get the rest of the night off."

Braun rolled his eyes, said something under his breath, and returned to the Humvee, glad to get away from all the reporters.

Polack seemed to enjoy the spotlight and continued to order, "You two ride motorcycles ahead to escort the patrol car, and you two ride behind. We'll interrogate them before hauling them before the judge."

"Roger," came from the teams.

"Back to work. Let's go, men." Polack climbed into the cruiser and slammed the door as the motorcade wove its way through the crowd.

Late Night Update

Sept. 11 – 9:45 p.m. EDT, Bunker Technical Lab, Washington, D.C.

Cordy was thankful that President Spendorf had made arrangements for Braun and her to stay at Blair House for the night. She wanted to be there with her husband, but for now, she set aside her growing exhaustion and made a fresh pot of coffee. She needed it to keep going, so she refilled her mug and added a tablespoon of cream to the steaming brew. Turning toward Evans, she asked, "Care for a cup?"

He shook his head. "I plan to sleep tonight. Aren't you heading out?"

"Not yet." She took a sip and headed back to her station. "Thanks for all your help. Before you leave, can you fill me in on the forensic evidence Braun collected from the Maven II drone earlier today? And what about fingerprints on Zinmansky's laptop the SWAT team found in the RV?"

Evans covered a yawn. "No time to waste, huh? Zac told me that you…oh, never mind."

"What did Zac say?"

"You're a taskmaster." Evans' smile lit up his brown eyes, but it didn't do much for the bags beneath them. He typed a text message to an FBI analyst asking for any fingerprint results on Zinmansky's laptop, pulled up a few additional files, and dragged them to the main screen for review. "I don't have results of Zinmansky's laptop, but the only fingerprints found on the outside surface of Carl's desktop computer were his, two security analysts', and his secretary's."

"That's odd," Cordy said. "Was the computer wiped clean, maybe a couple of days ago? There should have been more prints. According to our records, this computer is the same one Carl used for the past two years."

Evans nodded, "Right, but inside, I found more prints—mostly from Dell employees who probably built the equipment, and a few unknown, but the KeySweeper was wiped clean, and something else caught my attention—Congressman Justuso's prints were noted."

"Inside the computer?" Cordy clarified, "but not on the KeySweeper?"

"Right, and I have no idea when the Congressman accessed the inside of the equipment, but his fingerprints were also found on the desk, printer, and keyboard. Not on the outer computer itself, but the keyboard."

Cordy pursed her lips and paused in deep thought. "Justuso is the Chairman of the House Defense Subcommittee. I'm sure he meets with Carl routinely, but why would he have access to the inside of the computer?"

Evans shrugged his shoulders. "We're researching that."

Cordy jotted a note. "And did you check with Deputy Director Yelson about Zinmansky's laptop?"

"When would I have time to…?" Evans shook his head. "Not yet, but I will tomorrow when I'm fully awake. Is that soon enough?"

"I know we're both tired." She took another sip of coffee. "Did the FBI track down the bullet and metal shards that Braun gave you?"

"Yes." Evans dug through his leather bag. "It's in here somewhere." He removed an e-notebook, a pair of earbuds, an e-day timer, and a half-eaten candy bar. "Got it! We already discussed the first four items, but the last two even surprised me."

Cordy took the crumbled pink memo card that Evans handed to her. "Why didn't you get a digital report?"

Evans shoved a hunk of candy into his mouth and jammed everything else back into his pack. He chewed and swallowed. "They aren't done evaluating yet. Read it, and you'll see why."

Whoever wrote the memo used large, loopy letters and listed a few items:

- Bullet is undamaged.
- Made of a hardened polymer

- Red tip atop a black band
- Armor-piercing tracer—Illegal in U.S.
- ? made in Iran and smuggled across our border from South America
- ? supplied by Tree of Liberty Group

Gnawing on her lower lip, Cordy was startled when Evans asked, "You ever hear of the group?"

Cordy had heard of the Tree of Liberty Group but knew little about it. "Who are they?"

"A right-wing militia located at an ex-military campsite outside of Spokane, Washington. They have weapons of every variety." Evans gave a visible shudder. "Not anyone I'd want to meet. It could lead to another Waco event."

"Where do they get their weapons?" Cordy asked.

Evans said, "Don't know. I doubt even the government knows."

"What about the munitions on that drone?" Cordy asked. "Any of the shards give us a clue as to what was used?"

"Yes, a high-powered grenade like the weapons Iranians use in their Jihadi aviation," Evans said. "It explodes on impact. It isn't from the U.S., and the FBI is still researching where it came from."

Cordy ran a finger down her list and paused, "Braun left me a text message. The test was to prove the viability of using the RCV and drones to counter enemy weapons. What went wrong?"

"I checked the specs." Evans pulled up a diagram on the screen and pointed. "The drone used advanced seeker technology."

Feeling overwhelmed by the information, Cordy took a deep breath. "You're not talking to Braun. I don't know what you mean."

Evans leaned closer and whispered as if sharing a top secret. He got more excited as he talked. "The drone uses a kinetic energy interceptor to detect enemy drones, rockets, mortars, and even low-flying helicopters. Doppler radar technology identifies the type of weapon and payload and then tracks the enemy's actions. It captures and analyzes the speed and movement of the target for a more accurate hit."

Cordy groaned. "I'm sure Braun understands all of this, but…"

Evans nodded, "TMI? Okay. The drone collects and sends data back to the commanders so they can determine the best method to demolish the threat."

Cordy asked, "Why did the drone explode?"

Evans shrugged. "The system must have malfunctioned. Once a threat was identified, it went into destroy mode."

Cordy made several notes and hoped she could explain Evan's info. She rechecked Braun's text message. "He also wants to know what type of explosive was used in the attack."

"That's another interesting issue." Evans paused as if asking permission to continue and said, "There were traces of IMX-104 on the shards."

"IMX-104. How is that different from what the military usually uses?" Cordy poised her hands above the keyboard, ready to type his answer.

"DoD modifies explosives initially made in the Middle East." Evans half-whispered as if he feared a highly classified secret would be leaked. "The explosive is safer to use, and it costs 20% less than nitro-based munitions. Iran started using it around 2010, and it is the leading candidate to replace today's military explosives. That's why DoD is so eager to complete these tests."

Cordy was anxious to share the information with her husband. "How did the Department of Defense get access to these weapons?"

"That, I don't know, but the FBI referred Braun's fragments to the Bureau of Alcohol, Tobacco, and Firearms." Evans glanced at his watch and grimaced.

"Does the ATF have an inside contact with the Tree of Liberty Group?" Cordy asked.

"I'm sure they do—they have been watching the group for years." Evans stifled another yawn. "Their weapons get more lethal every year and penetrate even our best Kevlar vests."

"So, that's why the FBI changed to vests made of composite metal foam." Cordy tapped a few more notes into her computer. "Braun loves how lightweight the new ones are."

"I can't believe they're only 8 mm thick and can still disintegrate even armor-piercing bullets."

"Maybe it can save one's life, but if hit with one of those bullets, you can still end up with a fractured rib or collarbone. Braun knows from experience." Cordy glanced at her coffee cup but decided she'd had enough. "Anything new on the funds placed into the overseas account in Braun's name?"

Evans peeled the paper from the end of his chocolate candy bar, licked the wrapper, and popped the rest of the candy into his mouth. He spoke around the chocolate, "The U.S. funds came from a Wells Fargo transfer, but that's all I know so far."

His cell phone buzzed. "It's a text message with an update on Zinmansky's laptop. The FBI analyst found Zinmansky's fingerprints, along with Gregor's, Zahair's, and several others, on the laptop's surface and inside. A complete report will be released in the morning."

Cordy's VidChat dinged. "That must be Quint. I set up a meeting for ten. Do you want to stay, or should I update you in the morning?"

"If you don't mind, I'll pass." Evans wiped his hands on a tissue and packed his laptop. "Don't stay too late."

"Thanks, and good night." Cordy checked her messages and skimmed through two texts from Perry. He'd found a potential hacking group in Ryazan, Russia, and had tracked down the Wells Fargo link to Braun's overseas account.

Perry had also discovered the person at the bank who had set up the bogus account in Braun's name. It wasn't the first time this person had made false accounts. Cordy sent the information to the FBI to clear Braun of fraud charges and referred the information to the Federal Trade Commission.

Cordy stood up to stretch, repositioned the cushion, and settled back into the chair. It was time to switch gears. She opened Quint's link and found him still at the office. "We captured Zahair, freed Emma Sloan, and Secretary Hendrum, and I can't wait to see Braun. I hope you had a productive day."

"I'm sure better than yours, Girlfriend." Quint chuckled and appeared relaxed in his favorite green frayed V-neck T-shirt. "DoD and Homeland Security are both up and running smoothly. Ransomware has been quarantined and removed from the network."

Cordy pulled out her notes from Evans. "I discovered some information about the drones used during Braun's weapons test earlier today." She updated Quint about the forensic data. "Evans passed the information to DoD, Homeland Security, and ATF, who has an inside contact with the Tree of Liberty Group."

"We can't afford to waste any time on this," Quint said, his tone serious. "We need to find who planted the recovery partition before they strike again."

Cordy moved down to the next item. "Did you check into Zac's computer and that hidden drive?"

Quint nodded and moved closer to the screen. "That extra drive you found blocked my access to Zac's computer. I'm sure that's why I could shut down all the other equipment in the White House but not the president's station. It also allowed someone access to the entire network, including our defense system, and Zac's web camera allowed spying eyes into the Oval Office."

"My God," Cordy exclaimed. "A foreign agent or ANYONE could access our most confidential data! We need to find who planted the recovery partition."

"Yes, I know," Quint said. "We may need to replace the partition to capture the culprit. I've added a seeker code that will link everything back to me if accessed."

Cordy heaved a sigh. "Okay. I'll do that in the morning. Did you discover a way to enhance tracking possible terrorists at our ports of entry?"

"We've been working on that with CrowdStrike's help," Quint said. "So far, we've updated the code for their security camera software, which includes an algorithm to check additional ID data—iris and retinal scans, rims of the ear, and voice ID for the International watch lists on terrorists and violent extremists, as you requested earlier today."

"How soon before they can trial the system?" Cordy asked.

"I contacted CIA's IT department. They will implement our new code into the Interpol database, but rollout takes time. They'll test the program on a few local airport cameras first."

"Good." Cordy crossed that off her list.

"Svetlana has been analyzing government contractors in the last two years." Quint pulled up a list for Cordy. "She noticed a pattern, which would have taken me a month of Sundays to discover. There were 62 companies that made bids on providing overseas and domestic security. Of those, 38 bids were accepted, and 20 of them have merged through stock acquisitions—18 have sold short and use the same accounting system."

Cordy scanned the list. "Ansin Associates & Securities is on that list."

"So is Gonzalo Industries, another security corporation," Quint said.

"Gonzalo has contracts with the national defense system and our military," Cordy paused, "and they're connected everywhere—CIA, FBI, and defense."

Quint hopped from his chair. "Upon further investigation, Svetlana discovered its major investor is Congressman Conrad Justuso. And there's more!"

"More?" Cordy couldn't believe they had been working in the dark all year. "Oh wait, Justuso is the Chairman of the House Defense Subcommittee. Does Guy or Dr. Ping know about this?"

"I doubt they've made a connection," Quint said, opening the fridge and pulling out another Coke. "On top of that, Gonzalo just bought out Ansin Associates and Securities, Inc."

Cordy felt her heart thud in her chest. "So there's a race to privatize our Homeland Security. That's downright scary!" Her mind ran through the events of the last two years.

Quint popped the top of the Coke can and sat down. He leaned toward the screen. "Your eyes just lit up. Pupils are dilated—they do that when you're deep in thought, trying to find a solution. What are you thinking?"

Cordy blinked. "My, you're observant. Remember the latest school shooting—9 students killed, and the New Orleans incident at the gay bar? It wasn't Homeland that came to their rescue. It was crack sharpshooters—states deputizing their own teams, shooting American citizens who don't comply. And we all know what happened on January 6th a few years ago. Private citizens broke into Congress to prevent the transfer of power to a new president and built their own militia. This has to stop."

"If we don't act fast, they could gain complete control of our domestic security," Quint said, his voice filled with concern.

"If Svetlana's summary is correct, and I don't doubt it, over half of these companies have been consolidated already," Cordy said, emphasizing the urgency of the situation. "We need to act fast before it's too late."

Quint added, "Many through buying and selling shares, and I noticed something else. They all made investments through SkyUrsis Capital. Eventually, they may all gather into one huge company, taking control of our nation's security."

"We need to work together on this," Cordy said, her tone firm. "Send this report to Guy and Dr. Ping. I'll discuss our concerns with them in the morning."

"IYFTI is pushing the transit authority to sign their contract, and CrowdStrike is researching Ansin Associates." Quint leaned forward. "The NYSE claims it has an extensive firewall against intrusions, but I want access to the Stock market's daily backup to see for myself."

"What do you know so far?" Cordy asked.

Quint set up another screen. "Alysha and I discussed Guy's theory of the terrorist attacks on Washington, D.C., being linked to the assaults on the White House, and there's more. CrowdStrike did most of the research, so let's get an update. I'll link in Alysha."

Cordy ran a hand through her hair. Her wedding ring got caught in a snarl, and she finger-combed a stray lock back into a barrette. When Alysha popped up on the screen, Cordy greeted her, "Good to see you. Sorry, it's so late."

Alysha's dark skin stood out against a turquoise sweater, and her jet-black hair skimmed the cowl neckline. "It's been a busy day for all of us, and it's great to work with you and your team again." Alysha got straight to the issue. Her organizational skills meshed well with Cordy's, although, sometimes, Alysha's thoughts derailed and could be annoying. "You're calling about our findings on IYFTI and Ansin Associates, right?"

Quint scanned his list, "Yes, and any other updates from the Securities Commission."

Alysha said, "After reviewing the stock's activities, I agree the prices seem to have been triggered by a remote access tool. The RAT opened the back door to inject a second part—the payload of prices."

Cordy clarified, "So someone knew exactly what the prices would be and when to make a bid?"

"Yes," Alysha said, pulling up a computer screen. "I tracked down a contact that was not on security duty that day for the NYSE. We've worked together in the past. He insists their firewall would block any hackers and notify security upon any attempt to access. He also swears no unauthorized personnel could enter the secure computer room without logging in. All personnel who had access have been questioned and cleared."

"If that's true, how did the RAT get triggered?" Cordy asked. "Someone had to enter the payload—in this case, the stock prices, times, and record the names of the investors."

Quint added, "And this process happened more than once, first during the sale of IYFTI, with sales prices going up, and once again at the close of the day, with selling the stock short."

"Friday was also an eventful day for the Ansin Associates' CEO, Mierzany K. Ansin," Alysha said. "He sold IYFTI short, immediately cashing in the shares, making $6.3 million."

"Did Ansin invest through SkyUrsis Capital?" Cordy asked.

"I'll need to check," Alysha jotted a note, "but his transaction was the last trade of the day. Ansin barely transferred his funds to an overseas account before Saturday's late-night power outage, and by early Sunday morning, the city broke into chaos."

Cordy added, "And check if Ansin used SkyUrsis. So, do you also think the transfer of funds and the chaos in D.C. are linked?"

"Here are the facts, as I see them, and they all point in that direction. I'll start with the terrorist attacks." Alysha ticked off each item on her fingers. "First, Potomac Electric had a downed transmission line in Southern Maryland. One of the last banking transactions prior to the outage was a Wells Fargo wire transfer of $4.2 million from Ansin's account to Cypriot in Cyprus. Within minutes of the first transfer, Farzad Zahair had Wells Fargo wire a second transfer to the same location but with a different account number. Three minutes later, the power grid went down, and the power company was unable to reboot the system even after initial repairs—maybe a non-related event, but interesting to note. The power company attempted to fix the downed line without success. Finally, they reverted to a previous software update to regain power. The newest software system proved to be 'buggy,' as the supervisor put it."

"Do you think they were hacked?" Cordy asked.

"I wouldn't take it off the table, and Cyprus is renowned for money laundering." Alysha moved on. "Point two—during the power outage, a couple of subway trains crashed while underground leaving the Metro Station."

"I can't see how Ansin Associates had anything to do with that," Cordy said.

"Maybe not Ansin," Alysha agreed, "but what about IYFTI? They are putting intense pressure on the Transit Authority Commission to sign their contract. After the trains crashed," Alysha raised three fingers, "three bombs were discovered, and defused—not two, as we originally thought. One was found on the train, one in Metro Station, and the third outside a church across the street. Fortunately, they were defused before exploding."

"I didn't get many details about the bombs," Cordy said.

Alysha held up four fingers. "That's not all. It appears those metro buses heading for the airport were destroyed by IEDs, leaving traces of IMX-104. A bus accident also damaged the 14th Street Bridge. Traffic is still backed up with the bridge closed."

The comment piqued Cordy's attention. *It involved IMX—104, the same explosive used by the Maven II drone at Aberdeen Approval Grounds.* "Causing a train crash is extreme," Cordy said.

"Perhaps the crash was an accident," Alysha said. "I had my team research the upgraded code the subway system used that night, and they found a major glitch. It was an obvious revision that should have been easily identified if pre-tested. It shows the current Board wasn't prepared and didn't prevent this disaster from happening. It gives a new management team the opportunity to claim they could have prevented it. That's the spin I would take if I wanted to take over a company."

Cordy frowned. "Maybe so, but someone placed those bombs, so if the train hadn't crashed, the bomb would have gone off undetected, probably causing more casualties. Who's on the Board of Directors?"

"There are six voting members, two from the District of Columbia, two each from Maryland and Virginia, and two from the U.S. federal government. Funding is a major problem, and Congress may even get involved once again."

"And that could take months." Cordy shook her head. "I still don't see how Ansin fits into this scenario. Maybe the transfer of funds linked to the power outage, but..."

"Well, he's definitely involved in the selling short scam," Alysha said. "So maybe he's not our main focus, which is good since I haven't been able to find a trace of his existence. One of his clients must have tipped him off. I'm afraid he cashed out and ran."

This call captured Cordy's curiosity, wiping away the exhausted feeling she'd felt earlier. "Another question is, how many clients also invested, and who?" Cordy added Mierzany K. Ansin to her list just below IYFTI's CEO, Azinnea M. Krysin. Her mind clicked onto something, but then it flitted away.

Alysha was saying, "...Ms. Krysin has multiple citizenships—from Germany, the UK, and the U.S., so she uses different passports. However, one is under a different name. Delta Airlines confirms that Sinneya K. Marzin used a German passport and flew from Heathrow to Washington, D.C., two days ago, and then that same woman used a UK passport under the name Azinnea M. Krysin to fly to LA this morning and is scheduled to return to Heathrow this afternoon. When I ran an identity search for that photo, I got three hits. Interpol has tracked her on a number of occasions but has yet to prove anything to date, or she would be in a no-fly list."

Cordy made another note to do more research on Krysin when her thoughts were again interrupted by Alysha.

"We've tracked down two major investors besides Ansin," Alysha said, taking control of the screen. "One is an heiress named Lady Tiffany Hadsy. The UK's Foreign Intelligence Service, MI-6, knows her very well as the Shady Lady. She's in her early thirties and grew up privileged."

Cordy jotted down Lady Hadsy—Shady Lady. *Another odd name. Why are my internal alarms pinging me?*

"...with Daddy's help, Tiffany made her first million at age two. My bet is on her as the insider." Alysha popped a photo of a female on the screen—a platinum blonde with high cheekbones and an angular jawline. But what stood out most was the stunning heterochromia. Her eyes were different colors—a dark brown right eye and a blue as the ocean left. "She travels with Crayton Udesky, who's in his early forties. Both are from Liverpool, UK."

"Do you also have a photo of him?" Cordy asked, although something was brewing in the back of her mind.

"Yes, but it's not as flattering as Tiffany's," Alysha added a second image on the screen. The man had dark hair that curled slightly around his shoulders, and he sported a thick black beard. "His mustache covers a scar, and you can see his left lip droops a bit, even more so when he smiles."

There was a slight droop of his lip, but what caught Cordy's eye most was the dark splotch above his left eye. *Where did I hear about a dark spot above one's eye?* Cordy's mind flashed back to an earlier conversation, but she couldn't remember the details. "What's Udesky known for?"

"He owns a multi-billion dollar Greek restaurant chain and has a second home in Rome." Alysha popped up a stone Roman villa with a red-tiled roof and a mosaic courtyard. "Tiffany visits there on occasion."

"So, are they in business together?" Cordy asked.

"They jointly own a few restaurants in London. Tiffany travels all over the world and is currently in D.C., staying at the Hay-Adams Hotel. I understand they were in Russia last month and plan to open a new restaurant in St. Petersburg."

"Russia? Is there a link?" Cordy wracked her brain to remember what seemed trapped in her mind.

"Are Tiffany and Crayton a couple?" Quint asked. "There's quite an age difference."

"I don't think so." Alysha moved closer to the screen and rubbed her hands together.

A cue that Cordy dreaded—*here we go again.*

"I have another tip," Alysha gushed without pausing. "Tiffany had a lengthy meeting with Congressman Justuso this afternoon, and within the hour, he invested eight million in SkyUrsis Capital."

"I bet he didn't use his name," Cordy jotted down. "That kind of investment would raise some eyebrows on the Hill."

"No, Justuso used the name Gonzalo Industries, a private security corporation. Yesterday, they bought out Ansin Associates for $6.8 million."

"Quint mentioned that a few moments ago," Cordy said. "And I understand he also owns the controlling interest in Gonzalo Industries."

"He does now, but initially, it was Congressman Justuso's brother, José Carlos Justuso, who headed up the company," Alysha said. "Before José's death, he was suspected of heading up a Columbian drug cartel, which may have gotten him killed."

"So, did the Congressman inherit the corporation after José's death?" Cordy asked.

"Yes, and rumors are spreading that the company had been using the border to run drugs between Mexico and the U.S." Alysha rubbed her hands together once more. "They were also thought to be smuggling weapons."

Cordy couldn't bite her tongue any longer. "I'm not interested in rumors, Alysha. I need facts. Justuso ran against President Spendorf. He is a highly respected Congressman, and we must be certain before making any accusations. Do you have absolute proof of this?"

"Not yet. I'm still researching," Alysha admitted.

"Congressman Justuso is also the Chairman of the House Defense Subcommittee." Cordy also wondered about Justuso's actions. *Could he be the mole? We did find his fingerprints inside and on Carl's computer keyboard.*

"Lighten up, Girlfriend," Quint said. "We may be one step closer to figuring out what's happening."

Cordy knew she had been ready to pounce at a moment's notice. "Sorry, I guess we're all tired." Another idea popped into her head.

Before Cordy could speak, Alysha pushed on. "Anyway, Crayton dabbles in the stock market and knows computer programming. I wonder if he set up the RAT. I'll know more tomorrow. Tiffany is flying to Los Angeles, and I booked an appointment to meet her at 10 a.m. I hope to get some answers then."

"Is Crayton Udesky flying with her?" Cordy asked.

"No, and Tiffany said something that struck me as odd. She can't find him. They were to meet for breakfast this morning, but he never showed up, and he hadn't checked out of his hotel but was not in his room. He was to head back to Russia, but when she contacted the airlines, he never checked in, and the jet left without him. She was worried something happened to him, but she refused to call the police for some reason. Maybe she will have heard from him by the time I meet with her."

"Did Udesky also meet with Congressman Justuso?" Quint asked.

"Good question," Alysha said. "I'll ask about that, too."

"Talking about Justuso, does he have anything to do with the Supreme Court case, Texas vs. Zogster?" Cordy asked. "Zac mentioned that it's on the docket for this week."

"Yes, the Congressman is a major investor in Zogster's shares," Alysha said.

The case hit a nerve. Congressman Justuso's past oil business has made him millions. It helped launch his political career, and he vowed to rerun for president next term. Was this a ploy to undermine President Spendorf? Of course, Zac had already defeated the Congressman once, but it wouldn't bode well for the Democrats. Why does everything have to be so complex? Better tune in, as it could set precedence for future cases.

"…Zogster was accused of unlawful dealings and kickbacks to boost its already-dominant corporation, advertising with major online providers—some linked to a Mexican drug cartel, others dealt with buying and selling weapons." Alysha continued, "Congressman Justuso is a prolific advertiser with the company. The anti-trust case was appealed by a circuit court and taken before the Texas Supreme Court. The decision was appealed and landed in the Supreme Court."

Cordy's mind raced as more puzzle pieces floated through her head. Now, to link them—*Gonzalo Industries, a security company originally owned by the brother of a Texan Congressman, who allegedly headed up a Columbian drug cartel. The Congressman inherited the company and now has a controlling interest in Ansin Associates—a dynamic security and aviation corporation. What better way to transport illegal drugs and weapons safely across the border? It could also be an anti-trust issue.* Then, an idea that had been floating around in her mind for a while finally connected. *A dark bruised area above the left eyebrow like the body found in the bathroom next to the Roosevelt Room. Could it be Crayton Udesky? I wonder if the body has a scarred lip. And what about the names?*

"What's on your mind, Cordy," Quint asked. "I saw a spark, light up your face."

"We need to pass this information on to Chief Justice Sophia Hendrum. The Supreme Court is investigating Gonzalo Industries, and I understand Justuso also owns the controlling interest in Gonzalo Industries. Here's another mystery. Check this out." Cordy's fingers tapped out the three names.

Azinnea M. Krysin, maybe also Sinneya K. Marzin

Mierzany K. Ansin

Einar Zinmansky

"Rearrange the letters in each name. All have the same letters. They are anagrams. I'm sure it's more than a coincidence. What are their real names, and how are they working together? Or are they all only one person? No, Azinnea and Sinneya are females, right? The other two are males. I have a photo of Zinmansky but not of Ansin." Cordy tapped away on her keyboard in search of more information. Nothing immediately popped up.

Quint yawned. "Can we discuss that tomorrow? It's been a long day for all of us."

"Yes, but I'm sending this info to Judge Sophia Hendrum." It was already nearly midnight, and Cordy was anxious to spend some time with Braun. *He should be at Blair House by now.* "I think we deserve a break. I have a few more details to check out, and maybe something more will enlighten me during the night. Thanks for all your help. I'll check in with the team at 9:00 a.m. EDT. Get some rest. Tell Svetlana I'm proud of her findings, and let Perry know he did a great job of breaking through the Wells Fargo firewall to track those funds sent from Russia. One account eventually led directly to Braun's overseas account. He also found the culprit at Wells Fargo who set up the transaction."

"He did what?" Quint blurted. "Without telling me? I mean, I'll be glad to tell him that you put another gold star on his roster." Quint swore under his breath as he disconnected.

Cordy sent a memo and forwarded the data they found on Congressman Justuso, Gonzalo Industries, and Zogster. Then, she texted Guy and Dr. Ping with the latest updates and headed to Blair House to meet Braun. Her mind, still whirling with thoughts and images, made her feel excited, confused, and on edge, unable to relax.

Interrogation

**Sept. 11 – 10:03 p.m. EDT, En route to Metro
Police Department, Washington, D.C.**

Potomac Parkway seemed quiet as the motorcycle cops, two in front and two at the rear, escorted a patrol car with Farzad Zahair and Gregor in custody. There were no sirens, only the garish flashing of red and blue lights as they whisked the suspects to the Metropolitan Police Department.

Zahair couldn't help but stifle a smirk as he glanced over at Gregor. His luck had held once again. Instead of the FBI, they were being handed over to this Podunk local police agency. He knew this routine and how to manipulate the system. It must be Gregor's first encounter with the law. The poor man's brow blossomed with beaded sweat. His face grew paler with each passing mile. *He would probably piss himself before the night was over.*

Once inside, the station came to life—mug shots, fingerprints, and the usual processing of a suspect followed by hours of questions and interrogations. Zahair had already been charged with two counts of kidnapping, a serious felony, illegal entry into the country, planting explosives at the Metro Station, and possessing unregistered weapons, and was to appear before a magistrate later today at 10 a.m. An individual bond was expected to be over $1 million.

Zahair remained in the dingy, dimly lit, and undecorated interrogation cell, complete with four steel-backed chairs, two on either side of a metal table, bolted to the middle of the room. Three cement block walls lined the area, and a fourth wall had a two-way mirror facing Zahair. A camera was located on the right and left corners of the mirrored wall, and a red light flashed, indicating they were recording the interview. He knew from experience that the recordings had a blind spot when he placed his hands under the table just above his lap. He'd used this to his advantage once before. His lawyer knew the routine. His heart rate calmed, and his confidence raised a notch. This would be easy, the fools.

Mr. Bad Cop and Miss Good Cop entered the room and began asking questions. Zahair wondered why they always played this game, but he'd go along with the routine for now.

"We know you are guilty of kidnapping Mo Hendrum," Bad Cop said. "He was found unconscious as you attempted an escape from an RV located at Rock Creek Park. Why did you kidnap the Secretary of State?"

Zahair gave a blank stare with no answer to rile the interrogator.

Good Cop took the following question as Zahair knew she would. "I understand from your colleague, Gregor, that you had no part in Secretary Hendrum's injuries. In fact, you hadn't planned to hurt anyone, and you obtained a highly qualified ICU nurse to provide prompt medical attention as soon as you learned of his condition. Isn't that why you kidnapped Nurse Sloan?"

Zahair sat back in his chair as if he had all night. "I want a lawyer."

"A public defender will be arranged," Good Cop said.

"No, not a public defender." Zahair placed his cuffed wrists on the table and leaned forward. At least they hadn't chained his ankles. "I have a lawyer, Ichabod Bruchester. Ichy, and I go way back. He'll get me out of here. I'll be a free man soon."

Bad Cop cleared his throat. "Is he an American lawyer?"

"He's a lawyer," Zahair said. "He graduated from Harvard if that's what you mean, but no, he wasn't born in the U.S. He emigrated with his family twenty-three years ago from Russia before becoming a citizen."

Bad cop rolled his eyes. "I'll check with the boss."

Zahair knew this was a stall tactic. "You do that. I'm innocent until proven otherwise, and I know my rights. I invoke the right to counsel, and I have the right to choose my own lawyer. You can't ask me any more questions until he's present. My lips are sealed."

Bad cop mumbled something under his breath, but they left the room.

An hour later, Zahair met with his lawyer. Now, things would happen. He gave a broad smile. "It's good to see you again, my friend."

Ichy's dark brown eyes locked onto Zahair's as he took a seat. "And you, but I would rather meet at a fancy restaurant. What's on the menu tonight?"

So, Ichy wanted to talk in code—all the better. "A big, juicy steak with all the fixings would be nice, and before you leave," Zahair grinned. "You know, like my last visit? Oh, I know that's not possible. You don't have twenty minutes to spare for an old friend."

"Maybe I do." Ichy licked his lips and nodded. He made a show of sliding up his navy blue pin-striped suit sleeve to check his watch, gasped, and started to cough. He had a hard time catching his breath.

Zahair reached for his lawyer, dripping with concern. "Are you all right, Ichy? Can I get you something? Maybe some water?"

"No touching," Bad cop warned.

"Swallowed wrong," Ichy said between gasps, trying to breathe.

Zahair turned to the good cop. "He needs water. I'd appreciate it if you'd bring me a bottle, too. I'm thirsty." *Hopefully, she'll bring me one.*

Ichy thumped his chest, choking. "Water," escaped his lips. His face turned beet red.

The female cop stood ready to leave. "Okay."

She returned with only one bottle.

Zahair's heart rate kicked up a notch for the first time since his arrest. Now what? He glanced at Ichy, hoping he'd think fast and devise another plan.

Ichy coughed out, "Thanks." His hands trembled as he fumbled to open the bottle.

Zahair reached for the bottle.

"No touching." The bad cop grabbed the bottle and twisted off the lid. He shoved the opened bottle into Ichy's hands.

Ichy took a long swig and swiped one hand over his lips. Tugging at his necktie, he cleared his throat and wheezed out, "Thanks." He mopped his forehead, stood still, holding onto the bottle, and exhaled deeply. "It's hot in here." He shrugged off one arm of his jacket, covered the bottle, and dropped two tablets inside while removing the other sleeve. He heaved a jerky sigh and sat back down while setting the bottle on the table with his hands wrapped around the lower half.

"Can we get on with this interrogation?" the bad cop demanded, his voice cutting through the tense silence like a knife.

Ichy apologized once more and turned on the charm while absently monitoring the contents in his water. "Now, where were we?" All eyes were on him. Once the tablets dissolved, Ichy gradually agitated the bottle and pretended to take another swig of water between speaking legalese with the interrogators. He set his bottle down on the table close to Zahair.

"When am I scheduled to appear before the judge?" Zahair asked.

"You'll leave here, well guarded, at 9:45 a.m. for a 10 a.m. arraignment," good cop said. "You'll know the charges against you at that time."

Ichy pounded a fist on the table. "Whatever the charges are, we're pleading not guilty."

Zahair, with a calculated move, seized the opportunity when both cops were engrossed in an argument with Ichy. He swiftly emptied the bottle and returned it to the table, his heart pounding with the thrill of their daring escape plan.

Ichy smiled. "Okay, I'll be here at 9:40 a.m." He grabbed the bottle, pretended to drink the rest of the water, and scooped up his jacket. "See you then." He got up, thanked the officers once more, and left the room with an empty bottle in hand.

Meanwhile, Gregor, a low-level associate of the notorious criminal Zahair, found himself in a jail interrogation room. He couldn't believe his predicament, especially being across the hall from the man he feared the most. *What's going to happen to me? A small fish—expendable. Zahair is the last man on Earth I want to be in prison with. After all, his boss had shot Rugar in the back as he ran from the RV.* He kept replaying the scene over in his mind. Rugar's screams were etched in his brain. Scared to death, Gregor became a gem—a model prisoner and an informant. He tried to think like Zahair. *What would he do?*

"…answer me," snapped Gregor back to the interrogation room.

Gregor stammered, "Will you cut me a deal?" His voice was barely a whisper, and then he repeated the question, although his hands shook, and he couldn't keep his knees from knocking. "I'll… I'll tell you anything…I mean, everything you want to know—everything. I don't want to go to jail."

A female cop placed her arms on the table and stared at Gregor. "Why should we cut a deal?" Her gaze was piercing, her tone intimidating. This time, the female was the bad cop, and the good cop was the male.

"I'm not guilty…I mean, I didn't plan any of this." His voice tremored. "Zahair will kill me. I had to follow his orders." Gregor's heart thumped so loudly it echoed in his ears. "I did whatever my boss asked."

The bright light moved closer to his eyes, nearly blinding him. "Tell us about your boss."

He couldn't say enough about his boss, Zahair. He ratted on the guy, told about a plan to crash subway trains, plant bombs in metro buses, and launch a drone attack on the White House. Gregor knew he wouldn't live an hour if Zahair heard his tales.

Getting a public defender to represent Gregor didn't take long, and a deal was in the making.

"Who is Zahair working for?" Miss Bad Cop asked.

"A General H.Q., I don't know his last name," Gregor said. "He just goes by H.Q., but I do know he speaks fluent Farsi. I never heard him speak a word of English."

"When did Zahair come to the U.S.?"

"Eleven days ago, he flew from Mashhad, Iran, to Washington, D.C., but he used a fake passport." Gregor sat back in his chair, gloating over the fact that he'd forged a successful passport that had been unchallenged at Customs. However, Gregor neglected to share that tidbit of information.

"Why did he come to the U.S.?" Mr. Good Cop asked.

Gregor wiped his damp brow with his sleeve, scratched his left ear, and seemed to be deep in thought, then shook his head. "Don't know." Afraid he might end up in prison for life, his voice cracked. "Ah, I didn't ask."

"Did it have anything to do with Iranian weapons?" Miss Bad Cop asked.

"Maybe Zahair met with a government contractor, Einar Zinmansky, who was working on a drone project," Gregor said. "I wasn't with Zahair at the time. I had nothing to do with any weapons. Honestly, but I did drive him to the meeting at a local coffee shop at the Metro Station." Gregor glanced up and saw the cop's scowl. He rushed on, "Zahair seemed pleased when I picked him up. It was none of my business, so I don't know what happened during the meeting, but he brought back a laptop."

"What was on the laptop?" Mr. Good Cop asked.

Gregor shook his head and shrugged his shoulders.

"You didn't check out the laptop?" Good Cop asked.

"Well, yes, I was able to get into the computer, but Zahair took it from there. He made a few backup disks, but I have no idea where they are now."

"So what files did he back up?" the cop asked.

"Maybe everything?" Gregor shrugged his shoulders. "I wasn't allowed to see."

"Did you ever speak to this contractor?" Bad cop asked.

"No." Gregor gnawed on his lip. *Was that the correct answer?* "Well, yes, I talked to him briefly two days ago. He had a thick Russian accent." His mind seemed fuzzy as he hyperventilated. His fingers were going numb. "He was calling for Zahair, so I put him on hold."

Bad Cop rapped on the desk to get Gregor's attention. "But you did listen in on the call."

Gregor gnawed some more on his lower lip. "Umm…I may have overheard Zinmansky discussing a Maven II Drone Project he was working on. He wanted the drone to test out a few Iranian weapons that Zahair had somehow acquired. I'm not sure if Zahair delivered, but Zinmansky offered a large amount of money in return. I never saw one penny of that money."

"Yes, since you brought up the topic, let's talk more about money," Bad Cop said. "How much are we talking about for the capture of Secretary Hendrum?"

"That depends on who you talk to," Gregor said. "General H.Q. offered an unknown amount of funds. When we weren't sure if the general would deliver, Zahair made a ransom demand for $25 million given to Justice Hendrum for the return of her husband. He had Amir deliver the message to a coffee shop patron. He attached $10 to the note with a red paper clip, his calling card. The patron delivered the ransom demand to Justice Sophia Hendrum, but she went before a news team, so we never received any payment."

"Yes, we heard about that," Good Cop said, "but Zahair really didn't plan to release her husband alive, did he?"

"That I don't know." Gregor swallowed a lump in his throat. "He also offered a friend the plans to the most powerful weapon system used in the U.S. It was hidden inside a fake euro. I think that included an unmanned robotic vehicle along with the Maven II drones, and that included the release of Secretary Hendrum."

"How much money did the friend agree to?" Bad Cop asked.

"It was a lot, at least $50 million. I'm not sure if that payment included Hendrum, dead or alive, but we were to keep the Secretary alive, at least until we reached the private jet I arranged to fly us out of the country at 4:00 a.m. this morning."

"You arranged for a jet?" Good Cop asked.

"Yes, a private jet," Gregor said.

"Who was providing the jet?" Bad Cop ran a hand over her graying hair and tucked a lock behind her ear.

"Ansin Associates," Gregor said, "but we ended up here instead."

"How did you get in contact with Ansin?" Good Cop asked.

"Umm…through a power broker in London," he stammered.

"Who?" she asked.

"A Lady Tiffany Hadsy," Gregor said. "She hacked into several cell phone numbers, one of which allowed me access. She can summon influential people all over the world, and she has computer skills that put even mine to shame."

"What do you mean?" Bad Cop narrowed her eyes, debating if Gregor was telling the truth.

"I don't know if I should tell you this, but since we agreed to a negotiated deal, I will. Shady Lady, as Foreign Intelligence MI-6 calls her, broke into a cache of classified government intel, mainly government contracts," Gregor squirmed in his chair. "To my knowledge, she hasn't used any of the information. She did access data from her cell phone, which pinged off a server in Singapore."

"And what does that mean exactly?" Good Cop asked.

"She is a link between Ansin, Zinmansky, and Zahair," Gregor said. "She knows people who know powerful people. She may even know H.Q."

The lawyer raised his hands. "Look, we've been here for nearly four hours. It's time to take a break."

"I'll answer this last question," Gregor said. "Tiffany gave us Ansin's name two days ago when Zahair transferred money into a hedge fund. I drove him to Wells Fargo Bank, where the two met, made a few transactions, and then I drove Zahair back to our headquarters. He seemed pleased and said he was going to become rich. Perhaps he did make a lot of money, but I haven't heard anything since that day."

Suddenly, all hell broke loose outside the little interrogation room. Shouts came from across the hall and shuffled feet ran past the door. A female yelled, "Call 911. This is a medical emergency."

Good Cop flung open Gregor's interrogation door. Gregor saw officers in blue rush inside Zahair's interrogation room.

Chief Polack came into view. "What happened?" Polack's voice rose in pitch.

A pale female reported, "Zahair clutched his chest and collapsed on the floor. He isn't breathing and has no pulse."

Chief Polack shouted, "How did this happen? Get him to the hospital ASAP. The feds are going to have our hides."

Snatching A Moment

The original light-colored brick façade outside the four-story Blair House was nearly the same color as Cordy's two-story home in Fort Collins, Colorado, but it lacked the two polished double oak front doors with an oval of beveled glass in the center. Blair House also lacked her lush grassy lawn, the flagstone patio surrounded by a riot of colors that she had left so abruptly—the orange marigolds, purple phlox, and the bright yellow and purple pansies blooming into the early fall. She yearned to see her maple tree that had finally turned a blazing red only a week ago.

Instead, a curved green awning over a cement sidewalk led to a single front door. Cordy was warmly greeted as an honored guest when she passed through security. The receptionist completed her registration and informed her that Braun had already arrived.

Excitement grew the closer she stepped toward her assigned rooms in anticipation of spending time with her husband. Braun met her when she opened the door. Her eyes focused on him in a quick appraisal, dressed in faded jeans and his favorite navy flannel shirt, she barely noted the carefully decorated formal satin wallpapered foyer lined with artwork. The door closed, and she was wrapped in his warm embrace.

Braun brushed a stray lock of strawberry blonde hair from her cheek and lifted the shoulder strap from her arm. Her bag landed on the floor and joined Braun's SWAT gear piled by the door, along with her briefcase and coat. "You're shivering. Come by the fire." He led her to a large living room where flames crackled from burning logs in a marble fireplace, adding warmth, but she preferred the coziness of her home's humble moss-rock hearth.

She squeezed his hand. "It feels like an eternity since—"

He hushed her with a kiss, light at first. He didn't rush. She needed to throw off the job, which would be slower than usual, given the pressure of the day. The kiss, however, held promise, and Cordy found herself responding to the sheer pleasure of being held. She tasted wine and cashews—his favorite late-night snack. Still damp from a recent shower, his hair left an aroma of sandalwood and honeysuckle. Her heart beat so hard that she was afraid it would fracture. She wondered how she had been so lucky to become Braun's wife. "Braun…"

"Later, my darling, we can talk," Braun gave her another nibble. "I just need you." In a flash, he swept her into his arms and headed down a long hallway to the nearest bedroom. Pausing at the foot of a four-poster canopy bed, he peeled away her clothes as she tore madly at his shirt, managing to rip off a button in her haste.

"Easy there, tiger." Braun laughed. "We have all night," but he didn't stop undressing her until she lay naked on the bed. His hand caressed her shoulder and slowly glided down her body, past her ribs and waist, until it rested on her abdomen. "Have Katrina and her brother been behaving?"

Cordy felt a delightful response to his touch all the way to her core. "They've been quite active today, and I think they recognize your voice." The baby bump rippled beneath his hand. She wondered if the twins felt the rush of adrenaline and hormones flowing through her.

Braun bent down and kissed her belly by her navel. "Daddy wishes you sweet dreams, little ones."

As exhausted as she felt only moments before, sleep was the farthest thing from Cordy's mind, and she was sure Braun felt the same way. His lips were pure heat as they caressed and nuzzled her nipples. She moaned and pulled him closer, feeling his needs pulse against her own.

Not wanting to crush the precious cargo she carried, she allowed Braun to roll her on top of him and embarked on a rising journey. Tongues and fingers teased and taunted as their breaths grew jagged, hot, and steamy. Fiery shock waves sent shivers through her. She clung tightly to him as they climaxed.

Fear for his life, combined with the excitement of finding him healthy, washed through her mind. "How dare you go off and leave us. Katrina, her brother, and I need you here, need you desperately. You could have died. I can barely forgive you for that."

They must have been on the same wavelength. Braun's husky voice softened in the aftermath of the moment. "When that drone exploded, I was terrified that I'd never see you again. I'll never get enough of you."

"I love you, Braun. Don't ever leave me." Her eyes fluttered closed on a low moan—completely satiated—not just physically but emotionally reassured, her anger spent.

Sept. 12 – 3:00 a.m. EDT, Blair House, Washington, D.C.

It felt like only seconds had passed when a cell phone rang. Braun peeled back the covers, not wanting to move, but knew Cordy was resting for three. "I'll get it."

"Your phone or mine?" Cordy mumbled.

"Either way, it better be a wrong number." Braun lifted her arm wrapped around him, flipped on the small lamp on the bedside table, and padded toward the end of the bed to fish through the clothes heap. He groaned when he found his phone lit up. "Good morning, Chief Jackson. Do you know what time it is?"

"It's early. I can never repay you for saving Mo's and Emma's lives, and we're very grateful," Jackson continued without pausing, "but something has come up. I need another huge favor—your pilot skills."

"Can you repeat that?" Braun fumbled to get his jeans on straight, then tiptoed from the room and closed the door behind him.

"I need your pilot skills." Jackson's voice sounded strained as if he feared Braun would say no.

"Cripes, what the hell for, Chief? I haven't had a day off in a month." Needing coffee, Braun made his way to the kitchen and poured water into a pot. He splashed more water on his face and ripped off a paper towel from the roll to wipe away the sleep. "Can't it wait until morning?"

"I had planned to call earlier, but I knew you hadn't spent much time with Cordy lately, so I let you sleep in." Chief Jackson sounded apologetic.

"Sleep in?" Braun laughed. "How kind of you." He wondered what he would tell Cordy about this one. She was barely over the last debacle.

"I know. Here's the rub," Chief said. "Officer Peggy Wyller tracked down Einar Zinmansky. Do you know who I'm talking about?"

"His name came up once or twice," Braun said.

"Peggy's father is a retired cop, and he called in a favor," Chief said. "It turns out that Zinmansky is catching a private jet to Toronto, Canada, scheduled to depart at 4 a.m. He booked a flight from there to Russia, leaving today at 9:50 a.m. Rumor has it that the jet has armed security guards, so getting Zinmansky won't be easy. I want to replace the scheduled pilot with you."

"Why me?" Braun asked.

"We need an armed pilot who can defend himself," Chief said. "Zinmansky headed up that drone project that you tested yesterday. You capture him, and you might get some answers. Meet us at the designated site. I will see you there. Our target is to get Zinmansky alive and unharmed. We have a tight timeframe, and when I spoke with Russ Bracken, the SWAT leader, you popped into our minds. Agent Gray says you're already working undercover."

"What's going on?" Cordy came up behind him and wrapped her arms around his waist. Her green velvet robe felt soft against his back.

"Chief, I'm putting you on speaker. Cordy's here, and you might as well explain the details while I get ready." Braun poured two cups of coffee, added four spoons of sugar to his, and a good inch of cream to hers.

Cordy nearly gagged, pushed the coffee aside, and snacked on a few crackers while Chief Jackson explained his plan for Braun to meet him at the airport where Zinmansky supposedly hired a private jet.

Cordy asked Braun, "Are you sure you want to pose as the pilot?"

"I want answers to what happened to my team." Braun gulped his brew. "Zinmansky headed the drone project. He's suspected of an assassination attempt on the president, and I intend to get this bastard. It's the least I can do for Rusty and his family. You have questions for him, too."

"True." Cordy grabbed Braun's cell so she could share the details. "Evans found more forensic information about those bullets and metal shards. He also mentioned the explosive material used by the drone." She turned toward Braun. "I have notes in my backpack that I planned to share. Why don't I go with you and fill you in on the information? I also want access to Zinmansky's laptop."

Chief Jackson jumped into the conversation. "No, Cordy. I don't want you anywhere near Zinmansky. He's a prime suspect in the poisoning of the man found dead at the White House. This man is armed and dangerous. Stay away until we have him in our custody. Then you can question him for anything you want. And you mentioned forensics. Sophia and Peggy have a few facts to share as well."

"Okay, I won't get in harm's way, but I am riding with Braun, so I can update him on the forensic data."

"Better get dressed then." Braun kissed Cordy on the cheek, whisked the cell phone from her hand, and spoke to Chief Jackson, "Send me the GPS coordinates, and we'll be there shortly." He gathered his pilot and SWAT gear.

"What if the jet isn't leaving from the airport?" Braun asked. "It's too easy of a setup. It may be a decoy."

Chief forwarded a local map with a blinking red light traveling westbound along I-395 toward Dulles Airport. "An FBI helicopter has eyes in the sky monitoring a black SUV with three men, and

Zinmansky reported aboard. We'll send updates on the coordinates. They'll have to go through customs first and fly out of terminal one. Let's move!"

Cordy was dressed in a flash and standing by the door.

Braun felt his gut jolt as he watched her fling the backpack over her shoulder, uncovering her father's pistol tucked inside a shoulder harness.

Cordy grinned. "Don't worry, I'm not planning to use it, but I hate being unarmed."

"I'm not letting anyone harm you." Braun wrapped his arm protectively around her waist. "You stay in the car when we get there."

"Or I'll be at headquarters on the radio with you at all times," Cordy said. "I wish you still had that tie-tack."

"We'll have Quint make another one." Braun checked the updated GPS. "Ready?"

Cordy opened the door and peered around. The hallway was empty as they headed for the elevator doors. No one was at the front desk either, so she jotted a note for the receptionist, and they left Blair House.

Exit Plan B

Sept. 12 – 3:28 a.m. EDT, En Route to a private jet, Washington, D.C.

Einar Zinmansky, a rotund man in his late thirties, tried to get comfortable in the back seat of a black SUV as he fidgeted with his seat belt that pinched his hips. He'd been a nervous wreck ever since he'd heard the FBI had a warrant out for his arrest. He couldn't believe that he was now considered a criminal, accused of an assassination attempt at the White House and more. Proving one's innocence once deemed guilty was next to impossible. If accused of such treason in his native country, he'd be shot on sight. He had to get out of the U.S. undetected ASAP. He'd called the only person he dared to trust, his cousin, Mierzany K. Ansin.

Zinmansky had been initially thankful when Ansin agreed to book a private jet to Toronto, Canada. The plane was to depart at 4 a.m. From there, he'd travel back to Russia. It surprised him to see Ansin himself, along with two burley bodyguards, appear in the back alley of a run-down warehouse where he had been hiding most of the afternoon. He should feel relieved, yet his nerves remained frayed.

Next to him sat his disgruntled cousin, barking orders in Russian to the two bodyguards sitting up front. The older of the two was driving, but he was having difficulty navigating as wind gusts blew frigid sleet against the windshield. The driver had followed the preloaded GPS route, cursing when he misinterpreted the English voice system. After two mistakes, he paused as the GPS rerouted him again and swore in Russian, rolling his R's. "Rotten Rental! GPS has no brains. Only speak English."

Zinmansky's bushy black eyebrows came together in a frown. "We're going to be late."

Ansin leaned forward in the right rear seat and peered through the window. "Zes are dangeRous conditions." He turned to Zinmansky. "Eff I left ze flight to you, ve'd be on choppeR, and you'd never git to Canada. Good Zink, I book jet."

His cousin's thick Russian accent grated on Zinmansky's nerves. It had taken him nearly four years to lose the foreign accent, and he wondered why Ansin, who had been in the country for almost eight years, still rolled his R's, used a Z instead of th, an inK instead of ing, and a V instead of W. He felt his cousin was too lazy to learn English. Zinmansky had managed to curb the accent, but it still slipped out when he got angry. "You just passed the airport exit." His voice shook. "Where are you taking us?"

"Don't worry," Ansin said. "We can't go through customs, so we have another plan."

"Whose plans?" Zinmansky shouted. "I made arrangements. Where's our jet?"

"Tracking and on schedule." Ansin glared at Zinmansky. "You hire. We deliver." Ansin could have been Zinmansky's twin but thirty pounds lighter. "Trust me. I promised we'd get you out of the country."

A flutter in Zinmansky's gut warned him. *Can I trust Ansin?* His life was in his cousin's hands. He leaned back and tried to relax when lights in the sky caught his attention. He felt like he was losing control and had to regain it. "Someone's flying overhead. Are we being followed?"

"I already told you I'll take care of everything." Ansin fished through his suit jacket pockets and pulled out a small device.

"What's that?" Zinmansky asked.

"A GPS jammer." Ansin directed it toward the helicopter. "Take a left at the next exit. You know my motto, always be prepared. We're moving on to plan B."

The driver followed directions. "If we get lost, don't blame me."

"Just take the exit and pull into the nearest gas station." Ansin's right lip curled up in a smug smile. "I already arranged for a second car to meet us, and we'll split up. I have to call a friend over at Anacostia. We'll keep this GPS scrambled, and the other car will take our place. Won't they be surprised? I just love these gadgets."

When the driver pulled up, a black SUV was waiting at the gas station. Ansin got out. "Terrific, Zinmansky, you wait here. We need to divert their attention."

"But the helicopter is no longer above us," Zinmansky said. "Maybe they weren't tracking us after all."

"Let's just say they were, and we'll send them this decoy instead." Ansin snapped his fingers. "In the meantime, take off your suit jacket."

"You already borrowed one of my coats," Zinmansky said. "I never got that jacket back."

"Just do it. I'll buy you three suits when you get back to Russia." Ansin motioned to the new car's driver, who also got out to talk to Ansin. The two men disappeared around the rear of the station. When they returned, Ansin was wearing Zinmansky's suit jacket.

Zinmansky stared at Ansin as both men got into the other car. There were two other passengers in the rear. "Where's he going now?" He knew Ansin didn't want to be seen and certainly not by the police. After all, the man had been an enigma most of his life. Agents, detectives, reporters, and amateur sleuths had asked questions about his cousin's whereabouts in the past. Ansin had remained anonymous—his face only known by his family, and what a face. It was nearly a mirror image of his own except less pudgy in the cheeks.

Zinmansky's driver seemed confused when he heard his cell phone ring. He rolled down his window and called out to Ansin, who was sitting in the passenger's front seat of the other car. "My phone's ringing. What should I do?"

"Answer it," Ansin called out. "It's me on the phone."

"Why don't you just talk to me?" the driver asked and answered the phone. There was a pause. "You want me to what?" The driver turned and shoved the cell into Zinmansky's hand a few seconds later. "It's for you."

Zinmansky took the device.

Ansin said something about the two cars splitting up to make it more difficult for anyone to follow. "I look a lot like you, so they'll think they're tracking you. We'll meet up and share your ride with a friend of mine. He'll protect you until you get out of the country."

Zinmansky grunted. "Are you sure this will work?"

"Don't you trust me?" Ansin asked.

"Yes, but…I hadn't planned to share my ride."

"It works out better for all of us this way," Ansin said. "Have a safe flight."

"So you're not coming with me?" Zinmansky asked, already knowing the answer.

"I'll be heading off the police," Ansin said. "You don't want to be caught anywhere near me."

"Sure you will," Zinmansky muttered to himself, his voice trembling with the weight of the situation. He knew Ansin, the black sheep of the family just like his father warned, had no intention of tackling the police. The past day's events started falling into place. Furious with his cousin and maybe himself for being such a fool, he shouted, "Fine, have it your way, but don't frame me for another death. That's what you did at the White House, didn't you? You copied my ID badge and signed in as me. I thought I'd misplaced it last week, but you had it. That's how you got into my office. I bet you stole my laptop, too, and emptied my apartment. I'm no fool. I know it was you. You used Novichok to murder my contact, didn't you? They'll trace it back to me. I was shocked to learn the FBI was after me. Now I have to run for—"

"Einar, keep your mouth shut if you want to live." Ansin disconnected, and his car drove away.

Zinmansky's driver, a loyal and trusted ally, revved the engine and drove out of the gas station's parking lot in the opposite direction of Ansin.

Zinmansky felt a jolt of fear. "Where are you taking me?" His anxious voice was filled with confusion.

"Don't worry," the driver said. "Change of plans. I have my orders."

Braun and Cordy drove along I-395 and were in the middle of discussing the RCV and drone test that happened twenty-four hours earlier. Cordy had barely relayed the forensic data she had received from Evans when Chief Jackson spoke over the radio. "The helicopter lost Zinmansky's SUV somewhere over I-495, then picked it up again along I-395."

"Wait a minute," Braun said. "Are they flying out of Reagan instead of Dulles? That's terrific news. I'm much closer—"

"Breaking news," came over Jackson's radio. "Chief Polack here." He ordered, "All units. We have residents reporting beacon lights over Joint Base Anacostia-Bolling. It's after closing. Dispatch, deploy all available units to Anacostia. Surround the airport."

Sirens erupted in the distance. Flashing blue and red lights appeared out of nowhere as patrol cars, ambulances, and even fire trucks merged onto the highway.

"What's going on at Anacostia?" Braun asked Chief Jackson. "Why are the police being ordered to surround the area? Are they also looking for Zinmansky?"

"No, this has nothing to do with him," Chief said. "Peggy just got word from her father that Zahair collapsed and was pronounced DOA when he arrived at the Emergency Room. They took him to the morgue for an autopsy. When the ME pulled out the tray to get the body, it wasn't there. The morgue's surveillance camera captured video of a man dressed in an olive green camouflage shirt and pants, combat boots, helmet, and a Kevlar vest entering the morgue. Facial recognition software ID'd him as Amir, a member of the Iranian Revolutionary Guard. Fifteen minutes later, he left the building with a live Zahair. I'd say it was a miraculous recovery if I didn't know better. They hopped onto a motorcycle and drove away. Obviously, no one was watching the security screen at the morgue, and Chief Polack is on the warpath."

"Is he afraid someone will smuggle Zahair out of the country?" Braun asked.

"Highly likely," Chief Jackson said. "Gregor admitted that he arranged for a private jet to leave the country at 4 a.m."

"The same time as Zinmansky?" Braun asked.

"That can't be a coincidence," Cordy said. "And Polack's officers are surrounding Anacostia Airport just because of some lights? It makes no sense. Why would anyone at Anacostia turn on the landing lights and warn everyone that someone's flying out of the country in a private jet? Especially if that someone is trying to get away undetected?"

"That's true," Braun said. "Even a rookie pilot could fly out without landing lights on a night with a full moon. Well, maybe not in this sleet, but that has to be a ruse."

"Polack is sending in every man available," Chief Jackson said.

"Polack's an idiot." Cordy caught something out of the corner of her eye. "Look, there's a jet to your right flying very low near 14th Street Bridge. It doesn't appear to be heading toward Dulles, Reagan, or Anacostia. Could it land on a bridge?"

"Nonsense," Chief Jackson said. "How will a car meet the jet? The bridge is closed, and the wingspan will extend over the edges on either side."

"If the bridge is closed, it will be easier to land." Cordy grabbed the radio. "Chief, get helicopters overhead. Something is happening. I see headlights approaching the bridge."

Chief Jackson sputtered and cleared his throat. "Helicopter 40, check 14th Street Bridge. Small jet approaching."

"Roger, Helicopter 40 looking for traffic."

Cordy became more excited. "Yes, that plane is landing on the bridge. Where's the nearest police unit?"

Chief Jackson groaned. "Not close enough—five, maybe six minutes out."

"We're going in." Braun stepped on the gas, rounded another corner, and braked.

Cordy lurched forward and was caught by the seat belt, which prevented her from hitting the dashboard.

A few seconds later, the radio buzzed, "Helicopter 40. Affirmative. Jet is landing. Check Video stream over ShareLink," came over the radio.

The car's small ShareLink screen lit up. Cordy watched a grainy video of a jet below the helicopter. "A car just wedged its way between two cement barriers blocking the bridge and is heading for the jet. Zoom in."

The camera zoomed in as a black SUV pulled up. Cordy saw a shortcut on the GPS tracking device. "Turn left." She bounced with excitement. "Left, here!"

Braun took a corner on two wheels. "Better tell Polack he's missing the action."

Chief Jackson laughed. "Peggy's already on Polack's radio. That's one unhappy boss. He swore at Peggy until her dad took over. Once Polack discovered the ex-chief was on the call, he changed his tune. Now he's eating crow."

Braun pulled up to cement barriers at the edge of the bridge, climbed from the car, and threw open the rear door. "That's our target. Stay here. I'm heading in on foot."

"No," Cordy insisted. "It's too dangerous. We need to wait for backup."

"Backup is too far away." Braun grabbed his night vision goggles, slipped on a backpack loaded with gear, grabbed a duffle bag, and moved from the car. "Stay."

Loud voices came from the bridge, but it was too dark to see who was arguing. Cordy opened the car door and got out, straining to see what was happening. "They drove onto the bridge. There has to be a way to get closer."

"I mean it! Stay!" Braun shouted.

She ignored him, grabbed a pair of night-vision goggles from the back seat, and scanned the area. "There! Next to the barrier is a

Kawasaki dirt bike. It's smaller than your motorcycle but better than walking."

Someone was standing at the jet's doorway. Then Cordy heard Zahair's distinctive voice talking to a bulky man standing outside the black SUV. "There's only room for one of you."

"Get two passengers off the plane now," the man said. "This flight is already booked."

Cordy grabbed the radio. "We have a hostage situation. Zahair is ordering two passengers off the jet."

Braun didn't wait around. He rummaged around in his bag and grabbed something from his gear. He took off running toward the motorcycle as Chief Jackson, Peggy, and her dad pulled up behind Braun's car.

"Hurry!" Cordy said. "Braun's already on the bridge."

***

It took Braun a moment to locate the ignition cable and hot-wire the motorized bike. It was nearly out of gas, which is probably why it had been ditched. He wedged the duffle bag in front of him and pulled on the valve. The still-warm engine coughed momentarily before chugging to life. Braun kicked the lever all the way down and took off like a lightning bolt.

A fat man wedged his bulk from the rear of the SUV as he shouted, "We have company. He's coming fast."

Zahair held a pistol aimed at a man dressed in a navy suit standing at the top of the jet and yelled, "Get off the plane, or I'll shoot. Hurry!"

"Not without our son." The man grabbed a woman's arm. He yelled, "Do you know who I am? I have money."

"I don't want your money. I want your plane. Both of you, get off now, or I'll shoot your son and throw him off the plane, too."

The woman cried, "Take me instead. Please don't hurt my boy."

Zahair stepped forward and shoved the woman.

She tripped and lost her shoe. It tumbled down the steps to the bridge, but she stood her ground. "I'm not leaving without Arty."

Zahair fired his gun, and the bullet barely missed the woman's head. "That's my last warning. Get off the plane! I'll shoot you and your son if you don't move now!"

The man seemed to crumple. His shoulders were hunched, and his back curved as he yanked his wife's elbow, pulling her toward the steps.

"What about Arty?" his wife protested.

Zahair turned and pointed his gun inside the plane. "You want his body?"

"No, don't shoot," the man yelled and scrambled down the steps with one hand tugging along the female at his side. She swiped a sleeve over her face, snatched up the heel, and limped away, not bothering to slip on the shoe. The two nearly collided with Zinmansky as they raced past.

Zahair dashed down the steps and fired a warning shot into the air. "Keep running."

The escaping couple dropped to the ground and rolled toward the edge of the bridge unharmed.

Braun zigzagged the bike while firing at the airjackers. His first bullets bounced off the SUV and the metal steps as Zahair and the rotund man bobbed and weaved their frantic path to the jet's safety.

The two thugs turned their fire on Braun, who headed straight for them. He rode low in the seat behind the duffle bag, wound his way from left to right dodging bullets, and as he got closer, hugged the edge of the bridge. The thugs' bullets pinged off the frame as he slid the bike sidewise under the nose of the jet and hopped off. A flurry of shots pinged against the bike, but Braun wasn't at the right angle to fire back at the two thugs who knelt behind the SUV and covered Zahair and the fat man as they fled for the jet.

Zahair pushed the obese man's backside, shoving him up the steps. As they reached the top, Zahair yelled, "Amir, close the hatch!"

Motioning to the huddling couple, he shouted to the thugs, "Get in your car, and run them off the bridge."

***

Officer Peggy Wyller rounded the patrol's rear door, dashed to the end of the bridge, propped her semi-automatic rifle on top of a cement pillar, and fired, hitting the SUV's driver.

Her dad was close behind and shot the other thug, but not before the jet's engines fired to life.

The plane rolled toward Braun, who darted backward away from the SUV. The jet's front tire rolled over the dirt bike, skidded sidewise, and hit the vehicle. The plane stopped and tried to back up. The jet's wheels continued to screech in a deafening pitch as it dragged the car along the pavement, causing sparks and dark tread marks. The metal-on-metal collision shrieked in the night.

Braun exploded a flash grenade, hoping to blind the pilot, while Chief Jackson darted to rescue the fleeing couple stranded on the bridge.

Braun pulled a grappling hook gun from his gear, launched the dart above the jet's door, and hung on to the cable as the plane continued its backward motion. He grunted with effort to untangle himself from the line, but it held tight. Braun hit the ascension device, freeing his arm enough to grab his pick and tumbler, which drew him toward the jet door. When his feet reached the runner, he fumbled to open the door, cursing at his slowness. The latch finally clicked. He pulled a small dart gun from his pocket, opened the door a crack, and saw Zahair heading toward the door to greet him. Braun fired a drug-tipped dart at close range. It flew into the man's neck.

Zahair's gun clattered to the floor as he staggered forward and collapsed, nearly parting the curtain drawn between the cabin and the cockpit. Braun managed to wedge through the narrow opening and cuffed Zahair before the jet door closed.

"What's going on out there?" Amir yelled in his thick Persian accent. "Zinmansky? You okay?"

A gasp came from a heavy-set man who had been staring out the window at the left side of the jet. "Yes. Let's go!"

Braun stepped into the aisle.

Zinmansky startled and turned to face Braun. "Who are you?" His hands flew up in surrender when he saw the gun. "I didn't do it—he framed me! I love America!" Zinmansky spoke in a heavy Russian accent but was barely loud enough to hear over the racket. He pointed toward the curtain and mouthed, "There's a man in the cockpit. He has a pistol on the pilot."

"I can't think with all that clatter!" Amir shouted. "Lose the SUV, or I'll shoot."

"I'm doing the best I can," a man with a New Jersey accent said in a remarkably calm voice.

Braun figured he must be the pilot. Braun still had the dart gun in his hand. It wasn't loaded anymore, but Zinmansky didn't know that. "Put out your wrists."

The man, totally cowed by events around him, held up two beefy paws, and Braun cuffed him to his seat. He found a small knife in the man's boot, but otherwise, Zinmansky was unarmed.

A child sat huddled in a seat in the right corner of the front row. His eyes squeezed shut as he rocked his body and buried his cheek into the fur of a small brown terrier.

"Son, your daddy sent me," Braun whispered.

The boy opened his eyes but kept rocking. He whispered, "Grear. He has Grear. Save Grear."

Braun scanned the area and nodded. "Shh now," Braun warned with a finger over his lips. "Is Grear the pilot?"

"He has Grear." The boy's eyes moved back and forth between the cockpit and Braun while stroking his dog's fur. Still rocking, he kept muttering, "He has Grear. Save Grear."

The plane must have managed to dislodge the attached SUV because the racket stopped, and the jet quickly lurched backward for several meters.

"What's going on out there, Zahair?" Amir yelled. "It's too quiet." He shouted at the pilot, "Get this jet in the air, now."

***

"Over here. You're safe. The police have you covered," Cordy called out to the couple as they dashed off the bridge ahead of Chief Jackson. "What happened?"

Tears streamed down the woman's cheeks. "Save Arty. He has our son. You have to save Arty." Trembling, she wrapped her drenched fox fur coat around her.

"I'm Agent Cordy Hastings, and my husband is still on the bridge trying to prevent the jet from taking off."

"No, they'll kill Arty," the woman blubbered, her voice cracking with desperation. "We have to save him." She broke down into sobs and nearly collapsed. "My boy. My baby."

The tall, angular man wrapped her into his arms and held her upright. "Shh. Honey." He tried to reassure her, but he choked up. The couple shook with fear and the frigid cold. Clutching her husband's shoulder, she melted into his arms.

"We'll get them," Cordy tried to reassure the parents and escorted them to her car, hoping they would calm down enough to tell her what had happened on the jet.

The woman seemed so dazed and confused that the man had to nearly carry her to the car.

"Take the back seat." Cordy got a blanket from the trunk and handed it to the couple, "This should warm you up." Cordy returned to the front seat, cranked up the heat, and continued asking questions, "Do you know the pilot?"

"Yes." The man spread the blanket over their laps. "He's our neighbor, Goodwin Grear, and he is being held at gunpoint." He

392

wiped a sleeve over his watery eyes. Tears from the cold, or was it emotional stress? The man seemed to shrink in front of her. His eyes shadowed. He pulled off his soaking suit coat, baring a now rumpled blue cotton shirt. The once-creased sleeves lay limp and clung to his slender arms. Chilled to the bone, the harsh light of the plane made his skin appear like ghastly pale goose flesh.

Chief Jackson poked his head through the open front door. "I have Officer Polack on the line."

Cordy took the phone. "We have a problem on the 14th Street Bridge. A private jet was hijacked. The pilot and, hold a moment." She turned toward the couple. "How old is Arty?"

"Ten. The boy's autistic, and he has his pet terrier with him," his mother sobbed.

"We're going to bring him home." Cordy spoke into the radio, "A ten-year-old boy is also on board. His mother says he's autistic. His name is Arty. He has a pet terrier with him, and the pilot is also being held at gunpoint. The pilot's name is Goodwin Grear."

The plane roared louder as it ramped up speed, lifted its nose in the air, and gradually flew over their heads.

"Oh no! The jet just took off!" Fear flooded Cordy's system as she dropped the radio and pushed past Jackson as she climbed from the car. "Where's Braun?"

Two bodies lay prone not far from the crumpled vehicle. Cordy's breath came out in small pants, and her hands shook. Her heart hammered so fast that it felt like a hummingbird thudding against her chest, desperate to escape its cage. Her legs ached and threatened to collapse as she sprinted down the middle of the bridge. Her lungs burned with the exertion as the biting wind whipped her hair into a frenzy. The damp and now frozen ends slapped her cheeks as she searched. "Braun, where are you?" She felt like she was making no progress, placing one foot in front of the other—her legs felt wobbly. The cold stung her eyes. Numb fingers brushed away the tears. "Braun?" She stared at the bodies, felt relieved that neither was her husband's, and knew he had to be on that plane.

No Fool

Unlike manning the complex instrument panel of his fighter jet, Goodwin Grear now sat behind a simplified computerized dashboard of automated dials, knobs, and digital read-outs for altitude, speed, cabin pressure, and more. The forty-three-year-old, an Iraq war veteran with over 200 combat missions to his credit, was raring up for another fight. His nerves were steel-strong, and he wasn't about to let this schmuck Amir take over his plane. Nor would he allow Arty to be placed in harm's way. Oh, he'd play along until the time was right.

When his initial plan failed, refusing to land the jet, he deliberately ran into the black SUV on the bridge to buy some time. It was pure luck that the jet's wheel locked onto the vehicle, which dragged across the bridge when he reversed the plane. Acting like a doddering old fool also bought him time, but he was anything but an idiot. He was working on a plan that wouldn't threaten Arty's safety.

The loud clatter of the entangled SUV may have hidden the extraneous noise of something strange beyond that cockpit curtain, but Grear had heard everything. He knew Zahair was no longer a threat.

Amir had been concentrating on Grear's every move. Whenever an odd sound came from behind the curtain, Grear made sure to make some movement to distract Amir within the cockpit to keep him focused—now to neutralize the situation and free Arty. The kid had a special place in his heart. They were neighbors, and he felt like a step-grandpa. The boy's bright baby blues never missed anything, and seeing a despondent old man, at least old in Arty's eyes, he had brought Grear out of deep depression like a butterfly escaping its cocoon. Teddy, the rescued terrier, was Grear's gift of thanks to Arty. The child and dog were inseparable.

Amir stood beside Grear with a gun poised to blow off his head. Sweat beaded across Amir's forehead. His trigger finger twitched as he yelled, "Free up that wheel now, or I'll shoot."

Grear had to calm this excitable man, who was likely to blow off his head out of nervousness, although he wouldn't have a pilot. "I'm doing the best I can," Grear said with remarkable restraint and yanked the stick back. The jet lurched, the clatter ceased, and the pilot rammed the sidestick controller forward, lifting the nose nearly straight off the ground, hoping to topple the hijacker. *What kind of idiot would stand unrestrained during take-off?*

***

Braun raised his pistol and stepped toward the cockpit. The curtain slid open as the jet thrust forward, lifted, and knocked Braun backward.

Amir fell sidewise. The gun went off, and a bullet landed in the ceiling of the cockpit.

Before Amir could raise his gun again, Braun leapt to his feet and pounced on the man. His right fist aimed for Amir's head, but it was deflected when a quick block of Amir's left arm locked onto Braun's right wrist and smacked it to the floor.

Amir held Braun in an iron grip—that of a trained assassin. He followed it with a whip punch to Braun's face with the butt of the gun.

There was a loud crack, and blood dripped from Braun's nose. His whole face felt on fire, but it drove him to fight harder. He knocked the gun from Amir's hand with a kick. Grabbing the back of Amir's left leg with one hand, he twisted with the other hand and yanked the man forward. Amir screamed as his knee dislocated. Braun grabbed Amir's hair and slammed his face into the floor. The familiar crunch of Amir's nose made Braun smile.

The jet went into a dive, forcing both men off-balance, but Amir was no longer fighting. He was dazed and trying to catch his breath when Braun cuffed Amir's wrist to a seat.

Amir's nose dripped blood down his chin. He turned and spat at Braun.

Braun wiped his face with his sleeve and shouted to the pilot, "Turn the jet around." Placing his fingers over the bridge of his own nose, he gave it a tweak to straighten it with a crunch. A wave of nausea threatened, and he saw black dots float before him. Yep, it was definitely broken. He breathed through his mouth and stuffed a tissue into one nostril to block the blood flow. This wasn't the first time Braun had fractured his nose, and it probably wouldn't be the last. His nasal passages were already swelling. He'd have raccoon eyes within the hour. One look at Amir and Braun knew the Persian would suffer the same fate. He had made sure of it.

The pilot was already on the radio to the control tower, asking permission to land.

Braun checked on the boy, who continued rocking but was no longer chanting to save Grear. Zinmansky sat dazed in a wide-eyed stare and remained silent. Braun returned to the cockpit, stopped to pick up Amir's gun lying on the floor, and shoved it into his waistband. He took the co-pilot's seat and radioed Cordy. "Meet us at Reagan National Airport. I have Amir, Zahair, and Zinmansky in custody. The boy is unharmed, and this pilot has everything under control."

"What happened?" Cordy asked. "You sound all stuffed up."

"Broken nose, but you should see the other guys," Braun said. "I need ice and plenty of TLC."

"I'm glad you still have a sense of humor." Cordy chuckled. "See you soon."

"I'm serious, Cordy. I love you with all my heart," Braun said. "Please, take care of yourself and our family until I can hold you again. I can't lose you."

Clean Up

Cordy Hastings pulled into Reagan Airport's parking lot and couldn't wait to see her husband after his rescue of a pilot and a kidnapped 10-year-old boy from a hijacked jet. She wrapped her jacket closer around her shivering body, struggled to keep her teeth from chattering, and stepped onto the glazed ice, nearly losing her footing. Why hadn't she allowed Chief Jackson to drive her to the airport? He would have dropped her off at the front door, but no, she had insisted on taking her rental car, hoping to pick up Braun and spend a few precious moments alone together before starting another hectic day. Big mistake! What had started as a light drizzle turned to sleet, making the lot slick as snot. Puffs of steam escaped with every breath. Lightning cracked, and thunder roared overhead as she fought the storm, dodged an oncoming car, and finally reached the front door, thankfully without falling.

Mondays were hectic as members of Congress often took a red-eye flight to arrive in time to reach their chambers by 9 a.m. Out of habit, Cordy eyed the crowd, scanning the area for the small things—*Paranoia?* Could be, but that's what kept her alive until now. She paused next to a bookstore, absently perusing the shelves placed outside the store, lined with novels to entice one to enter for a better look. Something nagged at her mind. She noticed a tall blond man wearing jeans and a faded olive green and tan camo shirt walk briskly toward her. "Braun, over here."

The man glanced her way as he shrugged off a large blue backpack. He grabbed his cell phone and quickly dialed before ducking into a restroom.

She realized her mistake. *Of course, it's not him. Braun's still in disguise. I need to find an auburn-haired man with dark-brown eyes, a reddish mustache, and a goatee. Braun should easily stand out since he's a head taller than most men.*

A Latino man with a severe limp caught her attention as he haltingly followed the blond man into the restroom. The door closed, blocking Cordy's view. Her senses alarmed, but before she could follow her hunch, she heard a familiar voice.

"Wait up," Chief Jackson called out as he raced toward Cordy.

She turned toward Jackson. "Did you find Braun?"

"No. Chief Polack just radioed with new orders." Jackson paused to catch his breath. "His officers met the hijacked jet on the tarmac and took everyone, including Braun, Arty, and the pilot, down to the Metro Station. Peggy and her dad already left to file their reports. Arty's parents were anxious to see their son and went with them. We're to meet them there."

Cordy's mind resisted calming. *Something is wrong.*

Chief Jackson blew out a breath. "Are you coming?"

Deep in thought, she jolted, audibly sucked in air, and backed into a shelf, knocking a book from its rack.

"Sorry, I didn't mean to startle you." Jackson stepped closer. "So, are you coming?"

"One moment." She replaced the paperback, noting the title, "Ransomware," in large red letters against a black background.

Her neck muscles tensed instinctively—*that gnawing feeling again*. Glancing around, she saw the tall blond exit the men's room. He was now dressed in a navy sports coat and carried a briefcase. Even though he wore polarizing sunglasses, there was something familiar about him. Unsure why, Cordy grabbed her cell phone, snapped a photo of the book cover, and when the man glanced her way, she managed to capture a shot of him, too, before he turned to his right. *Where have I seen him before?*

The Latino opened the door to leave the men's room, glanced in each direction, and headed to his left. He now wore the blue backpack. Realizing Chief Jackson was staring at her, she asked, "Do you know that man in the navy jacket? Is he a Congressman or someone who works on the Hill?"

Jackson shook his head. "I don't think so."

Cordy also snapped a photo of the Latino, catching only a side view. "What about the limping man with the blue backpack?"

"Send me the photos, and I'll look into it later." Jackson turned to leave. "Braun will be waiting."

Cordy was torn between her desire to see Braun and her need to follow up on the blond. She opted to see Braun, "I'll be right there, but I need a pit stop before going anywhere. You go on ahead." Recalling her hazardous trek from the parking lot, she added, "Meet me at the curb. I don't want to fall racing to the car park. I'll leave my rental in the lot."

"Okay, but hurry." Jackson rushed into the crowd without another word.

Cordy crossed the hall and spotted the tall blond speaking to a guy emptying a trashcan. She couldn't hear what they said, but the sanitation worker turned and glanced her way, and then they both rounded a corner. Cordy shook her head, almost laughing at herself as she entered the ladies' room. *Now, I am being paranoid. It's probably pregnancy hormones.*

Cordy glanced around. *What luck—there was no line.* In fact, she was the only one in the restroom. She sent the photos to Chief Jackson and Quint, along with a text message: "Run a search for an ID. Gut feeling, get back to me." She did her business and darted from the stall as that same sanitation worker wheeled a cleaning cart into the room, closed the door, and blocked the entrance.

The tall blond popped from behind the cart. "Time to clean up."

Cordy recognized the man's voice. *Casper Grest, the co-pilot who hijacked the jet from Colorado. How did he find me?* Despite her heart pounding wildly in her chest, she forced herself to remain calm. Reaching for a paper towel with her right hand, she tapped the flag pin to alert Quint with her left. She refused to turn around to face Grest and watched his reflection in the mirror. Her mind raced when Grest raised his right hand. A roll of toilet paper covered the barrel of a gun with a silencer pointed straight at her back.

"I see the drug has worn off," Grest said. "You were better off unconscious and should not have gotten involved in this little matter. Now, I regret, we'll need to silence you permanently." He pushed the cleaning cart forward to get a better shot.

With no time to think, Cordy dove for the floor.

The sanitation worker caught her off guard and incapacitated her by plunging a needle into her neck. She lost all sensation but could briefly hear voices in the distance before her world turned dark.

***

"Stan, why did you drug her?" Grest asked. "I had a clear shot."

Stan glared at Grest. "The lady's pregnant! I'm not going to be charged with two murders—certainly not for killing an innocent child. What did she ever do to you, anyway?"

Grest frowned. "Nothing to me. We're paid to do a job, and if H.Q. wants her to disappear, that's what we do."

Stan's brow furrowed as he narrowed his eyes. "Disappear? Or murdered? Huge difference."

Grest hesitated. Zahair had wanted Cordy out of the country, and H.Q. hadn't actually ordered him to kill the woman. "Just get rid of her."

"Wise up." Stan opened the lid to the trash bin, "I have a better plan. Stuff her in here. I'll load her onto a jet and fly her out of the country. Whatever happens to her, it won't be our problem. We've already been paid half up front. I can live with that, but I don't want to be accused of murder. Do you?"

Grest holstered his gun and checked his watch. "My flight leaves in thirty minutes. I can't think of a better plan, so I'll help you load her into the bin, but you'll need to do the rest and make sure she's on a long flight."

After a fitful night, Quint squinted at the digital clock blinking a bright red 12:00. The power had gone out and returned sometime after 4:17 a.m., which was what the clock read the last time he checked. All he wanted to do was burrow his head under the pillow and go back to sleep. His eyelids felt like lead weights until he felt a vibration on his wrist. "Holy shit!" *Cordy activated her flag pin, but when? What happened?* She had also sent two images to ID and a text message.

Quint jumped from his bed, nearly tripped over his beige Dockers lying on the floor, and raced for his home office while hopping on one leg and then the other as he pulled on his pants. "Where is she?" He opened the tracker on his laptop. *Reagan International Airport runway? What is she doing there?* He called Cordy, but it went directly to voicemail. Braun's cell phone got the same results. Then he remembered Braun's phone had disintegrated during the deadly weapons test.

There must be someone I can call. Quint thought hard. *President Spendorf? No, she was working directly…*Quint speed dialed. "Chief Jackson, this is Quint."

Jackson heaved a deep breath, and didn't get a word out before Quint gushed, "Is Cordy with you?"

"No, but she's only been out of my sight for less than ten minutes. I just made it back to my car, and I'm going to drive to the curb to meet her. Why? Oh, I see she forwarded a text message. The images haven't even come through yet." Jackson sounded concerned.

Quint paced as he spoke. "Cordy hit the panic button. I've loaded the images into an ID detection program, but no hits yet, and the GPS tracker located her flag pin on the C-41 runway. What is she doing there?"

"I don't know, but I'll find her." Jackson barked orders over a police radio before he disconnected Quint's call.

Cordy blinked and tried to wipe her face with the palm of her hand. She winced when her wrist caught behind her back. Cuffs bit into her flesh. A chain ran between the cuffs and wrapped behind her waist, wedging her hands between the container and her hips. She tried to bring her wrists together behind her back. *If I can get my fingers under the cuffs, maybe I can slide them over my palms.* Wiggling, and jiggling, she couldn't wedge her hands together, no matter how hard she tried. Anger tinged with fear, she had to get free.

A pungent odor hit her nostrils—*diesel fuel.* Her heart jolted when engines roared to life. *Where am I?* The drug hadn't totally worn off, making her body feel jittery, jerky, and uncontrolled when she tried to move. Cordy sat with her knees tucked under her chin. Trash, paper towels, and clutter wedged under her butt, feet, and ankles. The space was too cramped to straighten her legs. The last thing she remembered was the cleaning cart in front of the bathroom door. She yelled, "Help! I'm trapped."

It was dark, but her eyesight gradually improved with time. She scanned her surroundings and discovered she was inside something. The cover was slightly ajar, allowing light and air to filter around her. Calling out at intervals seemed pointless, but it didn't stop her from trying, "Help! I'm inside—a waste bin." It was the only thing that came to mind. Her cries gave out a muffled echo, but no one came to her rescue.

Okay, what next? Thankfully, her ankles were unbound, although her feet felt numb like blocks of ice. It was cold, maybe 50° F., and she must have been crouched in this position for a while. As she flexed her toes, they felt prickly and ached. "Is anyone out there? I'm trapped!" She listened, then tried again, "Help! Someone, please. Anyone out there?"

With much effort, she moved side to side, inching the chain down from her waist, over one hip, then the other. Stopping at intervals, she continued to call out for help, but it was useless. Her throat was sore, her mouth dry, and she shivered to stay warm. The cuffs cut into her wrists, making them raw and chaffed. The metal links caught on the back pocket of her slacks, but she kept jerking the chain down to get free. The pocket finally gave way, probably torn, but she didn't care.

Feeling her side pockets, she sighed. *Empty—No cell phone. No keys, nothing.* Finally, she managed to drag the chain over her butt. She tried to slip her cuffs down far enough to get the chain over her feet, too, but the metal links were caught in debris and hugged tightly to her body. At least she felt warmer with all the effort to escape. Rubbing her sweaty brow over her knees, she refused to give up.

Instead, she dragged the blasted chain up her thighs, yanking, and pulling. Her wrists were now bleeding. At last, the chain was behind her knees, and she could remove a few paper towels that had made it more difficult to move. Panting, she took a moment to rest and listened for any movement outside. It didn't take long to scrape the cuffs along her calves, down to her ankles, and with great effort, she pulled the chain over one foot and then the other.

Heaving a deep sigh, relief didn't last long. The ride was getting bumpier. *Surely, Quint summoned help by now. When will they arrive? Will they be here in time?*

Her arms, although still bound, were now wedged around her waist with the chain in front of her. Readjusting her position, she managed to elbow her arms up the side of the bin, over her head, and tried to lift the lid. It wouldn't budge. Something weighed it down. *Probably baggage.* Cordy tried to stand and push the cover with her head and shoulders, but it still wouldn't move, and her head ached. Collapsing back on her feet, she felt nausea pulse through her.

She had to free herself. Her right wrist was caked in blood and stung with every movement, but she pulled her thumb into her palm, yanked hard on the cuff, and finally freed her palm and fingers. The chain still hung from her left wrist, but she could now move more freely.

Cordy found a rag at the bottom of the trash barrel, along with a few paper towels to wrap around her right wrist. She tried to blot the bleeding, but her main worry was her children. They were too quiet. She hadn't felt any movement, and that wasn't normal. *Wake up little ones. Are you sleeping, Katrina? Is that your name? It doesn't feel right, or maybe Vivian?* Cordy held her hands over her belly, trying to make contact with her most precious blessings. *Please. Just give me a nudge or a kick. I need a sign that you're both okay. Nothing.*

A loud, low rumble got her attention, and her surroundings vibrated and bounced. Recalling that her last known location was Reagan National Airport, Cordy feared she was now aboard a jet, and it had taken off. *What if something happens to our babies? I have to get out of here.* Cordy's mouth felt like it was filled with cotton, but she called out anyway, "Is anyone out there? Please, help me!" The noise reverberated, growing louder, and no one answered. She shut her eyes and realized someone was screaming. Her eyes flew open, she closed her mouth, and the screaming stopped.

Panic gripped her as she threw her body from side to side, wriggling and rattling her chain, trying to tip the barrel over to no avail. *It must be propped against something.* She continued to call out, but no one answered. "Someone, please." Her voice was nothing but a whisper, and she was hyperventilating so hard that she thought she'd pass out. Neither twin moved inside her womb.

Braun, where are you? I need you. Our family needs you. She took a deep breath, held a hand over her mouth, and felt tears pool in her eyes. What limited vision she had blurred. With a blink, warm streams flowed down her cheeks. Dizziness fell over her as she tasted salt on her lips. *I don't even have a hairpin to pick the cuff's lock.* Remembering why the flag pin was in the glove compartment in the first place, she recalled it only emitted a GPS signal. The recording device on the pin had malfunctioned, and she had planned to give it to Quint for repairs. *If only I had been more prepared and brought another recording device.* Her brain, still foggy, left her feeling helpless. Sobbing, she whispered, "Quint, I'm counting on you."

Flight Averted

Sept. 12 – 7:22 a.m. EDT, Reagan Airport, Washington, D.C./
5:22 a.m. MDT, Fort Collins, Colorado

The Boeing 747, located at gate C-41, taxied and lifted off the runway as usual until it reached its intended altitude of 31,000 feet and leveled off for the long flight to Frankfurt, Germany. Dark thunderclouds shrouded the jet. A staccato pulse of lightning burst from angry clouds to the east, but everything ran as scheduled, and breakfast started on time.

Three minutes into the meal, the plane hit violent turbulence, causing the cold and hot beverages to fall into the aisle. Passengers screamed as the overhead storage doors flew open, sending luggage showering down on them. Falling oxygen masks spun around the passengers' heads, darting away as they reached overhead. Some of the crowd prayed, others swore, and many panicked.

"Everyone, fasten your seat—" The purser at the front of the plane flew into the air. The microphone cable stretched and popped from the wall as she hit the ceiling and catapulted into the cockpit door with such force that it gave way. "Oof!"

She frantically grabbed the back of the co-pilot's seat. Blood flowed from a cut above her left temple and blurred her vision. She yanked the headrest cover from the captain's chair and dabbed the wound, then held pressure to stop the bleeding. "What's going on? The passengers are in a panic."

"Storm's brewing." The pilot, Rick Patterson, threw off the autopilot and grabbed the throttle, frantically working the controls to level the jet.

The co-pilot yelled above the noise. "Notify the passengers we're facing severe turbulence."

"They already know that!" the purser said.

"Calm them if you can." Patterson forced a lever forward. "Better strap yourself into the jump seat. It's only going to get worse."

Before she could work her way back out of the cockpit, the engine sputtered. The jet went into a nosedive and banked to the left. She managed to reach the door and maintained her balance as the pilot pulled and pushed more levers to stop the skid.

Crew members were clawing their way along the aisle, restowing luggage, and collecting scattered trash.

Patterson blew out a deep breath as the nose lifted, bringing the bank angle to 30°, which was normal for a jetliner. "Okay, it's safe for you to enter the cabin. At least for now." Sweat beaded his forehead.

Without the microphone, the purser had to yell, "Everyone, take your seats and buckle up. That includes the crew." The door slammed shut as she left the cockpit.

***

Patterson muttered, "Keep her steady."

Co-pilot Otto Hogan urgently grabbed the radio to contact air traffic control: "Flight 4180 is experiencing high wind gusts. We need to rise above the storm. Now!"

A message came across the overhead speakers as the purser addressed the passengers, but Patterson was too busy keeping the plane level to pay attention to what she said. The nose stayed up, but he needed more engine power to rise. The aircraft pitched once more to the left.

A female voice said over the ATC radio, "Flight 4180, we have you on the radar. We need to move you to someone working with upper area control."

A male voice joined the conversation, "Flight 4180, cleared to proceed to 35,000 feet."

The nose dropped and refused to level out. "Negative, can't rise," Patterson shouted above the chaos. He thought he'd encountered almost every crisis imaginable in his fifteen years as a pilot, but this was new to him. "The horizontal stabilizers won't move. Tail flaps will not budge."

"They must be frozen," Co-pilot Hogan said. "I don't see anything wrong with the electronic motor connected to the stabilizers."

"Turn off autopilot," came from ATC.

"Affirmative. Already did that." The pilot pushed several buttons and yanked the control panel toward him, but the nose refused to lift. "Come on!" He pulled harder. "The yokes stuck." He tried to maneuver a different lever made in a shape like a wing to free the stabilizers, but to no avail. "Won't budge!"

"Flight 4180, control panel levers and throttles are inoperable," Hogan reported over the radio. "The jammed wing control flaps and slats are forcing the plane to descend directly into the storm."

"What's the altimeter reading?" Patterson asked. "The needle is all over the dial."

"Flight 4180, I have you at 28,500 and falling," came from ATC.

"Roger," Hogan said.

ATC's operator asked, "Are you sure you disengaged autopilot?"

"Affirmative!" The pilot continued to struggle. His heart was beating in his ears, and his sweaty hands shook. He had to remain calm.

"Flight 4180, Pull back harder on the yokes." This time, a man with a deeper voice took over ATC's radio. "This is Leroy. Raise the nose of the plane ASAP. Try the elevator flaps. Use all your strength to throttle up."

The pilot and co-pilot pulled on throttles, one on the horizontal stabilizers and the other on the elevator flaps. They rode the levers to make the necessary changes. "The nose is lifting, but I don't know how long I can hold it," Patterson said in desperation.

Leroy barked a few orders in the background. "Get me someone from maintenance. We need immediate technical assistance."

A man with a thick New Jersey accent said, "Maintenance 261 here."

Leroy asked, "Any logged faults on that jet in the last 30 days?"

There was a pause, then 261 replied, "Negative. I recommend landing at the nearest airbase for repairs."

Leroy came back with, "Flight 4180, divert to Washington Dulles Airport. I'll make the necessary arrangements."

Someone said over the radio, "The diversion will cause several delays," but Leroy cut the chatter with, "Safety has a higher priority. Let's get the plane on the ground and worry about passenger destinations later."

The pilot heard a loud commotion coming from the cabin, but his hands were full, and he was exerting a constant 10 pounds of force to maintain the course. "I can't turn this plane around. It's taking both of us just to keep the plane level." He felt as if he was running in place and getting nowhere—seconds felt like minutes.

"Now that you're at a lower altitude and out of the storm clouds, try the trim system," the maintenance man said. "Maybe that will unjam the stabilizers and maintain altitude. Those flaps may be iced, but they aren't frozen in place."

With a great deal of effort, Patterson used the backup flight control system and managed to free the stabilizer, but an alarm blasted as the nose again dipped. "Holy crap! Nose is down. We're descending at 1,000 feet a minute."

Hogan shoved harder on his throttle, but it got worse. "Elevator flaps won't move. The nose is going lower."

The rattling vibrations tugged the wheel forward, nearly jerking it out of the pilot's hand. Alarms blasted. The engine started to sputter, and the whole plane bucked like a bronco, then stilled. He checked his panel. "Jet stalled."

The purser's voice came over the speakers, "Everyone, stay seated and put on your oxygen masks." Then the pilot's radio cut through the now silent cockpit. "What's our flight status?"

Patterson ran a sleeve over his moist brow. Although his heart raced like a jackrabbit, he said, "Buckle up and stay calm."

"Stay calm?" Hogan muttered. "We have no power." He frantically radioed ATC once again, "Engine's stalled. What do we do now?"

Patterson punched the igniter unit one more time, hit the clutch, and the turbine's blades whirred again.

"I hear the engines." Leroy's voice remained calm. "Push the nose back into the dive."

Patterson pulled the wheel and column toward him and tried the throttle, but the plane kept falling in altitude. "Can't hold the yokes steady."

"Negative, release the yokes, let it glide back to level, and slow down," Leroy warned. "You're at 23,000 feet."

"I'm deploying speed brakes and high-pressure props. It's worked in the past." The pilot's hands flew across the front panel, punching buttons, pulling, and pushing throttles and controls. "Okay, we're leveling off but veering to the right."

Hogan's voice was raspy. "Get us on the ground."

"We're doing everything we can," Leroy assured him.

"The plane continues to pitch as we fight for control," Patterson said. "Maintenance 261, are you still on?"

"Affirmative, your nose was full down, and you're having trouble keeping the plane level. Is that right?" 261 asked.

"Affirmative, and I'm not fool enough to repeat what we just did. We'll crash. That dive scared ten years off my life."

"We need to get you on the ground," 261 said.

"Tune frequency to 121.900," Leroy said. "I'm handing you over to JFK International before you reach open water. They have an expert on hand to talk you down. We're summoning fire trucks and police. Ambulances are already enroute."

Hogan changed the radio frequency. "JFK here. Radar intermittent…you've dropped speed…285 to 230…hour. Ten minutes to land."

Patterson held the throttle steady. "Affirmative, we're slowing down, but I can't prevent the plane from going in a huge pitch and—"

"Mayday! Mayday! Mayday! We're inverting!" Hogan shouted. "Rolling over. Out of control."

"Push…rudder," came over the radio.

Now upside down, blood rushed to Patterson's head, causing a throbbing headache. Fighting gravity, his mind raced, trying to get the jet back on track.

Hogan yelled, "Can't reach the rudder."

The roar of the slipstream deafened Patterson, but one look at Hogan's flushed face, pale lips, and bulging eyes, he guessed Hogan's plight. He was as scared as Patterson felt, but he had to stuff the feeling deep into his soul. The entire crew and passengers depended on his actions in the next few seconds. They were about to crash.

"…rudder." The radio went to static.

Hogan's voice rose in pitch. "Repeat. I can't reach the rudder."

With a burst of desperation, Patterson tugged and yanked on the levers, but the plane remained upside down. He moved to his left. "I'll kick it." His sweaty hands slid on the wheel as he fought gravity, scooted to the left, and finally swung his booted foot against the rudder's foot control. It gave, allowing the aircraft to gradually roll back upright.

"Flight 4180…lost radar… read me?" came across the radio and then steady static.

Hogan tried the radio again. "I've lost communication."

"Try emergency channel," Patterson shouted over the engine's noise. He searched for a place to land, but all he saw were buildings, trees, and no open space before him.

Hogan flipped to 243 MHz. "Still nothing. We've lost all communication."

Patterson realized the ground was coming up too fast to meet him. He held his breath, saying a silent prayer, knowing this was the end. He'd tried every maneuver he knew, but he'd failed. Then, a miracle happened. "Tarmac below." Instinct took over.

Hogan leaned forward and peered out the front window. "Can we land safely?"

"Notify our flight team." Patterson lowered the landing gear.

Hogan contacted the purser, "Prepare for an emergency landing."

The purser's voice cracked, "Finally." She notified the passengers to get in the crash position and prepare for landing.

The plane was so close to the ground that it slid sidewise and touched the runway, bounced into the air on two attempts, bending the wheel axle, and finally relanded at a tilted stop. Some passengers screamed, infants cried, and bags flew out of the overhead bins once again, landing on the passengers below. It wasn't the correct runway, but fire engines, ambulances, and police cars raced across the tarmac and surrounded the plane.

***

Cordy instinctively held her abdomen as the massive jet jerked her body from side to side. Her heart sped up, her limbs felt numb and cold, and her vision sharpened with fear when the jet's engines sputtered, and alarms blasted. She was trapped and abandoned in the unlit baggage area below, left to live or die, powerless to even help herself. Unable to think clearly after being drugged, she imagined the round waste container closing in around her like a constricting snake, slithering through the wastepaper and trash that clung to her feet and legs. She gagged on the diesel fumes mixed with a sickeningly sweet odor of banana peels. Her voice was barely a whisper, and she could no longer scream for help. Another wave of fear shot through her when she realized she felt no baby movements.

Before she could concentrate of what that meant, there was another jolt, and she flew into the air as the plane rotated, now completely airborne, she scrambled out of the trash bin, clawing her way above several cases and bags, avoiding golf clubs and all manner of tourist paraphernalia. The plane continued to roll until it was upside down, flinging bags and debris like missiles into the air. She ducked, wrapped one arm over her belly, and raised her other arm over her head to ward off incoming debris. She quickly turned as a large dog crate flew across the deep space. It launched against the wall, rebounded, and hit her cheek before she could shove it away.

Every bag was now a potential murder weapon. Breathing deeply, her jacket sleeve snagged on the Flag pin still attached to her collar, and a scratching sound echoed inside the plane. "Cordy…hear me?" The voice sounded like Quint.

"Quint? Are you there? I'm trapped in the baggage compartment of a plane, and it's flying out of control." Cordy's voice rose to barely a hoarse whisper, although she felt as if she shouted directly into the pin, hoping someone would answer.

"…plane…diverted…JFK…get you home…" came across the flag pin.

Cordy gasped as the plane dove again. She hung onto a leather strap attached to the side of the aircraft. With another bump, she was briefly airborne again. Then the plane rolled once again and became upright, causing equipment and debris flying like dangerous airborne rockets. Cordy held on with all her strength but lost her grip and landed hard. Grabbing her pin to keep it from being damaged further, she spoke directly into it. "Repeat," was all she could whisper. She found herself wedged against a wire mesh, a fortunate spot of safety, surrounded by luggage, some cracked and others opened, spilling contents everywhere.

The cargo area looked like a hurricane had been through, and in a way, perhaps it had. The space was cramped, cold, and there was no answer from Quint. Cordy kicked away the larger suitcases and climbed up the mesh to sit on top of the overturned trash bin.

She tried the flag pin again, but there was still no answer. A few minutes later, the plane bounced hard, wheels squealed, gears whined, and luggage threatened to explode forward once more. She heard sirens in the distance and hoped the plane was on the runway. Relief flooded through her as she felt the first small flutters in her abdomen. Wrapping her arms around her precious twins, she anxiously waited for someone to open the cargo door, hoping she had landed in friendly territory.

***

An hour later, a paramedic had checked fetal heart tones, treated Cordy's swollen and bloody wrists, iced her swollen lip, and bandaged a cut on her right cheek before medically clearing her and the twins. She was now inside the JFK International Airport Security Office for a debriefing. She and Todd, the head of airport security, were on VidChat with Guy from Homeland Security, Nick, the Secretary of Transportation, and Dr. Ping with National Security.

"What do we know so far about this flight?" Cordy asked.

"System malfunction was not due to the storm as the pilot originally thought," Todd said. "Security found malware on the plane's navigation system. It's a sophisticated virus that took over flight control and knocked out all communication with ATC at the end of the flight."

Nick added, "Fortunately, the pilot was very experienced and managed to land the aircraft safely, but it took a lot of planning, engineering, and research for the hackers to plant that virus."

Todd nodded. "Thank God for the airport tower people, who were able to bring the plane down safely. Without them, this would have ended in a worse disaster. There were several injured passengers being treated at St. John's Medical Center, but no fatalities."

"Why this plane?" Cordy gently rubbed her throbbing cheek, and still swollen lip, after being smacked by a dog crate. Her head ached, and a dull roar persisted in her ears, adding to her discomfort. "It couldn't have been a spur-of-the-moment decision, and since I wasn't scheduled to be on that flight, there had to be another intended victim. Who was the actual target, or was the object to just cause the plane to crash? Have you reviewed the flight list?"

"Briefly, and thanks to trial software implemented at JFK, a TSA camera discovered a powerful Zeta drug lord among the plane's passengers, and the CIA has him in custody," Dr. Ping said. "Ernesto Vincent De La Gutierrez was on his way to Iran, allegedly to meet his former partner, José Carlos Justuso. Rumor has it that José is on Zeta's hit list. Fortunately, Agent Usher Hastings got to Justuso first and is bringing him back to face espionage charges. Usher also intercepted plans to steal the Maven II drone and RCV specs hidden inside a fake euro. He sent me the euro's specs, and I'll forward a copy for your review."

One of the security officers said, "According to our records, José is already dead. Are you sure of Ernesto's mission?"

"José's death was faked," Dr. Ping held up the death certificate. "This was traced back to Mexico. It's a forgery."

Guy added, "Ernesto was José's Zeta partner, and he's been on our terrorist watchlist for years. Of course, he's not flying under his real name, but his fingerprints and ear markings match Ernesto's. No matter what his original mission was, we'll interrogate him."

Dr. Ping put a photo of Ernesto on the screen. "This is the man we have in custody."

Cordy's hand flew to her mouth. "Wait, I saw that man coming out of the men's room at Reagan Airport before I was kidnapped. He has a limp, right?"

"Yes," Dr. Ping agreed.

"I believe he met Casper Grest, the co-pilot who kidnapped me. I saw Grest enter the men's room. He wore a blue backpack. Then I saw this Latino man follow him. Grest was dressed in a sports coat when they left the restroom, and the Latino wore the blue backpack. Was the pack with him on the plane?"

Todd checked his records. "We didn't find it among his carry-on luggage, but everything's a mess, luggage scattered throughout the plane, the hull, and with so many injured, their treatment came first."

"The backpack is probably still there," Guy said. "Can one of your security officers recheck the baggage log, or is it still in the jet's overhead bin?"

Todd radioed his request, but shook his head. "It could be hours before we find it.

"Are you sure we also have Grest in custody?" Cordy reached into her coat pocket and groaned. "I snapped a photo of both men as they left the men's room and went in opposite directions, but I don't have my cell phone. Wait, I sent the photos to Quint and Chief

Jackson. They can verify for me." Cordy reached for a phone on the desk, and hesitated. Her head throbbed so much, she had a hard time concentrating.

Guy waved his hand, indicating there was no need to worry. "Quint already forwarded your photos to Dr. Ping, Braun, and me. As I mentioned earlier, the FBI has Grest in custody. He was trying to board a flight to California, with plans to catch another flight to Moscow from there. Along with him, they have also detained Lady Hadsy, who was on the same flight. According to Quint, she is a person of interest in a DOJ investigation regarding the NYSE. She was sitting next to Grest on the plane, and she also had a boarding pass to Russia, again seated next to Grest."

"I understand that MI-6 has also dealt with her in the past," Cordy said. "You might check with them. Since Hadsy was sitting next to Grest, I think that we can presume that they know each other? It would be quite a coincidence if they did not."

"I don't have all the information yet," Guy said. "Braun called in a few favors and is on a private jet coming to get you, Cordy. He's beside himself with worry for you and the twins. I'm glad you're safe, and everything checked out with the paramedics."

Dr. Ping added, "Chief Jackson found your purse and cell phone in a trash can in the ladies' room in Dulles Airport where you were kidnapped. He also tracked down and the police arrested a sanitation worker who admitted to dosing you with propofol."

"Is propofol safe during pregnancy?" Cordy's concern resonated in her voice. "If anything happens to my children, I'll—"

Dr. Ping jumped in to reassure her, "I understand. We've already checked, and it crosses through the placenta, but our triage physician assures me it has no permanent effect, especially since you're into your third trimester and it's gradually leaving your system since you're now awake, I checked because I knew you would want to know. We have some more details to cover, but they can wait until tomorrow after you get back to Washington, D.C. and get some rest.

Braun insisted that he see you and demanded you take the rest of the day off."

Cordy rolled her eyes. "As long as the twins are unharmed, I'll take off a couple of hours, but I need to meet with you and my staff. Also, Alysha at CrowdStrike can fill you in on more details regarding Lady Hadsy. Let me call Quint and get an update. Then I'll be back to the White House this afternoon."

"Braun's not going to agree," Ping said, "I know him."

"Then we'll both come to the White House," Cordy smiled. "That way, he can keep an eye on his family while we discuss the details of this attack. Braun's no longer wanted for treason, right? You got my memo, didn't you? Perry found the people who placed funds into that fake overseas account."

"Yes, he's been cleared," Ping said, "and he's no longer working undercover. Loran Sloan is also back on duty as the FBI Director."

"Good," Cordy said, "and I want to know who planted that malware on the plane. It sounds like someone planned to take out Ernesto, but we're not sure if anyone else on the plane was a target."

"You can go through the passengers' roster," Todd offered. "If we're done here, I'll pull up the list."

"Thanks." Cordy gratefully accepted the offer. "Should I look for anything else while I'm here?"

"If they find the backpack, it will be submitted as evidence," Dr. Ping said. "And I want your team to investigate that malware virus on the plane. I believe it could have taken total control and crashed the jet, but it didn't."

Cordy frowned. "But Nick just said the pilot's expertise prevented the plane from crashing—"

"Yes, but it could have been a disastrous crash. I'm worried it's just a warning," Dr. Ping said. "What if whoever planted the virus wants us to know they have the power to crash our planes at any time? Just research the malware."

"Okay. Someone also crashed the subway system, and we're checking that out, too. Anything else?" Cordy made a note.

Guy, Nick, and Dr. Ping shook their heads. "Stay safe," Dr. Ping said.

"We'll see you this afternoon." Cordy disconnected the VidChat and followed the security officer to another office.

The blue backpack was on the desk. "Good, is this the blue bag you were referring to?"

"Yes," Cordy said. "Can we see what's inside?"

Todd called over another officer to help go through the pack. They put on latex gloves, dusted everything inside and out for fingerprints, and checked for any evidence of gunpowder and explosive residue.

Cordy anxiously waited for them to remove the contents. Tucked inside were a pair of jeans and a faded olive green and tan camo shirt. "That's what Casper Grest was wearing when I first saw him at the airport."

The back jeans pocket bulged. Upon further investigation, the officer discovered a cell phone, an encrypted note, and $25,000 in cash tucked inside an envelope folded in half with a rubber band around it. After testing for fingerprints, Cordy asked the officer to snap photos, signed for copies of the documents, and got permission to forward everything to Quint, hoping he could translate the encryption. Tucked into the shirt pocket was also a map of the New York subway system. "Look at this circled date at the top of the page—September 27. That's a week from tomorrow." She held up the photo of the map. "There's also some chicken scratch along the side."

The guard slid the map into a plastic bag and dug out a magnifying glass from a top desk drawer. "Looks like it says, 'Hit each borough at 1-minute intervals—Bronx, Queens, Brooklyn, and Manhattan.'"

Cordy texted Quint and Homeland Security, while Todd called New York City's chief of police. The original documents, contents, and phone were bagged as evidence, and the Todd sent them to a forensic lab. Now Cordy had to work with copies, but with after recently earning her law degree, she was a stickler for following legal procedures when it came to the chain of evidence.

Guy called Cordy and agreed to work with federal, state, and local authorities, and then spoke to Todd, "I want Cordy to have access to the cell phone data. Can you arrange for her to make the necessary phone recordings and replicate the SIM chip info, including the contact list?"

The guard agreed, security made copies, and Cordy replayed messages for Quint and Dr. Ping. The first one was a recording of Ernesto's call to Congressman Conrad Justuso. At least, Cordy believed it was Ernesto, but he used a mechanical scrambler, so the voice was hard to detect. Quint would put it through a voice descrambler after the call, but it was the details that Cordy wanted ASAP.

"You don't know me, but I know all about you," the mechanical voice said. "And unless you meet me in the next half hour, I'm taking your little secret public."

"What secret? Can you repeat that? I don't think I heard you correctly," Conrad sounded panicked.

"You can't lie to me," the disguised voice said. "I know your family secret and where you got your money."

Cordy found another recording between Conrad and his lawyer, and this time the voices were natural, "…beware, you'll be brought before the Intelligence Committee."

"Intelligence Committee?" Conrad asked.

"Yes. According to my sources, Congressman, you're making promises to rebuild America, making her much stronger and safer, and to wipe out the National deficit during your first term as president. My concern is that you've tied your businesses with a retired Soviet spy, Ansin, an old KGB follower of the last Chairman, Vadim Viktorovich Bakatin. He also has hidden ties to our top brass in the military. Did you lie to the public?"

Cordy turned off the recording. "I had wondered if the Congressman was involved. José is his brother, after all, but how did Ernesto get a recording of the Congressman's lawyer?"

Dr. Ping said, "That's confusing, since attorney/client privilege should have made this impossible."

"True," Cordy agreed, "unless Ernesto bugged Conraad's phone."

"We'll need to talk with the Congressman to get more details. Is there more on the recording?"

"There's more." Cordy hit replay where she had left off.

Conrad snapped, "I never lie. I don't need to. I give a hint of what I'm going to say. The more I repeat the message, in private and in public, Tweet, Twitter, and Truth Social, it soon becomes truth. I wait until that settles in, ask pertinent questions, and sooner or later, my hinted words come back from their lips. I make sure to praise their brilliance, wondering where they obtained such insight into the situation. Now, what I say is absolute truth."

"Ansin's a Soviet spy?" When Cordy finished the recording, she disconnected the VidChat call with Quint and Dr. Ping. Wanting to know more about Ansin, she texted her Russian colleague, Cracker, for more information.

Quint texted, "I found two encrypted messages along with maps of Heathrow Airport, terminals 3 and 5 security points, and restaurants, dated September 27, the anniversary of the opening date of terminal 5. The second file has details of Frankfort International Airport Terminal 1 A-Z. I'm worried there will be a terrorist attack on both of those sites. I'm forwarding the info to the CIA, Homeland Security, and the National Counter Terrorism Security Offices in the UK and Frankfort, Germany. There are two more files that I'm working on, but they used a different encryption system from the rest. I also forwarded that data to Cracker. Perhaps they've encountered this in Russia."

"Thanks," Cordy texted Guy, "More data. We need to talk ASAP."

Cordy was on a conference call with Homeland Security when a guard escorted Braun into the room. She concluded, "Thanks, Guy, for all your help. Keep me informed. Braun just arrived, so I'll talk to you soon." After she disconnected the call, she turned to the guard and thanked him, too.

"I just got word the preliminary forensic results are in. I'll be back in a few minutes with the report before you leave." Todd left the two alone for a moment.

Braun rushed to her side and held her out at arm's length. "Cordy, your lips and right cheek are swollen, and your wrists are bandaged. Are you all right? I've never been so afraid in all my life." He crushed her into a bear hug.

"I'm fine," Cordy was shocked to see his swollen face and two black eyes, "but you look awful!" Remembering he had broken his nose, she kissed him gently on the cheek. He was still in disguise, his blond hair was still dyed auburn, and his chin seemed more pronounced with a goatee. She could get used to the hair, but she preferred him clean-shaven. However, right now, she didn't care about anything but his being alive. Feeling choked up, she leaned into him and whispered in his ear. "Aren't we a sight for sore eyes? Thanks for flying here to get me."

"I will always come for you, no matter what happens." Braun backed away from Cordy when Todd approached with the forensic results but refused to let go of her hand and turned. "Is she free to leave? Do you need anything else before we go?"

The security officer asked Cordy. "Did you find anyone else that could have been a target on the passenger list? Or maybe you haven't had enough time to research that,"

Cordy released Braun's hand and stepped forward. "Not yet, but I'd like to send this report, a digital copy of the passenger list, and the names of the aircrew sent to my office, and please, include Homeland Security when filing your reports."

An officer sent the requested lists to her team and Homeland before Cordy left. "Thanks for all your help." She shook the officers' hands and then walked into the hallway. "Nausea's gone for the moment, and I'm starving. Can we stop for lunch before going to D.C.?"

Braun smiled. "Now that sounds like my wife. How about a Lombardi pizza to go? I know you love pizza, and we can update each other while we wait." He guided her through the airport and to a side door. "You look pale. Are you really feeling well, or putting on your usual brave face?"

Cordy gently slipped an arm around Braun's waist and whispered, "There is much to do yet, and there are many questions unanswered. I used to think international terrorists just sneak into our country from overseas to target an attack and then leave, but today, these terrorists have boots on our ground. They could be our next-door neighbors walking and living among us. It's never been so important for our intelligence agency to have total cooperation between federal, state, and local organizations to work together. Look how close we are to another potential crisis two weeks from now. We have to stay one step ahead of them, and it's not easy."

Braun pulled her into his arms. "Whatever happens, we'll fight this together. I can't lose you, Cordy. I meant it when I said I've never been so scared in all my life. I wake up with you on my mind, think about you throughout the day, and can't wait to hold you at night. I don't know how to say this. I love you and need you as much as I need air to breathe, so please be more careful."

"I love you, too, and I knew when I married you that you were no couch potato. I worry about you every time you go on a special mission. That's why I gave you that tie-tack, and talking about being more careful, I believe you destroyed it earlier today."

"Sorry." Braun pulled the tack from his back pocket and held it up. "It served me well, but you're right. I think we each need an update. I'm sure we can create other built-in devices."

"A few," Cordy laughed. "Your smart wedding ring didn't warn me either. I already knew you were at Aberdeen Proving Grounds—your ring needs an upgrade. I'll talk to Quint about designing twin tie-tacks while you order pizza. Did I mention I'm starving?"

"You did, and maybe Quint should make our new wedding rings, too." Braun smiled his crooked grin. "Then I can define a few tracking devices of my own, and next time you fly off into the sunset, I'll be able to find you."

"It's a deal."

Missing Puzzle Pieces

"I could sleep for a week," Cordy whispered as she climbed aboard the jet to Washington, D.C., after her kidnapping experience to JFK International Airport.

"Then sit back and take a catnap while I fly us back to civilization." Braun gave her a peck on the cheek and smiled his breath-taking grin, making her heart flutter. "Loran called, and he's lined up an interrogation with Farzad Zahair today, but he'll record the session so you won't miss anything. He's also scheduled an interview with Einar Zinmansky for 1 p.m. this afternoon. I know you're anxious to find out what's on Zinmansky's laptop, and I want to know why Zahair sent funds to that overseas account to frame me, so I'm okay with you listening to a recording of the interview, but we're not going back to the White House this afternoon. Get a little rest, and we'll be there soon."

"I need to reinstall a partition into Zac's computer—"

"Not today!" Braun snapped. "Have Evans replace it."

Cordy opened her mouth to protest, but she saw his eyes narrow as he shook his head.

"I mean it," Braun used his, "I'm not arguing with you" voice. "You're not leaving my sight for the rest of the day. Evans is perfectly capable of installing the partition. You can call him if you must, but you're home with me, resting with the twins in my eyesight at all times."

Knowing he wasn't going to change his mind, she sighed in surrender. "Thanks. I don't want to leave you either." Relaxed and stuffed to the gills after eating two slices of pepperoni, sausage, and mushroom pizza slathered with extra cheese and black olives, Cordy slid into her seat and buckled up. Her mind kept racing while she tried unsuccessfully to locate some mental solitude.

Thankfully, Braun came to my rescue, and our twins survived the ordeal. It has been a long, rough week, and the main culprit behind the cyberattack is still a mystery. Who is the ringleader—Farzad Zahair, Amir, Einar Zinmansky, General HQ, or someone else? In her mind, each suspect fit on a puzzle piece linking to others. How did Pilot Stone, Casper Grest, Ansin Associates, Ernesto, and José Justuso fit into the plot? Then there was something Alyssa mentioned: a Shady Lady and some restaurant owner who visited Russia. Someone caused the Maven II drone to explode, derailed Washington, D.C.'s subway system, and launched a drone attack on the White House. Her mind felt like it would explode with unanswered questions. *I'm still missing too many puzzle pieces to link together for a clear photo, and I'm too tired to think clearly.* Cordy closed her eyes. *Maybe with some rest, things will become clearer.*

Instead of sleep, she relived the events of the past few days, starting with a power outage causing a subway derailment and the assault on Washington, D.C., creating riots in the streets. Awakened by a Code Q cyber alert, she countered an attack on the government cybersecurity system, a shutdown of all White House computers, except for Zac's, and a threat to President Spendorf's life. Perhaps another attack is being planned for Minute Maid Park in Houston, Texas, during Zac's scheduled pitch at the World Series a week from Friday. Someone stabbed Secretary of Defense Carl Wyller while escorting the president to the bunker. Secretary of State Mo Hendrum and Emma Stone had been kidnapped, and an unknown man was murdered at the White House. SWAT had freed Mo and Emma during last night's raid, captured the Iranian terrorists, Farzad Zahair and his IT guru, Gregor, and turned them over to Chief Polack. Unfortunately, Polack allowed Zahair to escape.

With a stroke of luck, Braun was able to recapture Zahair, along with an Iranian Revolutionary Guard, Amir, and Einar Zinmansky earlier this morning. The FBI has Casper Grest, Lady Hadsy, and José Justuso, but they are all pawns. Who is the mastermind? The threat goes beyond the United States.

After airport security captured Ernesto, they made a great discovery of future plots to sabotage the New York subway, a potential terrorist attack at Heathrow and Frankfort International Airports. *Are these all pieces of the same puzzle, or yet another?* Yawning for the third time, sleep swept her away into a blessed relief.

A Day of Rest

Cordy was confined for the rest of the day and felt her energy return. It allowed her time to reflect, and the puzzle pieces of the past few days' events started aligning themselves into a full-blown picture. Although she stayed at Blair House at Braun's request, she spent the afternoon making VidChats with her team members—Evans, Quint, Perry, and Svetlana. She and Braun also touched base with President Spendorf's security team via a conference call with Dr. Ping, Guy at Homeland Security, Quint, DoD's Deputy Director, Chet Yelson, and her CrowdStrike team.

Braun asked, "How is Emma?"

"My wife is a bit shaken, but she's safe," Loran said. "Thanks for asking."

"Any update on Carl?" Braun asked.

"Carl is off the ventilator and out of ICU, but he's still on pain meds, and he's a bit fuzzy on the events leading up to the stabbing," Loran said. "He keeps repeating, 'My only concern was to get President Spendorf to the Bunker.'"

"I'm glad Carl is recovering." Cordy fired up her computer, "How's Mo doing? I know he had surgery and moved to the ICU, but Emma was worried Mo had a head trauma. Did the doctor rule that out?"

"Mo had a CAT scan, and it showed a concussion," Loran said. "He was alert enough to identify the man who attacked him as the driver who died on the bridge after delivering Zinmansky to the hijacked jet. Mo said the man probably wasn't planning to harm him, but he attacked when Mo caught him breaking into the car parked next to his."

"Bum luck," Braun said, "a matter of being in the wrong place at the wrong time."

Loran added, "Our team discovered that car belongs to Congressman Conrad Justuso. We think there might be more to the story, but unfortunately, Congress is currently out of session, and the Zogster case is in recess, so we haven't been able to reach Justuso to ask him any questions about his vehicle. He is expected back to work on Thursday."

"I hope we don't have to wait that long to get answers," Cordy said. "I want to resolve a few issues today."

Evans agreed, "I replaced the partition on Zac's computer, but no activity has been captured yet, and I'll bring over Zinmansky's laptop, copies of the two thumb drives, the hard drive, and an e-tablet that the SWAT team found in Amir's pouch shortly." Evans also reviewed the modified software system from the jet that nearly crashed at JFK, discovered a Russian hacker had modified it, and Cordy referred the data to Cracker. Agent Gray said he'd also send Zinmansky's original RCV and Maven II drone specifications with Evans.

Cordy browsed through several notes that needed clarification, "I understand the FBI caught Casper Grest and Lady Tiffany Hadsy at LAX after they boarded a flight to Moscow, Russia. Can anyone give me a summary of their interrogation?"

Guy reported, "An FBI agent recorded the interview and shared the MP4 file with various departments for review. Cordy, a copy was also forwarded to your team, but you might not have heard it yet. Here are the main points: Lady Tiffany Hadsy confessed that she and her colleague, Crayton Udesky, recently made millions of dollars by buying and selling shares short on the NYSE. She also admitted that Crayton dabbles in computer programming and may have tampered with stock pricing. She knows nothing about computer programming."

Cordy perused her notes from past criminal interviews. "That's not what Gregor told the interrogator. He said, 'Shady Lady, as MI-6 calls her, broke into a cache of classified government intel, mainly government contracts. She has hacking skills better than mine.' It sounds like Lady Hadsy could have also accessed the stock exchange files."

"Interesting," Alysha sounded excited. "We think someone used a remote access tool that opened a back door to set stock prices, and the U.S. Market went crazy last Friday—buying and selling short shares. The Securities and Exchange Commission is doing further research and sent us a link to review the past month's activities."

"Did you find a remote access tool?" Cordy asked.

"Yes," Quint added. "As we suspected, it was a RAT, which is quite sophisticated. If Crayton programmed the tool, he knows his coding. Or maybe it was Lady Hadsy. Will she face an injunction for illegal gains?"

"Probably," Guy said, "but she is plea bargaining for lesser charges by revealing the names of those involved in the scam and explaining how they operated. So far, she has named Crayton, Mierzany K. Ansin, and Azinnea M. Krysin as accomplices. We don't have much on Krysin, except she is IYFTI's CEO."

Dr. Ping cut in, "Right, and Intercity Future Transport, Inc. shares also sold short on Friday, making millions. The company is pressuring the transit authority to sign its contract. Did they also invest through SkyUrsis Capital?"

"Yes," Alysha interjected, "and so did Ansin Associates and Gonzalo Industries."

Cordy glanced up from typing on her computer. "I wonder if the transfer of funds and the terrorist attacks on Washington, D.C., are linked—maybe even to the assaults on the White House."

Dr. Ping asked, "How so?"

Cordy summarized her thoughts from the time Potomac Electric lost power right after Ansin and Zahair transferred funds. "According to Ernesto, Ansin is a Soviet spy, and he could be working with Congressman Conrad Justuso. Anyway, those funds somehow triggered the loss of electricity, which led to the subway system going to a battery-operated backup that caused a crash. Metro bus and transportation lines exploded, damaging the 14th Street Bridge," and she added, "The same bridge was used by a private jet booked through Anson to land and pick up Zinmansky, and to divert Zinmansky's and Zahair's escape."

"How does that lead to an attack on the White House?" Guy asked.

Cordy thought briefly. "Creating chaos downtown drew everyone's attention away from a chopper landing on a building across the street from the White House. Within the hour, Zahair launched a Russian drone from that site. If Avenger hadn't knocked it from the air, it would have been a successful hit on the White House."

"How does that link to selling short?" Dr. Ping asked.

"That's another issue. Did you find Crayton?" Cordy asked.

Dr. Ping cleared his throat, "We may have found his body in the Roosevelt restroom at the White House, but I have no idea how he slipped past our agents. We don't know who murdered him, and we're still working on a positive ID. His fingerprints were removed with some sort of acid."

"Did he have a dark area over his left eye?" Cordy asked.

Alysha popped up a photo of Udesky on the screen, showing a discoloration. "Is this the man? He also has a scar above his lip. You can see it in his mustache."

Ping tapped the screen. "Send me that photo, and I'll discuss this with the ME, it could be a match."

"If you get us a photo of the body, I'm sure we can identify the man, but I won't be surprised if the body is Udesky's," Cordy added to her to-do list. "Does Lady Tiffany Hadsy know about the body?"

"No," Guy said, "and we won't release any information until we have a positive identity and have informed the family. Hadsy says she doesn't know what happened to Crayton, but they were supposed to meet with Ansin for breakfast. Crayton never showed up, and he missed his flight to Moscow. She also said that Ansin notified her that he had flown to Canada and couldn't make the meeting."

"Ansin is in Canada?" Cordy clarified. "Is he seeking asylum?"

"President Spendorf is speaking with the Prime Minister, but I don't know the details yet," Guy said.

"What about Hadsy's meeting with Congressman Justuso?" Cordy made a few more notes on her computer.

Alysha piped up, "I was planning to meet with Lady Hadsy yesterday, but the FBI aborted that meeting. From what I did learn, she met with the Congressman to discuss details of Ansin Associates' sale to Gonzalo Industries, which is a shell corporation owned primarily by the Congressman."

"I don't think that issue was addressed during her interrogation," Guy said, "at least not on my recording, but we will check into it. If Congressman Conrad Justuso is involved, he'll be in front of the House for disorderly behavior, for starters, and could be impeached."

"What about Casper Grest?" Cordy asked. "Who is he working for?"

"Grest claims he's working for H.Q., and so is Zahair," Dr. Ping said. "We also recorded Zahair's interrogation yesterday. We just received a copy of his interview, and charges of air piracy were added to Zahair's list. I'll forward a copy to your team, Cordy."

"Where is H.Q.? And what is his full name?" Cordy asked. "President Spendorf mentioned that General H.Q. is number 4 on the 10 top terrorists list."

Dr. Ping rubbed his chin, "H.Q. is known to have connections with the underworld and has managed to evade being photographed. Plus, he disguises his voice whenever he speaks, and neither Zahair nor Grest has any idea where his headquarters is located."

Loran added, "Zahair admitted to having a direct line to General H.Q., but he only texts and waits for H.Q. to return his call on a burner phone."

"Did you find Zahair's cell phone?" Cordy asked. "If so, we can trace all calls, the time, and the GPS location. What about Grest's phone?"

"No calls to H.Q. on Zahair's or Grest's phones. They're burner phones, and Grest's was activated 12 hours before he kidnapped

Cordy," Ping turned to Cordy and added, "Grest admitted he helped place you on that jet to Frankfurt before he departed Washington, D.C., to Los Angeles. He denies drugging you. That wasn't in his plans, but his cousin, a sanitation worker at the airport, gave you the drug to prevent Grest from shooting you."

"What about the phones on the jet from Fort Collins to Washington, D.C.?" Cordy flipped through her notes. "Buckley answered the red phone, and someone with a thick Arabic accent said, 'Orders from General H.Q. Change of plans' and hung up. Then, the jet's controls locked in a dive. Buckley stumbled and hit his head. He didn't remember anything after that until he woke up tied to a chair in that warehouse where the FBI freed us."

"I'll check with the FBI," Loran said. "They collected the evidence from the scene, and we'll forward a report to you."

Guy added, "Zinmansky's interrogation tape should also arrive soon, but he denies everything and says his cousin, Ansin, stole his laptop and delivered it to Zahair. He swears Ansin stole his ID and used it to access the White House the morning of the murder. He also believes Ansin stabbed Carl by mistake instead of President Spendorf and murdered Crayton Udesky, leaving his body in the White House. Using Novichok and removing fingerprints with acid has been used for years by the KGB. Zinmansky admits that before coming to the U.S., his cousin, belonged to a Russian counterintelligence group. Ansin and Udesky were supposed to meet to discuss the sale of Ansin Associates and Securities, Inc. to Gonzalo Industries. Review the interrogation recordings when you get a moment. That's it for our summary. Is there any more news from your team?"

Quint and Alysha shared Svetlana's discovery of consolidation of government contracts over the past two years.

"How could so many companies providing overseas and domestic security merge through stock acquisitions without anyone noticing?" Guy asked.

"That's not the only scary part," Cordy admitted. "As Lady Hadsy mentioned, Gonzalo Industries is on that list, and they contract with the national defense system—the CIA, FBI, and our military. Last Friday, they acquired Ansin Associates & Securities, doubling their contracts."

Quint mentioned, "Although Tiffany Hadsy said Congressman Conrad Justuso has a controlling interest in Gonzalo Industries. It was Justuso's brother, José Carlos Justuso, who was the head of the company until José's death. The government suspected José of leading a Colombian drug cartel, which may have resulted in his murder. There are rumors that the company used the border to transport drugs between Mexico and the United States."

Ping corrected Quint, "José Justuso's proposed death was a ruse to ward off the Zeta drug cartel—probably running from his old partner, Ernesto. José's alive. Usher Hastings captured him in the process of delivering the Maven II drone specs to a Quds Force in Tehran, Iran. The specs were on a microchip hidden inside a fake euro. Usher brought José back to the U.S. for further investigation. José's brother, the esteemed Congressman, may not be as loyal to our country as he portrays."

"Are you suggesting Congressman Justuso may also be involved in smuggling that euro?" Chet bolted upright and sounded shocked. "I can't believe it. Conrad is Chairman of the House Defense Subcommittee."

"Maybe not smuggling the euro, but if you recall, privatizing Homeland Security was one of Congressman Justuso's campaign promises when he ran for president against Spendorf. Being head of Gonzales Industries gives him power over our defense systems. Remember, he supports states deputizing their own security teams without federal oversight. Now, he could be working behind the scenes to make it happen."

Cordy reminded the security team, "Congressman Conrad Justuso also has ties with the Zogster Case currently before the Supreme Court, and we know his brother, José, has smuggled weapons across the U.S. border in the past. He fled to Mexico to avoid U.S. penalties. We also found the Congressman's fingerprints on the inside of Carl's laptop. That's a big red flag. Do you think Conrad is our government mole?"

"Highly likely," Braun paused, a crease crossed his brow. "Does the Congressman have ties to the Tree of Liberty Group? The Maven II drone was weaponized with illegal firearms similar to those touted by the Group, and Evans has the proof."

Dr. Ping rubbed his chin. "We're currently researching that. Thanks for bringing these concerns to our attention. Now, we need to find General Shyler."

"As a U.S. Chief of Staff, he must remain available at all times, so where is he?" Quint finished his Coke and threw the can in the trash. When he got no answer, he added, "Keep us informed. I'll talk to you again after I run through the recordings."

"I'll stop by shortly with Zinmansky's laptop, hard drive, two thumb drives, and an e-tablet." Evans was already gathering the items. "Signing off for now." His line went dark.

"Thanks, everyone. I'll talk to you soon," Cordy disconnected the VidChat call.

She got up, went to the kitchen to refill Braun's coffee cup, poured one for herself, and returned to the dining room table.

"Thanks," Braun seemed in another world as he typed a few lines, muttering to himself, taking a sip of coffee, and then going back to typing.

"You're thinking so hard, I can hear your brain hum," Cordy laughed.

"Making plans, trying to clarify discrepancies, and get some facts about that drone test," Braun admitted. "Kip's death was senseless, and I can't let this go unresolved. I owe it to Brit and their son to get the facts."

Cordy leaned over his shoulder and gave him a hug. "We'll work together on this as soon as Evans brings over those specs."

"Thanks," Braun went back to work, so Cordy sat next to him, leafed through her notes from the other day, and ran across another puzzle she hadn't solved yet. A list of names floated through her mind: Azinnea M. Krysin, CEO of IYFTI, has multiple citizenships and flies using three different passports. Last week, she flew from Heathrow to D.C., under a German passport with the name Sinneya K. Marzin. A few days later, she flew to LA using a UK passport: Azinnea M. Krysin—the same name as her U.S. passport. Why not fly within the country using her U.S. passport?

Then there's Mierzany K. Ansin, cousin to Einar Zinmansky. Why are these all anagrams? Are they related? Ansin and Zinmansky are Russian. Cordy blinked as if she had an aha moment. She dialed Cracker and Rozalina to discuss this dilemma.

Rozalina laughed, "You're just now asking? Ansin and Zinmansky are both grandsons of Kenya S. Razinmin and Myrian Zensinka. They are anagram fanatics, and challenged their children to use the same letters as their names. Kenya passed away two years ago, but Myrian is still alive in Moscow. I'm not sure if Azinnea is related to this family, but I wouldn't doubt it. Let me do some more research and get back to you."

Cracker updated Cordy on Usher's latest mission trip, "Uncle Albert wasn't able to destroy the missile factory, but the three missiles headed for Syria were dismantled. Now Albert's team is hunting down H.Q."

Rozalina asked, "Did the president exonerate Braun after Perry found the culprit who had hacked into the defense department and located the origin of the funds sent overseas in Braun's name?"

"Yes, Braun's sitting next to me, and we're taking the rest of the day off," Cordy laughed, "or at least, taking a break."

Rozalina gave a few more updates on the latest developments, and had signed off when there was a knock on Cordy's door.

It was Evans. He took one look at the dining room table, where the huge screen lit up with data coming from six different locations and files spread out on one end. He added to the clutter with Zinmansky's laptop and other devices. "Do you call this resting?"

"Absolutely," Cordy laughed at his expression as he wiped his brow.

Evans stepped away from the table. "I trapped the culprit who placed that partition into Zac's machine."

Cordy brightened, "Who is it?"

"JCJ300 and Quint tracked that back to Mierzany K. Ansin. He tried to access the drive from somewhere over the Atlantic Ocean. Ansin didn't get any useful data, but we can now track him wherever he goes, as long as he uses his cell phone."

"I bet it's another burner," Cordy said. "The last I heard, he was still in Canada, so he must have managed to catch a flight out of the country."

"Yup, Quint says he's on his way to Russia," Evans admitted, "and Cracker and Rozalina were notified. They'll meet the plane when it lands and they'll contact Usher."

"When did Quint contact Cracker?" Cordy asked, "I just got off a conference call with them, and they didn't mention Ansin."

"I was talking to Quint as I rode up here on the elevator, so you must have just missed the call. Quint says to get in touch when you have a moment. I got to go."

***

Braun grabbed the hard drive and booted it up. "I can't wait to review the Maven II and RCV schematics."

Evans waved and left.

"Wait another minute while I run the documents through Gnatcatcher." Cordy scanned the documents and uploaded them to Braun's machine.

Braun carefully examined the blueprints and compared them to the updated specifications on Zahair's hard drive. Upon analysis, he tapped at the screen. *Something isn't right. The entire triggering mechanism has been reworked. Initially, the government mandate was for defensive weaponry, but someone modified the drone that was delivered to Aberdeen Proving Grounds.*

Cordy glanced over Braun's shoulder. "The revised specs have a radio signal jammer to disrupt GPS and a spoofer to manipulate the drone signal, instead of using the drone as a weapon."

"Look at this button," Braun pointed toward the RCV specifications. "I had noticed it during testing, but no one had pressed it. As per the modified specifications, this button activates a high-energy laser beam that can destroy the drone when activated. My guess is that this button caused the explosion of the Maven II drone during our test."

"So this proves both the Maven II drone and the RCV were weaponized, but who activated it?" Cordy reached around Braun and enlarged the diagram.

Braun exclaimed, "Bingo! There was a timer on that trigger. See here, it's set for 0422."

"That's the same time your tie-tack turned black," Cordy gasped. "Did Zahair make the modifications or just relay the specs?" Upset that she hadn't made it back to D.C. in time for Zahair's interrogation, she had to settle on sending over a list of questions, and she hadn't heard back from Loran.

"Good question." Braun took the chip Usher retrieved from inside the euro. "I wonder how this compares to what we have reviewed."

Cordy mentioned that drones not only save lives, but are also more accurate, can operate 24/7, and are cheaper to produce than Javelin anti-tank missiles. "What new features are included in the euro's drone specifications?"

"An upgrade in AI capabilities and algorithms for starters," Braun said. "It can detect threats, deliver targeting data using satellite imagery, and give weapon responses at lightning speeds."

✳✳✳

While Braun reported his findings to Loran and Dr. Ping, Cordy moved to her computer to review the data on the two thumb drives found in Amir's pouch. One had recordings of several phone calls to Zahair.

Three calls were marked from General H.Q. One was made to Amir two weeks ago, and it was about the specific details of capturing Mo Hendrum, as requested by a member of the Iranian royal family. The second call was made 12 days ago, and it was about Zahair joining Amir's military force. Amir was ordered to hand over the unit to Zahair and follow orders. In both calls, General H.Q.'s voice was altered mechanically to remain anonymous.

However, on the third call, dated Sunday at 4:38 a.m., H.Q. called, and Gregor had video recorded the transaction. There was no image of H.Q., but his voice was undisguised. Gregor said in the background, "General H.Q. is on the phone."

"What does he want?" Zahair sounded perplexed.

Gregor held out the phone, his brown eyes wide with fear. "He's asking for you and says he heads up a Quds Force of the Islamic Revolutionary Guard Corps. They will be in position within the next 24 hours."

Zahair ordered Amir to leave the office, but Amir stood his ground before leaving, "Didn't you hear Gregor? If it's truly General H.Q., you should be shaking in your boots. Of course, he always disguises his voice, so it's hard to know who you're really talking to, but surely, you've heard of the general. He's everyone's boss. You'd be wise not to anger him. He will hold you responsible for any mistakes. So, beware."

Zahair scowled and pointed to the door, motioning for Amir to leave.

"You have been warned." Amir saluted and let the door slam behind him.

Zahair greeted the general, "Salam Alykum."

The general launched into a rant in Farsi. Cordy paused the video. "Braun, can you interpret this for me? It's a call from H.Q. to Zahair. At least, that's what Gregor said, but it's in Farsi. I don't know what they're saying, but the general's voice isn't disguised, which is a first. I'll run it through a voice detector shortly."

Braun listened and interpreted, "That drone attack on the White House failed. You can't trust Russian drones. We should have relied on our own. Did you plant the test weapons on Maven II, as I ordered? It's essential. They don't know they're really testing Iran's malware." Braun paused the recording when Cordy motioned to stop for clarification.

"So H.Q. ordered Zahair to attack the White House and to modify the Maven II drone and RCV. I need to pass this on to the president's security team." Cordy made a few notes. "Continue."

Braun restarted the recording as the general gloated, "It's one thing to launch rockets on the U.S. Embassy in Baghdad, but an attack on U.S. soil? That's a real coup, and with their own weapons. That will shock the whole world. There is another issue of grave concern." H.Q.'s voice became serious, "I ordered a robust cyberattack, but you need to take care of certain analysts to ensure success. Do I make myself clear? That analyst and her team could muddy the water."

"Yes, General," Zahair said. "Perfectly clear."

Braun paused the recording. "H.Q. is talking about you. How does he know about the team? Zahair must have sent that jet to take you to Washington, D.C."

Cordy thought back to the jet ride. "I need to do more research, but this is proof that Zahair weaponized the drone sent to Aberdeen. What does the rest of the recording say?"

Braun listened and then summarized, "General H.Q. is angry that Zahair kidnapped Mo Hendrum and Emma. It wasn't part of the plan, but H.Q. admitted to creating the cyberwarfare and the drone attack on the White House." Braun frowned, replayed a portion of the tape, and paused it again. "It seems the general changed his mind while on the call and told Zahair to make a ransom demand for Sophia to pay $25 million. It also sounds as if Zahair was to take Secretary Hendrum with him out of the country and leave Emma, but the SWAT team aborted his plans."

Cordy shook her head. "That doesn't make sense, the first call from H.Q. discussed Mo's capture, and the last call questioned the orders. I wonder if that last call was really H.Q.—he didn't disguise his voice. Is there anything else on that recording?"

Braun pressed play, and a few moments later, he hopped from his chair. "General H.Q. is angry, and his shouts sound just like General Shyler's, except in Farsi. I'm going to play this for Loran and the investigative team to get their opinion, but if Shyler is H.Q.—"

"He can't be H.Q., can he?" Cordy said, "Remember the recording from your bug? That was H.Q. calling Shyler. They're not the same voice. H.Q. has a much deeper voice even noticeable when disguised."

"Listen to Zahair," Braun hit the recording, "for your information, I'm the one responsible for waking three more secret cells within the U.S. over the past week, starting with an attack on the Securities and Stock Exchange, disrupting the subway systems causing riots in Washington, D.C., and a cell to launch next week in Texas. With that comes many risks, so do not bully me. I do not believe you are H.Q., and if you are, why are my orders changed?"

"So, is Azinnea M. Krysin, IYFTI's CEO, one of Zahair's sleeper cells. It sure sounds that way, and those shares have created extreme chaos." Cordy sighed. "Maybe you're right. That last call might not have been H.Q. There are too many discrepancies that H.Q. would have already known. It was as if Zahair had to remind H.Q. of his earlier actions. Run this through your voice detection system, and in the meantime, I'll share this with the team."

Twenty minutes later, Braun got up and stretched. "Let's take a break. Will your stomach accept food? I'll whip up something and meet you at the kitchen table."

"Yeah, but maybe just some fruit. I'll be there shortly," Cordy said, but she continued listening to the thumb drive calls. The call to General Shyler from General H.Q. was followed by an outgoing call marked to JCJ300. *JCJ300?* Cordy made another note. *I saw that scribbled on the back of a business card when Casper Grest showed me his ID.* She rubbed her chin and closed her eyes, replaying what she saw in her mind. *I think it was written on the back of Ansin Associates' business card. So, Ansin is JCJ300. I guess that makes sense. He has a whole security team working for him.*

Braun was on the phone.

Cordy listened to the JCJ300 call and then texted Quint, "Check the following bank account in Cypress for a transfer of $50 million. It was in exchange for drone schematics and source code. I don't know if it was ever delivered or who received it, but track the money if you can. There was also a note attached to an envelope with a red paper clip. The letter was addressed to our office in Fort Collins."

Quint called in a panic, "What did the letter say, and who was it addressed to?"

Cordy held the note up to the light, "It's addressed to the Cybersecurity team and says, 'A coin should arrive in Tehran by midday. No one will suspect that euro has a hidden chip inside.'" Cordy sounded upset. "It's signed, Vlad, so maybe it was sent to Perry, but we both know Vlad was in Iran with Usher, destroying those missiles bound for Syria, and how did Amir get it? This is a direct assault on our team."

"It's not the first time," Quint admitted. "We also received a letter two days ago from Vlad, and Svetlana thought it was for Perry. I found it in Perry's desk, and I nearly terminated his job over it. I guess I owe the lad an apology."

"Wait a moment," Cordy said. "I see an impression of another address on this note. It must have been written on the sheet above this, and it's addressed to someone in Virginia." She took a photo of the original envelope and used an electrostatic detection apparatus to decipher the hidden address. Once the address was translated, she forwarded it to Quint and Loran for further research. Braun stood over her, making notes of his own.

When Cordy glanced his way, Braun set a sliced apple next to her. "Break time." He handed her a cup of steaming coffee with a lot of cream. "Chief Jackson called. He wants to meet us for dinner tonight. Do you feel up to going out?"

"I've been cooped up for nearly six hours," Cordy said. "Does he have a hidden agenda?"

Braun gave that lopsided grin. "You never know with the chief."

"I've been thinking about the message detected by the bug in Shyler's office," Cordy said and sipped her coffee. "The message was from H.Q. or at least someone with a disguised voice. They were demanding a shipment to be sent by 10 p.m. tonight. Shyler's supposed to ship a delivery of weapons overseas. I wonder who the recipient is and where the weapons could end up."

"I've been researching that, and Chief Jackson has a few ideas, but you're not to worry yourself over any of this," Braun said.

"Where is Shyler?" Cordy asked. "It appears someone captured him as he was leaving the parking lot, blowing up his car, and the FBI found Shyler's blood on his key fob. Do you think H.Q. is behind this?"

"I believe that Shyler is playing games," Braun stated. "He would never let someone catch him off guard in a secure parking lot. He was aware that his car was beyond the coverage of the security cameras, and I am confident that he is hiding. He is likely waiting for the situation to calm down."

"How did Chief Jackson get involved in this?" Cordy asked, pausing before nodding in realization. "Usher must be back in town, and you guys are on a special mission to find those weapons. We're not really going out to dinner with the Chief, are we?"

"All right, you caught us," Braun winked, "but Loran doesn't want me involved. And he certainly doesn't want you risking your life again, so we'll be going to a small restaurant located a block away from that hidden address you sent to Loran, which happens to be an old, abandoned warehouse. The diner will be a perfect place to set up a stakeout."

Scammed

Sept. 12 – 7:50 p.m. EDT, Rundown slum area in Huntington, Virginia

Cordy shielded her eyes against the setting sunlight, reflecting below the car's visor as she gave Braun directions from Google Maps, "Turn left at the next intersection and stay in the right-hand lane for two blocks, then turn right at the light."

Braun drove down the curvy highway, hugging the river's edge, avoiding the busy bike path where motorcycles roared in both directions, weaving between cars, going much faster than the speed limit of 25 miles/hour. Braun slowed to take the turn and was on a narrow, one-lane street for two blocks.

"What light?" Braun asked, "It looks like someone knocked it over ten years ago. It's bent and rusted."

"Turn here," Cordy pointed, but not before he passed the corner. "Sorry. Turn around if you can find a way to intersect a road in the opposite direction."

"Are you sure we're going the right way?" Braun's cell pinged. He pulled over to read the text. He sighed, "Usher and Chief Jackson are already at the diner. They say it's a dump, and they're the only customers so far. Jackson asked to be seated upstairs where he could survey the abandoned warehouse across the street."

Cordy handed her phone with Google Maps to Braun, "See for yourself," An abdominal cramp made her moan. Her back had been aching for the past fifteen minutes, and she couldn't get comfortable.

"Are you okay?" Braun asked. "You're bracing yourself with every turn, and now you're holding your stomach."

"I'm just nauseated, I guess," Cordy said. "My back hurts. Can we just get there? We've been searching for this place forever."

Braun looked at his wife for a long moment before resetting Google Maps directions to the warehouse district and pulled back into the street. "I'm sure you're right, Honey, if twenty minutes is forever."

"Whatever," Cordy snapped and leaned forward, "I think Vivian wants out. She's kicking from the inside, and her brother doesn't like it. She's going to be a feisty redhead, I can tell."

"Vivian?" Braun asked. "Where did you come up with that name?"

"She must have slipped me a secret message because that's what I've been calling her all day, but her brother hasn't claimed his name to fame yet. I guess he's counting on you."

Braun turned the car around and found the correct road. "Ten more minutes, and we'll be at the diner. So, we've discussed several names, but this is the first time I've heard Vivian." He thought a moment. "I like it, but what happened to Katrina?"

"She didn't like the name, and Vivian popped to mind," Cordy squirmed. "Can we just get there already?"

"You're a bit testy tonight. Are you sure you're up for a stakeout?"

"You're not going alone," Cordy insisted, "and don't tell me Usher and Chief Jackson aren't relying on you. What are your plans?"

"Chief Jackson has been working with Perry, and they tracked down a phone number from Shyler's burner phone, which he believes was destroyed in the car fire, but two phone calls came into the office, and Miss Ward, Shyler's secretary, had recorded the calls. Fortunately, they were able to track one call that bounced off a cell tower near a Huntington, Virginia warehouse, so Jackson started a surveillance of the area."

"What kind of surveillance?" Cordy asked, "Did he get Russ Bracken involved?"

"Yes, they used two X-ray drones and got a 3-D image of what's inside the building. They located our suspects' floor. Are you familiar with the 3-D system?"

"Yes, Jackson used it to locate Sophia Hendrum last year when she was kidnapped. One drone sends a continuous Wi-Fi signal while the other measures the power as it passes through the building. It sends us a clear image of everything inside. Did the drone also have a sniffer for explosives and drugs?"

"You bet it did, and the sniffer came in hot as a habanero pepper," Braun said. "I'm sure the weapons are inside that warehouse, and Jackson tracked cell activity from the roof to Tehran, Iran. He's sure that's where H.Q. is currently headquartered. Usher has Albert's team in Iran on alert to take out H.Q. as soon as we capture General Shyler."

"You can't believe General Shyler is alone," Cordy said.

"No, but we don't know what he has planned." Braun drove past a block of old, rusted-out trucks, trailers, and vehicles parked on the cracked pavement with long grass poking through the crevices that led up to a tall, four-story warehouse with many broken windows. "Here's the place."

Cordy gasped, "There's torn crime scene tape across the front door. Are we too late?"

"That's from a month ago. This isn't the best neighborhood." Braun pulled into a near-vacant parking lot in front of a rundown diner next to Chief Jackson's rental, a white Mazda. "I don't see another vehicle, so Usher must be with Jackson."

Cordy stretched when she got out of the car, trying to work out a kink. Just walking in the diner's front door, Cordy knew something was really off about this place. The entryway had an antique Spartan radio dating back to the 1930s. The once multi-colored round dial was now so dusty she couldn't read the numbers, but the rich tiger wood grain with dark veins and deep reddish-orange stripes captured her attention. Two knobs were cracked, and one was missing. An old gramophone sat on top of the radio, but the stylus was also missing, and the large, dulled brass horn was dented. The place reeked of garlic, stale olive oil, and an old attic. "We don't really plan to eat here, do we?"

"Maybe we'll just have a drink while waiting for action." Braun stepped up to the host stand and was greeted by a young man dressed in blue jeans and a frayed gray sweatshirt. "Your friends are waiting for you upstairs. They said you'd have a pregnant lady with you, so follow me. My name's Max. Call if you need anything. Just yell over the railing. I'll hear you, and it's easier than coming back down these stairs to find me."

"Thanks. I'd like a glass of water when you have a moment." Cordy hung onto the loose railing as Max escorted them up a dark, narrow staircase with uneven steps.

"A glass of water. Got it," Max said, "anything else?"

Chief Jackson glanced up from eating a chicken wing, "The food is better than you'd think. I'll have another root beer."

Usher handed Braun his menu. They ordered, and Max went back downstairs.

Cordy glanced outside the window, "Any action yet?"

Usher turned a laptop in her direction, where two heat images moved along the roof of the building across the street. "If that's Shyler, he's not alone, but we don't know who is with him."

"It's definitely a male," Cordy said after studying the images. "Are there any more phone calls from this site?"

The waiter approached with their order and set the plates on the table. Usher and Braun had a salad, while Jackson topped his meal off with Key Lime Pie. They seemed quite content.

Cordy couldn't sit still. Her nagging backache refused to ease. "I can't tolerate more than water, so you finish eating, and I'll call Perry for an update."

Her phone rang before she could dial. Perry burst forth with, "Russ Bracken set up two cameras on that old warehouse, and Svetlana got access to all the city security cameras within a ten-block radius. Not much is happening where you are now, but check four blocks from the restaurant. I'll send you a link."

"What's Quint doing?" Cordy asked as she uploaded the link.

"Quint's in his office, monitoring Marshal Albert's operation in Iran. H.Q. is visiting the missile site in Tehran, and he's surrounded by Albert's team, and they want to capture H.Q. alive, if possible."

Cordy opened Perry's satellite image and felt her heart skip a beat. "We're missing all the action. Come on, men. Svetlana tracked down a street camera close by. Three tactical trucks and a Humvee left the warehouse and are now parked outside of Warehouse G, four blocks from here. I bet they're loading more weapons. Where's Bracken? Are you still in contact with him, Perry?"

"No, Jackson—"

Braun hopped up and grabbed the laptop. "Perry, call Loran and update him. Get Dr. Ping, too. We'll meet them at the scene. We can't let those trucks out of our sight."

"Where's Bracken," Cordy asked.

Chief Jackson was already on his cell phone, "I'm on it."

"Usher, Quint needs to talk to you, but he's tied up," Perry said over the chaos, "The Russian team captured H.Q., and Albert's asking for you. It appears H.Q.'s Quds Force is inside the missile silo but not beyond the sealed blockade to the missiles where Albert is holding H.Q. The Force is demanding that Albert release their boss, or they'll attack."

Usher dialed Albert on his watchlink and moved away from the noise. "Is it safe to talk?"

"Give me a minute," Albert whispered. "Dimitri, load that helicopter on the top level of the silo. Take off with H.Q. while Vlad and I go underground, and we'll meet you back at headquarters." Albert returned his attention to Usher, "Okay, I need a distraction. Usher, here's what I need from you."

Albert spoke quickly, and Cordy couldn't quite catch what was said with all the chaos around her. Jackson was talking to Russ Bracken, Braun talking to Loran, and Perry shouting for her to set up better surveillance in a new location.

"Can I do that from the U.S.?" Usher asked.

"Just broadcast the speech I downloaded to you," Albert said. "Vlad already linked the microphone to the loudspeakers. The speech is in disguised Farsi, so I hope the Quds Force believes it's coming directly from H.Q. That will keep the Force occupied while we make our getaway."

Usher tried to download the message, but he couldn't get access. "Cordy, I need your expertise." He explained the problem, and she made a few behind-the-scenes access tweaks, and the link opened.

"Okay, we're ready," Cordy said. "I'll broadcast so you can stay in contact with Albert via the watchlink." Cordy also tapped a code into her watchlink: "Dimitri, can you hear me? Are you ready to commence?"

"Yes," Dimitri said, "I launched the plan three minutes ago."

Albert sounded out of breath, "We're moving underground, and Dimitri and the team are loading H.Q. into the helicopter. I can hear banging on the outer doors. Start the recording. We need enough time for the men to get back down here and go underground."

Cordy pressed play and heard, "Salam Alykum,…"

"How long is the speech," Cordy asked through Usher's link.

Albert gasped in a deep breath, "Five minutes. It gives us time before the blockade door is set to open, and if they blow up the missiles, even better. We're safe, but they won't know that."

Braun was on a conference call with Loran, Dr. Ping, and Chet Yelson, who were taking a helicopter to the area.

Chief Jackson was downstairs getting orders from Russ as his team geared up. "We're going with you." Jackson shouted upstairs, "Coming, Braun? Russ has the Humvee loaded. We're all wearing helmets with internal vision screens and two-way radio links, so Cordy and her team can see and hear all activity."

"Perry's monitoring, so I'm going with you," Cordy said.

"No way! I only brought you along so I could keep an eye on you. I'll be fine. Stay with Usher and help Perry and Quint monitor as needed," Braun shouted over his shoulder as he bounded down the steps. "I mean it! Do not follow. Stay safe. Usher, watch over her until I get back."

Cordy heard communication from her watchlink and realized Braun was right. She needed to stay and help Usher. She asked Dimitri, "Are you in the air?"

"Yes, and most of the Quds Force are inside the silo, so they didn't hear us take off. We're nearly to headquarters. Is Albert safe?"

"Yes, he and Vlad are underground, but does the tunnel go all the way to headquarters?" Cordy asked.

"I'm sorry, I need to concentrate," Dimitri said. "H.Q. is stirring, and I'm landing soon."

"Okay, let me know when you've landed." Cordy turned toward Usher.

Dimitri cut in, "An explosion is set to blow—" A deafening blast made Cordy visibly jolt.

Usher said, "Albert wondered how he could destroy those missiles without getting caught. Now it appears the Quds Force blew up the missiles—well-timed."

"What about Albert and Vlad? Are they safe?" Cordy asked.

"The tunnel goes to one of Leo's contact's homes. From there, Leo will drive them to headquarters," Usher said. "I met the family when I was in Tehran. The team trusts them. I'll check in with Albert."

"We hear you," Albert said. "Leo met us at the entrance, and the team's safe. We're flying back to Russia with H.Q. He's wanted for treason, and if he makes it to Russia, he knows he's dead."

"Great job," Usher said. "Do you need anything else from me? We're in the middle of a mission of our own. Braun and Chief Jackson are stopping General Shyler from making a weapon's transfer to H.Q."

"General Shyler?" Albert asked. "That must be what H.Q. was talking about. He mentioned a transfer of the world's most deadly weapons would happen on Friday at 0600. I guess we don't have to worry about that shipment making it to the Quds Force. Oh, wait, he also mentioned a Maven II drone is heading to Texas. H.Q. laughed and said, 'Watch the World Series. The game will knock your socks off, and the U.S. will never be the same.' Dimitri got him to admit the Maven II drone will attack as President Spendorf makes his pitch."

"Thanks for the heads-up," Cordy said. "I already warned the FBI, and Secret Service agents are taking care of the threat. Keep in touch. We'll want to know what happens to H.Q."

"We're heading for headquarters." Albert sounded out of breath as if he'd run the whole way underground. "All hell is breaking loose at the missile factory. Sirens galore, and I'm sure that Quds Force Squadron is history. Talk to you soon." Albert signed off Usher's watchlink.

Cordy moved back to her screen and noticed activity across the street. The two heat images had moved from the roof. One went to the ground floor, and the other had disappeared entirely. "Usher, look at this."

Usher studied the screen, slipped into his Kevlar vest, and checked his pistol, "I'm not letting Shyler get away!"

Cordy said, "Be careful—"

A blast sounded as the restaurant windows shattered, and a burst of hot air blew Cordy backward. She plowed into Usher, and they both landed on the floor. The building next door had burst into flames.

"Cordy, what happened?" Perry shouted over the screen.

"Are you okay?" Usher scrambled out from under Cordy and helped her up.

"Fine, and you?" Cordy didn't get an answer as Usher raced down the stairs. She moved in front of her laptop and shouted over the roar, "Perry, do you have eyes on—"

"Yup, a man dashed from the building just before the explosion. I see Usher running from the restaurant in pursuit."

"Did only one person leave the warehouse?" Cordy peered through the glassless window. "There were two heat signatures, then I lost one, and the top floors are gone."

"Only one man," Perry said. "The other person didn't make it out of the building."

"Usher's out there alone. Call Bracken. I'm following Usher." Cordy dashed for the steps and stopped as water gushed down both legs. An abdominal cramp made her double over in pain. "What's happening?"

Perry yelled, "Cordy, are you all right?"

"Get, Braun!" Cordy gasped. "It's too soon, but the twins don't know how to tell time yet, and they are coming. Now!"

Miracles

It had been a wild and crazy 32 ½ weeks when twin cells, the size of a pinpoint nearly invisible to the naked eye, divided and grew inside her uterus. It seemed that, in a blink of an eye, the time had flown by with dreams of parenthood, preparing to enjoy the twins, and relaxing—that's when the rude reality hit Cordy. *Their room isn't finished. Not enough baby clothes, blankets, and what about milk? Will I be able to breastfeed? What's wrong with me? Usher's out there alone, Braun's, who knows where at the moment.* The feeling of being unprepared for the challenges of parenthood was overwhelming. *Focus, Cordy!*

The twins were making their debut in the middle of Daddy's ops mission while Cordy was on a special reconnaissance team, operating behind enemy lines, avoiding direct combat, and monitoring enemy activity. Stranded on the top floor of a rundown restaurant, and she was still responsible for surveillance to obtain information of the rival forces and counter any attack with weaponized drones—well, with Perry's help.

Cordy grabbed a napkin from the table and tried to clean up.

"Cordy?" Perry called out. "Braun's heading your way. He says he called for an ambulance."

Cordy scanned to the screen, searching, "Did you find Usher?"

"Yes, Usher has Congressman Conrad Justuso in handcuffs. He says he argued with General Shyler, trying to prevent him from shipping those weapons. As soon as the military caravan left, the general seemed to go crazy. He threatened to blow up the building before Conrad fled for freedom. He believes Shyler was inside the building when it blew but denies knowing where the weapons were to be shipped. Bracken's team stopped the two military trucks. Loran's team has the Humvee driver in custody, and they're wrapping up the mission. How are you and the twins?"

Max stood at the top of the stairs. The waiter's eyes were wide with fear. "Ma'am, can I help?"

"I'm sorry about the mess," Cordy felt embarrassed, then another contraction had her using her Lamaze breathing.

"I'll take care of it," Max scampered down the stairs and returned with a pail of water and a mop.

Braun raced up the steps, "Cordy?" He reached her side and wrapped his arms around her. "Honey, you look pale. Are you feeling all right?"

"I may have overdone it today, as you warned me," Cordy said. "My water broke. Our twins will be here soon, and we aren't ready." She straightened up.

"I'm here now, and we are ready to welcome them into the world," Braun balled his fist and checked his watch. "How long does it take for an ambulance?" He pulled up two chairs. "Do you want to sit down? Or maybe lay down on the table?"

"No, I'm not going to deliver our children in this place."

Perry cleared his throat. "Um, what can we do for you?"

Quint came into view on VidChat. "We'll close up this case, check in with the president's security team, handle the Securities Exchange, and work with Cracker. Braun, the ambulance will be there soon. Usher handed over Congressman Justuso to Dr. Ping, and he's heading your way. He says Zina is flying to D.C. and will be here tomorrow. She's anxious to see the twins. We're signing off now, but keep us posted. Uncle Quint can't wait to see all of you and hold the babies." He disconnected the call.

"Uncle Quint?" Braun asked, "Really?"

Cordy laughed. "I'm sure our twins have more aunts and uncles than you realize." Sirens sounded in the distance. "Help me to the bathroom. I want to clean up before we leave."

Braun helped Cordy downstairs to the restroom.

Usher and Chief Jackson entered the restaurant. Usher said, "What do you need me to do?"

Braun turned. "Can you pack up the equipment upstairs and load it in Chief Jackson's car? We'll collect it later."

Jackson helped Usher gather the laptops and surveillance equipment and brought them downstairs as the ambulance pulled up to the front door.

The attendant was loading Cordy into the back of the ambulance. Braun handed Usher the keys to his car. "I'm going with Cordy. Take my car. I'm not sure I'm safe to drive at the moment." His face was pale, and sweat beaded his forehead.

"Don't you dare faint, Daddy!" Usher punched Braun in the shoulder. "Buck up."

Braun took a deep breath and squeezed Cordy's hand. "I'm excited, scared, and you're a real trooper. I won't let you down." He turned back to Usher and the chief, "We'll meet you at St. Mary's Medical Center OB-GYN dept."

"You bet Daddy, take good care of those twins," Jackson waved as Braun climbed in next to Cordy, and the paramedic shut the ambulance doors.

Sept. 12 – 9:38 p.m. EDT, St. Mary's Medical Center
OB-GYN dept., Huntington, Virginia

Rushed to the maternal child unit, Cordy was examined by Dr. Kate Benson, "You're in active labor and already dilated 6 cm." She turned to Cordy. "You're doing great. Just breathe with the contractions." Kate grabbed Braun's hand and placed it on Cordy's abdomen. "Feel the muscles tightening under your hand. Here it comes. Now focus, and help her breathe with the contractions." Kate moved toward Cordy. "Take a deep breath, and slowly let it out. If they get too intense, try to pant a little, but not enough to get dizzy."

Cordy took a deep breath, gritted her teeth, and exhaled slowly with a jagged edge. Her eyes narrowed with the pain, but she didn't complain.

"Yes, that's it," Kate said. "It's easing now. Just relax until the next one. Now, it's your turn, Braun, to do this on your own."

Cordy could see Braun's pulse pound in his neck with each heartbeat. He whispered, "I don't know if I can do this."

She gently took his hand. "We're in this together, and I've never been more proud to be your wife. You'll do whatever it takes to get us through this birth." Cordy gasped, "Here it comes," and took another deep breath.

Braun nodded, "For you, I'd do anything. I love you, Cordy, and I love our children, both Vivian and," he started breathing with her, taking it slow. "That's it."

She breathed hard with a curious mixture of intense pain and determination to birth healthy twins—their babies.

"I can't begin to describe my love for you." Braun's hands shook as he placed them over her abdomen. "I'm afraid I'll mess up."

Cordy turned to her side. "You won't. You're my strength, my rock. I need you. Please, rub my back."

Braun started to massage between her shoulder blades.

"Lower," Cordy said. He moved down to the small of her back. "Yes, that's the spot."

At the next strong contraction, fear made him grip her hand once again. "You're doing great."

"Tell me what you started to say. You love both Vivian and, have you decided on a name for our son?"

"I think his name is Zane. I'm not sure why that popped into my head. I was going to say, Brian, but I like Zane better."

"So do I," Cordy beamed. "Vivian and Zane, I can't wait to hold you."

Braun moved to the edge of his seat. "This may be a long night. Can I get you anything? Coffee, tea, water?"

Cordy smiled, "I thought you were going to say, 'or me.' I want you, Braun, now and forever. Thank you for marrying me, and thank you for our children. We are so lucky."

Usher knocked on the door, "Talk about lucky, I just heard from Zina. She's at the Dublin Airport heading here, so she can help with the babies once she arrives and you return home."

"Great," Cordy chuckled, "and maybe you'll want to add a little one to your family."

Usher blushed, "I'll let my baby brother experience fatherhood first and see how well he does before committing."

Braun admitted, "You may not have a choice. We hadn't planned for this."

Cordy rolled onto her back. "Braun maybe hadn't planned for this, but I'm not sorry."

Braun stood and scratched his head. "I didn't say I was sorry." He turned to Usher, "See what trouble I get into when I'm with you?"

"It's not my fault." Usher smiled. "Let's have some coffee."

"Don't leave me." Cordy moaned and squeezed his hand. The contractions grew stronger and closer together now, as Cordy tried to breathe through the next contraction.

"Never," Braun wiped the sweat from her brow. "Have a cup with Chief Jackson. I'm sure he's in the waiting room by now."

"We'll wait outside," Usher kissed Cordy on the cheek. "We love you." He headed for the door and turned back, "It just dawned on me. I'm going to be Uncle Usher soon. Wow, I hope I can live up to that title."

Braun chuckled, "We'll make sure you do. Go have your coffee, Uncle."

Braun refused to leave Cordy's side the entire time as they worked their way through the labor. By 11 p.m., the contractions intensified, and Braun winced through each pain as Cordy fought to breathe. "And they say women are the weaker sex."

Dr. Kate asked if Cordy wanted anything for pain, but she refused. "I want to be totally awake to see our babies."

She checked Cordy, "I can see a head. Push hard with the next contraction."

The swell of pain was excruciating. Braun supported Cordy as she pushed with all her might. She squeezed Braun's hand so hard his fingers turned white, but instead of complaining, he found himself breathing with her as she worked so hard, and watched in awe.

Dr. Kate said, "I see dark hair. Another push, and we'll have one birth."

Cordy pushed until Dr. Kate supported a dark-haired baby. She guided the baby's shoulders through the narrow canal, quickly cleared the infant's airway, and the baby announced its presence into the world.

The nurse held a blanket under the child and caught it as the next contraction pushed it free from the womb. The bundle was so tiny and yet so perfect—ten fingers and ten toes, and before Cordy knew it, Kate said, "It's a boy." She handed Braun a clamp and sterilized scissors, "You can cut the cord, and then I see a little redhead crowning."

Braun cut the cord, and a nurse placed the infant into Braun's outstretched arms.

"Zane," Braun hugged the little boy, who let out a loud cry. "What did I do?"

The nurse wrapped the blanket more snuggly around the boy. "You didn't do anything wrong, he's just greeting you, and we want his little lungs to fill with air."

Zane quieted, and his wide blue eyes opened as he saw his daddy for the first time. Cordy held his little hand.

Everything happened so quickly that Dr. Kate barely had time to catch the little redhead as the baby's head popped out. "She's anxious to see the world," Kate said, clearing the airway.

"Vivian," Cordy cooed. "They're both beautiful."

Kate laid Vivian on Cordy's abdomen, and the nurse had to pry Zane from Braun's arms. "I need to wash and weigh him, and you need to cut Vivian's cord."

"Okay, I have this," Braun said, taking the scissors and snipping the cord between the clamps. Then, Braun grabbed a blanket, wrapped his little daughter, and handed the baby to Cordy. "She looks just like you—a feisty redhead, bright-eyed, and curious."

The nurse brought Zane back to the room. "He weighs 4 pounds 3 ounces and is 16 inches long, can I weigh Vivian?"

Braun took Vivian from Cordy so she could hold Zane for the first time. "He has your square chin and dimples."

Zane was already nuzzling, so Cordy breastfed him while the nurse cleaned up Vivian. She returned the little girl, announcing, "She's only 3 pounds, 12 ounces, and 15 ¼ inches, but she has a powerful voice. I think she's hungry, too."

Cordy had a hard time balancing one baby on each side, but Braun helped hold Zane until he started to doze. Then Braun proudly stood. "Can I show them off to their Uncles?"

Cordy nodded. "Usher and Chief Jackson can come in. Vivian seems happy at the moment."

Braun leaned over and kissed Cordy. "We did a great job. They're both beautiful. I was afraid they'd be bald, blotchy, and ugly, but not so." He kissed each of his children on the forehead. "I love Zane's cute, little, upturned nose, and his hair is so silky."

Braun couldn't smile wide enough as he returned with Usher and Chief Jackson. "They're the cutest children in the world."

Tears streamed down Cordy's face. "Aren't they beautiful?" She briefly peeled Vivian's blanket back, counted her fingers and toes, did the same with Zane, and then hugged both close to her. "They're perfect."

Reluctantly, Braun handed his son over to Usher and Vivian to Chief Jackson, then he took a cool, damp rag and wiped Cordy's brow. "You amaze me." He leaned over and kissed her.

Usher insisted on taking photos to share with Zina and, of course, with President Spendorf, VP Harris, Guy, Loran, Dr. Ping, Quint, Perry, and Svetlana. Braun stroked his daughter's tiny hand. "She has her mother's slender fingers."

It was after midnight when Usher whispered to Chief Jackson, "Let's leave Braun and Cordy alone to admire their twins." He set Braun's car keys on the overhead table, and closed the door.

Moments later, Braun opened his eyes and noticed his brother and Chief Jackson had left the room. He noted the car keys and knew they had left the hospital. Braun gazed over at his wife, silently sleeping with Zane at her breast. Vivian was napping in his lap. He couldn't wait to bring his little miracles home—feeling truly blessed.

The End

Thank you for reading *Caught Unaware*. I loved writing it and hope you enjoyed reading it. If you did, please tell a friend and consider leaving a review on Amazon. Your sincere feedback means everything to me. Please visit me on my website and continue to read the next adventure. ***https://jillsflateland.com.***

Get ready for the next book, a prequel to the entire series that's packed with action and suspense. Join Cordy's father, Josh Cordelia, as he assumes the dangerous persona of Skid Monroe. Alongside his partner, Fritz Von Schlegen, they plan a high-stakes jewel heist in the bustling streets of New York City. Their target? The formidable mafia underboss, Vinny Corenelli. Brace yourself for the adrenaline-pumping *A Jewel's Sting*, and start the journey with the first chapter below.

Preview of A Jewel's Sting – Chapter 1
It's A Son

March. 6, 1974 – 2:08 p.m. CET, Palermo, Sicily

Honor, respect, and loyalty had never been a problem for Poppy Corleonesi until the day it exploded in his face. He had been betrothed to the mob boss's youngest daughter, Maria since she was four years old. The boss had seven sons, but only one daughter, and marrying into this household was highly esteemed. Poppy had watched Maria grow from a carefree child to a lovely, resilient, and charming young lady. He cherished their long walks together, her inquisitive nature, and lengthy chats. Her honesty, sense of humor, and generosity inspired Poppy, and he fell madly in love. Overjoyed to wed Maria, his marriage strategically sealed a family alliance, ensured cohesion within the ranks, and solidified a partnership of utmost control over everyone around them. Like the crowning of a monarch, he had been blessed with the regal authority of an underboss on his wedding day and would be next in line to lead the powerful Sicilian Corleonesi Mafia. However, the dynamics within the mafia and the tension and intrigue it created would never interfere with his love for his wife.

April 12, 1977 – 7:20 a.m. CET, Palermo, Sicily

Personally and professionally, Poppy's life couldn't have been better. He admired the strong, devoted patriarch—the most powerful guardian to protect mankind. Poppy was quick to learn and followed in the boss's footsteps. Now second in command, he was responsible for all capos and soldiers and ready to take over when the time was right.

The rift came three years later. Poppy was deeply in love with Maria, the most beautiful woman alive. The young couple had been trying for a baby for what seemed like forever. Each month, they waited in anticipation, hoping for a little miracle to enter their lives, but like clockwork, Aunt Flo came for a visit.

Then, one spring day, Maria's eyes lit up as she ran into the office and announced, "I'm pregnant." Those two small words filled their hopes and dreams for the future. "Poppy, you're going to be a daddy."

"That's terrific. I hope it's a son." Poppy's unsteady heartbeat thrummed in his neck as he swept Maria off her feet and kissed her. "Are you sure?"

Maria nodded.

"I love you. You're beautiful." Overjoyed with the greatest blessing of his life, Poppy grabbed her hand. "Come on. I can't wait to see the look on your father's face when he hears the news. This will be his first grandbaby. Can you imagine, after seven sons, he still has no other grandchildren?"

Maria let go of his hand and stood firm. "No, we can't tell Papa yet. We must be sure the baby is healthy and will survive." She turned away with tears in her eyes.

"Nonsense," Poppy pulled her closer. "He'll be thrilled. What man wouldn't love to have a grandchild in his life?"

"Haven't you wondered why my brothers have no children?" Maria asked. "We have a family curse. An ancient family secret—one I'm not at liberty to tell." The weight of these words hung heavy in the air, casting a shadow over their joy.

Poppy's voice was firm, "What do you mean? Surely you can tell me. I'm your husband. I'm understanding and will protect you from whatever you fear." He would stand by her side always.

"You can't protect me. Not from Papa." Maria sobbed.

Poppy gasped, "You're afraid of your Papa?"

She nodded. "Please, don't tell him until it's too late." Maria ran from the room crying.

Poppy was left standing there, his mind racing with questions and fears. *What is so terrible that Maria is afraid to tell me? And why is she scared of her father?*

It was as if her words finally hit him. "Wait. Too late for what?" Poppy followed her down the hallway to their bedroom.

She slammed the door in his face and locked it. "We need to go away, Poppy. He'll make us go away."

"He wouldn't do that?" Poppy turned the knob, but it wouldn't open, so he pounded on the door. "Honey, please, open up." To his surprise, Maria refused to obey. It was so unlike her that he had to get to the bottom of this.

Maria's fear must be due to pregnancy hormones. Indeed, her Papa will be thrilled to hear the news. Poppy marched out the front door and raced across town to share the exciting information with the mob boss. Bursting through the door, he announced, "Gather around. I have great news. Maria's with child."

Papa's dark eyes flashed with anger. "This can't be happening. No, I won't allow it." His fists clenched, and he ranted as he paced before Poppy. "Why didn't you tell me you wanted a family?"

"Why wouldn't I—"

"Stop the pregnancy!" Papa continued to rant.

Poppy tried to step into the boss's path to get him to explain some stupid comment that he kept repeating. "...get an abortion ASAP. We can't allow this..."

"No. Why?" Poppy asked.

"I've had three sons, little people, dwarves, as you might call them," Papa yelled.

"You have more sons?" Poppy asked. "Where are they? I've never met them."

"Of course not," Papa said, "they are all with their maker—in heaven with God." Papa paused and softened his tone, pleading with Poppy. "Please, listen to me. Have Maria get an abortion before it's too late."

Poppy's mind spun. He couldn't focus. "No, this is my family. I am free to have children, and Maria will have my baby."

"I'm not arguing with you." Papa glared. "I gave you Maria. I made you a full-fledged member of this family, and this child will not be born. Not in this country. Not in my house. I will not have another misfit."

"Misfit?" Poppy said in horror. "This will be your grandchild! An innocent infant to be loved. Besides, how can you be so sure? And even if the baby is of short stature, I'll still love him. This is the family we are talking about. Not yours!"

"I am your wife's father, your boss, and head of this family," Papa shouted. "You will do as I say."

Poppy was a man of staunch principles, and Papa's words only triggered hatred. Poppy was proud to be a father and stood firm in his decision to forbid an abortion. "Maria is my wife! We will have my baby, and that's final!"

Poppy pounded a fist on his desk. "Then you and all of your family are ousted from the clan! You know what happens to outsiders."

Poppy flinched at his words. "I am a Corleonesi. You can't take that away from me."

Maria's Papa narrowed his beady, dark eyes, now throwing fire darts. "Watch me. Don't be surprised if you end up in some dark alley one night. It could happen, and I refuse to protect you any longer."

This rift was unforgivable—a betrayal of trust. Poppy sucked in a deep breath, stood his ground, and confronted the boss. Something he never thought he'd ever do. "So you have a genetic defect, and you're sure it's been passed down to Maria. How could you keep this family secret, hidden away for decades, only known to immediate family members? I have news for you. There's no shame here. So what if Maria's three brothers were dwarves? What happened to them anyway?"

"That's none of your business," Papa snapped. "Get out of my house. I never want to see you or Maria again."

Poppy lowered his head and turned, shocked at his response. "You'll change your mind. You'll see."

"Don't count on it," Papa said as he had the butler show Poppy to the door.

The feud lasted two days, with the boss refusing to see Poppy or Maria. Then, at 2 a.m., Poppy was awakened when his neighbors, some of his closest friends, dragged him from his bed, beat him to unconsciousness, and warned Maria, "Leave town, or the next time, he won't survive, and neither will you."

Fearing for their lives, Poppy, Maria, his parents, four siblings, and their children left all their belongings behind and moved to New York City, where they changed their names to Corenelli. Despite the fear and uncertainty, the family remained resilient. Maria's greatest fear was realized—she had inherited the recessive trait. Tragically, Maria died giving birth to a son.

Poppy was devastated, raising a child alone, not just any child: he named the boy Midget.

Despite the hardships, the family's bond was unbreakable, their loyalty steadfast, and they remained united. Poppy's fourteen-year-old niece, Aurora, moved in to help him raise the precious boy. Poppy, in turn, fell deeply in love and married her when she turned fifteen. The gorgeous, brown-eyed beauty became pregnant on her wedding night. At least, that's the story, and no one dared dispute it.

Eight months later, Vinny arrived in the world. He grew up an intelligent, cunning, and opinionated young lad. Leading a mafia was all Poppy knew, but he vowed he would welcome all of his grandchildren. He would not be a tyrant like Maria's Papa had been. He started his family clan with a few loyal, mostly immediate family members. They initially targeted the stronghold of five businesses, and their influence grew, as did the family, now nine sons, trained in the family business. They eventually became a formidable force in New York City, taking control of the teamster's union and becoming a name that sent fear throughout New York.

It was time for a reckoning, and FBI Agent Josh Cordelia was the perfect agent to force the clan to deal with the consequences of their misdeeds. Standing at six-foot-one, with hair longer than FBI-issue length, mahogany color, and an avid swimmer's athletic build, he didn't blend into the shadows. His piercing blue eyes scanned the area, constantly alert for trouble, and it seemed to follow him wherever he went. As a chess grandmaster, Josh's strategic thinking was as intriguing as his skills. He thrived on adrenaline, craved creating solutions to complex puzzles, and planned three steps ahead for any complications. Ready to defeat the mob, Josh went undercover, assumed the dangerous persona of Skid Monroe, and teamed up with Vinny.

When Josh's longtime partner, Fritz Von Schlegen, stumbled upon the news of an auction of the most exquisite handcrafted jewelry in the world, set to take place at a downtown Brooklyn, New York Depot over the weekend of November 13-15, it was a golden opportunity to bring down the Corenelli mafia. With the clock ticking, Skid knew he had to act fast.

About The Author

Jill S. Flateland,
RN, BSN, CCRN, MBA

Caught Unaware is the fifth book in the Dr. Joshtine Cordelia Hastings Series. Cordy has been promoted to a new cabinet position, the Cyber Crisis Agency. A massive cyberattack on Washington, D.C., challenges the team to pull out all stops to defend the president, especially when drones attack the White House. General H.Q., number 4 on the top 10 terrorists list is behind the attack and is waking sleeper cells across the nation to create additional havoc and to destroy U.S. democracy.

Sweet Revenge is the first book in this action-packed thriller series. The mafia is back on her turf, causing a life-changing event. A re-acquaintance with an old flame rekindles sparks that haven't died. He's trapped inside a Bunker. A timer is set to explode, and Cordy must break the code to rescue him before villains snuff out his life. Her cybersecurity skills are stretched to their limits.

Her venture continues in *Rapid Response*, where Cordy fights a bioterrorist attack. An astronaut unknowingly transports a potent virus, created without gravity on the space station, back to Earth. This virus is more deadly than our recent Covid epidemic. Not only does it devastate the lungs, but it also attacks the brain. Risking exposure, Cordy rushes to find a cure when U.S. President Spendorf, his key advisors, and many members of Congress become infected.

Next in the series, *Crashing The Grid*, sends Cordy and her team to reverse a cyberattack on NYC that shuts down the power grid, water treatment plants, and more. Cordy's adventures continue in *Combating Chaos: All Systems Down*. Cordy and her new husband, JSOC Agent Braun Hastings, hunt down a Russian terrorist, General Okueva. He enlists student hackers to disrupt the New York Stock Exchange and major financial systems. Foreign forces have also attacked London and Rome. Cordy and her team risk their lives to stop the terrorists. I hope you enjoy these fast-paced novels.

Although my background is over 40 years in healthcare as an ICU and ER nurse and the CEO of an Urgent Care Corporation, I've been a writer all of my life. I've created 26 audio/video courses for nurses' continuing education and published 21 volumes of healthcare pathways for disease management throughout the U.S., Japan, Europe, and Australia. My husband and I live in Colorado, and we travel extensively.

In 2006, I retired and ventured into the wider writing world. In 2011, I published *A Lightning Slinger's Tales of the Rails*, which tells of my aunt, Dr. Vera E. Williams, life as a female telegrapher during World War II. She worked for the railroad to make enough money to get her degree in teaching.

In 2014, I published *Ding Dong! The Rural Schools Are Gone*, a story of my two aunts, Vivian V. Lund (age 97 at the time, died at 104 in 2022) and Dr. Vera E. Williams (age 88 at that time, died at age 90 in 2016), who were both teachers during the early twentieth century.

I entered my fifth novel, *Until We Meet Again*, in the 2014 Colorado Gold Contest at the Rocky Mountain Fiction Writer's Contest. The novel became a finalist in the suspense category. Tobias McFitzroy's tombstone lay shattered in a cemetery outside a Colorado ghost town northeast of Fort Collins. *The stonemason had carved his own epitaph. It read, "Until we meet again. 1830 – 1899." Unlike most people, it didn't mean when he'd meet them in heaven. He couldn't. He hadn't made it that far.*

Sales Support a Worthy Cause

Byron and I are actively involved with two Non-Governmental Organizations (NGOs). The first is **Angel Covers**, who helped open Vill-Angel Medical Clinic in the center of a rural farming community in Endebess, Kenya, allowing poor families to receive high-quality healthcare.

As Director of Healthcare Services, my goal is to help expand the clinic to offer maternal-child care. Many families have no car to travel to a hospital, the nearest being 17 kilometers from the clinic. Some have a motorcycle, others have a cart pulled by a donkey, but many walk on foot.

Most women deliver babies at home, but the infant mortality rate in Kenya is six times higher than in the U.S. (Kenya has 30 infant deaths/1000 births compared to the U.S., which has 5 infant deaths/1000 births.) Some women travel up to two hours on foot while in labor to receive care during high-risk pregnancies. Plus, children are at the highest risk for death within the first 28 days. Most die of pneumonia, diarrhea, and sepsis. Our clinic can treat these ailments and provide follow-up care as needed.

The second is **Seeds of South Sudan**, where donations help rescue refugees from Kakuma Refugee Camp in Kenya, allowing orphans to attend boarding school in Kenya. Once these students graduate, they plan to return to South Sudan to help rebuild its economy, infrastructure, and create a stabilized country.

You, too, can help. Part of the proceeds from the sales of these books help support these causes, and I thank you from the bottom of my heart. We know you have many choices when purchasing mystery novels and methods of donating to worthy causes, so I'm grateful that you chose to help support these charities.

Other Books Written by Jill S. Flateland

Thriller Series:

Sweet Revenge
Rapid Response
Crashing The Grid
Combating Chaos: All Systems Down

Suspense Series:

Until We Meet Again

Secret Series:

Secrets & Chandeliers
Family Secrets & Betrayals
Secrets Lost Among Forget-Me-Nots
Secrets of Grayson Mansion

Family Memoirs:

A Lightning Slinger's Tales of the Rails
Ding Dong! The Rural Schools Are Gone
Chugs & Hugs: Growing Up In A Train Station Vol 1
Chugs & Hugs: Growing Up In A Train Station Vol 2
Chugs & Hugs: Growing Up In A Train Station Vol 3